NIGHT ASYLUM

Tales of Mystery & Horror

DOUGLAS CLEGG

ALKEMARA
PRESS

CONTENTS

Also by Douglas Clegg   v

Get Douglas Clegg's Newsletter   ix

Preface   xi

The Stain   1

The American   29

Belinda in the Pool   43

The Skin of the World   67

A Madness of Starlings   83

Subway Turnstile   107

Where Flies Are Born   111

Becoming Men   127

People Who Love Life   153

Fries With That?   169

The Machinery of Night   209

The Wolf   235

The Wicked   247

265 and Heaven   273

Ice Palace   301

Why My Doll is Evil   329

The Five   331

The Dark Game   353

Read the Nightmare Chronicles   403

About the Author   409

ALSO BY DOUGLAS CLEGG

STAND-ALONE NOVELS

Afterlife

Breeder

The Children's Hour

Dark of the Eye

Goat Dance

The Halloween Man

The Hour Before Dark

Mr. Darkness

Naomi

Neverland

You Come When I Call You

NOVELLAS & SHORT NOVELS

The Attraction

The Dark Game (Two Novelettes)

Dinner with the Cannibal Sisters

Isis

The Necromancer

Purity

The Words

SERIES

THE HARROW SERIES

Nightmare House, Book 1

Mischief, Book 2

The Infinite, Book 3

The Abandoned, Book 4

The Necromancer (Prequel Novella)

Isis (Prequel Novella)

THE CRIMINALLY INSANE SERIES

Bad Karma, Book 1

Red Angel, Book 2

Night Cage, Book 3

THE VAMPYRICON TRILOGY

The Priest of Blood, Book 1

The Lady of Serpents, Book 2

The Queen of Wolves, Book 3

THE CHRONICLES OF MORDRED

Mordred, Bastard Son (Book 1)

COLLECTIONS

Lights Out: Collected Stories

Night Asylum

The Nightmare Chronicles

Wild Things

BOX SET BUNDLES

Bad Places (3 Novels)

Coming of Age (3 Dark Novellas)

Dark Rooms (3 Novels)

Criminally Insane: The Series (3 Novels)

Halloween Chillers

Harrow: Three Novels (Books 1-3)

Harrow: Four Novels (Books 1-4)

Haunts (8 Novel Box Set)

Lights Out (3 Collection Box Set)

Night Towns (3 Novels)

The Vampyricon Trilogy (3 Novels)

With more new novels, novellas and stories to come.

GET DOUGLAS CLEGG'S NEWSLETTER

Get book updates, price drop news flashes, and exclusive offers—become a V.I.P. member of Douglas Clegg's long-running email newsletter:

http://DouglasClegg.com/newsletter

PREFACE

Welcome to the Night Asylum – you may walk alone down its dim corridors but beware of those who lie in wait, scraping the dark.

This asylum sits upon a lonely hill, hidden from the world by dense woods. Within these walls of stone and beneath razor wire, the dreams of madness roam, and every patient has a story to tell.

This collection, in its second edition, contains eighteen tales of the strange, weird, horrifying, and mysterious — including those previously published separately in the mini-collection, *Wild Things*.

I hope you enjoy your stay in the asylum – just watch out for the other inmates...

— Douglas Clegg

NIGHT ASYLUM

THE STAIN

Jason hunted for the T-shirt just outside the walls of the hotel compound.

He haggled over the price of a particular shirt — the kind Kyle would love. It was boiling hot out; the sea breeze did nothing to cool down the market stall. After an extended back-and-forth with the seller, Jason got a sweet deal: the shirt, flip-flops, plus a few knickknacks for his son's collection.

The guy selling souvenirs under the plastic awning lived — no doubt — among the squalor of hut and shack that ran the length of road between hotel and airport. The man's teeth were a mess. Bright-eyed but malnourished, he sweated in the sauna of noon.

Jason felt a twinge of guilt, having bargained so aggressively just to shave off a buck or two. He recalled his wife's phrase, spoken on their honeymoon a decade earlier, at a coastal resort in that kind of country: "The misfortune of being born in the wrong place."

Still, Jason closed the deal with American dollars.

The seller chattered in the universal language of pissed-ness to the short woman who wrapped the items and slipped them into a brown paper bag.

Jason gave the shirt to Kyle the minute he got home from the airport that night.

"LOOK WHAT IT SAYS," JASON TOLD HIS SON.

Kyle, who was nine, read it out loud.

"Wow," his son said, after. "Wow."

"Wow is right," Jason said. "When you're a little older, I'll take you there. It's got cool cliffs and these islands out in the ocean that you can actually swim to. Your dad para-sailed. It's like flying."

Over dinner at the sushi place in town, his wife Amy said, "Don't I get a T-shirt?"

"Maybe next time. I brought in three new clients, one trip."

"And that means…"

"Well, we can probably put an offer on the beach condo."

She took a sip of her soda, picked up a chopstick and jabbed it at the air. "Do we really want to do that? We may take a hit for it."

"It's for Kyle, too."

"I think we should just save the money. Invest some more," she said and reached over to harpoon a piece of dragon roll off his plate. He crossed chopsticks with hers and knocked it back in his court.

"Yeah but a condo, just think," Jason said. "Income property, plus vacations. It'll pay forward. Add a little to our investment portfolio."

"But can we make a business of it?"

"It's a start," he said. "You never know where it might lead."

When they got home, Jason drove the nanny back to her little apartment, paying her double for the extra time.

After Amy fell asleep, Jason went to look in on Kyle.

In bed, Kyle's head was nearly covered by the blanket. Jason drew the cover down a little, kissing his son on the back of the scalp.

Kyle wore the T-shirt. A slight discoloration ran along the collar where the manufacturer tag had turned upward.

Jason turned on the flashlight of his cell phone to look.

A brown-red stain.

He checked the back of Kyle's neck, but there was no cut.

He wondered if the stain had been there when he'd bought the shirt.

A few weeks later, Jason — at home, contacting potential clients — was interrupted by a call from Kyle's school.

Jason met with the headmistress that afternoon. Her office looked out over the vast grounds with its soccer field and swimming pool. She mentioned Kyle's moods, his disruptive behavior among the other boys, his outbursts.

"But that's why he's here. You're handling it," Jason said.

Then, she mentioned the T-shirt.

"I still don't understand," Jason said.

The headmistress, her eyes a bit too kind, said, "He wears it under his school shirt every day."

"That against the rules?"

"Of course not," she said. "Our nurse suspected he was using it to hide something. We've seen this before."

Earlier that day during recess, one of the teachers noticed some bruises at Kyle's neck. Boys got bruised all the time, but these seemed odd. Sent him to the school nurse. The nurse noticed that the bruise disappeared down behind the collar of his T-shirt. Kyle told her about having problems sleeping. Waking up in the middle of the night. A scratchy feeling on his back. She asked him to take the T-shirt off. He wouldn't. She had to physically draw it off. He became uncontrollable.

"That's when she saw it," the headmistress said.

"Saw what?"

"The blood. The markings."

Before four, Jason wrangled an appointment with Kyle's pediatrician, who examined the bruises and sores on his back.

"IT'S NOTHING — LOOK." THE DOCTOR WIPED THE

trace of blood away and smoothed out the faint scars with his fingers. "I don't think this is anything serious. Just a skin thing."

"How could it happen?" Jason looked from the doctor to his son.

His son looked down at his feet.

"Kyle?" Jason asked.

His son looked up at him. "I told you. I don't know. Maybe I fell. I don't remember."

"Yep, that's probably it," the doctor said. "Probably scraped himself a little. It's not as bad as it looks. See? Might have brushed against something, scratching it. That would account for any blood."

"You sure it's not something worse?" Jason asked.

The doctor would run some tests. He took a little blood, gave an overdue booster shot, suggested a specialist of some kind if it kept up.

"I'm okay," Kyle said. He looked at his father.

"Did anyone hurt you?" Jason asked.

Kyle shook his head. "I already told you a million times."

That weekend, Jason and Amy set up camcorders all over the house.

THEY HID THEM AMONG SHELVING, BEHIND HANGING plants.

Every night, they watched video of the nanny and Kyle from the previous day.

The nanny —from Ecuador — proved efficient for the

most part but did push Kyle away when he went to grab a second cookie after he got home from school.

Jason didn't quite like Maria that much after this, but it was hardly cause for firing her.

When asked — frequently — Kyle denied any knowledge of the origin of the bruising and sores.

The bruises faded in a few days.

"My brothers were always bruising themselves," Amy said in bed one night. "Boys play rough. You must've been in a few fights as a kid. That alcoholic school nurse just over-reacted."

The next afternoon, while doing laundry, Jason drew the T-shirt from the hamper.

THE STAIN WAS STILL THERE, RIGHT NEAR HIS SON'S side. Jason saw a new stain at the collar and another down along the lower part of the shirt, and yet another by the sleeve edge.

He scraped at the stains with his fingernail.

Little dried flecks came up.

He remembered how — as a boy — he once or twice scraped up his side falling off his bike. He'd bruised himself all over after accepting a dare to jump from a boulder. Suspended over a bridge, he'd burned and blistered his hands. No one had ever thought — in those days — to mention it.

Jason bleached the shirt three times, but the stains wouldn't quite come out. He kept seeing them, faint as they'd become.

He threw the shirt out in the trash.

When Kyle discovered it was missing, he slammed his bedroom door and told his father he didn't love him.

Jason and Amy both laughed at this over a drink before bed.

"I'M PRETTY SURE I SAID THAT TO MY MOTHER HALF A dozen times before I was fourteen. Maybe after that, too," she told him. "Don't worry, he still loves you. He's being silly. Maybe we spoil him too much. Your mother thinks so."

Jason didn't respond. He did spoil Kyle, but when he thought of his own childhood, he didn't want Kyle to ever feel the way he felt as a boy — going without when it came to things every boy wanted.

In bed, finishing up the last of several spreadsheets on her laptop, Amy clicked over to a travel site to book their flight to Costa Rica.

"THERE. WE'RE SET," SHE SAID.

"When?"

"Two weeks from now. Sun, sand, sea — and vacation home hunt."

In the days leading up to the trip, Jason felt coldness from Kyle — still angry at the loss of his favorite shirt.

Just before hugging his son goodbye, Jason promised

he'd bring back a bunch of "T-shirts, sunglasses, sandals. Cool stuff."

When the airport limo drove off, Jason looked back, waving from the open window.

Kyle stood in the driveway with Maria.

His son turned away a little too quickly, grabbing Maria's hand, tugging her back to the house.

In Costa Rica, Jason and his wife spent mornings checking out dozens of condos and houses on the coast. Their afternoons and evenings became bouts of windsurfing, sailing — and drinking a bit too much.

"I don't think I ever want sex again," he laughed after their second go-round in one afternoon.

Every night at seven, they had video chats with Kyle on the laptop. Jason spent a half hour asking him about his day, what he'd done and what friends he'd seen.

They'd play a brief game of Turtle Races on the computer before shutting it down. He always let Kyle win.

"You miss him already?" Amy asked.

"Yep. Next time, we'll bring him. It'll be fun. I want to teach him how to wind surf."

"I'll be worried he might drown. You know me. He's too young."

"Plenty old enough to go out on the water — with me there to catch him. Maybe kayaking, too. That'd be fun."

Amy leaned into him. "Remember when it was always like this? Just the two of us?"

He put his arm around her. "Okay, one more time before shut-eye. Just one more and then this old man's got to sleep."

~

THEY SETTLED ON ONE OF THE CONDOS IN A colorful complex called *Cabeza del Mar*.

The property management company was first-rate. A handful of laborers worked on the floors as Amy stepped around them, inspecting their work, suggesting the kitchen appliances.

The agent told them that if they signed the contract soon, they could decide all the upgrades, including the *en suite* bathroom.

"We'll take a few weeks down here a year, rent it out the rest of the time," Jason told Amy over margaritas at their new favorite watering hole. "By the time we're fifty and taking early retirements, it'll be paid off, and maybe we'll spend winters here,"

"Or sell it when the market revives," Amy said. "I bet it'll be worth a million then. Maybe more."

"Given what we're going to be paying, it better be more."

They had a goal of reaching eight million dollars in savings and investments — minimum — by the time they were fifty. They looked for new business opportunities whenever they could; that's where Amy's market research skills came into play.

Jason was certain they'd make more than their goal if they were careful. They weren't doing too badly, although they had friends who were doing much, much better.

"Still," Amy said, "Not bad for two kids from the suburbs."

On their last day in Costa Rica, Jason remembered the souvenirs for Kyle. One of the cute little shops near the beach had several T-shirts.

"Very cool," Jason said as he sifted through the mountain of shirts, all with printed sayings on the front or back, most of them about the beach and islands and surfing.

"You know, the whole T-shirt industry isn't a bad one," Amy said. "At the company, we've seen growth in this kind of stuff."

"T-shirts? But they're so cheap."

"You'd be surprised. High volume, low costs, high sales. Resorts like this. I'll bet millions of people come through here annually. And every one of them buys a tee or a beach blanket. A memento, gifts for friends."

"But we're not exactly up on this kind of business."

"One of our clients is in textiles — they have a varied industry, but making cheap clothes is big for them."

"In Malaysia?"

"Various countries," she said, rattling off several, some of which he'd never heard of.

"These are made here, there and everywhere," the shop owner said.

Jason looked over at the wizened old American with mottled skin.

"Little factories," the man said. "Nice clean places, each one of 'em."

"You're from the states," Jason said.

"New York," the man said. "I own this shop and three others down the beach. Run them during high season, on my vacation. I'm in Manhattan most of the year. Started in boxer shorts and went to tees. My wife — died five years, November — used to tell me I'd moved up in the world. Underwear always does well. Resort business is on the upswing."

He went on: in America, in summer, T-shirts were huge. Tourist resorts in Central and South America, year-round profits. Big profit margin, low overhead. "Most people can afford to buy a T-shirt — a great way to pull in cash. Souvenirs are big. We had shops in Cancun, Mazatlan, Cozumel, along this coast, of course. Miami and San Diego, too. Used to have three shops in Tokyo. Closing most of these, year by year."

"Really," Jason said, looking at the shirts in his hand. "Must be a boatload of work."

"Not these days," the man said. "Overseers run the factories. The accounts are pretty basic. You don't need to have an American down here — or anywhere. You get a local who knows the laws, knows how to crack the whip, so to speak. Here, China, Africa even, India, other parts of Asia, too. Big production, cheap, and a ton of sales. Even online. We've had the biggest growth online. Used to be, I had to fly all the hell over the world to check on factories. Now I just hire these overseers who run these places independently. Throw a rock in any port city, and you'll hit some guy just waiting to start up a factory. They take a percentage off the top, including production costs — I don't ever have to worry about it. Everything shows up, inventoried, and everything sells to the point where I don't even discount it. Nothing ever *doesn't* sell."

After buying several of the shirts, they took the old man out for lunch. Jason and Amy shot a barrage of questions at him from across the table.

LATER, IN THEIR HOTEL SUITE BEFORE CHECKING OUT, she said, "You really think this is worth doing?"

"Well, we can research it a bit. But I always see people buying souvenirs — and those cheap shirts are popular."

"Everybody has at least one," Amy said.

"And you're always making up funny sayings and stuff."

"True," she said. "It's my one dumbass talent outside of corporate bullshit."

"And we're always talking about diversifying our income."

"Yeah, but there'll be start-up costs."

"Maybe instead of buying a condo, we should create a company. Just a little one."

"Aw, but I loved the condo."

"Sure, but maybe in a year, we'll buy ten condos. Think about it that way."

"But there's a hell of a lot of T-shirts out there."

"We'll differentiate," he said. "We'll do T-shirts just for kids. Or something."

"Sure. We can test it."

"Then, we get them out there," he said. "Get the process going and if it breaks even, fine. If it takes off, we sell it for a big payday within three years. Or less. Who knows? Then, we're not around when it crashes."

KYLE WAS THRILLED TO GET THE SHIRTS FROM COSTA Rica. He fell in love with one that had a picture of a palm tree and said, "Fun, Meet Sun."

The boy wore it everywhere.

WITHIN FOUR WEEKS, AMY AND JASON GOT THEIR prototypes up and out. They launched some small online stores with various names, took out banner ads and made a few deals with established vendors.

Jason kept up with the old man on business trips to Manhattan, frequently taking him to lunch and sometimes drinks and dinner, asking him questions, getting advice, until finally, the old man said, "When is enough *enough*? Now's the time. The market's down, but T-shirts are up. If not now, when? Get this going. You'll expand into other areas, once it's running smoothly."

"You don't mind competition?"

"Please. I'm getting out of the business. I'm too old.

Time for me to go to my little shops in Costa Rica year-round. Just enjoy the sun and my grandchildren."

He recommended various regions around the world for the factories but settled on one or two as sure bets. "You'll get your best bang for your buck, and you'll never have to see it if you don't want."

"Are you kidding? I'd love to see the place where they make our shirts."

"I can't advise that," the old man said. "Let them do their thing, you just do yours."

Still, Jason got on a plane within a week, heading to a small, obscure country the old man recommended.

THE FACTORY WAS A LARGE WAREHOUSE THIRTY MILES from the coast.

Jason met the overseer — a local with an unpronounceable name, in his late thirties, smart, educated, confident.

The overseer pointed out the factory floor where the workers would go at it, the bathrooms, his own office, and the machines.

"You'll never have to worry about a thing," the overseer said. "I take care of it all. You'll check spreadsheets and run sales and marketing. And think of this: all the people you're giving jobs to. I thought my little factory would go under, but you're saving it."

Jason had a good trip.

"Production's already begun," he told Amy.

A FEW WEEKS LATER, A PROBLEM CROPPED UP.

Kyle.

The nanny was upset because a woman had come to the door one afternoon demanding things, bothering her, bothering Kyle when he got home from school.

A neighbor, it seemed, had called the local social service agency.

The next morning, Jason met up with the caseworker.

"WE GOT A REPORT," SHE SAID, AFTER CHECKING HER computer. "Someone noticed your son had scarring around his throat."

Jason stared at her. "*What?*"

She glanced up from her desk. "We didn't find anything wrong with him. We spoke to him. He showed us his neck. It was fine. Still, we had to follow up."

There was a procedure, she told him. She passed him some paperwork. He filled it out.

Jason wondered if he needed to call his lawyer.

He wondered which neighbor had done this.

That night, Jason sat on the edge of Kyle's bed as his son got into his jammies.

KYLE KEPT THE T-SHIRT ON. JASON ASKED HIM TO take it off and put on his pajama top.

"But I like to sleep in it."

"I need to wash it. Sleep in another one."

"But this is my favorite," Kyle said.

"Come on, Kyle. Just change into another one. That one's filthy. *Stinky*." He tried to make the word "Stinky" sound funny so that Kyle would loosen up. But the boy didn't.

"You're being stubborn."

"I sleep good in it," his son said.

Jason got up, pulled out the middle drawer in the pine dresser by the bed, and reached for a T-shirt.

"This is a cool one."

"No."

"Kyle," Jason said. "Just change."

A strange look — one Jason had never seen before — a kind of *dread* brushed across his son's face.

The boy looked frightened and embarrassed in a much deeper way than Jason thought he would be.

"Kyle, what's going on? What are you hiding?"

"Nothing."

"*Kyle*."

His son began crying.

"You're being a baby about this. You have other things to sleep in."

"I don't want to take my shirt off."

"Why not?"

Kyle looked down at his hands. "I just don't. Don't ask me to."

"Look, one way or another, that shirt's coming off your back. My advice is: just forget all this nonsense. Take it off. *Now*."

Jason did his best to remain patient. He spoke with a gentle tone to his voice with warmth in his glance despite the direct order. He was, after all, a loving, understanding, and patient father — for the most part.

"Please, Dad. Don't make me take it off. *Please.*"

Jason caught his breath. He felt a strange power rising up in his throat. He coughed it back. *Breathe. Just breathe. Don't get angry.*

"Kyle, look," Jason said, calming. "I'm your best friend, right? And I'll never hurt you. *Never.* But this is important. I think you know why."

"Please," his son whimpered.

Reluctantly, Kyle raised the shirt over his head.

The boy didn't look at his father when he grabbed the other T-shirt.

"Stop. Freeze." Jason said, just as Kyle began drawing the new shirt down over his neck.

His son stood still.

Jason flicked up the bedside lamp to its highest setting and lifted off the shade.

The room lit up.

Kyle's side and chest looked bruised. Jason grasped his son's shoulders lightly, turning him around.

The boy's back had a series of crisscross scars raised up in a pattern that made him think of…a *whipping.*

"Holy shit," Jason said. He felt kicked in the gut. "Kyle, what happened?"

Kyle closed his eyes as if he'd dreaded this moment. When he opened them, he looked down at his feet.

"Who did this to you? Was it someone at school?"

Kyle glanced up at his father. He whispered something.

Jason couldn't hear him. He crouched low in front of his son, looking at the scars and bruises.

"Just tell me who did this," Jason whispered. "I'll take care of it. It won't ever happen again."

"I don't *know*," Kyle whispered. "I don't *know*. It just happens."

IN BED WITH AMY, JASON TOLD HER.

"Holy shit," she said.

"Exactly what I said."

She wanted to bolt out of bed and check it out for herself.

Jason told her that would only embarrass Kyle more. "I washed his back. Put some lotion on. He said it doesn't hurt."

"You think it's psychosomatic or something?"

"We'll get him to the doc tomorrow. Don't worry."

"Who the hell is doing this?" she asked.

"It's not Maria, obviously."

"Maybe we need to change schools," Amy said. "If they're not doing something about this, it may be time to lawyer up. Maybe they're protecting some fucked-up little sociopathic bully."

In the morning, when Jason helped get Kyle ready for a trip to the doctor's, he noticed that some of the bruises had faded.

By the time they got to the doctor's office — and

waited another forty minutes for Kyle's pediatrician — the bruises were mostly gone.

THE CRISSCROSS PATTERN ON THE BOY'S BACK WAS barely visible when the doctor had Kyle undress.

"Sure, I've seen this sometimes," the pediatrician said. "We don't quite know what it is. Sometimes kids are allergic to stuff. We can test him."

"Allergies?" Jason said. "To what?"

"Maybe it's the material. What's this made from?"

Jason shrugged, touching the edge of the material at Kyle's shoulder. "Natural fibers, I think."

"Where's it made?"

"Does that matter?" Jason asked.

The doctor nodded. "Sometimes these factories have other things going on in them. You never know. I've certainly seen this before. Cheap goods, lower standards."

Before he left the doctor's office, Jason set up two more appointments — one with the child psychiatrist recommended by the social worker — and one more to double check the bruises the following week.

After Kyle's session with the psychiatrist, Jason was handed a prescription.

"HE SEEMS STRESSED," THE PSYCHIATRIST SAID. "We'll get him on a couple of good meds and see how it goes. He may be a little sleepy after the first dose. If you notice erratic behavior, call me."

"Did he talk about anything I should know?" Jason asked.

"Don't worry about this," she said, ignoring the question. "It'll pass. Get those pills. They'll kick in within a week. I'll bet this clears up by the weekend. I'll call social services about the other thing."

"That's it?"

The psychiatrist nodded. "Bottom line, your son is fine. Kids go through phases. He's not in pain. He's not being bullied. My only concern is that he gets some rest."

THAT NIGHT, JASON CALLED THE OVERSEER OF THE factory, who swore up and down that the factory was clean. The workers weren't sick. The fibers were not only natural but had been tested for allergens.

"Don't worry," his overseer said. "I make shirts for a ton of suppliers. Hell, we make sheets now, we make towels, place mats, scarves, purses — you name it. I've got deals with a lot of great places. You'd be surprised all the stuff we make here."

He mentioned several brands to Jason, who noticed — as he went through the house later — that in fact, most of the upholstery was from that region, and the 750 count sheets on the bed were exclusively from this particular factory.

Unable to sleep that night, Kyle crawled in bed with his mother and father.

Given the rough week and the new course of pills that Kyle was on, Jason decided to allow this bending of the rules.

In the morning, after Amy left for her commute, Kyle still snoozed, head on his mother's pillow. He wore the T-shirt that Jason had just thrown out the night before.

Looking at his son's back under the shirt, Jason saw a crisscross of faint scars, bloodstains along them.

He reached out to touch one of the scars. It was slightly raised. His son flinched, waking up.

"Daddy?" Kyle turned around to look at him. "It happened in my dream again."

"Again?" Jason asked. "What do you mean 'again'?"

Kyle nodded. "That's when I see him."

"Who?"

"The boy. The one who's hurt." Kyle said. "I dream about him. He says he dreams about me. He likes seeing where we live."

"Bad dreams?"

Kyle nodded. "They beat him."

Thoughts raced through Jason's mind:

Kyle was going to tell him the truth. He was going to tell him it was a dream, but it was really and truly the truth. His son was going to tell him now who had done this.

It was no allergy. No psychiatric problem.

Some other boy was hurting him. A boy in the city. A boy in school. A boy in the neighborhood.

"Who beats him?" Jason asked.

"Others."

"Who are the others?"

His son squinted, tilting his head to the side.

"You can trust me," Jason said, almost frightened of what his son might say. "Have these 'others' threatened you?"

Kyle shook his head, slowly.

"Tell me what happens in the dream."

"The boy gets hurt. The others make him hurt."

"And who are they?"

"People," Kyle said.

"Do they live near us?"

Kyle shook his head.

"Please, son. This is important. Tell me more about the boy."

"He's not fast enough."

Jason remembered all the bullies in gym class from his own childhood, the boys who just liked to pummel other kids who were slow or less athletic or seen as weak by them.

"Is the boy not a fast runner? Or good at basketball?"

"Not fast enough," Kyle said. "They make him bleed. They make him cry. Sometimes he can't sleep for days. He's afraid they might kill him. He thinks they've killed someone he knew. Someone who's not around anymore."

Unable to control himself, Jason nearly leapt for his son, grabbing him in a bear hug.

"Daddy? Are you okay?"

"Nobody's ever going to hurt you. Nobody," Jason whispered. "You just need to tell me. You need to trust me. I'm your father. I love you. I love you no matter what you do, no matter who you are. You could do the most terrible thing in the world, Kyle, and I would love you anyway. I will love you until the world comes to an end. Even after that, I'd still love you."

Kyle struggled against his father's embrace, but then he began crying, too.

"You're scaring me," he said.

Jason let go. He took a few heavy breaths, calming.

After a minute, Kyle told him more about the boy and what he remembered from the dreams — the bruises on the boy, the scars and welts on his back and shoulders, even the name.

"I think it's his name. I'm not sure he told me. But I think this is his name."

After pulling Kyle into another school — a better, more expensive one — Jason banned all T-shirts from the house.

KYLE EXPERIENCED MINOR SIDE EFFECTS FROM HIS medication but slept through most nights. He seemed better behaved and more alert during the day.

The bruising and scarring became a distant memory.

The dreams of the boy hurt by others no longer happened, according to Kyle.

The side business of T-shirts took off. Within two years, a buyer approached Jason and Amy about buying the whole operation from them.

Amy felt the offered price was too good not to sell.

Before the sale, they'd take one last trip down to the

shirt factory, give a big fat bonus to the overseer and the office workers, and then a great "goodbye" bonus to every single worker on the floor.

IT WAS A BIG DAY AT THE FACTORY, WHICH HAD grown into three large buildings.

Amy *oohed* and *ahhed* over the operation. Jason marveled at the ambitious production schedule; the blocks of apartments for the workers; the canteen; the offices. The overseer and his secretary took them to the little area where their shirts were manufactured.

The line workers remained busy, down on the floor, a humming hive moving in and around a variety of machines. There were several older women, some middle-aged, at least one expectant mother among them. The men were younger, some of them in their teens.

Jason was surprised to see children there, too, running errands, sewing, cutting fabric, rolling it out.

He knew this was the standard of the country, and even children needed to bring money home to their poor families. He didn't love seeing it and mentioned it to the overseer.

"Only fourteen and up in my factory," the overseer said with pride. "The laws here allow for much, much younger. Children need work, just like anyone else, but some of these boys come from families with nothing. Absolutely nothing. It's a pleasure to find some kind of work for their children."

"They look way too young." When Jason said this, he felt Amy's elbow in his side.

"We're short, young-looking people," the overseer's secretary said. "Not tall and strong like you people."

All of this did little to reassure Jason. He and Amy exchanged glances.

They went around to the happy and grateful employees, many of whom wept when they were handed cash.

The boys — they seemed not much older than Kyle — came up, grinning, thanking, speaking the few words of English they could manage. The girls at the machines kept their eyes downcast but thanked both of them for the money with nods and closed-mouth smiles.

One little boy — *could he have been fourteen? Looked younger.* He was Kyle's height, but much thinner. He ran up and hugged them both, speaking bad English, thanking them but not daring to look up at their faces.

Jason felt an unexpected tug at his heart. He gave the boy double the amount.

The boy wore one of their T-shirts, the one that Kyle had loved back when he was allowed to wear it.

As the boy turned to run back to his station, Jason saw the crisscross bloodstain marks along his back where the shirt had been torn. He remembered seeing a long strip of thick cowhide hanging above the door of the overseer's office. When Amy had mentioned it, the secretary remarked that it was hers "so I can whip the boss into shape when he gets lazy," and they all had a good, polite laugh at this.

"You gave him too much," the overseer said, mentioning the boy by name as he ran off among the aisles of machinery. "He's a daydreamer. Never fast enough, never on top of his work. I don't know why I keep some of them on."

"You have a big heart," his secretary said.

Jason recognized the name of the boy.

JASON FELT LOST FOR THE REST OF THE TOUR through the factory. He could not look Amy in the eye, nor did he manage much in the way of conversation with the others.

He canceled dinner but nodded when Amy said she wanted to go as a final thank you to the overseer and his secretary. She was sorry he felt ill.

Jason went to lie down in their hotel room.

Amy returned from dinner, very excited, and woke him at midnight.

"OH MY GOD, JASON, YOU WOULDN'T BELIEVE IT," HIS wife said, her voice rising with excitement. "I think we can make a killing with high-end sheets and pillowcases. We all crunched numbers tonight. They showed me some printouts regarding the competition. He can bring it in under budget. He told me that our business made him rich enough to keep expanding product lines and now…"

She kept talking about the millions they could make and maybe even attach products to a celebrity and market them through some big box stores to appeal to middle-class people who wanted great bedding at low, low prices.

He felt as if he were gasping for air with every word she spoke.

He ran his fingers along bruises at his throat and felt the skin of his back rise slightly to meet the edge of the whip.

THE AMERICAN

Quested's, a cafe in the old Fire District, looked out on a triangle of park lined with sculptures and trees.

The barman brought out an espresso, tinged with lemon, on a small round tray. He set the cup down in front of the latest arrival.

The American stared at the small cup for a moment as if deciding whether or not to order something else.

"I tried to kill myself tonight," he announced to the couple at a nearby table.

HE SIPPED HIS DRINK AND GLANCED OUT INTO THE night, not caring if they listened.

"I smoked every cigarette I could find. Drank everything. I swam in the filthy river and then went to a brothel where the whores were shapeless and ancient."

"Now, that's the way to do it," one woman said, from the table nearest his. "Good for you. Bon voyage."

"So you come to a dark little cafe like the rest of us," said the Italian gentleman beside her, his face lit by candle glow from the table's center. "More drinks, good sir. This time, two shots. I feel lucky tonight."

The barman stood by, a small white towel draped across his arm, an emptiness in his gaze. "We're closing in a half hour."

"Why's that?" the tourist from Scotland asked.

"I have a life, that's why," the barman said.

"It's a lovely night," the Italian said, and then began singing, lightly, a beautiful old song in a reedy voice. The handful of ex-pats and tourists, all of them, smiling; with the exception of the American, who glanced face to face, table to table.

The slender branches of nearby trees, full of summer leaf, waved slightly, then, the breeze died.

The American began laughing.

"What's the joke?" said the woman.

"I want to obliterate myself. Somehow."

"Why's that?"

"I am one of the great unloved."

"You can't be more than twenty-three. You can find love next year."

"I don't think that's how it works. I think it begins at birth and goes from there. Then, one day you just recognize it. You're outside the joke that others get. You're not in on what they seem to connect with."

"You're just inexperienced," she said. Then, turning to

her the man beside her, she whispered a few words in Italian.

He whispered back.

She said to the American, "Come sit with us. Would you like a cigarette?"

IN A MINUTE OR TWO, HE'D CHANGED SEATS AND SAT across from the woman and her friends.

She introduced the young man to the others: the Italian gentleman, and a young couple from Bristol who were only in Rome for a week.

One of the Scottish tourists at the next table began whispering to one of the others as if he knew something about the American.

The woman said, "You look familiar to me."

"I'm here a lot, sometimes. I come late at night. I suppose I drink too much," the American said.

The woman looked at the older Italian man and smiled. "We like Quested's. So many people come here who speak English. My Italian is still a little rough, but I'm getting better, aren't I, Dario?"

The Italian nodded, "Yes. Every day you mispronounce a new word in my language."

"Oh," she said, nudging him with her elbow. She offered a sorrowful smile to the American. "I'm sorry you're not feeling yourself tonight. But that's what drinking's for."

"Have you ever burned for anyone?" the American asked. "Burned? I have. I do."

"Someone must've broken your heart," the woman said. "Here in Rome?"

"A whore," the American said.

"if you really mean 'whore,' you might be smart not to give your heart where you put your wallet," the Italian said. "But I suspect you exaggerate."

"Well, a whore in spirit."

"All of us should be whores in spirit," the Italian said.

"Darling," the woman said, placing her hand on the Italian's wrist. "Give him a little space to grieve for his lost love. Don't all men call women whores when they've been thrown over?"

"It's a man, not a woman," the American said.

"*Aha*," the woman said. "That explains it. Men are all whores. No exaggeration there."

"*I'm* not a whore," the Italian said.

"Of course you're not. Darling, go get us another drink. The barman's too surly."

After the Italian left the table, the woman — who seemed to the American like every British woman he'd met — leaned over and whispered, "You're gay, then. What's that like?"

The American grinned. "Here we go."

"No, I mean, what's it like to feel the way we — women — always feel, and yet have the same instincts as any man?"

The other woman at the table laughed. "It's true. It must be terrible."

"It's exactly the same," the American said. "Nobody feels differently. We're all looking for love, and we're all messed up at the same time. Some people are meant to be loved. I am not."

"That's ridiculous. Utterly ridiculous. Everyone is meant to be loved. Is this about your mother?"

"What?"

"Well, in my experience, men get screwed up by their mothers because mummy wanted a perfect little husband in the perfect little son. It's incestuous. I see it all the time. Especially with you American boys."

"My mother died when I was three, so I suspect that's not the issue."

"That destroys my theory," the woman said. "Do you really want to kill yourself? I mean, honestly, kill yourself?"

He thought a moment but did not answer. He leaned back, looking up at the tree branches. "It's impossible to see the stars through these trees."

"No, it's not. I see them."

"I can't."

The Italian returned with a round tray of small glasses filled with greenish-brown liquid.

"Here we are," the woman said. "Do you like absinthe?"

"Absinthe-*lootly*."

No one laughed.

He added, "I like everything that's bad for me."

"Maybe that applies to the men you pick. Tell me about this recent love."

"Recent one? My only love."

"Wait. You're joking."

"No, I'm not," the American said. "Before him, I hadn't been with a man."

"With a woman before?"

"A few times. In my teens."

"But this was your first real love. That explains a lot," the woman said. "First loves are dreadful unless you're the one who dumps him. So this was just your learning experience."

"No. He was the only one until he had me do things. But that was all for his benefit. It's over. My life."

"Don't be ridiculous," the woman said. "Here, drink. You'll feel better. You'll burn away those feelings along with a few brain cells tonight."

The Italian began speaking to the barman who stood by.

"He wants to close up," the Italian said. "He has a sick child at home."

"Just one drink to go," the woman said. She raised her glass and sipped. "Do you feel it yet?"

"I feel too much," the American said.

"I mean the absinthe. They say it's terrific for destroying the brain."

"And hallucinating," said the Italian.

"I need hallucination to do what I need to do," the American said. "Here's the thing." He took a few sips. "Here's the thing. He told me he loved me. He made me do things that I wouldn't ordinarily do."

"Like?"

"I'd rather not say."

"I see," the woman said "*Sexual* things."

"And other things. He had me...do things. With others. He says it's what will bind us. I was stupid. I don't know who I am sometimes."

The American drank down his glass of absinthe too quickly. "I must be a terrible person. I've done things that I never thought I'd do. I've humiliated myself. I've crossed boundaries I thought I would never cross. For him."

"You'll get sick if you go at it like that," the woman said. "Sip. That stuff'll give you the biggest headache of your life by dawn. And dawn is coming up soon enough."

The Italian took his glass and set it down in front of the American. "For you."

The American glanced up at the Italian. He picked up the glass and took a sip. He kept his nose near the drink as if inhaling something delicious. He watched the Italian as he drank.

"This is a fine drink."

"It's terrible for you. This is really the way to kill yourself," the Italian said. "If you're going to do it. This, or perhaps gelato — or pastries."

The American looked at the glass and swirled the green liquid around in it. "How beautiful."

"This man of yours sounds terrible," the woman said. "Just awful."

"He sounds unusual, that's true," the Italian said. "But why do these things? Why do what he asks?"

"I love him. I loved him. I still do."

"Love means hurting yourself?"

"Sometimes."

"Did you enjoy any of this wickedness?" the woman asked.

"Enjoy?"

"Well, it sounds like a dirty movie. There must be some fun to it. You were asked to do things you wouldn't ordinarily do. You must like the authority of it. Being told what to do. And doing it."

"I suppose I do like it. And I hate that I like it."

He drank the rest of the Italian's absinthe.

"You've just lost some brain cells," the woman said. "Well, as terrible as that love affair sounds, there are others in the world for you. You're just starting out. There may be dozens of men you'll love before you find that elusive right one."

"I can't do that," the American said. "There's only one man for me. I am not going to live that life, from one to another. I've known people who did that. It is awful. It turns love into a machine."

"But what did this man do to you?" she asked. "He didn't care for you. He used you. No matter how you would like that to be, that's not love. That, my friend, is a machine of some kind. That love of yours." A slight laugh. "It may be fun. It may be a good memory for when you're old and gray and want to think of misspent youth. But it's not love."

"You don't understand," the American said. "Love is about giving yourself up. Body and soul."

"Is it? I thought it was an action. I love Dario," she leaned into the Italian and gave him a squeeze. "But by love, I mean, I do things with him, for him, we have fun, we think about life together. But if he asked me to do something I couldn't do, I'd draw a line."

"Would you?" the Italian began laughing. "Well, I guess I know the limits of our love life now."

"Ha ha," she said.

"No, truly," the Italian said, kissing the top of the

woman's scalp and watching the American. "I would draw no line for you. If you wished me to sleep with others, I'd do as you wished."

She swatted at the Italian. "Oh, you. This young man is serious." She leaned across the table and touched the top of the American's hand. "Love is when you trust each other. Like good friends. Best friends."

"I don't think that's love. That's complacency," the American said. "Love is a lot more extreme. It's everything or nothing. I'm not sure trust is part of it."

"That's because you're young."

"You're not old. How old are you?"

"Nearly thirty."

"I bet at twenty you felt differently."

"Perhaps I did. But you grow up." Then, seeing the stricken look on his face, she added, "I think sometimes in life, to learn about love, you have to break at first. You can't have those illusions you have when you're a child. And you will break, first, before you find out what love is. You break and are hurt. As you are now. But then you mend and grow stronger, and you come to realize what love is and what it isn't. And you avoid what looks like love, but is really just some wild animal that has no love in its soul."

"I want to burn from love," the American said.

The woman took a sip from her glass and then lit up a cigarette. "This is such a serious topic. We should talk of lighter things."

"All right," the American said. "How about the war?"

"Oh, no, let's go back to your sex life."

The American, his eyes glazing a bit from the drink, looked at his glass as if he could see the past in it.

"He had me sleep with soldiers, several at a time. Then, with the wife of a friend."

"A woman?"

"Yes. Then, one night, a man of seventy. He had me steal from people. Just to see if I would obey him."

The woman inhaled deep from her cigarette. "You're taking the piss now. This sounds made up."

"It's not," the American said. "I did it for him. I'd do anything for him."

"Well," the woman said, glancing at the others. "Then you need to separate from this person forever. You need to go get some help."

"Did he make you kill anyone?" the Italian asked.

THE AMERICAN DIDN'T ANSWER.

The woman and the Italian glanced at each other. The other couple began to talk about going home for the evening, back to their flat that was a quarter mile away.

After they left, the Italian said, "I think you're troubled. I think this love you talk of is very disturbing for you. Perhaps you just need to sleep."

"Who can sleep?" the woman asked. "I can't. Not until I put myself out with these." She lifted her glass, then noticed that the American's was empty. "More? Look, Tina's left some in her glass. Have it."

She passed the glass over to the American.

"You asked me if I ever killed anyone for him," the

American said. He drank the absinthe down. "'Not yet' is my answer. But I would."

"Would you? That's terrible," the woman said.

"I know. I'm lost. That's why I tried to kill myself tonight. I want to end it. I am never going to be loved. I am not going to ever have him again. I know it. I know it."

"Did he ask you to kill someone?" the Italian asked.

The American glanced at the woman, then at the Italian. "He's out of my life."

"But he did ask you?"

"Yes. But I don't think I can."

"Why not?"

"Dario!" the woman said, giggling as if she had drunk a bit too much. "Of course he wouldn't kill anyone."

"I'm just asking. It sounds like a fantasy anyway. Who would have this young man sleep with an old man — or with soldiers — who loved him? Who would do that?" the Italian said. "What kind of man? I don't believe he exists."

"He does," the American said. "And I'd do everything I did again. And then some."

"But not kill."

"I might. I might. I think everyone is capable of killing someone."

"I'm not," the woman said.

"You just haven't met the right person who needed killing," the American said.

"Why do this? For *love*? What does that mean?"

"It means I have no other choice."

"How are you going to kill?" the Italian asked. "If you decide to do this. Hand to hand?"

"That's what he wants. He told me who. He told me where and when. He wants me to use my bare hands."

"You don't seem that strong," the Italian said. "You don't look like you could kill a man."

The American glared at him and slipped a cigarette between his lips.

The Italian leaned forward with his lighter and lit up the American's cigarette.

The woman glanced at the two of them as if she were capturing the moment in some mental photograph. The way the American cupped his hand around the Italian's hand, encircling the heart of the flame as it touched the tip of his cigarette.

"Who did he ask you to kill?" the woman asked, a slight anxiety in her voice.

"Someone I don't know. Someone I don't care to know very well."

The Italian closed the lighter and drew back in his chair. He glanced out into the dark morning. "What I love about the night is that we're all alone in it, even if we're together. Like this."

The woman went silent for a bit. Then, after a minute or two she said, "You should get away from this man completely. You should leave Rome. Go to Paris. Go back home if you need to. Stop drinking. Stop taking whatever drugs you take. Go discover life. There's more to life than love, anyway. You don't need to burn from love, or even burn from liquor. You need some rest and to get away from this terrible human being."

"I don't think I can live without him," the American said.

The woman glanced at the Italian, who still looked out at the night. Then, at the American. Then, to her empty glass.

The barman came out and told them that he was closing up whether they stayed at the tables or not. "I don't have this endless night that you people have."

"All right, all right," she said. "Let's go."

"We can't leave this young man here," the Italian said.

"Oh yes, we can. Do you need a taxi?"

The American stared at her but didn't answer.

She stood up and reached into her purse for money. "You need sleep is all." She said this indirectly. It could've been to anyone — the Italian, the American, the barman, or even to herself.

The Italian remained in his chair but looked up at her. "We can walk down to the fountain."

"No," she said. "Let's go home. Back to my place."

"Let's go to mine," he said.

The American stared at them both, and the woman was nearly certain that tears rolled down his cheeks. She drew a tissue from her purse and passed it to him. "It'll be all right. Whatever it is."

The American took the tissue, swiping it around his eyes. "I've never killed anyone before."

"And you don't have to. Don't talk nonsense. Please."

The Italian finally rose, pushing his chair back. "You shouldn't have been drinking the absinthe," he said. "It's not good."

"Let's go," the woman whispered, loudly enough for the American to hear.

"All I'm saying," the American said. "All I'm saying is

that I'm thinking of killing for him. That's all. I don't know why he drives me to this. I don't know what he wants. I only know I have to do what he wants."

The Italian stepped back from the woman and nodded. "Love is a cruel thing, sometimes. It needs proof. These are dangerous times in the world. We've met an assassin over drinks at Quested's."

As she passed by the American on her way out, the woman said, "Just go home and go to sleep. It'll seem different when you wake up."

She nearly touched him on the shoulder as a way of comforting him but withdrew her hand at the last second.

The woman and the Italian gentleman left Quested's, walking out under the trees, through the park.

As she stepped into the path between some thin sculptures, she shrugged off the touch of the Italian as if she were annoyed with him.

AFTER A MINUTE, THE AMERICAN GOT OUT OF HIS chair, as well. The lights of Quested's shut off and the barman went home.

The American stepped into the park and moved through the shadows to catch up with the couple.

BELINDA IN THE POOL

S itting just in front of Michael and his daughter, the woman — white of hair and coat — lifted her card.

"Three hundred!" the auctioneer said. "Number 17!"

"If she'd just quit bidding," Belinda said, under her breath.

Michael — Number 5 — glared at the back of the annoying whiteness of Number 17. Belinda gave him a nudge. He held up his card.

Twenty people in sweaters and coats sat on hard plastic chairs crammed into the cold, dusty little shop.

Belinda squeezed his arm. "You can get it, Dad."

Nobody's going much over 500 dollars for this, Michael thought. It wasn't even worth three hundred to anyone in the market for antique watches with silver bands.

In that second between his most recent bid and the auctioneer's next mouthing, Michael tasted something bitter at the back of his throat.

After years of searching, here we are, he thought. *In a*

junk shop with Belinda, a twenty-minute drive door-to-door,
the watch right there in front of us.

"Your mother's not going to be happy," he said. "I
wasn't even supposed to go over two-fifty. Holy cow."

"But we're almost there," Belinda said. "And it's just
money. You'll make more. You always say that."

His daughter — verbally expressive beyond her fourteen years, curious, inquisitive, advanced in her thinking
— constantly surprised him. Belinda of the dark hair,
slightly bowed shoulders, fresh-faced, the last of
summer's freckles still faint on her cheek, green pond-
water eyes, unremarkable nose, barest hint of mascara,
vanishing dimple at her chin, most of the baby fat gone
now, at the beginning of her swan years, a little silver
crescent moon on a slim chain around her neck, fog-
gray wool sweater pulled over orange T-shirt above blue
jeans, fake tattoo — the Eye of Horus — at the back of
her hand; she of the swim team, of the annual Charlotte
Russe, made with the flourish of a great chef abandoning
messy pans and spattered bowls in her wake, of sweet
crushes on pretty male pop idols with wavy hair who
posed in posters tacked up around her bedroom, of the
little squeal of delight in sampling gelato at a shop on
the *Via di San Simone*, of the amusement park obses-
sion, of the junior debate team, of the long chess games
with her old man where they talked endlessly of the
world and school and how things used to be and how
they were now, of the trips to Spain and England and
Italy, of the bruised knees made better by a father's kiss,
of the treasure hunts, of the late night movie marathons
with stove-hot popcorn dripping in butter and parme-

san; so much like her mother and so much unlike her, too.

And Belinda in the pool, Michael thought, suddenly cold.

"Dad, don't let anyone else get it. It's meant for you. I can feel it."

The woman in white raised her arm again, yellow card in hand.

When the auction was over, Michael and his daughter remained in their chairs, waiting out rush hour traffic.

Belinda passed him a mint from the small flat tin she kept in her pocket.

"Sorry, Dad."

"Sometimes ya win, sometimes ya lose," he said.

"That's what losers say."

"Very funny."

He thought he might tell her, right then, about why that watch meant so much.

But why should she be burdened with his reasons?

Belinda was still a baby in his eyes, despite her womanly form emerging, *oh god,* he thought, here come the breasts, her waistline narrowing as hips curved and legs lengthened; and the way her hair sparkled after she'd brushed it; the strange silences during which he imagined her a captive in some newly-minted cell of that hormonal prison called adolescence, unable — suddenly — to talk openly about private feelings.

It came back to him as he sat there, a thud at his heart, the nightmare moment — those dreadful few seconds earlier that week when the reality hit him.

Somehow, it made the search for the watch that much more important.

HE'D DRIVEN OVER TO PICK HER UP AT THE YMCA. Tired of waiting in the parking lot, Michael went inside. He passed through the men's locker room, pushed the door into the swimming area.

He stood by the folded bleachers.

Belinda emerged from restless water and ascended the metal ladder at the edge of the pool. She wore a midnight blue bathing suit, her skin glistening. She'd only just drawn off her bathing cap, unleashing a cascade of thick, shiny hair that curved along her still-tanned shoulders.

Michael became aware of the boys. All those seventeen and eighteen-year-olds standing by the edge of the pool, towels flung over shoulders, their tell-all Speedos, mouths agape, eyes burning with intensity, an electrical, musky charge in the chlorinated air as they watched his daughter in a way that disturbed Michael to no end.

The kind of boy he had once been.

Oh god, Belinda. Not yet.

He could feel her slipping from his grasp. She'd be under the waves, carried by dangerous currents to some distant shore he'd never reach. No more gelatos with dad, no more squandering of Saturdays in junk shops, no more buttery, cheesy popcorn, no more *Michael-Belinda Misadventures.*

He tried to push the moment from his mind.

MICHAEL LOOKED DOWN AT HIS YELLOW CARD WITH the number 5 scrawled on it in magic marker. He passed it to her.

"A souvenir."

"Yee-haw." She folded up the card until it fit in the palm of her hand.

"Come on, it's been fun," he said. "Not a bad way to spend an afternoon off."

Belinda slumped further down in her chair. "There's absolutely no other watch you want in the entire world?"

"Sounds silly when you put it like that."

The shopkeeper's son began sweeping the floor around empty chairs. The boy — roughly fifteen, Michael guessed — glanced at Belinda and smiled.

"He's not very smart," Belinda whispered, leaning in close. She smelled of French soap and raspberries. "Look. He's doubling his work. You clear chairs first, then sweep."

"You should tell him."

"Like I care."

Belinda moved her legs to the right to avoid the broom. She didn't look at the boy. She swiveled in her chair. Her knees brushed against her father's. Instinctively, Michael pulled his legs away.

"Makes me angry," she said, after a full minute. "That lady just grabbed what's supposed to be yours."

"I was outbid."

"No, she grabbed it. It can't possibly mean as much to her — not like it does to you. Just look at her."

He turned his attention to the far right, beyond the chairs.

THE COUPLE THAT RAN THE SHOP SAT ON ONE SIDE OF a long narrow table. The lucky bidders took the chair directly across, one at a time, signing checks and paperwork.

Passed across the table: a 19th century painting of the mill stream with its chipped ornate frame, a little bronze art deco nude, two giant blue and green glass globes, the small cast-iron table with pink marble top, a doll with its face pushed in and dollhouse without doors that went with it, a mangy full-length mink, a small cardboard box filled with what Belinda had called "old lady jewelry," and a few other things that Michael mostly considered crap.

And then, the woman of white, taking a little square box from the owner.

He couldn't see what she did — her back was toward him — but guessed that she opened the box and drew out the watch.

Belinda arched her back, stretching out. "You could've bid more."

"Your mother would kill me."

"But this was the one time we found it," she said.

"It's just a watch. It doesn't really matter."

"If you want it, it matters."

"Sometimes it's good to want something but not get it."

"Yeah, except you never get what you want," she said. "Remember Italy? All your meetings were over. You wanted to go to Florence. Mom wanted two more days in Rome. We stayed in Rome."

"Well, we had a good time," Michael said. "And we can always go back."

"But we won't. You only go where work sends you. You never take a vacation just for you. And you won't ever see the Uffizi. Let's just write that little dream off."

"Well, I say we'll go again," he said. "Someday. Florence ain't going anywhere."

"You never know," she said. "A war. A tsunami. A world cataclysm. Things happen. I'm betting a couple thousand years ago somebody put off a summer trip to Pompeii and then — well, that's that."

"You're a little too smart for your old man."

"It's just that things only come around once. Sometimes."

Belinda crossed and uncrossed her legs. She tapped her foot against the empty chair in front, kicking it just enough that the chair moved forward.

"I don't know if I want to live in the same universe where that lady gets the watch, and you don't," Belinda whispered as she glanced around. "It's…It's an injustice."

He wasn't sure, but it looked like her eyes shone with tears.

He reached over and hugged her. She pressed her face against his shoulder.

"Aw, come on," he whispered. "Sometimes the hunt's better than the treasure."

Belinda drew back, a glint of tear at her cheek. She wiped it away. The Eye of Horus, now a smudge on the back of her hand.

"I wanted you to get it," she said.

"Me, too."

"It's not fair."

"Life's never fair." He kissed her on the forehead. "And it's not all about me, anyway. But you've got to be the sweetest kid on the planet to stick up for your old man. We'll find that watch someday."

"And someday you'll see the Uffizi Gallery," she said, with a slow drip of cynicism.

The shopkeepers' son began clearing chairs away. Again, the boy glanced over at his daughter.

"See? He's going to have to sweep all over again," Belinda said, momentarily distracted from her mood. "If he'd done it right the first time…"

Michael closed his eyes. *Don't think of the pool.*

"Dad, Dad — look, quick," Belinda said as if she were waking him up to an emergency.

Michael opened his eyes.

BELINDA TURNED HALFWAY AND POINTED TOWARD the front window of the shop.

The woman of whiteness stood out at the street, glancing one way and then the other, waiting for a gap in the heavy traffic. She stepped off the curb only to be chased back to the sidewalk by a car.

"They need to put more traffic lights downtown," Belinda said.

The shop was on a strange corner, jutting out like a peninsula into a choppy sea of streets.

"She won't get across any time soon," Belinda said. "She should walk down to State Street and then go over. Or wait it out in here. Someone should tell her."

Michael watched the back of the woman of white.

"Dad, remember how you're always saying I should take fate into my own hands?"

"Of course. Seize the day."

"You can still get the watch."

"It's too late," he said.

"She's standing right there. You could offer her fifty bucks more."

Michael stood up to get a better look out the window.

Belinda slipped outside and went to stand just behind the woman. She glanced back at her father through the shop window, motioning for him to follow.

"Excuse me," Michael said. "Miss?"

The woman of white didn't look his way at first.

"Hello?" he asked.

She glanced over. Younger than he'd expected, given the white hair.

Belinda stepped up. "My dad just wants to see if he can buy that watch off you."

"I'm sorry," the woman said. "You bid on it, too?"

"We sat right behind you." Belinda brought out the yellow card from the back pocket of her jeans, unfolding it. "See? Number 5."

The woman looked from Michael's face to his daughter's.

"My daughter, Belinda."

Then, he introduced himself.

The woman of white smiled at Belinda.

"I'm Carolyn. What a beautiful sweater." Then, she looked over at Michael, her smile fading. "I could never give this watch up. You could pull out five thousand dollars cash right now. I wouldn't be able to hand it over. And I'm not rich. I could use five thousand. Couldn't we all."

She held up her wrist, drawing the coat sleeve back. The silver and turquoise gleamed in the moody slant of November's dimming light.

"It's really a man's watch. Seems old-fashioned to say it. As if watches could be male or female." The woman dragged her sleeve down again.

"My dad's been looking for that exact watch for years," Belinda said.

The woman looked from Belinda to her father. "I'm sorry. Maybe you'll find another one."

Belinda walked behind the woman's back. She mouthed a word that Michael thought might be: "fate," or perhaps, he thought: "hate." Or "wait."

"Sure I can't change your mind?" Michael asked.

The woman held her hand up, a stop sign. "Please leave me alone."

Carolyn turned and looked back toward the shop.

Michael wondered if she might run inside and claim he was harassing her. He had to be sensitive. He took a step back.

"No," he said. "I understand. Honestly…"

Belinda, on the other side of the woman, made a rolling motion with her hands, which Michael interpreted as *keep talking, Dad.*

"Just name a price," he said, worried that the woman might throw out some astronomical figure and then he'd have trouble saving face in front of Belinda.

"Look," the woman said. "Fuck off."

She stepped into the street.

Something about Belinda caught his eye.

His daughter darted to the edge of the curb, a blur of motion reaching for Carolyn's white coat.

In the same second that Belinda did this, a truck came out of swift traffic, brakes squealing and slammed into the woman of white at the dead center of her body.

Belinda stepped back to the curb. Instinctively, Michael nearly leapt for his daughter, and they both crumpled down to the sidewalk in each other's arms.

Carolyn flew like a great white bird to the truck's windshield, reaching upward.

The woman of white slid down across the hood and then fell to the street.

MICHAEL RODE WITH THE WOMAN IN THE ambulance, after making sure that the police would give Belinda a ride home.

He felt responsible. He wondered if he'd scared the woman a little, making her want to get out into the street, away from him.

Michael noticed that the sleeves of her coat had torn, but her arms were pristine. The watch seemed to have survived perfectly well.

AT THE HOSPITAL, CAROLYN OPENED HER EYES.

Michael told her where she was, who he was, and why she couldn't move.

The nurses flitted around the gurney, doctors chattered, someone called for a specialist, someone else called for someone named Bobby, and Michael felt a thud in his chest knowing he had a few seconds before anyone might see.

He thought of Belinda, all those times they'd scoured auctions and shops, looking for a watch he was certain they'd never find.

And then, found.

And lost.

Right here, inches away.

Carolyn's eyes opened, watching him.

He slipped the watch off her wrist and into the pocket of his jacket.

She'll forget this. After the anesthesia, it'll all be a weird dream to her when she recovers.

Later, he called his wife and told her what happened —accident, hospital; nothing about the watch. His wife snarled at him for abandoning Belinda; for riding with some stranger in an ambulance.

"Who does that?" she kept asking as if he'd been unfaithful.

He managed to get Belinda on the phone.

"You okay?"

"I'm fine, don't worry," she said.

He was just about to hang up when Belinda asked, "Did you get it?"

MICHAEL ARRIVED HOME LATE. HE SLEPT IN THE DEN on the couch, the watch cupped in his hands.

He woke up several hours later in the dark.

He remembered a dream: the woman of white, her face a bloody mess, rose from the depths of a swimming pool to strangle him.

He took Belinda to the city hospital the next afternoon.

"I STILL DON'T SEE WHY WE'RE HERE," SHE SAID AS THEY sat in the waiting area. "I mean, we don't actually know her."

"I want to make sure she's okay."

"You're giving it back, aren't you?" Belinda glared at him, then picked up a magazine and began flipping through pages, breathing heavily, making her disapproval known with little grunts and sighs.

CAROLYN LAY ASLEEP IN HER ROOM IN THE MIDST OF a labyrinth of tubes, hook-ups, and machines.

Michael set the wristwatch on the dresser by the bed.

HE BROKE OUT IN A COLD SWEAT IN THE HALLWAY, just beyond the double doors.

Belinda looked over at him from her seat at the end of the corridor.

WHEN HE REACHED HER, SHE STOOD UP.

"I need to use the bathroom."

"Over there," he pointed.

Michael sat down and closed his eyes. A headache came on. He pressed his hands over his eyes, leaning forward. A throbbing pain, suddenly, a build up of tension; guilt; the poor woman of white; a memory in the past that meant so much to him; the moments of loss in his life; the damned vision of Belinda in her bathing suit rising from the waters of the YMCA pool with all those boys.

After a minute or two, Belinda returned and put her arm over his shoulder.

"Dad, it's okay. I'm not mad at you or anything," his daughter whispered.

A month later, closing in toward the holidays, Michael

got a letter from a law firm claiming he'd stolen — from their client, Miss Carolyn Hoskins — an expensive wristwatch.

THE FIRM PRICED THE WATCH AT FIFTY THOUSAND dollars.

"The value may be higher," the letter stated. "Our client believes the item is priceless."

He could only guess what had happened.

"That's ridiculous," Belinda said after he showed her the letter. "She didn't even pay six hundred for it."

They were both in the warm kitchen, a Saturday leaning toward noon. They shared a grilled cheese on rye and a bowl of tomato soup at the breakfast counter by the window overlooking the patio, which was covered with snow.

"Besides, you didn't take it," Belinda added after she'd read the letter a second time.

"Someone else — a nurse, maybe a relative — must have stolen it. After I put it back," Michael said, pausing to take a sip of orange spice tea, one of Belinda's winter concoctions. "Of course she thought I did it. She saw me pick it up."

"Oh come on," Belinda said. "Nobody's going to remember that after they get hit by a truck. Her lawyer probably got your name and address from the cops. She just *thinks* you did it. What a greedy little piggy she turned out to be."

"Not sure what the next move'll be," he said, setting

the letter down by his plate. "I guess I'll need to shoot a note back about that damn watch."

"Why'd you even take it back in the first place?" Belinda asked.

"I was wrong to steal it."

"If she died, she wouldn't have cared."

"But she didn't die."

"But she might've."

Michael cocked his head to the side, looking at his daughter's face.

"Is this the kind of stuff the debate team argues about?" He waved his spoon in the air as if making a point.

Belinda ignored the question. She picked up a paper napkin and leaned over, wiping up some of the soup spatter on the front of her father's shirt. She frowned slightly at the result.

"Listen, when I die, I don't care if someone takes my red shoes," she said. "And I love those shoes. I'd fight for those shoes."

"But wouldn't you care who'd get them?"

"Not if I'm dead."

Michael narrowed his eyelids. "Carolyn Hoskins isn't dead."

"She's seriously injured, Dad. She may slip into a coma or something. Anything could happen. And you're out your watch."

He bit down on his lower lip. He should've told her by now why they'd hunted for that watch. It seemed too late. What was the point?

"It's not my watch," he said. "It never was."

"It *is*," his daughter insisted. "You want it. As long as I've known you, we've been looking for it. She doesn't need it. Not if she dies, anyway."

"Belinda, I don't like this kind of talk."

"It's not like you didn't think about it. If she died, what'd she need a watch for? She wouldn't care."

There was more to his little girl than Michael had ever realized.

He wondered if she had misinterpreted all those little chats and negotiations while they sought their treasures — the coins on the beach, the sulfite marbles, the amethyst glass bottles, the onyx elephant, and *the watch, the watch, the watch*.

"So, now it's okay to steal?"

She shook her head. "No, that's obviously *wrong*. If someone's *alive*. But I'm talking about if she died. A watch would be pointless to her. What's a wristwatch going to matter to someone who's out of time?"

"But could you live with that?"

She shrugged. "Maybe. If I'd been hunting for that watch since the world began. Like you have."

"Stealing from the *dead*, Belinda?"

"Listen," she leaned in, twirling her spoon lightly in the soup bowl. "Remember that red granite lion? The one in the British Museum. And all the other stuff. Did Lord Carnarvon really care that he was raiding tombs?"

"Well," Michael hedged a little. "It was a long time after King Tut died. Maybe if you give someone a few thousand years, a little thievery's forgivable."

"In fact, isn't it true that Lord Carnarvon and Carter and their team of thieves did the mummies good? They made King Tut famous all over again. We all love Egyptian history because of thieves. And don't even get me started on the Elgin Marbles."

"You might want to consider the legal profession," he told her.

They joked back and forth about the various museums built on theft from one group or another, the wonderful kingdoms built on extortion and skullduggery, the terrible De Medicis and the fantastic Renaissance (with Belinda reminding him yet again that he would never see the Uffizi), about auctions themselves being a kind of tomb plunder.

"I bet that watch shows up at auction again," Belinda said. "Maybe we can get it, after all."

"You miss the part where I'm being sued?"

His daughter shook her head slightly as if he were being an absolute fool of a dad.

"It's not a lawsuit," Belinda said. "It's a shakedown. She's lying there in the hospital. She got some ambulance chaser to send it. Don't be afraid. What can she prove? Who'll believe her? Who's going to even back her story?"

A week or so later, days away from Christmas, Michael saw the obituary in the newspaper.

"CAROLYN HOSKINS," HE SAID THE NAME THREE times.

"Who?" His wife asked as she went to grab her purse from the coffee table.

He glanced up. "Oh, that poor woman. The one who got hit."

"The one who's suing you?" Belinda asked.

"She died," Michael said.

"You're being sued?" His wife stopped in the middle of the room.

"Not anymore," Belinda said.

His wife glanced at their daughter with a mysterious expression. "I'm always the last to know in this house."

"She was in her late thirties," Michael said. "Single. New to the area. They'll do the funeral back in Chicago."

"Long way from home," Belinda said. "Does it say what she died from?"

His father looked over at her. "I'm sure it was the accident."

"Poor thing," Belinda said. "How awful. We should send flowers, Dad. We really should."

After her mother went upstairs, Belinda settled down beside Michael on the sofa. She tugged the newspaper from his hands.

"Such a dinosaur, still reading papers," she said.

"I like the feel of newsprint."

"Like I said. *Dinosaur*." Belinda folded the paper in half and read the obituary silently.

"It's sad," she said.

She reached over and picked up Michael's cup of coffee. Lifting it to her lips, she checked to see if he disapproved. Took a sip, made a face, put the coffee back down on the coaster.

"You must feel a little better, Dad."

"Not really."

"I mean, because of the lawsuit."

He thought a moment. "I guess that's all in the past."

Belinda leaned back, one leg over the other, head on the cushion as she flipped through the rest of the paper.

"Isn't it weird, Dad? We spend years looking for this particular watch, right?"

He nodded.

"It's something you really, really want. Ever since I can remember, you talked about the watch."

"It was a little crazy, I guess."

"So we find out about the auction for some old stuff, and — *voila* — here's the exact watch. Right nearby. And then this woman outbids you. Only she gets hit by a truck. And then you take the watch when she's in the hospital, but you feel bad about it. So you return it the next day. And sometime after that, someone else steals it."

Belinda took a deep breath. "It's almost like she wasn't meant to have it."

"I guess we weren't meant to have it, either."

Belinda laughed. "That's not what I'm getting at. What I mean is, maybe the watch didn't want her. *Fate*."

"Well, poor Carolyn. Not a great fate."

"Yeah, if only she'd sold you the watch in the first place. She'd probably still be walkin' around with her white coat on."

Michael thought no more about this until Christmas day, when Belinda pulled him aside after all the presents were opened, after stuffing themselves on eggnog and pie, and after his wife took the dog out for a walk in the snow.

Belinda drew him into her bedroom.

SHE PATTED THE EDGE OF THE BED. MICHAEL sat down.

She wore her Christmas red sweater and gray sweat pants. Her feet were bare, toenails painted frosty pink.

He noticed — for the first time — that no pop star posters remained on the walls.

Belinda shook her hair out and drew it behind her ears so it wouldn't flop in her face. She wore the small diamond earrings they'd given her that morning.

From behind a pillow, she brought out a wrapped box.

"More Christmas?" he asked.

"I didn't want mom to see it."

"A secret?"

"Kind of." She shrugged.

Belinda passed him the box.

Michael looked down at it. He undid the knot of silver string and tore the neatly folded paper with its red and green snowflakes.

"Dad, remember how you once said to me how fate doesn't just happen — you have to make it?"

Opening the slats of the cardboard box, he saw a gently curved glimmer of silver.

Oh, Belinda, he thought, looking at her intensely. Eyes like pond water, faint freckles, barely-perceptible dimple in her chin. He felt as if someone kidnapped his child and put this girl — a replica, a changeling, almost Belinda but not quite — in her place.

"You stole it," he whispered as he held the watch in his hands.

"No guessing," she said.

But several other guesses began streaming through his mind as he thought of the events — of fate — of the woman in white so hesitant to step out into busy traffic, Belinda with that rolling motion of her hands standing behind Carolyn Hoskins and mouthing a word — *Fate? Hate? Wait?* — reaching out to pull the poor woman back at the last second before she went into the path of the truck.

But had Belinda really tried to save her?

Michael imagined his daughter stepping forward and pushing the woman of white into traffic.

Impossible.

He looked at his daughter — really studied her face as if he'd never taken the time to see her. Not as a little girl but as an adult slowly emerging from some outer sheath of innocence as boys in speedos watched her and as a woman in a hospital bed looked up to see her pick up a watch from the dresser.

Had she returned to the hospital later, after the letter arrived? Had she pushed a pillow on Carolyn's face, unplugged machines or done any of the dozen things you could do to stop the life of someone who couldn't move much, who went in and out of consciousness, who lived on a morphine drip?

No, she wouldn't. *Ridiculous. She's smart and stubborn, and she can make your head spin with those moods of hers, but she'd never murder someone. What kind of father are you to even think it?*

But that memory of Belinda in the pool, the way she stopped near the top of the ladder as she let her hair fall from the bathing cap to her shoulders. He'd seen her glance at the boys — for just a second. As if she knew what she was doing to them.

Who was she? Who had she become?

"Belinda," he whispered, holding the watch in the palm of his hand. He could barely get the words out. "How'd you get it?"

"I'll tell you. After you tell me something."

"All right," he said, breathing slowly, trying not to imagine.

She slid back, up against the headboard, drawing her knees toward her chest.

"It's something I've never understood — all these years."

"And then you'll tell me how you got this," he reminded her, the sense of an undertow in the room.

"Sure. Right after."

Belinda rested her chin in her hands, her elbows atop her knees, looking up at him with that sense of wonder she'd never quite lost from childhood.

"So, Dad," Belinda said. "What's this watch really mean to you?"

THE SKIN OF THE WORLD

"I gotta go, anyway," my brother Ray said.

He had a look on his face that I only now understand, a look of wanting to do something without regard to consequences. He had a face like a raccoon, dark-encircled eyes, and a need to get into things he wasn't supposed to. I remember that face with fondness, not for his smile or his wildness, but for what came after.

It was 1969, and a man had landed on the moon the day before which is why we'd been staying at my uncle's. My uncle had a color television set and my father didn't believe in them until the day a man walked on the moon.

It had been an unpleasant family outing, and my brother was giving my father some lip. We drove past the sign that said Vidal Junction, and my father turned to my older brother, Ray, and told him to just keep it shut tight or he'd be walking from there back to Prewitt. As if to show he meant it, my father slowed the car to ten miles an hour, and pulled off on the shoulder.

My mother was quiet. She kept facing forward, as she always did, and I pretended I wasn't even there.

Vidal Junction was just a sliver of a gas station and maybe an old diner off the railroad tracks, but it had been abandoned back in the thirties.

When I was much younger my mother and I had stopped there to collect some of the junk she took to her junkshop dealers, like old telephone pole insulators and bits from the gas pumps. It had looked the same since I was four, that junction, a ghost place, and that sign just sitting up there: *Vidal Junction,* as if it would continue, lifeless, into infinity.

"It's damn hot," my father said, parking the car so we could all look at the old gas station, and my brother Ray could get good and mad about my father's threats to make him walk.

"Look at that big heap behind the pumps."

My mother was trying to remain silent, I could tell. But she wanted to say something; she ground her teeth together so as not to let anything out.

"What do you boys think it is?"

"I don't know," I said. It looked like a piece of a car, but I didn't know cars too well, and it could just as easily have been a piece of a rocket. I smelled something from my cracked window, something sweet like candy.

"Maybe you can sell it to one of your junk shops," my father said to my mother.

"Antique stores," she said.

"This place is strange," my father said, "you'd think somebody would plough it over and put up some stores or maybe grow something. Maybe that thing's from outer space. Or Russia. Or maybe it's like space trash. Everything's space-*something* these days. Right, Ray? That's right, Ray? You think it's from Mars?"

I heard a click, and there was my brother Ray opening the door on his side of the car.

"Maybe I will walk from here," Ray said. "Just maybe."

"Just maybe my ass," my father said. "It's a sure thing."

Ray got full out of the car and left the door hanging open.

"Coop," my mother said. She reached over and touched my father gently on his shoulder. He shrugged. "Coop," she repeated, "it's twenty miles home."

"Only fifteen, by my estimate," my father said. "He's old enough. Or is sixteen still a baby?"

My mother was silent.

Ray walked across the steamy asphalt on the highway, over to Vidal Junction and I wondered if he was going to burn to a crisp. As if he sensed this, he took his shirt off and rolled it up and stuck it under his right armpit. He was so bony that kids at school called him Scarecrow, and I swear you could read the bones of his back, line by line, and they all said *Up Yours*.

My father started up the station wagon.

"Coop," my mother said. Coop wasn't my father's name, but it's what Ray used to call him before I was born and my father was a Corporal and wanted to be called Corporal but Ray could only say Coop. My mother had called him Coop since then. To my father it must have been the kind of endearment that reminded him that he was a father after all and no longer a Corporal. My mother probably figured it would soften him, and it probably did.

"He wants to walk, let the boy walk," my father said. "I didn't make him walk. I didn't. His choice."

That was the end of that, and my father started up the car, and as we drove off toward Prewitt, I looked out the back window and saw Ray just sitting down by one of the old gas pumps and lighting up a cigarette because he knew he could get away with it.

We crossed the railroad track, and the road became bumpy again because nobody in the county much bothered to keep up this end of the highway, and it would stay bumpy until we got out of this side of the valley.

"FIFTEEN MILES," MY MOTHER SAID. WE SAT ON THE front porch, just sweating and wondering when Ray would be home.

"Daddy said he used to run fifteen miles every Saturday."

My mother looked at me, and then back to the road.

"Used to," she said under her breath.

"Ray walked ten miles in the rain last March."

My mother stood up and said, "oh." I thought at first it was because she saw Ray coming up the road, but there was nothing there. We had four neighbors, back then, before the development came through, and the nearest house was a half-mile down the road. Across the road was a pond and some woods, and beyond that the mountains and the Appalachian Trail. It was pretty in the summer, if the temperature dropped, to sit on the porch and watch the light fade by slow degrees until the sun was all but gone by nine-thirty and it was past my bed time.

My father looked out through the screen door.

"They still teach math?" My father said. "At a slow pace, given the sun and other factors, you can figure on maybe three miles an hour, and that's only if he keeps a moderate pace. So he won't be home 'til eleven. Maybe midnight. Ray's stubborn, too. Got to factor that in. He may just sleep out back of Huron's, or by the river."

"Mosquitoes'll eat him alive if he does," I said.

"He's done this before," my mother said, more to herself than to anyone.

"He can go to hell for all I care," my father said.

A brief silence followed this. I thought about my parents and my brother who seemed to ruin any peace we had as a family; I thought of the pain my mother felt; I was already tired of the fights between Ray and my dad.

"Huron said he might carry some of your junk," my father said, softly.

"Oh," my mother said. She walked out into the yard and called for the collie to come in for the night.

I wondered what Ray was thinking right now, or if he was sneaking a beer at Huron's, or if he was just out of sight but almost home.

SEVEN DAYS LATER, I WAS FAIRLY SURE WE WOULD never see Ray again, and we eventually moved, when I was twelve, to Richmond, where my father got a job that actually paid, and where I was sure we had arrived because it was so different from Prewitt. I thought of Ray often, and what our family would've been like if he had ever returned from his walk that day when I was ten and a half.

I have to admit that our family was the better for his loss. My father became a tolerable man, and the violence that I had known from early childhood transformed into a benevolent moodiness, an anger that took itself out on, not his family, but his employer, or the monthly bills, or the television set. No longer did he throw furniture against the wall when he and my mother argued, and never again did he raise his voice to me. I missed my brother some-what, but he had never been kind to me, nor had he been my protector. Ray had always dominated things for me, and had even gone so far, once, to piss on my leg when I was five (and he was just about eleven) to prove that he was the brother with the power.

Although my mother suffered greatly for a few years after Ray disappeared, I think even she finally blossomed, for Ray was a difficult child, who, according to her, since birth had been demanding and unreasonable and quick of temper. I think that Ray did a great service by walking the other way from Vidal Junction, or wherever I assumed he had marched off to, for my mother had the tragedy of loss, but over the years she drew strength from the thought that Ray was, perhaps, living in some rural Virginia town, and functioning better without the burden of his family.

Perhaps he was even happy.

Never once did it cross anyone's minds that Ray was dead. He was a cuss, and cusses don't die in the South. They become the spice of the land, and are revered in the smaller towns the way unusually beautiful women are, or three-legged dogs.

When I grew up, I moved around a bit, raised a family, and then got divorced.

When my son was five, I decided we'd take a trip to his grandma's for a belated visit. I had custody of Tommy for six whole days, which was generous of my ex-wife

I took the surface roads through all the small towns in the mountain valley. It would be nice to drive to Prewitt and show my kid the failed horse farm.

But my memory of the area was bad, and I was too proud to stop at gas stations for directions.

We got a little lost.

Tommy wanted lunch, and I pulled off at a coffee shop that looked like it was made of tin and was shaped like an old-fashioned percolator.

The waitress was cute and told Tommy that he was the red-headiest boy she had ever seen. The place smelled like rotting vegetables, but the ham biscuits were good, and I taught my son the lost art of *see*-food with the biscuits and some peanuts thrown in. His mother would hate it when he returned to Baltimore and kept opening his mouth when it was full of food.

"You know which way to Prewitt?" I asked the waitress.

She went and got a road map for me, and I moved over so she could scooch in next to me and show me the route down past Grand Island, and off to the south of Natural Bridge.

"All these new highways," I said, "got me confused."

"I know what you mean," she said. "They just keep tearing the hills up. Pretty soon it's gonna look like New York."

Because I wanted to keep flirting with her, I began the story of my missing brother, which never ceased to interest Tommy whenever I told him. While I spoke, I watched the girl's face, and she betrayed nothing other than interest. She was years younger than me, maybe only twenty, but it was nice that she enjoyed my attentions at least as much as I enjoyed hers. I ended, "...and to this day, we don't know where he went."

She looked thoughtful, and reached over, combing her fingers through Tommy's hair to keep it out of his eyes. "Well, I've heard about that place."

Tommy asked for more milk, and the girl got up to get him some. When she returned I asked her what she'd meant.

"Well," she said, her eyes squinting a bit as if trying to remember something clearly from the back of her mind, "they don't call it that, anymore, Vidal Junction, and the railroad tracks got all torn up or covered over. But it's still there, and people have disappeared there before."

"You talk like it's a news story," I said.

She laughed. "Well, it was one of those boogeyman kind of stories. When I was a kid."

You're still a kid, I thought. It struck me then, that she reminded me in some way of Anne, my ex. Not her looks, but the girl in her.

"What's a boogeyman?" Tommy asked.

"Someone who picks his nose too much," I told him.

The waitress looked very serious, and she spoke in a whisper. "There was a girl in Covington who ran away from home. My cousin knew her. She got to that place and she didn't get further. My aunt said she was taken by her stepfather, but my cousin said that was just to keep us all from getting scared."

"It's one of those stories," I said, but then I started to feel uneasy, as if the child in me were threatening to come out. "You know, like you hear from a friend of a good friend about a dead dog in a shopping bag that these punks steal, or the hook in the back of the car."

"What's a hook in the back of the car?" Tommy asked.

"Fishing hook," I said by way of calming him. His mother had been telling me that he had severe nightmares and I didn't want to feed them.

But the girl went ahead and scared him anyway, by saying, "well, folks around here I grew up with think it's something like the asshole of the universe."

I paid our bill, and I raced Tommy to the Mustang, because the girl had finally given me the creeps and convinced me that Tommy would have more nightmares —for which I would be rewarded with fewer and fewer weekends with him.

But, instead, Tommy said, "I want to go there."

"Where?"

"The asshole."

"Never say that word again as long as you live."

"Okay."

"She was weird, huh."

"Yeah," he said. "She was trying to scare you."

"I think she was trying to scare *you*."

He shrugged. "I don't scare."

I DIDN'T HUNT VIDAL JUNCTION DOWN intentionally, but we happened to come upon it because of my superb driving which, at the rate we were going, would set us down at my mother's in Richmond at midnight. It was only five-thirty. I didn't recognize the Junction at once. It had changed. The sign was gone, and the old gas pumps, while they were still there, were surrounded and almost engulfed by abandoned couches, refrigerators, and old rusted-out clunkers along the roadside.

I would've just driven by the place if it were not for the fact that Tommy told me that he had to pee. He could not wait, and what I had learned in my five years of fatherhood was that my son meant he had to go when he said it.

I pulled over and got out of the car with my son, and told him to pee behind one of the couches. I didn't stand near him just because I was afraid of the waitress' apocryphal warning, but because I worried about copperheads and perverts.

I glanced around the junction and noticed that the girl in the coffee shop had lied: the railroad tracks were very much in evidence.

"Lookit," Tommy said, after he had zipped up. He grabbed my hand and pointed to the bottom of the torn up old couch.

"It's asphalt," I said. *Or oil*, I thought.

Or something.

"Don't touch it," I told him, but I was too late. Tommy stooped over and put his fingers right into it. "I hope it's not doggie doo."

I pulled him up and away, but as I did he let out a squeal, and then I saw why.

The skin of his fingers, right where the pads were, appeared ragged and bleeding. The top layer of skin had been torn off.

"Owee," he said, immediately thrusting his fingers in his mouth.

The asshole of the universe is right, I thought.

"Hurts bad?" I asked.

He shook his head, withdrawing his fingers from between his lips. "Tastes funny."

"Don't eat it, Tom, for God's sakes."

He began crying as if I had slapped him — which I never did — and he went running across the drying field of junk.

I called to him.

I heard a door slam.

I WENT TOWARD THE SOUND, BEHIND THE OLD GAS station, and there stood a man of about forty, with long hippie-style hair, and a white cotton T-shirt on and jeans, covered head to toe with dirt. "Tried to stop him," the man said. "He went in, and I tried to stop him."

"Tommy!" I called, and heard something that sounded like him from inside the gas station. The man blocked my way to the doorway, which had, in its last life, been the gas station restroom. It was odd that it had a screen door, and it seemed odder that this man standing there didn't move as I came rather threateningly towards him.

He wore a puzzled look, briefly. Then, he nodded to me as if he'd sized me up in a matter of seconds. "It's a kind of attraction they smell. I don't smell it much now, but at first I did. The younger you are, the more you catch it."

From the restroom, I heard my son cry out.

"You don't want to go in there," the man said. He remained in front of me, and I felt adrenaline rush through my blood as I prepared for a fight. "I tried to stop the boy, but it's got that smell, and kids seem to respond to it best. I studied it for three years, and look," he said, pointing to his feet.

And then I understood why he stood so still.

The man had not feet, but where his legs stopped, his shins were splinted against blocks of wood. He squatted down, balancing himself against the wall of the building, and picked up a small kitchen knife and a flashlight, and then slid up again.

"Be prepared," he said, handing me the knife, "I was smart, buddy. I cut them off when it started to get me. Cauterized them later. It hurt like a son-of-a-bitch, but it was a small sacrifice."

Then he moved out of the way, and I opened the screen door to the restroom, and was about to set foot inside when he shined a flashlight over my shoulder into the dark room. I saw the forms, and the beam of light hit the strawberry-blonde hair of my son, only it was not my son but something I can't even give a name to, unless it can be called skin, skin like silk and mud, moving slowly beneath the red-blonde hair, and from it the sound of my boy as if he were retreating somewhere, not hurting, and not crying, but just like he was going somewhere beyond imagining, and was making noises that were incomprehensible. Skin like an undulating river of shiny eels, turning inward, inward.

Knife in my hand, I stood on the threshold, and the man behind me said, "they go in all the time. I can't stop them."

"What in god's name is it?"

"It's a rip in the skin of the world," he said. "Hell, I don't know. It's something living. Maybe anything."

I felt something against the toe of my shoe, and instinctively drew back, but not before the tip of my Nike was torn off by the skin. The toes of my left foot were bleeding.

"Living organism," he said, "I don't know how long it's been here, but it's been three years since I found it. Could've been here for at least a decade."

"Maybe more," I said, remembering my brother Ray and his cigarette in front of the gas station, and his words, "I gotta go, anyway." He would've gone around back to take a leak, maybe smelled whatever you were supposed to smell, and then just went in.

The skin of the world.

"Does it hurt them?" I asked.

The man looked at me, startled, and I wondered for a moment what I had said that could startle a man who had cut his own feet off.

And it dawned on me, too, what I had just asked.

Does it hurt them?

The man didn't have to say anything, because he knew then what I was made of. That I could even ask that question. And what that question meant.

He looked like he was about to tell me something, maybe advise me, but he knew and I knew that only a man who had given up would ask that question.

Does it hurt them?

Because, maybe if it doesn't hurt, maybe it's okay that my son went in there, and got pulled through the seam of the world, the asshole of the universe. That must be what a man like me means when he has to ask.

"How would I know?" the stranger said, and hobbled across the grass, moist with the sweat from the skin of the world.

I STOOD IN THAT DOORWAY, AND COULD NOT BRING myself to call to my son.

I shined the flashlight around in that inner darkness, and saw forms rising and falling slowly, as if children played beneath a blanket after lights out.

Soon, the evening came, and I was still there, and the man had gone off somewhere into the field of junk.

I thought of Tommy's mother, Anne, and how worried she would be, and perhaps the need she would have that I could respond to.

I began to smell the odor that the man had spoken of: it was gently sweet and also pungent, like a narcissus, and

I remembered the day after my brother Ray had not come home, and how my mother and father held each other so close, closer than I had ever remembered them being before.

I remembered thinking then, as now, *it's a small sacrifice for happiness.*

A MADNESS OF STARLINGS

What possessed me to retrieve the little fledgling, I can't say for sure. I rescued the baby bird from the jaws of the tiger-striped tomcat that had been stalking it. I wanted to show my boys that the smallest of life sometimes needed protection from the predators.

I brought it into the house, hoping to wait out the cat's bloodlust. My two boys came out to look at it. I warned them not to touch the bird just then. "The less contact it has with people, the better."

After an hour, I took the bird outside again. My kids watched from the living room window.

It hopped in the tall summer grass that I had not gotten to with the mower. Its mouth opened wide, up to the skies, expecting its mother to come with food.

I stepped back onto the porch and scanned the area to make sure no cat returned. I hoped that the bird's mother would return and feed it so that the balance of nature could be restored and I'd have no more responsibility.

An hour later, the fledgling continued to hop and squawk and open its mouth to heaven. No mother arrived. I had lost my own mother when young, and did not like remembering this when I saw the bird I came to call Fledge. Loss was the bad thing in life. I hated it, and didn't wish it on a baby bird.

I took the little guy in, and my wife, Jeanette, and the boys (little William and tall Rufus) helped me build a cage for it as part of our "Saturday Family Project." At first, Fledge would not eat from my hand — or from a straw. But we picked up some mealworms and crickets from the pet store in town, and soon enough, the little guy hunted them up on the floor of his cage.

Devouring fifty worms a day and perhaps ten crickets, Fledge grew fast.

WITHIN FIVE DAYS, THE LITTLE GUY HAD FULL feathers and the boys and I took him into the rec room from flight training. He flew from Rufus' fingers to the bookcase.

I had to put a stepladder up to rescue him from the highest shelf.

"We have to let him go," I told the boys. "He's ready to fly. He's eaten a lot and knows how to catch crickets and peck for worms on his own."

"Isn't he a pet?" William pleaded. "He's ours now."

Rufus, the elder at nine, added, "He can't survive out there, Dad. He can't. He's too used to us."

"It's only been a week," I said. "He belongs out there."

"I heard birds only live a couple of years out there," Rufus said. "I bet in his cage, he'd live a long time."

"He's a wild bird, he's meant to be out there. Besides, when we go to Florida in February, who's going to take care of him?

Will you clean the cage for the next twelve years if he lives that long? Every day that cage needs cleaning," I said.

Rufus looked very sad, and William's eyes glistened with the easy tears of a little boy who won't accept loss. "But Daddy," he said. "Daddy, I love Fledge."

"I know," I said. "But don't you want Fledge to be happy?"

William nodded. "I want him safe."

"He's happy here," Rufus said. "Now. He won't be happy when a cat gets him. Or when an eagle gets him."

"We don't have eagles around here."

"Or when he gets some disease and nobody takes him to the vet."

"I'm going to miss him," William said. "So long, Fledge."

"Look, he'll be around the yard. He's a starling. They're always here. He'll probably fly around and make a nest under your bedroom window."

William's eyes brightened. A smile crept across his face.

Noticing that I had turned the corner on William's emotional rollercoaster and now things were heading upward, I said, "And whenever you see him hurt, you can run out and bring him in and we'll take him to the bird doctor, if you want."

Rufus had begun to scowl. "I saw a dead bird out by

the curb. That's what's going to happen to him if we let him go."

"Roof," I said. "Roof, look. When you grow up, we're going to let you go. You're going to fly away. And as much as I'd like to put you in a cage here so I can always see you, I know that's going to be wrong."

Of course, he didn't understand this. Rufus felt he'd never leave the house or his parents or the protected world of childhood.

But *I* knew he would.

I knew the bird needed to get out and live just like my kids would one day need to get out and spread their wings. Even when the tomcats of life got them.

The shelter of childhood was temporary, at best.

The boys put up more protests, with Rufus cataloguing the bleak prospects of a bird in our suburban world. I countered his arguments with tales of birds flying over the treetops, or Mother Nature, or how Fledge saw us as giant monsters that were not like his parents or brothers and sisters. "Starlings have to fly twenty miles a day to really enjoy life."

Finally, I let the discussion die down. When the boys were out playing with friends, I took Fledge onto my fingers, and leaned out the second floor window of our house.

The bird flew off.

Just as it got up into the air, clearing an overgrown azalea bush, another bird came down and began attacking it mid-air.

I felt panic and genuine terror.

I worried about the little guy, trying his wings out for

the first time. Fledge continued flying toward a crabapple tree in the front yard. Fledge turned, almost as if he were looking at me. His mouth opened wide as he squawked like a baby. In that moment, I didn't see the bird; I saw my boys.

I HAD A PREMONITION OF A MOMENT OF TERROR IN life when I would let go of my sons' hands and they would go off and the world would do its own version of attack on them. My imagination went haywire as I imagined Rufus in his early twenties in a foreign land, felled by bullets in a war; and William, injecting heroin into his arms, surrounded by lowlife friends in some crack house.

As I watched Fledge, he fluffed up his feathers and spread his wings wide and flew over the rooftop. I raced to the bathroom window, and saw Fledge flying over other houses, off through the neighborhood.

Fledge had made it past the attacking bird. Past the trees. We had done it, I thought. We helped Fledge get strong and healthy and become an adult, and he was going to live his life the way he was meant to live it. My brief insanity, those split-second visions of my boys, the dreadful futures I imagined for them — all of it dissipated and I laughed at myself and the way my mind worked.

Later, I told the boys that Fledge had flown off, and that he was fine. They moped a bit, but the more we talked about Fledge and Fledge's life, the better my children seemed to understand why Fledge had to go.

That first night, I went and sat in front of Fledge's

empty cage. Beyond the cage, a window looked out on trees. I opened the window and lifted the screen. Part of me felt that Fledge might come back, or if he was hurt, he might show up for food again.

I kept the window open for three days, and then shut it.

I MISSED THE BIRD.

We had kept the little guy for five days, but it was enough for me to begin to think about life and nature and to wake up each day hoping Fledge had not died in the night. Out the window, other starlings and robins and mockingbirds flew around, but I kept watch for Fledge. I brought out the old binoculars from the cabinet in the garage, and, early in the morning — before even my wife awoke — I went to the window and looked out. I whistled sometimes when I was in the yard, thinking Fledge might hear my voice.

Then, at twilight, I spoke to my wife, Jeanette, about the bird.

"It's a starling," she said. "They're nuisances. I bet the state would've paid you to kill it."

"Stop that," I said. "It needed help."

"I know. I'm kidding. Really. I'm kidding. But the bird's fine. Believe me. You protected it. You got the boys to think about nature a little. And now that bird's off doing what birds do."

"I never really noticed starlings before," I said. "I mean, I knew they were out there."

"God, in the fall they just swarm. Freaks me out sometimes. Like the Hitchcock movie."

"I was out in the yard this morning," I said. "I couldn't stop looking in the trees. And on the roof. I just figured he'd stick around."

She gave me a funny look, as if she were trying to figure out if I were joking or not. "Honey? It's a bird. You really want a bird, we'll get a cockatiel. But I don't really want a bird," she said.

"I don't want a bird, either," I said. Then, I laughed at myself, and she giggled, too. We had some coffee and went out on the patio. We sat in the old deck chairs that were gray from years of neglect. "But it's funny."

"What's that?"

"Loss. All of life is about loss."

"No, it's not." She laughed and told me I had better not get depressed on her.

"Life has loss in it," she said, when she saw that I was a little hurt by her laughter. "But look, we both have great jobs, the kids are great. We're building to something. We have love. There's a lot in life besides loss."

"Someday, we'll lose everything. I mean it. I'm not sad about it. I guess I'm wistful."

"Wistful is sad."

"No it's not. Someday, the boys will go out into the world. Not everyone survives it. God, maybe I'll get heart disease. Or some...some accident will happen."

"You're getting morbid," she said. "I hate this kind of stuff. You shouldn't say it. It's too dark."

"I'm trying to grasp this thing. I'm nearly forty, and I want to be prepared. I want a good mindset."

"That bird," she said. "It got you thinking like this."

"It's nuts, I guess," I said.

"Not nuts, honey. But it's…it's useless. We have a good life. Bad things don't always happen. That bird. That bird is probably off flying around, happy as hell to be out of the cage and back in its natural environment. It's probably flocking with other starlings, devouring someone's grass seed or chasing off squirrels from a nest that it's building with a mate. It's an adult by now. It's fine. That's how life goes."

"Did you hear that?" I asked, startled as I glanced over at her.

She held her coffee mug near her lips, watching me. "What?"

"That sound. Was that Fledge?"

I heard it again. The bickering squawk of a starling. Somewhere among the trees.

"No. Wait," she said. "No."

Then, I heard a chirp at the rooftop. I looked up — it was a sparrow.

"Come here," Jeanette said.

I glanced over at her. She had raised her eyebrows ever so slightly, her version of close-up seduction.

"What for?"

"Just come here." She set her mug down on the little table, and scooched back in her chair. "Sit with me."

"We'll break the chair."

"Throw caution to the wind."

I went over, and she put her arms around me. Kissed me on the forehead. "My big baby who loves birds."

Deftly, she slipped her fingers to the buttons of my

shirt, and opened them, her hands going to my chest, combing through the patch of hair. I kissed her, and she whispered, "The boys won't be back from the Nelson's 'til nine. Nobody can see us."

We made love in that uncomfortable deck chair, in that desperate way that old marrieds do, trying to recapture the wildness of premarital sex. Somewhere in the rapture of it all, I heard the chattering of starlings in the trees, and glanced up.

"What is it?" she asked. "Why did you stop?"

"I thought…" I didn't want her to know what I was thinking, so I kissed her on the lips. "Maybe we should do this later."

"Why?"

"I feel funny. What if someone sees us?"

"Nobody can see us."

"I feel like someone can," I said.

"So, we give 'em a show. Greatest show on earth."

"Naw," I said, trying to sound warm and cuddly and friendly, but I drew my underwear and pants back up, and buttoned my shirt. She left hers open, but drew her knees together.

"Since when do you turn down outdoors sex?" she asked.

"We've never had outdoors sex till now."

"I remember a certain hot August night on a lake in a little boat with life preservers as pillows," she said. "August 18th."

"You remember the date?"

"Sure. We were out at the lake. It was when we…"

She didn't have to finish the thought. It was the year

before we conceived Rufus. It was to be our first child, the one who came from sex in the boat out on the lake at midnight. But she had lost the baby within four months. Eight months later, she was pregnant with Rufus.

I didn't like to be reminded of the first child.

THAT NIGHT, AFTER MY WIFE FELL ASLEEP, I WENT out to the patio for a cigarette. My first in three years. I kept the pack of Gitanes in an old backpack I'd had since college. It hung on a nail in the garage. Inside the pack, besides the French cigarettes I'd learned to smoke on a post-graduate trip to Paris, there was a bottle of Grand Marnier that had never been opened, a T-shirt with various obscenities written on it, and a pair of swimming trunks I had not been able to fit into since my twenties.

The cigarette tasted great, and I followed the first with a second. I thought of Fledge, up in one of the trees, his little leg hidden under his feathers, with the other leg down, small claws clutching a tree branch.

THE FOLLOWING SATURDAY, I TOOK THE BOYS FOR A hike. First, to a drug store to get some candy, and then up to the unincorporated area of town where there was a bike trail by the old railroad tracks. The boys seemed to have fun, running ahead of me, climbing rocks, finding a penny or quarter, balancing on the railroad ties. But I had begun hearing the birds. I heard more and more of them as we got deeper into the woods. Starlings, certainly, but also the caws of crows; the songbirds, too, with their chirps and whistles. I felt like I would hear Fledge's distinct squawk, but did not, and even while I told the kids to watch out for broken glass on the trail, or not to touch the poison ivy, part of me had blocked even my own children out.

I had never noticed so many birds before. Most of them were unseen, but their voices seemed loud, even annoying. Bickering in the skies, chattering in treetops, their language must have meant something to them. They must be communicating with each other. Mating. Attacking. Flocking.

Twilight came, and back at home, Jeanette made it bath time for the boys because of the dirt all over their faces.

I went to the second floor bedroom window, and climbed out onto the ledge, and sat on the roof. Smoked a cigarette. Leaned back, and looked up at the veiled sky and the darkening clouds in the distance.

Distinct voices of the birds. Not just the usual cacophony. I felt as if my ears had begun to notice precisely how one sparrow chirped, how the swallows spoke to each other, and those starlings — their nastiness, their territorial voices that spoke of battle and ownership. I began to hear something in the world I'd never really heard before.

"ARE YOU ALL RIGHT?" JEANETTE ASKED THAT NIGHT.

We lay in bed. Lights on. She had just put down the book she'd been reading.

"Of course."

"You're staring at the ceiling."

"I'm thinking. You know, there must be something weird about life. We took that little guy in for five days, and now I just notice birds. I've never noticed them before."

"What's that called?"

"What do you mean?"

"It's called something. When you didn't notice something. Then you do. Then you notice it's all around you all the time."

"Crazy?"

She grinned. "No. No. And it's not about something being ubiquitous, either. It's something else. Like when you've never heard a word before, and suddenly, once you've heard it, it's everywhere you look."

"I keep listening for him."

"For who?"

"Fledge."

"Honey," she said. "Aw. Poor baby. I miss the little guy too. You should be proud of yourself. You rehabbed a bird and set it free. That's what life should be about."

"I read about starlings. Online. They're non-native. They were brought here by a guy who released a hundred of them in Central Park in 1890. He wanted to introduce birds that were in Shakespeare's plays. So he brought starlings, among others. I read that in the wild they don't live all that long. In captivity, they can live up to twenty years."

She lay down and turned to me, her eyes like warm

muddy pools. "I would rather have a few years among my own kind, with a life of mating and birth and, yes, even death, than twenty years alone in a cage."

"He wouldn't have been alone," I said. And then, "Aw, this is silly. I'm silly."

"Yes, you are. It's not about the bird, is it?"

"I told you before. It's about loss."

"I know. Life does have a lot of loss in it. You're almost forty. You'll probably start buying sports cars and chasing blondes."

"No. I'm not that guy," I said. "I just hate how life takes everything away."

"That's ridiculous. Think of all the people in the world and what they don't have. Now, think of all that you have. And tell me how life takes everything away from you."

"Not from me, personally. From everyone. Nobody really tells you that when you're Rufus' age. We protect our kids from it. But it's there."

"God. That fucking bird," she said.

She turned away from me, and reached over to flick the light off.

THAT WAS ORDINARY LIFE, BUT THE EXTRAORDINARY had entered my life through the voices of birds. Whenever I went outside, or opened a window, I heard them. Too many of them. The voices all going on about food and shelter and war and children and work and flight and anger and joy. I could tell that much from the tones of their voices. I noticed that when a storm came, the gulls from the bay — a good hour from us — suddenly were on our rooftop. But then, I began to hear the voices of the birds change when a storm was predicted, as if they knew, many hours before a thunderstorm reached us, that it was going to descend. Any changes in their voices, or the amount of bickering, heralded nestlings. I began to hate crows, for I saw them dive for the babies, and heard the awful wailing of the mother birds at the death of a child.

Then, one evening we watched a TV show on a Wednesday night; it was still light out; I began to hear the birds squawking and thought I heard Fledge, so I went to the window, opening it.

"What's up?" Jeanette asked.

"I heard something."

She turned the television's volume down, and listened. "I don't hear anything. What was it?"

"Nothing," I said. I had begun to lie to her about hearing the birds outside. Listening for Fledge, trying to see if there was a message I should be hearing. That's what I had begun thinking: there was a message that might be delivered to me. Delivered unto me — it had begun to seem religious to me. Birds brought omens. God might speak through birds. I knew that was just my imagination, but something spiritual had entered my life through the sounds of the birds.

I took a day off from work, but didn't tell my family. Instead, I took some binoculars and spent the day up in my sons' tree fort, which nearly went into the thick woods behind our house.

I took water and sandwiches and soda; when I had to pee, I just peed off the tree. I listened all day to the birds, and I began to feel a change within me — toward nature. It made me sad in some way, because I began to see my wife as someone who would never truly understand me, and with whom I might never genuinely communicate what was within me. I loved my boys, but I knew they had other lives to live.

They, too, would develop their own secret languages and matings and lives.

I might never understand them fully as I could never fully comprehend my wife.

I began to take personal days off from work, and just wander the woods, or walk along the bike trail. I'd get lost for hours at a time in the deep forest that should not have been there — for there was a shopping mall two miles away, and a town on either side. Yet, a forest existed, and I could lose myself in it for half a day without seeing another human being.

There were arguments at home that escalated into shouting matches.

I became less tolerant of the boys' behavior when they crossed a line. At work, I just didn't deal with others much and spent most of my time pretending to be buried in projects that I knew I'd never finish. On my lunch break, I'd go out to the park and sit and listen to pigeons and yet more starlings, and watch as they flew and stole bits of food from near the trash cans and dive-bombed someone who sat too close to a hidden nest.

On a bitter day of bad reports at work, and a wife who didn't even want me to come home, I walked along the bike path in the woods, and could not stand the voices of the birds anymore.

I wept in my wife's arms that night, and told her I had some kind of madness in me. She cooed into my ear and told me she loved me and that it would pass, whatever it was, and if it didn't, we'd get help.

"It's all the loss," she said. "You didn't cry when we lost the baby. You didn't cry when your mother died. That bird did it. It reminded you of loss. It got to you."

The bird had changed me. The bird had never left me. I longed for the kingdom of birds rather than the kingdom of men. The voices of birds seemed, to me, to be more about life than the voices of mankind.

A CALL CAME IN TO WORK FOR ME, BUT I DIDN'T PICK up. I just let my voice mail get it, and it wasn't until my wife messaged me on the cell phone that I paid attention.

She wrote:

Emergency Room.

When I got there, she was trembling and pale. I held her, and she whispered, "William."

Strangely, I noticed a man nearby who looked as if he had just done something terrible. He spoke to a nurse and mentioned "birds."

I suppose that was why I noticed him at all. Later, I learned that he had been the one driving the car.

DURING THE SIX MONTHS AFTER MY SON'S DEATH, I began to listen only to the birds. I barely acknowledged Jeanette, and though I loved Rufus dearly, I could not bear to look at him for he reminded me too much of his little brother. I smoked my Gitanes in the open now, for my wife could not chide me during this time.

I spent long afternoons and evenings out on a lawn chair, beneath the sycamores and maples, my eyes skyward as I watched the dark flocks of starlings readying for winter. Their words comforted me, and took me elsewhere as they spoke of distant places of warmth and insects. Though I often thought of William's warm fingers in my hand or his soft whisper at bedtime, the birds told me about life and death and loss and continuations and how the spring brought hope and summer brought plenty. I also heard about the deaths of birds, of sorrow, of a mate shot down by a thoughtless boy with a gun, of marriages and the ends of marriages, of wounds that never healed, and feuds between siblings that continued to the end of life.

Laid off from my job by October third — in a massive layoff that left thousands without work — I came home to an empty house. By empty, I mean, bereft, without human voice. Jeanette and Rufus had left a couple of weeks earlier to stay at her sister's in the next town over, but they would be back (so my wife promised) or things would change or something. I wasn't clear on the details.

In the early morning, I went out in my boxers and sat on the back lawn. The earth had turned hard and cold, and the wind was strong. I listened for the birds, and leaned back, my arms crossed behind my head. Still sleepy, I began to doze when a voice brought me up from sleep.

What the voice had said, I am not sure. It seemed like my name or a name. The sound was nearly like a child's voice. Perhaps I had been dreaming that it was my dead son's voice.

I opened my eyes. There, on a slender leafless branch above me, a starling. Dark, and mottled with the yellow stars of adulthood, and — I was sure — it was Fledge himself. Watching me.

"Fledge?" I asked, but then laughed at my foolishness for asking a bird its name.

The bird cocked its head to the left and the right, and then hopped down to the ground. It fluttered over and hopped up on my chest. It began squawking and making a whistling sound that was a fairly good mimic of my own whistle.

Then, it hoped closer to my face.

Instead of a whistle, it spoke to me. "William," said the bird.

As I lay there, stunned by this hallucination, the bird flew away.

NOW, OF COURSE I THOUGHT I HAD LOST MY MIND, but I had to know something I didn't know before. Something I'd never really asked or followed up on.

I went to visit the man whose car had hit and killed my little boy.

"Yes?"

The door opened, and the man, who I guessed was about fifty, opened the door to his apartment. He lived in a rough neighborhood near the city, but had not lived there at the time of the accident. He had lived, the day when my son stepped off the curb, in a nice house, larger than my family's place, but the death of my son had changed him as much, if not more, than it had changed us. His own life had fallen apart. His wife and he had divorced. He had a grown daughter who blamed him, though it had been apparent that he had been driving the speed limit and had done what he could to avoid hitting my son and several children who had stepped into the street in heavy traffic. He had only hit my son, but four children's lives had been spared, including my eldest, Rufus.

Yet, his life had spiraled downward.

I saw it in the apartment building, which was dark and filthy.

I saw it in his eyes, as well. "Oh," he said, recognizing me. He didn't ask the next question, but it hung there as if he had: What do you want?

"You said something. I barely heard it. I guess I wasn't listening."

He opened the door a bit wider, but looked at me with a kind of anticipation as if I might swing a punch at him. "I'm sorry," he said. "I really am."

"You said something about birds," I said.

"Oh." He looked over my shoulder as if expecting others to be with me. "The birds."

"What was it about birds. I overheard it. We were standing there, at the hospital. But I just caught the tail end of it. I didn't even know who you were at the time."

"I can't remember," he said.

"It's important. To me." Without realizing it, I had begun sobbing, and I suppose my body heaved with each exhalation of grief.

He came out into the hallway, and put his arm around my shoulder. "Come in. I'll get you some water."

INSIDE THE APARTMENT, ON A GREEN, WORN COUCH, I sipped from a glass. Vodka, not water. It tasted good.

He sat across from me. Behind him, the television was on, but the sound had been muted. "I don't remember about birds. Look, I'm sorry. I have nightmares about what happened. I see his face."

"Me, too."

"I see all their faces. If I had only…if I had only stopped for the ice cream my wife wanted. If I had just taken the short cut instead of driving down Apple Valley Road."

"I know. I think if I had just made him stay home from school. If I had just told Rufus not to play after school. 'If only' drives you nuts. I'm weary from it."

"Yeah."

"You said something about birds. At the Emergency Room. You were speaking to a nurse."

"Oh," he said. A shadow passed over his face. "Oh. The birds. I saw them. Blackbirds. I think that's what the kids were doing. There was a bird in the street. I saw it, too. Just sitting there, and I thought it was going to get hit by somebody. I think that's why the kids went in the street. Maybe I'm wrong. I don't know." He emptied his glass, and sighed. "Does it matter? I'm sorry. I'll be sorry for the rest of my life."

"It was an accident," I said, and then rose, setting my glass on the glass table.

I WAITED FOR RUFUS AFTER SCHOOL. WHEN HE SAW me, he looked at me as if I were the enemy. He walked cautiously to the car, and leaned into the open window.

"Come on, I'll drive you to Mom's."

"She's gonna be mad."

"She'll be mad when she sees me. At least she won't be mad at you."

Driving him to his mother's place — which really was his aunt's large home where they were staying for a few weeks until everything somehow either worked out or didn't — I said, "You doing okay?"

He remained quiet.

"I want to ask about something."

Again, no response from my boy.

"All right. Look. That day. That *day*. Was there a bird? Or a flock of birds?"

He looked at me, his eyes seeming to flash with anger. Then, back to the road ahead. Then, he blurted, "Don't ever talk to me about that day again. I mean it. I never want to think about it."

As I dropped him off at his aunt's house, he slid out of his seat and had not yet swung the door shut. I said, "Just tell me. Why did you go in the street at all? There was traffic."

"Ask William," Rufus said, his face a mask of child-hood fury, which was both pale and burning. "He's the only one who knows. I was trying to stop him. I was trying to stop him. Nobody believes me. I was trying to stop him!"

MY WIFE CALLED ME ON THE CELL PHONE TEN minutes later and yelled at me for making Rufus upset. She said he had gone all fetal and wouldn't talk to anybody and that if I showed up at his school again she didn't know what she'd do, but she'd do something.

I barely heard her — the birds were talking outside, and I went out to them and tried to decipher what they were saying.

Winter had not quite come 'round the bend, but autumn had exploded briefly like a firecracker and stripped the trees bare.

On the twisted branches, the dark swarms of starlings began chanting.

I STOOD THERE, IN AWE OF THEM, THEIR BEAUTY AND their language and their flight.

They spoke of journeys to sunlit lands, and of love among them, and of the legends of their ancestors and of the anger and fury at the deaths of those they raised up from birth. I wandered back through the yard, into the woods, and followed them.

I, earthbound, watched as they danced tree to tree to sky to telephone wire to rooftop.

I began speaking in the tongues of birds and all else fell away, the whistles and warbles from my throat seemed perfectly natural. The starlings told their secrets to me.

I knew my son's final moments. The starlings told me what they had seen, what my boy William had done. It was in their songs, their exaltations, their chattering squawks as they surrounded me, a cathedral of dark birds.

They shared with me the love I had taught him for even the smallest bird, the tiniest creature, in the road, to be rescued from the traffic of human monsters. I heard his footsteps on the street as he raced into traffic.

The birdsong grew deafening. I clutched my hands to my ears, for I could not take what they told of my little boy.

I pressed my fingers deep into the skin of my ears — and deeper still to the wax — to plug them up and keep the sound of the last moment's of my boy's life from entering my brain. The pressure was enormous as I pushed my fingers deeper still.

And yet, I heard his voice as he shrieked, and the thud of the car against him — they warbled each note of his last moments of life so that I might feel I was there with him. I begged them to stop, but the birds continued their praise of my little boy. They mimicked his cries and the wheezes of his lungs and throat until he breathed his last.

I felt as if I were there, with William, in the street, his head upon my lap, his eyes turned upward, his small body shivering.

As if I held his small body and looked up to God in the sky, but only saw the birds that had witnessed his death. The birds that had lured him into the street. The birds that had begun to drive me to madness with their terrible words and sounds.

Their voices, telling me of other secrets, of those who had died in the past, and the deaths to come.

SUBWAY TURNSTILE

W alks through the turnstile, dropping tokens, grasping the boy by the elbow.

"Pull through," he says, but the little boy won't budge.

Glances at the others, behind them, waiting.

A friendly woman behind him suggests they hurry.

"The train's coming. Please," she says.

"Come on," he says, and again grasps, and again, the boy manages to stiffen.

"Are you scared?" he asks, and glances up at the others. "He's not usually scared."

Gets a kind look from the woman behind him.

She is wrapped up in a thick tan winter coat. A large handbag over her shoulder.

"Come on," he says, and this time reaches around and places his fingers against the child's throat.

"Davy," he says. "People are waiting."

"Let's go," the woman says, on the edge of polite.

The train comes and sounds of annoyance rise from a low grumble behind the woman who stands at the back of the man with the boy.

"Just push him," someone says.

The heat of the train against his face.

Davy looks up at him. Shakes his head.

"I know what to do," the wrapped woman says, and steps beside the man.

SHE LOOKS AT DAVY AND SMILES SWEETLY.

She lifts him up in her arms and carries him through the turnstile.

"See? Not scary at all."

The boy whispers against her ear, "He's not my daddy. I don't know him."

She feels a shock go through her. Lowers the boy to the platform.

The man has come through, and takes the boy's hand.

"Thank you for that," the man says.

The little boy looks up at her.

"Come on, Davy," the man says.

The boy looks back at her as the man tugs at his hand.

They board the train.

The woman watches them, nearly about to do something. She glances at the others on the platform.

At the face of the boy through the smudged window of the train.

The train leaves the station.

She picks at her coat, unwrapping herself.

She finds a place on a bench and waits for the next train, but the heat of his whisper remains.

WHERE FLIES ARE BORN

The train stopped suddenly. Ellen watched her son fill in the coloring book with the three crayons left to him: aquamarine, burnt sienna, and silver.

She was doing this for Joey. She could put up with Frank and his tirades and possessiveness, but not when he tried to hurt their son. *Her* son. She would make sure that Joey had a better life.

Ellen turned to the crossword puzzle in the back of the magazine section to pass the time. She tried not to think of what they'd left behind.

She was a fairly patient person, and so it didn't annoy her much that it was another hour before anyone told the passengers it would be a three hour stop — or more.

Or more, translated into *overnight*.

Then her patience wore thin and Joey began to whine.

THE TOWN WAS A QUARTER MILE AHEAD, AND SO THEY would be put up somewhere for the night.

So this was to be their Great Escape. February in a mountain town at thirty below. Frank would find them for sure; only a day's journey from Springfield. Frank would hunt them down, as he'd done last time, and bring them back to his little castle and she would make it okay for another five years before she went crazy again and had to run.

No. She would make sure he wouldn't hurt Joey. She would kill him first. She would, with her bare hands, stop him from ever touching their son again.

Joey said, "Can't we just stay on the train? It's cold out there."

"You'll live," she said, bringing out the overnight case and following in a line with the other passengers out of the car. They trudged along the snowy tracks to the short strip of junction, where each was directed to a different motel or private house.

"I wanted a motel," she told the conductor. She and Joey were to be overnight guests of the Neesons', a farm family. "This isn't what I paid for," she said, "it's not what I expected at all."

"You can sleep in the station, you like," the man said, but she passed on that after looking around the filthy room with its greasy benches. "Anyway, the Neesons run a bed-and-breakfast, so you'll do fine there."

THE NEESONS ARRIVED IN A FOUR-WHEEL DRIVE,

looking just past the curve of middle age, tooth-rotted, with *country* indelibly sprayed across their grins and friendly winks.

Mama Neeson, in her late fifties, spoke of the snow, of their warm house "where we'll all be safe as kittens in a minute," of the soup she'd been making. Papa Neeson was older (*old enough to be my father*, Ellen thought) and balder, eyes of a rodent, face of a baby-left-too-long-in-bathwater.

Mama Neeson cooed over Joey, already asleep. Papa Neeson spoke of the snowfall and the roads.

Ellen said very little, other than to thank them for putting her up.

"Our pleasure," Mama Neeson said. "The little ones will love the company."

"You have children?" Ellen winced at her inflection. She didn't *mean* it to sound as if Mama Neeson was too old to have what could be called "little ones."

"Adopted, you could say," Papa Neeson grumbled. "Mama, she loves kids, can't get enough of them, you get the instinct, you see, the sniffs for babies and you got to have them whether your body gives 'em up or not."

Ellen, embarrassed for his wife, shifted uncomfortably in the seat. What a rude man. This was what Frank would be like, under the skin, talking about women and their "sniffs," their "hankerings." Poor Mama Neeson, a houseful of babies and *this man*.

"I have three little ones," Mama Neeson said. "All under nine. How old's yours?"

"Six."

"He's an angel. Papa, ain't he just a little angel sent down from heaven?"

Papa Neeson glanced over to Joey, curled up in a ball against Ellen's side. "Don't say much, does he?"

THE LANDSCAPE WAS WHITE AND BLACK. ELLEN watched for ice patches in the road, but they went over it all smoothly. Woods rose up suddenly, parting for an empty flat stretch of land. They drove down a fenced road, snow piled all the way to the top of the fence posts. Then, a farmhouse with a barn behind it.

We better not be sleeping in the barn.

Mama Neeson sighed. "Hope they're in bed. Put them to bed hours ago, but you know how they romp…"

"They love to romp," Papa Neeson said.

THE BED WAS LARGE. SHE AND JOEY SANK INTO IT AS soon as the door closed behind them. Ellen was too tired to think, and Joey was still dreaming.

Sleep came quickly and was black and white, full of snowdrifts.

Ellen awoke, thirsty, before dawn.

HALF-ASLEEP, SHE LIFTED HER HEAD TOWARDS THE window: the sound of some animal crunching in the snow outside. She looked out—had to open the window because of the frost on the pane.

A hazy purple light brushed across the whiteness of the hills—the sun was somewhere rising beyond the treetops. A large brown bear sniffed along the porch rail. Bears should've frightened her, but this one seemed friendly and stupid, as it lumbered along in the tugging snow, nostrils wiggling.

Sniffing the air; Mama Neeson would be up—four thirty—frying bacon, flipping hotcakes on the griddle, buttering toast. *Country mama.* The little ones would rise from their quilts and trundle beds, ready to go out and milk cows or some such farm thing, and Papa Neeson would get out his shotgun to scare off the bear that came sniffing.

Ellen remembered Papa's phrase: "the sniffs for babies," and it gave her a discomforting thought about the bear.

She lay back on the bed, stroking Joey's fine hair, with this thought in her mind of the bear sniffing for the babies, when she saw a housefly circle above her head; then, another, coming from some corner of the room, joining its mate. Three more arrived.

Finally, she was restless to swat them. She got out of bed and went to her overnight bag for hairspray. This was her favorite method of disposing of houseflies. She shook the can, and then sprayed in the direction of the nine or ten fat black houseflies. They buzzed in curves of infinity. In a minute, they began dropping, one by one, to the rug. Ellen enjoyed taking her boots and slapping each fly into the next life.

Her dry throat and heavy bladder sent her out to the hallway.

FEELING ALONG THE WALL FOR THE LIGHT SWITCH OR the door to the bathroom—whichever came first. When she found the switch, she flicked it up, and a single unadorned bulb hummed into dull light.

A little girl stood at the end of the hall, too old for the diaper she wore; her stringy hair falling wildly almost to her feet; her skin bruised in several places—particularly around her mouth, which was swollen on the upper lip.

In her small pudgy fingers was a length of thread.

Ellen was so shocked by this sight that she could not say a word—the girl was only seven or so, and what her appearance indicated about the Neesons...

Papa Neeson was like Frank. Likes to beat people. Likes to beat children. Joey and his black eyes, this girl and her bruised face. I could kill them both.

The little girl's eyes crinkled up as if she were about to cry, wrinkled her forehead and nose, parted her swollen lips.

From the black and white canyon of her mouth a fat green fly crawled the length of her lower lip, and then flew toward the light bulb above Ellen's head.

LATER, WHEN THE SUN WAS UP, AND THE SNOW outside her window grew blinding, Ellen knew she must've been half-dreaming, or perhaps it was a trick that the children played—for she'd seen all of them, the two-year-old, the five-year-old, and the girl.

The boys had trooped out from the shadows of the hall. All wearing the filthy diapers, all bruised from beatings or worse. The only difference with the two younger boys was they had not yet torn the thread that had been used to sew their mouths and eyes and ears and nostrils closed.

Such child abuse was beyond imagining. Ellen had seen them only briefly, and afterwards wondered if perhaps she had *seen* wrong. But it was a dream, a very bad one, because the little girl had flicked the light off again. When Ellen reached to turn it back on, they had retreated into the shadows and the feeling of a surreal waking state came upon her. *The Neesons could not possibly be this evil.* With the light on, she saw only houseflies sweeping through the heavy air.

At breakfast, Joey devoured his scrambled eggs like he hadn't eaten in days; Ellen had to admit they tasted better than she'd had before.

"You live close to the earth," Papa Neeson said. "And it gives up its treasures."

Joey said, "Eggs come from chickens."

"Chickens come from eggs," Papa Neeson laughed, "and eggs are the beginning of all life. But we all gather our life from the earth, boy. You city folks don't feel it because you're removed. Out here, well, we get it under our fingernails, birth, death, and what comes in between."

"You're something of a philosopher," Ellen said, trying to hide her uneasiness. The image of the children still in her head, like a half-remembered dream. She was eager to get on her way, because that dream was beginning to seem more real. She had spent a half hour in the shower trying to talk herself out of having seen the children and what had been done to them: then, ten minutes drying off, positive that she had seen what she'd seen. It was Frank's legacy: he had taught her to doubt what was right before her eyes. She wondered if Papa Neeson performed darker needlework on his babies.

"I'm a realist," Papa Neeson said. His eyes were bright and kind—it shocked her to look into them and think about what he might have done.

Mama Neeson, sinking the last skillet into a washtub next to the stove, turned and said, "Papa just has a talent for making things work, Missus, for putting two and two together. That's how he grows, and that's how he gathers. Why if it weren't for him, where would my children be?"

"Where are they?" Joey asked.

"We have to get back to the train," Ellen said. "They said we'd take off by eleven."

Papa Neeson raised his eyebrows in an aside to his wife.

"I saw some flies at the windows," he said. "They been bad again."

Mama Neeson shrugged her broad shoulders. "They got to let them out at times or they'd be bursting, now, wouldn't they. Must tickle something awful." She wiped her dripping hands on the flower print apron, back and forth like she could never get dry enough. Ellen saw a shining in the old woman's eyes like tears and hurt.

Joey clanked his fork on his plate; Ellen felt a lump in

her throat, and imaginary spiders and flies crawling up the back of her neck. Something in the atmosphere had changed, and she didn't want to spend one more minute in this house with these people.

Joey clapped a fly between his hands, catching it mid-air.

~

"MAMA'S SORRY YOU DIDN'T SEE THE KIDS," PAPA Neeson said, steering over a slick patch on the newly-plowed road.

"But you're not." Ellen said. She was feeling brave. She hated this man like she hated Frank. Maybe she'd report him to some child welfare agency when she got back to the train station. She could see herself killing this man.

"No," Papa Neeson nodded. "I'm not. Mama, she don't understand about other people, but I do."

"Well, I saw them. All three. What you do to them."

Papa Neeson sighed, pulling over and parking at the side of the road. "You don't understand. Don't know if I should waste my breath."

Joey was in the backseat, bundled up in blankets. He yawned, "Why we stopping?"

Ellen directed him to turn around and sit quietly. He was a good boy. "I have a husband who hits children, too."

"I don't hit the kids, lady, and how dare you think I do, why you can just get out of my car right now if that's your attitude."

"I told you, I saw them," she said defiantly.

"You see the threads?"

Ellen could barely stand his smug attitude.

"You see 'em? You know *why* my kids look like that?"

Ellen reached for the door handle. She was going to get out. Fucking country people and their torture masked as discipline. Men, how she hated their power trips. Blood was boiling now; she was capable of anything, like two days ago when she took the baseball bat and slammed it against Frank's chest, hearing ribs cracking. She was not going to let a man hurt her child like that. Never again. The rage was rising up inside her the way it had only done twice in her life before, both times with Frank, both times protecting Joey.

Papa Neeson reached out and grabbed her wrist.

"*Don't hold me like that,*" she snarled.

He let go.

Papa Neeson began crying, pressing his head into the steering wheel. "She just wanted them so bad, I had to go dig 'em up. I love her so much, and I didn't want her to die from hurting, so I just dig 'em up and I figured out what to do and did it."

WHEN HE CALMED, HE SAT BACK UP, LOOKING straight ahead. "We better get to the junction. Train'll be ready. You got your life moving ahead with it, don't you?"

"Tell me about your children," she said, feeling a slight shiver as she thought of the flies. "What's wrong with them?"

He looked her straight in the eyes, making her flinch because of his intensity.

"Nothing, except they been dead for a long time." He let this sink in. He took a deep breath and looked out at the snowy world. "My wife, she loves 'em like they're her own. I dig 'em up, see, I thought she was gonna die from grief not having none of her own, and I figured it out, you know, about the maggots and the flies, how they make things move if you put enough of 'em inside the bodies."

She wanted him to stop talking. She couldn't stand the pain in his voice.

But he continued.

"I didn't count on 'em lasting this long, but what if they do? What if they *do*, lady? Mama, she loves those babies. We're only humans, lady, and humans need to hold babies, they need to love something other than themselves, don't they? Don't you? You got your boy, you know how much that's worth? Love beyond choosing, ain't it? Love that don't die.

"You know what it's like to hug a child when you never got to hug one before? So I figured and I figured some more, and I thought about what makes things live, how do we know something's alive, and I figured, when it moves it's alive, and when it don't move, it's dead. So Mama, I had her sew the flies in, but they keep laying eggs and more and more, and the kids, they got the minds of flies, and sometimes they rip out the threads, so sometimes flies get out, but it's a tiny price, ain't it, lady? When you need to love little ones, and you ain't got none, it's a tiny price, a day in hell's all, but then sunshine and children and love, lady, ain't it worth that?"

～

Ellen had a migraine by the time Papa Neeson dropped them off down at the junction. She barked at Joey. Apologized. Kissed him on the forehead.

She bought Joey an orange soda and made him promise to stand just over by the long bench near the soda machine and not go anywhere.

Ellen went into the restroom to wipe cold water across her face

The mirror in the bathroom, warped, distorted her features. She thought she looked stunning: brown eyes circled with sleeplessness, the throbbing vein to the left side of her forehead, the dry, cracked lips. She thought of the threads, of the children tugging at them, popping them out to let the flies go. Ran a finger over her lips, imagining Mama Neeson taking her needle and thread, breaking the skin with tiny holes. Ears, nostrils, eyes, mouth, other openings, other places where flies could escape.

Flies and life, sewn up into the bodies of dead children, buried by other grieving parents, brought back by the country folks who ran the bed-and-breakfast, and who spoke of children that no one ever saw much of.

And when they did...

Ellen imagined *Mama Neeson kissing the bruised cheek of her little girl, tears in her squinty eyes, tears of joy for having children to love.*

Behind her, someone opened the door.

Stood there.

Waiting for her to turn around.

"Look who I found," Frank said, dragging Joey behind him into the women's room.

TWO WEEKS LATER, SHE WAS ON THE TRAIN AGAIN with Joey, but it was better weather—snow had melted and the sun was exhaustingly bright.

Frank was dead.

She could think it.

She could remember the feel of the knife in her hands.

FRANK HAD COME AT JOEY WITH HIS OWN TOY DUMP truck. She had grabbed a kitchen knife—as she'd been planning to do since Frank had hauled them back to Springfield.

She had gone with the knowledge of what she would have to do to keep Frank out of her little boy's life forever.

Then, she had just waited for his temper to flare.

She kept the knife with her, and when she ran in the living room to see Frank slamming the truck against Joey's scalp, she let the boiling blood and rage take her down with them.

The blade went in deep.

She could not stop stabbing her husband.

SHE LIFTED HER SON IN HER ARMS AS SHE STEPPED off the train, careful on the concrete because there was still some ice.

Joey, wrapped in a blanket, sunglasses on his face, "sleeping," she told the nice lady who had been sitting across from them; Ellen, also wearing sunglasses and too much make-up, a scarf around her head, a heavy wool sweater around her shoulders, exhausted and determined.

Joey's not dead. Not really.

IT HADN'T BEEN HARD TO TRACK DOWN THE NEESONS. She had called them before she got on the train, and they were not surprised to hear from her.

"It happens this way," Mama Neeson told her. "Our calling."

Ellen was not sure what to make of that comment, but she was so tired and confused that she let it go.

Later, she might think that something of the Neesons had perhaps rubbed off on her and her son. That, perhaps just *meeting* them might be like inviting something into life that hadn't been considered before.

Something under your fingernails.

SHE CARRIED JOEY TO THE PAYPHONE AND DROPPED A coin in; she dialed the number from memory.

"Mr. Neeson?"

"Here already?" he asked.

"I took an early train."

"Mama's still asleep. She was up all night. Worries, you know. Upset for you."

"Well…"

"I'll be down there in a few minutes," he said. "You're sure this is what you want?"

"Love beyond choosing," she reminded him.

A spool of white thread fell from Joey's blanket, bouncing once, twice as it hit the floor, unraveling as it rolled.

BECOMING MEN

A match struck; its tiny yellow flame illuminated the circle of boys, casting their faces in flickering.

Ralph went first, his breath coming slowly because he still hadn't recovered from the way they'd held him down; his asthma had kicked in slightly and they'd taken away his inhaler so he had to be careful.

Slow, deep breaths. His eyes hurt just from the memory of the interrogation's bright lights and then the bitter tears that followed his confession. Was he still crying? Even he wasn't sure, but he tried to hold it in as much as possible, to hold in the little boy inside him who threatened to burst out and show the others that he was what he'd always feared himself to be: a weakling.

The darting light of the match slapped yellow warpaint on all of their features.

He closed his eyes and began, "I had just barely gotten to sleep — halfway in a dream and it was all kind of like a dream when I heard all the shouting, it was my dad, he was shouting like crazy."

Jesus de Miranda, the smallest boy of thirteen that Ralph had ever seen, said nothing but his eyes widened and he had a curious curl to his lips like he was about to say something, even wanted to, but could not. There was something compelling to his face, something withdrawn yet very proud.

Ralph tried not to only look at him, because it made him feel little and ready to break down crying again, so he laughed like it didn't matter, "And my dad is such a loud son of a bitch."

Jack jumped in, "My dad didn't say a word. The bastard."

Hugh coughed. "My dad went nuts, he was just shouting, and my mom was crying, but even when the big guy grabbed me—"

"The big black guy," Jack added, then glanced at the others. The match died. Another one burst to life immediately; Ralph and his matchbook again.

"A big white guy," Marsh said, slapping Jack across the top of the head.

"Yeah, a big white guy, wearing camouflage shit and his face was all green, it was freaky, I tell ya," Ralph said, holding the piss-colored fire in his hands like a delicate small bird in front of the others so they could all see their own fear. "And I was so scared I pissed myself and my dad, when I saw him, he was practically crying but since I could tell they weren't beat up I knew somehow that they had something to do with this, and it had something to do with that thing with my cousin from three days before and maybe with the fire that burned down this old shack, but I never really thought they'd do something like this, I mean, shit, this kind of Nazi bullshit—"

"It's scary," Marsh said, and his voice seemed too small for his six-foot tall frame. He grasped his elbows, leaning forward on his knees. "I just smoked some pot. That was it. Not half as much as my friends."

"What did you do that got you sent here?" Ralph asked Jack.

A silence.

Match died.

"Ralph," someone said in the dark.

Ralph wasn't sure who it was, but he waited in the dark for a moment because the ghosts of their faces still hung there, photographed by the last light of the match.

Scraped another one against the matchbook. The little flame came up.

Marsh continued. "With me, I thought they'd killed my folks and my sister and they were gonna do something terrible to me. And then I wished it was a dream. All of it."

"They hit you hard?" Hugh asked.

Marsh shrugged. "Yeah. They hit me. That's all. I barely felt it by then. I just figured they were gonna kill me. I figured if I just concentrated or something it would all happen and then it would be over. I thought it was because of the time I bought pot and got more than I paid for. That's what I thought. I didn't even think. I just figured that was it. It was over."

"And it's worse than that," Jack said. "You know what I

heard my mother say when they put the blindfold on me? I heard her say—"

"No one cares," Ralph said, too wisely. "They all lied."

The boys fell silent for a minute.

"I thought it was gonna be like tough love or something."

"They sold us up a river."

Jesus opened his mouth as if to speak, but closed it again. Fear had sealed his lips.

"They did it because they love me," Jack said, but he was crying, he was fourteen and crying like a baby and Ralph decided then and there that he didn't care what the others thought. He leaned over and threw his arm over Jack's shoulder. It reminded him of when his little brother got scared of lightning or of nightmares, and even though Jack was his age, it seemed okay, it seemed like it was the only thing to do.

Jack leaned his head against Ralph's neck and wept while the others watched.

Jesus de Miranda wept, too. Ralph asked him why, and he said it was because he was afraid of the dark.

Ralph gave him one match to keep.

"For an emergency," he said, and all the boys watched as the little de Miranda boy put it in his pocket, as if the match were hope and someone needed to keep it.

Ralph kept lighting his matches as other boys gathered around in the darkness and told their stories of woe, and wept, and gave up what fight they had in them.

By the time Ralph's last match died, morning had come, and with it, silence until the foghorn blasted its wake-up call.

TO BE A MAN
  YOU MUST KILL THE CHILD
  YOU MUST BURY THE CHILD
  YOU MUST GROW UP
  YOU MUST ACCEPT RESPONSIBILITY FOR
YOUR ACTIONS
  YOU MUST TAKE ON THE RESPONSIBILITIES
OF OTHERS
  YOU MUST BURN
  YOU MUST FREEZE
  YOU MUST GIVE YOURSELF TO US

The words were emblazoned on the side of the barrack wall, and every morning, Ralph knew, he would see those words, every morning, no matter how hard he tried to resist them, they would enter his soul. In the line up, they had to shout out the words, they had to shout them out loud, louder, I can't hear you, louder, over and over until it seemed as if those words were God.

"Number one!" the big man named Cleft shouted so loud in rang in their ears, pounding his chest hard as if he were beating it into his heart, "I am your priest, your father, your only authority, understand? I am Sergeant Cleft, and my colleagues and I, your superiors in every way, are here to drill you until you break. We are not interested in bolstering your gutless egos. We are not interested in making men out of you. You are the worst kinds of boys imaginable, every one of your families has disowned you, and we intend to break you down as far as is humanly possible to go. Then, if you have what it takes, you will build yourself up from the tools we give you here. Right now, this is Hell to you. But when we are through grinding your bones and spirits, this will be heaven. I don't want any quitters, either. You never give up, do you understand me, grunts? Never ever give up! This isn't a camp for sissies and pansies, and you aren't here because you been good little boys! You got sent here because you are headed for destruction! You got sent here because you couldn't cut it like others your age! You got sent here before someone sent you to jail! Before you destroyed your families! Before you could keep up your stupid antisocial ways!"

His barks sailed over them, for by dawn, even the terrified ones were ready to put up some resistance, even Ralph's tears were dry and he spent the time imagining how to escape from this island in the middle of nowhere, how to get a message out to the authorities that he'd been kidnapped against his will, and then he was going to sue his parents for kidnapping, endangerment, and trauma.

He looked at Cleft with cold eyes, and wished the big man dead. Cleft was muscle-bound, large, a baton in his belt strap, pepper spray too, and something that looked like a stun gun looped at his back. Ralph glanced around at the others, the twenty three boys, all with dark-encircled eyes, all looking scrawny from a night of no sleep and dreadful fear, and he shouted inside his mind.

How could they do this? How could all these parents do this to their children? What kind of world was this?

Morning had come too soon, and they'd been roused and tossed in the open showers (like the Jews, Ralph thought remembering the show on the History Channel, like the Jews being thrown in showers and gassed, or hosed down before they started on their backbreaking labor, treated not like people but like cattle), and then they all had been given uniforms, and the boys had complied. It struck Ralph as strange how everyone accepted it all; as if this was the Hell they were all consigned to, and there was no way around it. The uniforms were brown like shit, that's what Cleft had told them, "Like you, you are shit, and you will look like shit until we make men out of you!" Then no breakfast, but barrels of water just outside the showers, and each boy, if thirsty, had to stick his head in the barrel like an animal and drink. Some didn't, but Ralph did. He wanted water badly, he wanted to drink the entire barrel despite the other boys' spit he saw floating in it, and the insects that had fallen in. The bugs were everywhere, from sucking mosquitoes to huge winged beetles that flew at the screen door on the barracks. And what kind of island was it? Where? Was it the Caribbean? Ralph thought it might be off the coast of Mexico somewhere, something about the light of the sky, something about the water, but his experience was limited. He knew the island was flat where they stood, raised like a plateau. There were cliffs diving down to the sea, he'd seen them when the helicopter had brought him in the night, when the blindfold had slipped slightly and he'd glimpsed the rocky cliffs and the crashing waves far below.

"Grunt!" Cleft shouted, and Ralph looked up. Cleft pushed his way through the front line of boys in their shit-colored uniforms, and found him. Cleft looked like a parody of a marine, a steroid joke, a pit bull-human love child, and when he stood right in front of Ralph, Ralph wished he would wake up. Just wake up, he told himself.

It's a dream. It has to be a dream. Piss your pants. Roll out of bed.

Cleft barked, "You worthless sack of owl dung, you keep your eyes on me, you understand? I seen a lot of boys come through here, and you are the sorriest ass piece of shit I ever saw. You hear me?"

Ralph kept his gaze forward, staring at a place just below Cleft's eyebrows, not *in* the eyes, but between them.

"I said, you hear me?"

Ralph trembled slightly, feeling his knees buckle. Hunger grew from a place not in his gut, but in his extremities, his fingers, toes, the top of his head, it was like a spider tingling along his skin, squeezing his nerves. His mouth felt dry.

"I hear you like to set fires, Pig Boy," Cleft almost whispered, but a whisper that boomed across the heads of all the other boys. "I hear you did something really nasty to another boy back home. I heard you—" Ralph shut his eyes for a second and in his mind he was flying over all the others, he was going up to the cottony clouds. He felt hunger leave him, he felt tension leave him, he felt everything fly away from his body.

With a sickening feeling, he opened his wet eyes.

Then Cleft glanced down from Ralph's face to his chest, then his crotch. Cleft laughed, a nasty sound. "Baby Pig Boy here has pissed his panties!" Cleft clapped his hands together. "He's pissed his panties like a big Baby Pig Boy, haw! You can put out a lot of fires with that piss, can't you Pig Boy?"

Then, Cleft shoved him hard in the chest, so hard Ralph fell backwards on his ass. He looked up at the big man, the bulging muscles, the sharp crew cut, the hawk nose, and gleaming teeth. "Let me show you how to put out a fire, men!" Cleft laughed as he spoke, unzipping his pants and Ralph screeched at first — like an owl — as the piss hit his face. Cleft continued shouting, telling him that to be a man, one had to first prove himself worthy of manhood, one had to accept humiliation at the hands of one's superior, one had to take what one deserved whether one liked it or not, one had to know one's place—"You like to set things on fire, grunt, but you need a man to put out the fire inside you!"

Just kill me, Ralph thought. *Just kill me.*

We are just like the Jews in the concentration camps, Ralph thought, glancing to the others who still had their eyes forward, their lips drawn downward, looking scrawnier and weaker than boys of thirteen to sixteen should look, looking like they would all have been happy to not have Cleft pissing on *them*, happy that Ralph was the first sacrifice of the day, happy to die.

Just die.

IT BECAME A ROUTINE THAT THEY NEITHER LOOKED forward to, nor complained about, and the others who had sat up with Ralph the first night never spoke together again. Ralph would give Marsh a knowing look, and Marsh would return it, but for a millisecond before his eyes glazed over in what Ralph came to think of as "Cleft-eye." It was the zombie-like way they were all getting, Ralph included. When he lay asleep in his lower bunk, he could hear Hugh weeping in his sleep, then whimpering like a puppy, and sometimes Ralph stayed up all night listening for Hugh to cry, and it would help him fall asleep if only for an hour or two. Food got better, but not good. From the first two days of water only, they went to bread and water.

By the end of the first week, they were having beans, rice, water, bread, and an apple. By the second week, it was beans, rice, water, bread, milk, apple, and some tasteless fish.

Ralph noticed that his diarrhea had stopped by the third week, as did most of the boys'. The labor was grueling, but Ralph didn't mind it because while he hacked at the logs, or while he chipped at stone with what seemed to be the most primitive of tools, he remembered his family and home and his dog, and it was, after awhile, almost like being with them until the workday was over.

The maneuvers began at night.

Cleft, and the six others who ran the camp, had them running obstacle courses in the stench of evening when the mosquitoes were at their worst, when the mud was hot and slick, when the sweat could almost speak as it ran down his back. Wriggling like snakes beneath barbed wire, climbing ropes to dizzying heights, leaping from those heights into mud, running across narrow, stripped logs, piled end to end, it all became second nature after the initial falls and screams.

Foghorn, as they called a large boy in Hut D, fell and broke his leg the first day of the obstacle course, and Jesus, the little boy that Ralph had never heard say so much as a word, got cut on the barbed wire, badly, across his shoulders, and then got an infection when it went untreated.

After the third week, none of the boys saw Jesus anymore. Some said he'd been sent back home. Some said he'd died. Some said he'd run off. Some said it was all bullshit and he was probably back with his dad in New York City, lucky bastard, with a scar on his shoulder, and an excuse for not being in Camp Hell.

Rumors circulated that Jack and Marsh had been caught jacking each other off. The next time Ralph saw them, he also noticed bruises around their eyes and on their arms.

Boys had ganged up on them, but Ralph didn't want to know about it. He was somewhere else. He didn't need to be among any of them, he was in a place of family and fire in his head, and although his muscles felt like they were tearing open when he lay down in his bunk at night, he knew that he was growing stronger both inside and outside.

And then, one day, Jack came to him.

"Got any more matches?"

Ralph opened his eyes. It had to be four a.m., just an hour or so before First Call.

The shadow over him gradually revealed itself in the purple haze of approaching dawn.

"What the—"

"Matches?" Jack asked again. "You're like the fireboy, right?"

"No."

"Liar. Come on, wake up. We have something to show you."

"I don't care. Leave me alone." Ralph turned on his side, shutting his eyes.

"He pissed on you. Don't you hate him?"

Ralph kept his vision dark. If he didn't open his eyes, it might all go away. "I don't care."

"You will care," Jack said. The next thing Ralph knew, it was morning, the horn blasted, the rush of ice cold showers, the sting of harsh soap, the barrels of water and then chow. Out in the gravel pit, shoveling, someone tossed pebbles across Ralph's back. He looked over his shoulder.

"Leave me alone," Ralph spat, the dirt sweat sliding across his eyes; he dropped his shovel, looking back at Jack.

"You set fires back home, I know that," Jack whispered. "We all know it. It's all right. It's what you love. Don't let them kill that. We need you."

"Yeah, well, we all did something. What did you do to get you sent here?"

Jack said nothing for a moment.

"We found Jesus," Jack said, and tears erupted in his eyes. Ralph wanted to shout at him not to cry anymore, there was no reason to cry, that he was weak to cry, just like Cleft said—

Ralph asked, "Where is he?"

"Dead," Jack said. "They killed him. They killed him and they hid him so we couldn't find him. Did you know he was only ten years' old?"

"Bullshit," Ralph gasped. "He's thirteen."

"Ten years' old and his father sent him here after he left his mother. His father sent him because his father didn't give a damn about him. You, Ralph, you set fires. And me, I maybe did some stuff I'm not real proud of. But Jesus, all he did was get born in the wrong family. And they killed him."

RALPH CLOSED HIS EYES.

Tried to conjure up the vision of his family and home again, and the beautiful fires he had set at the old shack in the woods, the fires that had made him feel weak and strong all at once and connected with the world. But only darkness filled his mind.

Opened his eyes.

Jack's face, the bruises lightening, his eyes deep and blue, the dark tan bringing out the depth of the color of those eyes, a God blue.

"Dead?"

"Yep." Jack said.

"How?"

Jack glanced over at Red Chief and Commodore, the two thugs disguised as soldiers who stood above the gravel pit, barking at some of the slower boys. "Keep digging, and I'll tell you, but do you know what I think we're digging?"

Ralph cocked his head to the side, trying to guess.

"Our own graves."

JACK CONTINUED. "ME AND MARSH BEEN TRYING TO find a way out every single night. We wait till three thirty, when the goons are asleep with only one on watch, and we get mud all over us, and we do the snake thing and Marsh and me get away from the barracks until we go out on the island, and we see that there's no way anybody's getting off this island without killing themselves, that's why security ain't so tight. It's a nothing island, maybe two square miles at the most, with nothing. The thugs' huts are in the east, and between those and ours and the work pits, there ain't a hell of a whole lot. But we find this thin crack opening between these rocks just beyond the thug huts, and we squeeze in—that's all the bruises—"

"I thought you got beat up."

Jack held his temper. "That's what we said, dumbshit, so nobody would know."

"I thought you two…"

Jack cut in. "We spread that story, fool. So we squeeze through the opening, and it's too dark to see, and this cave that we're hoping will take us out ends within six feet of entering it, only we feel something there in the dark, we feel something all mushy and stinky and only when Marsh falls on it and screams does he realize it's a body."

IT WAS JESUS DE MIRANDA, THE LITTLEST BOY AT camp, dead not from an infection but from something that smashed his hands up and his knees, too. Ralph heard the rest, tried to process it, but it made him sick.

"Where are we?" he whispered, leaning against Jack.

"All I know is, I think we're all dead."

"All?"

"I think," Jack said. "I think they're going to just kill all of us. I don't think any of us are leaving."

Jack stuck four small rocks in Ralph's pockets.

"Later. They'll be useful," Jack said.

"Just like the Concentration Camps," Ralph whispered, and then Commodore shouted at him, and he returned to shoveling while the blistering sun poured lava on his back.

"I said get up here, you worthless Pig Boy!" Commodore yelled.

By the time Ralph made it up from the pit, crawling along the edges, he scraped his knees up and was out of breath.

"Something you want to share with the rest of us?" Commodore said, his eyes invisible behind his mirrored sunglasses. "I saw you chattering down there, Pig Boy."

"Don't call me that," Ralph coughed.

"Something wrong?"

Ralph covered his mouth, hearing the balloon hiss of air from his lungs.

"Asthma," he gasped. "I don't have...my inhaler..."

"It's all in your tiny brain, Pig Boy, you don't need some inhaler like a mama's boy, you just need to focus.

You need to be a man, Pig Boy," Commodore laughed, and shoved Ralph down in the dirt. Ralph felt his windpipe closing up, felt his lungs fight for air. He could not even cough. His eyes watered up, and he opened his mouth, sucking at air.

Commodore lifted him up again, bringing his face in line with Ralph's. Eye to eye, Commodore snarled, "Breathe, damn you!"

Ralph gasped. He knew he would die. He knew his lungs would stop. His vision darkened until all he could see were the man's brown eyes. He thought of little Jesus, dead, his hands smashed into bloody clay. Dust seemed to fill his mouth.

"Breathe!" Commodore continued, and reached over, pressing his hand down hard on Ralph's chest. "You want to be a man, Pig Boy, you breathe like a man, open up those lungs, make 'em work," and suddenly, air whooshed into Ralph's mouth.

The darkness at the edge of his vision erased itself into the light of day.

Ralph sucked at the air like he was starving for it.

"There," Commodore said, and pushed Ralph back down in the dirt. "You boys, you think you can create the world in your own image. That's your problem. You think you can keep from growing up. Well, growing up means accepting the burden just like the rest of us. Accept it, accept the truth, and you'll thrive. Keep doing what you've been doing, and you'll die."

Ralph sat on the ground, staring up at the man. The air tasted pure. He gulped it down, feeling his lungs burn.

TO BE A MAN
  YOU MUST KILL THE CHILD
  YOU MUST BURY THE CHILD
  YOU MUST GROW UP
  YOU MUST ACCEPT RESPONSIBILITY FOR YOUR ACTIONS
  YOU MUST TAKE ON THE RESPONSIBILITIES OF OTHERS
  YOU MUST BURN
  YOU MUST FREEZE
  YOU MUST GIVE YOURSELF TO US

They shouted it in the morning, still shivering from the icy waters that erased their dreams, standing in the shimmering day, a mirage of day, for in their hearts, they never felt dawn.

At night, Last Call, the bells ringing three times, running for a last cold shower, running for the latrine, and then Light's Out.

"HE'S UNDER THE HUT," JACK SAID.

He'd gathered Hugh, Marsh, a boy named Gary, a boy named Lou, and Ralph wanted to see, too, to see if they were telling the truth about Jesus. At three a.m., they all hunkered down, crawling like it was another maneuver under barbed wire to get out of the hut unnoticed; then under the hut's raised floor, down a narrow tunnel that might've been dug out by jackals.

Jack and Marsh had dug an entrance that led down into a larger hole, and there, in the dark, they all felt Jesus' body, smelled it, some vomited, others gagged.

Ralph reached into the dead boy's pocket and drew out the last match, the one he'd given the little boy the first night they'd met to keep him from the dark.

Ralph struck the match against a rock, and it sputtered into crackling light.

They all looked at Jesus, at the rotting, the insects already devouring his puffy face, the way his hands were bloody pulps, his kneecaps all but destroyed.

"Holy—"

"—Shit"

"They did it," Jack said.

"Mother—"

"Yeah—"

"Holy—"

"Is that really him?" Gary asked.

"It has to be," Marsh said.

"Who else?" Ralph said, and then the last match died.

Sitting in the dark, the stink of the boy's corpse filling them, Ralph said, "If we let this go, we'll die. Right here. You all know about concentration camps in World War II. You all know what happens. This is just like it."

"Yeah," Lou said. "They killed him. Man, I can't believe it. I can't believe my mom would send me here. I can't believe…"

"Believe," Jack said. Ralph felt Jack's hand give Ralph a squeeze. "Maybe our folks don't know what they do here. Shit, I doubt Jesus' father even knows."

"I can't believe it either," Ralph said. "They're monsters."

"They aren't human, that's for sure," Marsh added.

"What are we gonna do?" Jack asked the darkness.

"What can we do?" Ralph countered.

"Someone should so something," Gary moaned.

Then, they crawled out of the ground, up to their hut. The diffuse moonlight spattered the yard, lit the barracks and huts and showers and the boy's faces were somehow different in the night, flatter, more alike than Ralph had remembered them being. Before they went inside, Jack turned to Ralph and said, "Too bad you wasted that match. We could've set fire to this place with it."

Ralph said almost to himself, "I've never needed a match to set a fire."

IN THE MORNING, A QUIET PERMEATED THE CAMP, and when the boys trooped out to shout their pledge of allegiance to the dawn, their mouths stopped up as if their tongues had been cut off.

On the side of the barrack wall, the words:

TO BE A GOD
YOU MUST KILL THE ENEMY
YOU MUST BURY THE ENEMY
YOU MUST NEVER GROW UP
YOU MUST BURN THEM
YOU MUST FREEZE THEM
YOU MUST GIVE YOURSELF TO THE CAUSE
OF JESUS

There, besides the hastily scrawled revision, written in rough chalk, the body of Jesus de Miranda, held up by barbed wire twisting like vines around his limbs and torso.

Ralph glanced at Jack, who laughed, and then to Marsh who had a tear in his eye. Behind them, Cleft came striding, whistle in his mouth, wearing a green baseball cap and green fatigues. "Into the showers, you pansy ass bitches!" Cleft shouted, blowing the whistle intermittently.

Then the whistle dropped from his mouth. He saw the writing. He saw the boy's body.

Cleft reached up and drew his baseball cap off, letting it fall to the ground. He let out a whisper that sounded like, "Holy."

And then the rocks.

Jack had made sure there were enough, just enough, for ten of the boys, Ralph included and they leapt on Cleft, stronger now, their own biceps built up from weeks of labor.

Cleft tried to reach for the pepper spray, but he had to raise his hands defensively to ward off the blows. Cleft was like a mad bull, tossing them off to the side, but the rocks slammed and slashed at his face, tearing his hawk nose open, a gash above his eye blinding him with blood flow, and as the red explosions on his face increased, Ralph felt something overpowering within him.

He became the most ferocious, ramming at Cleft with all his weight, cutting deep into Cleft's shoulder with the sharp edge of a rock, bringing the big man to his knees.

Ralph grabbed for Cleft's belt, tearing it off the loops, holding up the pepper spray and stun gun and baton.

Ralph lifted the baton in the air and brought it down hard on Cleft's skull.

And then all of the boys leapt upon Cleft.

"YES!" RALPH SHOUTED, HIGH-FIVING JACK, RUNNING with the others — a pack of wolves — across the muddy ground, through the steamy heat, rocks held high, Cleft's pepper spray in Ralph's left hand.

Jack held the stun gun, and Marsh, the fastest runner of them all was in the lead, waving the baton that still had Cleft's fresh blood on it.

They shrieked the words of rebellion they'd written on the Wall. Several of the boys had taken down the body of Jesus de Miranda and hoisted it like a battering ram between them as they flew to the sergeants' barracks.

They caught the masters in their showers, mid-coffee, shaving, cutting at them with their own razors, scalding them, beating them, until two more were dead, and the others unconscious.

Later, Ralph remembered the feeling of all of them, all the boys together, moving as one, storming the island, like lava overflowing a volcano.

WHEN IT WAS MOSTLY FINISHED AND NIGHT COVERED them, Ralph leaned toward Commodore; the man was tied to a chair, his great muscles caught in wire. Ralph held out a cigarette lighter, a souvenir from a downed sergeant.

Stepping forward, Ralph struck the lighter, the flame coming forth.

"Arsonist, murderer," Commodore said, his eyes bloodshot, his face a mass of bruises.

"Shut up or I'll cut out your tongue," Jack laughed. Ralph looked back at him, and wondered if, like Jack, he was covered with blood as well. He heard the shouts of the other boys as they raided the food supply.

"We didn't kill that little boy, you dumbfuck," Commodore said.

"Okay, here goes the tongue," Jack said, coming up to the bound man, clippers in hand.

"Liar," Ralph said, twisting the lighter in front of Commodore's face.

"One of you must've done it, "Commodore spat, but it was the last thing he said, for Jack had the clippers in his mouth. Ralph couldn't look, it wasn't something he enjoyed, but Jack had that glow on him, his whole body radiated with his joy.

The man didn't even try to scream.

Ralph looked at the blood on Jack's hands.

"Jesus, Jack," Ralph said, feeling the spinning world come back to him, the world of sanity that had somehow gotten out of control. "Jesus, Jack."

"What?" Jack laughed, dropping the clippers, clapping his red hands together.

Ralph looked back at the man, his mouth a blossom of bright red.

The man's eyes did not leave Ralph's face.

Ralph was amazed that the man didn't cry out in pain, that he kept his eyes forward, on Ralph, not pleading, not begging, but as if he were trying to let some truth up from his soul.

"Jack," Ralph went over to his friend, his blood-covered friend, his friend who had helped him get through this time in Hell. "Was he lying?"

"Yep," Jack said, averting his gaze. The blood ran down his face like tears. "He's one of them. They always lied to us."

"You sure?"

Jack closed his eyes. "Yep."

Then, "Did you and Marsh kill Jesus?"

Jack opened his eyes, staring straight at him. "If that were true, would it change anything? Jesus is dead. He came here. They did all this."

Ralph felt his heart stop for a moment, and then the beating in his chest became more rapid.

"We're just like them," Ralph whispered, mostly to himself.

"No," Jack grinned, blood staining his teeth, "They're weak. We're strong. They're time is up. Ours is just beginning."

"What did you do that got you sent here?" Ralph asked for the last time.

"Nothing," Jack said. "Nothing that you need to know about."

"You killed someone, didn't you?"

"It was nothing, believe me," Jack smiled. "And you've done some killing yourself today, haven't you?"

"I wouldn't have if—"

"You'll never know," Jack slapped Ralph on the back. "But it's okay. I understand."

Later, the man they called Commodore died.

JACK FOUND RALPH IN THE DARK, SITTING ON A bench outside the barracks. He put his arm over Ralph's shoulders and whispered, "Now we can go home. We can go home and make them all pay."

"Are we men yet?" Ralph asked, feeling an icy hand grab him around the chest, under his skin, closing up his throat until his voice was barely a whimper.

"No," Jack said. "We're better than men. We're gods. Come on, let's play with fire. You'll feel better after that, won't you?"

He stood, drawing Ralph up by the hand. "You're good at fires, Ralph. We need you. I need you."

"I don't know," Ralph said. "Yesterday it was one thing. It seemed different. Jesus was dead. They were like the Nazis."

"I need you," Jack repeated, squeezing Ralph's hand tight, warm, covering Ralph's fingers in his. "You as you are, Ralph. Not what they wanted. As you are. I want you."

Ralph felt his fingers curl slightly under the weight of Jack's. He looked down at their hands and then up at Jack's face. "I can't."

"No shame," Jack said, "Let's set it all on fire. Glorious fire. Let's make it burn all the way up to the sun."

"That's my dream," Ralph whispered, a shock of recognition in Jack's words, a secret between the most intimate of friends. "How did you know my dream? My first night here, I saw it in my mind, a fire going all the way to the sun."

They stood there, frozen for a moment; then, Jack slowly let go of Ralph's hand, leaving in his palm a new silver lighter. "Go set fires across the land."

BEFORE THE SUN ROSE FROM THE SEA INTO AN EMPTY sky, the fires got out of hand.

Ralph realized — putting aside other considerations — that it was the most beautiful thing he had ever seen in his young life, the way fire could take away what was right in front of his eyes, just burn it off with no reason other than its own hunger.

Jack said it was the best day he'd ever had, and when the burning was done, the boys ran off to the showers, all except for Ralph who went in search of something new to burn.

PEOPLE WHO LOVE LIFE

W hy did he always have to follow her wherever she went and bring her back?

Irene liked to go down to the schoolyard because of the children, the little children. Their faces, *their faces*, their tiny hands, their dresses and shorts and shirts and shoes, so small, so perfect. It bothered her when he volunteered to go, too, because the edge of the schoolyard was her special place, the children were there, and he didn't know anything about children.

Children had that edge; they could *smell* things when they were bad, and they weren't afraid to say it. And when things were truly good, children sensed that, too. Children were the thing.

"Oh, but when *we* were children," the girl had said in the kitchen, and Irene had had to stare at her younger sister long and hard before she realized that she wasn't a girl at all, but a woman in her early forties: Gretchen was still pretty and adolescent, even with her slightly etched face and graying hair.

Irene could not stand her sometimes, although Gretchen on her own was one thing—sweetness and light even though she *knew*, but Gretchen with this man she'd married was quite another. Irene had never really enjoyed his company, although she couldn't ever tell Gretchen how she felt; and so, she was often stuck with him, this William person, even when she went to the schoolyard to watch her children play.

"When *we* were children," Irene replied. "Good lord, I can't even remember, barely."

Gretchen loaded the dishwasher. "I remember like yesterday. Days like today, just like today. Look outside the window, it's just like when we were children and mother was in here cleaning, looking out at us."

But, of course, there were no children out the window now.

Gretchen was the most self-assured person that Irene had ever known, but she lied. Irene knew that about Gretchen: she lied. Gretchen could not possibly remember their childhood accurately, she had no head for memories. She blocked them purposefully, like closing doors on useless rooms. Irene remembered just about everything, but she had lied, also. Irene was not fond of remembering: *days like today, indeed. All days, like today. Unending. I just want to leave. Why won't they just let me leave?*

They had been a family of liars, and had never quite grown out of it, although Irene was tired, today, lying to herself about what she felt and what she wanted. Truly wanted. *I just want to go by myself.*

"You were undoubtedly two of the most spoiled girls in creation, all those toys and the way your mother used to dress you up for Sunday school like little dolls," William had said, and Irene thought:

Why do you live here with us when you're so awful to Gretchen? How you did to her what you did, let alone how I must pay for it, is beyond imagining. But you have no imagination, do you? You think it is the way you see it. In front of your face. The way you see it, with no one else allowed to look.

He was an old man who pretended to be young, but she saw right through that, right to that middle-aged heart with its bloodless beating. He pretended things were all right, that there was good to every purpose.

"We were never really spoiled," Gretchen said, "but there's always been someone to watch out for us."

"Amen to that," William said, clasping his hands together.

He had decided to come with her this day, and so there he was at her right arm, helping her every few steps as if she were a complete cripple.

"I can handle the steps quite well, thank you, William," she said, and knew she sounded testy. Her right leg twisted as she stepped down to the sidewalk. Again, she had lied; stairs were difficult for her, the way her feet went, one moving almost against the other, but once she was on flat ground she was fine. But she was tired of his help.

"All righty, then," he said, and he made it sound like he was trying to be funny.

She could not stand people who spoke like that. People who made fun of everything. People who love life.

If only he'd let her *go* sometimes, instead of following after her like a yappy dog.

"I am not so far gone," she told him, "that I can't walk by myself. You know that, don't you?"

"Oh, Irene, I was trying to be helpful."

"Don't think me ungrateful. You and Gretchen have been kind, since the accident. More than kind. But I don't want kindness, not anymore." She had given up on direct sarcasm, and never thought he would get it, anyway. Why couldn't he just let her go?

"You're almost all healed." He reached over and touched around her face.

Irene gasped.

He was always close to touching her, and *there* of all places, but he had never accomplished more than the slightest graze. She stood still as if he were pulling a stray hair from her forehead.

He touched her scars. His fingers were soft along the place where the skin had bubbled and obscured the vision of her left eye.

Why did his fingers seem so warm, when she knew him to be so cold, so empty? Was he laughing at her, the way he laughed at the whole of creation?

Finally, he removed his hand. "Does it hurt?"

"Not now. Like a headache, sometimes, but the pills take care of that, but please, let's not talk about it, I feel all talked out, and I see it in the mirror every morning, so I don't find it interesting." Would that shut him up? She would like to just have a nice day and watch the children in the schoolyard.

"God loves you, you know, Irene. He really does, and in His infinite wisdom," and he would've gone on with his smug little litany, too.

But she spat at him, "I don't care for your God, William, and I don't care for you. I was going to spend the day alone, in my own way, and you have to come along with your almighty creator and ruin everything once again."

"I know you don't mean that," he whispered, like a hurt child. "I know you're saying it because of great pain."

"You," she said, "you are my great pain. You and your miracles."

HE WAS WALKING SEVERAL STEPS BEHIND HER, AND she thought of trying to lose him in the village, but she really must go and see the children when they went out to the playground. She must not miss them.

Perhaps she'd stop in for a cup of coffee, but only for a minute, because the children would be waiting to see her.

Only the children knew how to treat her, how to respect her wishes. They had almost come through for her last time: their tiny hands, so willing, so lovely. It was because children knew things instinctively, they had gut reactions, they were so close to the real pulse of life.

Grownups had lost it all, and certainly men like this William person that Gretchen had married were so out of touch, so *clueless*, that everything was like a car: maintenance and repair, tinkering around with things that were best left to the junkyard. And always the male need for possession.

Well, I do not belong to you.

She limped another quarter mile through the village, and it was empty. It had been mostly empty when she and Gretchen had been girls, and it was empty when they were in their twenties and thirties, and now it was desolate. She had wanted to leave the village for as long as she could remember, but she'd never had the nerve.

Now she knew of only one route, and damn him, he was going to shadow her.

The sunlight was flat and nothing escaped it: she saw her reflection in the bookstore window. The scars weren't healing at all, they were simply drying. Her mouth looked terrible, and she couldn't bring herself to look at her jaw. Her hair was mostly gone, but the scarf hid that.

The clerk inside the bookstore pretended not to stare at her from behind the counter, but she saw him stealing glances. *I don't mind*, she thought, nodding to him, *let this be a lesson to you. When it's time, it's time.*

William stood behind her. She saw his reflection. "My sister told me once that life was precious," Irene said aloud, knowing he would hear. "And I believed her. But she meant something different than this."

"Life is the greatest gift," he said. He sometimes had a voice like nails on wood, and in the county they said he had a voice like thunder, but he sounded to her most like teeth grinding. Nothing more than teeth, one bone wearing away at another.

She turned to face him. She counted to ten, silently. Her tongue went dry in her mouth. "I am going to have some coffee, and I want to be alone."

She walked on down the sidewalk, trying to stay in the shade.

She passed Fred Smith, whom she hadn't seen since just after the accident when the town meeting was called, and he actually tipped his baseball cap to her, which seemed a rather pleasant gallantry, considering what he'd said about her in the past. *"Way I see it, you belong somewhere between a freak show and a wienie roast,"* Fred had *muttered from the safety of his pickup truck, but she hadn't blamed him because he was right.*

"Well, hey, Miz Hart," he said this time, but he didn't look at her, not directly. Her shoes, but not her face.

She didn't blame him: she was surprised that the young man in the bookstore had tried. *They're all afraid they're going to turn to stone.*

She walked around him into the Five & Dime, but not before she heard Fred say, more stiffly than when he'd greeted her, "Hello, preacher."

And William's absurdly heartfelt reply, "This is the day the Lord has made, Fred, rejoice."

"Yeah, well…" Fred had nothing more to say.

THE LUNCH COUNTER WAS GREASE-SPATTERED AND vacant.

Ever since the freeway had been built closer to Blowing Rock, the village didn't even have the trucks coming through. *As if the world knew not to come through here. It's a cursed place. Unclean, like in biblical days.*

Jeannie Stamp came out from the washroom and leaned over the counter, nodding when Irene sat on the stool.

"It's dying, all my business is gone, just about," Jeannie said as she poured out the coffee, "Black, you like it? I told that old fart Harry to make sure the county money got thrown our way, but he said wait, and look what's happened now we been waiting long enough, we ain't even on the map. Used to be, ten, twelve people in here by noon, and now, just you and me, Renie."

Jeannie never looked at her directly, either, but Jeannie was always nicer than the rest of the village. Irene had been to school with Jeannie, and had never thought in all her youth that she would ever depend upon her for friendship, but it was the best that was offered these days.

"I'm going to the school," Irene told her, leaning her elbows on the counter, sipping her coffee. It was lukewarm and smelled like dirty socks, but this was the only place to get coffee in town since the trouble when they'd burned down the ice cream shop. It was the older kids, just going crazy and setting fire to things. Even the teenagers knew when something was wrong, when things needed to be torn down. *Maybe the whole village will go. If I can't leave, maybe it will leave me.*

"You think that's a smart move?"

Irene shrugged. "What's smart?"

"School. All those kids I heard about the other day. What happened."

"*Almost* happened, *almost.*"

"Well, it could."

"Yes, hon, it could," Irene set the half-empty cup down and could not decide if she should go out in the summer heat again and face Gretchen's husband, or if she should wait another fifteen minutes.

The children would be in the playground soon, and if she didn't see them today, it would be tomorrow, and if it didn't happen today, they might get used to her presence and never do what she knew they wanted to, never be free to be children, *just be children.* Less than twenty children left in the village at all.

"Preacher's talked about the Lord in our lives," Jeannie said. "He says we should be grateful, that God shines His light on us, even here, to the lowliest."

I am so tired of this fundamentalist town, Irene felt a headache coming on, and all her pills were back at the house, so the headache would just have to hammer away at her. *Gretchen and I should've left long ago, back when we had choices, back when we wanted to get out in the world. I should've learned to drive when I was in my twenties. Not wait until I was forty-six and in a stick shift with a sixteen year old. But they would've laughed at me. Luke was the only one who could teach me, the only one I could trust not to tell William, or even Gretchen. They would've laughed, and then he would've wondered why I wanted to leave so badly, and he would've stopped it. He did stop it. And I should never have been pulled from the car. Not back to this godforsaken place.* "If that's true, Jeannie, about God, what about Luke?"

Jeannie looked like a girl who had been scolded. "That's different. Preacher says God helps those He chooses."

"Who chooses? God, or the preacher?"

"Preacher don't have a choice, way I see it. He just got the gift. Always been miracles, always will be. Ain't you happy, being so special and all?"

Irene put two quarters on the counter. "Look me in the eye and ask me that."

"Oh," Jeannie said, "you know I can't do that. You know what happens. You don't want it to happen, do you?"

IRENE WAVED TO WILLIAM AS SHE CAME BACK OUT, into the sunlight.

No one else was on the street, and there he was with his grin, his hopeful grin, like a dog waiting to be kicked. He had that charm, which she found so dull. But in a village like this, he would be king. He would be adored. So he had come here and found Gretchen.

He was the big fish in the small pond.

He was Preacher, and this was his Flock.

Irene had once liked him, a little, but not at all since the accident. She had not even been feeling kindly towards her sister. "I don't understand you," she'd told Gretchen, "why do you even want me here? Isn't it painful?" But Gretchen was so brainwashed by this William person, by his laying on of hands and speaking in tongues, that she was not really the same girl that Irene had grown up with. Gretchen could not see her way out of things, never had been able to; for Gretchen, things were the way they were. Only once had Gretchen asked her about that day, about what happened. And Irene had pretended to have forgotten, as if the accident and the darkness had wiped it away.

"IRENE," WILLIAM CALLED OUT, HIS HANDS TUCKED almost sheepishly in his pockets; he was rocking back and forth on his heels, "I was afraid I'd lost you."

He stepped into the street and crossed over to her. He walked like a boy, all bounce and uncertainty.

"I'm going to see the children."

"I'd like to come along."

"Do what you like," she closed her eyes and he touched her elbow with his hand. The bone was broken there, and had not healed where it poked out from her skin. She could move it fine, but she didn't like to be reminded of it.

She wondered how he could touch her the way he did; she sensed his discomfort each time he was close, but now, this day, he seemed more relaxed, as if he were no longer fearful of what had happened to her body. She often wondered: *Do you like what you see? Does it please you to be so close to this monster? Do you love life this much, even when it looks this way?* But she had never been beautiful; Gretchen was always the pretty one, which bothered her until the accident, because afterwards, Irene was happy with Gretchen's beauty. She felt her little sister *should* be the lovely one, the one whose flesh was pleasant and fragrant and satisfying. Irene needed no beauty, she needed nothing.

What she longed for was death, truly, and in death, an escape from this ravaged flesh.

"You're beautiful in God's eyes," he said, his breath like a warm humid wind along her neck.

"You should have left me."

"I couldn't."

"The children, the ones in the ice cream shop. Told me."

"Liars."

"You let him die."

"Those children are liars."

"Your own son."

"God called me to you. To save you."

"But Luke was still *alive*. You could've saved him." She felt exasperated. He was so dense, so stupid. He only saw what he wanted to see. She moaned in frustration, wanting to hit him as hard as she could. "I was dead. Why can't you just let me go?"

THE SCHOOLYARD WAS EMPTY, AND SHE WENT TO SIT on a swing. He followed her, but didn't speak again for awhile, so she acted as if he were not there.

This would be a place for miracles.

She saw their faces in the school windows, staring and pointing, some calling. She knew their parents.

Places like this, you know everyone, you had no secrets.

"It could happen again," William said.

She tried to wish him away.

"You should come home with me now," he said.

When she didn't respond, he added, "You want it to happen, don't you?"

IRENE WATCHED THE CHILDREN IN THE WINDOWS: some of them had been at the ice cream shop when the car had smashed into the truck, and the fire had started.

She remembered their faces, fascinated, their screaming, excited voices, as they watched the burning wreck. Her last sight had been of them holding their ice cream cones, and she had felt a peace, even in the pain of death, the numbing cold of fire, a peace from those lovely faces, knowing that the world would pass on without her there, that she would leave them, and they would still eat ice cream, and still talk out of turn, and still grow up into the world without some woman they barely knew by sight named Irene Hart who had stayed her whole dull life in the village.

Her last thought had been, *children.*

It had been a death she enjoyed, and the suffering had only come when she was pulled from the darkness, and opened her eyes to hear him, this man that Gretchen had married, saying, "And as Christ brought Lazarus from the dead, so I call His servant, Irene Hart, come, come to us, live again in the flesh with us."

Irene sat on the swing and began crying. She felt the weight of his hand on her shoulder.

She could not help herself, and in spite of her repulsion at his touch, she asked, "Children are closer to God, aren't they? Closer than us? 'Suffer the little children to come unto me', isn't that the quote?"

"God is close to all of us. All who believe, anyway."

"Oh," she stopped crying and laughed. He came and stood in front of her. She hadn't laughed in ages, and he smiled, probably thinking he was finally seeing the light within her. "Oh, that explains it, *that's it*. It's not God who lifted me up from the burning car, it's something else entirely. It was Luke who God took care of, not me. I get it now, oh, William, you should've told me at the time. It was Luke that God loved, not me."

"Irene, you don't know what you're saying."

"Well, if it's not true, why didn't you save your son? Why did you raise me up?"

William looked her in the eye, and she almost fainted because no one had done that since the accident.

He whispered something, but she knew it before he whispered it, and she wanted to stop up his mouth before the words had formed, "Because I love you," and she knew he was ashamed and humiliated to have to say it in a schoolyard, in the light of day. "Ever since I saw you, I loved you. I want to be near you. I never want to let you go."

So that was it.

Love.

"You go home now," she said softly.

She turned away from him, swinging to the side, her heels scraping the dirt, happy that he had let that awful feeling out, what he called love, out to evaporate in the shimmering heat of August. It had burned all these years within him, and she had been singed by his fire. She had not known what to call it, and she knew that it was not love, not love at all, but desire.

Had it been only his desire that had brought her back from the dead? *Well*, she thought, *let desire die, then, and let it have no resurrection.*

"I'll see you at supper," he said, and she heard his footsteps on the soft grass as he headed back to the street.

THE SWING SAGGED BENEATH HER WEIGHT: *IT WAS made for a child and I am not meant to be here. The children will know, too*, she thought.

The bell rang, and the children poured out onto the playground, and some saw her and some were involved in their games.

Children like golden light on the grassy field, coming slowly, curiously towards her. They called her the names she knew children called, their small, delicate hands, and their wondrous faces, their perfect thoughts.

She had come before, and they had been close to it, but they had not done what they longed to do.

Their hands, their eyes, their instinct so much a part of their flesh.

But today.

Today.

One of the little boys was bold, she thought he must be twelve, and he came up and stared at her fiercely.

"You're ugly," he said. "My daddy said you should be dead. You look dead. You even smell dead."

She looked him in the eye, and did not even flinch.

One of the children behind this boy picked up a small stone and threw it at her, hitting her just above her left eye. Irene smiled, *the children know what to do, they are closer to things, to nature.*

She felt another stone, this one larger, hit the back of her head, and then she was surrounded by beautiful, joyful children.

Irene waited for the darkness as they looked her in the eye and knew what she was.

It was later, when she thought the Kingdom was opening for her that she regained sight, and she welcomed whatever Kingdom there was, whatever light seemed to grow in the dark as the place where she belonged, but it was nothing other than the beam of a flashlight, and the lid of a coffin opening, and a madman above her who had scrambled in the earth to dig up a grave, only to say, "Come to us, live again in the flesh with us!"

FRIES WITH THAT?

When we got interviewed by *People* magazine, Maggy said that I'd always known about my talent, but that isn't true.

She didn't say it to the guy interviewing us, just to me in private. She told him that the gun had felt good and warm in her hand.

"Like a kiss," she said. "Every time I took a shot."

Mags doesn't tell the truth in interviews.

The truth is, I never really knew about my talent much until things started to happen over a long period of time. My gramma didn't even know for sure, at first, at least not till I told her. Now, I wish I had listened to that old woman. She knew how bad it could get.

My mom should've known, too, after that cat. But she didn't catch on too quick, and now, look at the mess. Sure, we could hire good lawyers because of how much both my mom and dad make, and who my dad knows, and we did what we could for Maggy. She's not mad at me or anything, but every now and then she gives me that glare.

But gramma knew, once I told her about the cat and other things. She told me without really telling me about how bad it could get.

Mags said it would've happened anyway, what she did.

I HAVE TO ADMIT, IT WAS FUN GOING ON TELEVISION, and meeting big celebrities like Oprah Winfrey.

They were all nice and really sweet. I thought I looked ugly in that white dress my dad made me wear. He told me that young ladies going on television should look virginal, as if this has ever been a problem for me.

Maggy only wore her usual black, from head to toe. I call it her witch phase, although she thinks she looks thinner like that. She doesn't like me calling her a witch or a bitch, mainly because she's both—she hasn't been to church since confirmation, and the bitch part…well, if you saw her on television, you'd understand.

When she started yelling back at the studio audience, I just about died.

But it figures.

She was up there flailing her arms around and cursing and I know her grandmother just about had a cow watching on the old RCA back at the trailer park.

Maggy doesn't like being called trailer trash either, but that's really what started it all when she and I were show-ering off after field hockey (which is neither, since we have to play it on what might best be referred to as a gravel pit, and our team has always been lame).

It was before fourth period, and Alison Gall had stolen Maggy's clothes.

ALISON, WHO IS THE KIND OF BITCH THAT NO ONE ever calls bitch, is not exactly the cheerleader type even though she made the squad finally after years of trying. It was her mother pushing her that made her crack the squad, and ever since then she's just been looking for scapegoats for unresolved anger all the time.

So she calls Mags a trailer trash dyke, and Mags throws her against the tiles. And Mags, sounding like some other-worldly monster, says, "I'm gonna kill you someday, Alison, and when I do, you're gonna wish you'd never been born."

Alison picked on a lot of girls, but mainly Mags.

Maggy is a good scapegoat since she doesn't quite fit into Glasgow High (named for a famous writer, like I want to be someday soon).

Maggy is not exactly Glasgow material. She smokes too much, tells everyone but me to fuck off, and some-times me, and she has what Mr. Herlihy writes on her report card all the time.

"An unusual sense of justice." Mr. Herlihy's easy going, which is why we like him. But Mr. Green always writes, "Margaret has trouble forming bonds with other students due to issues."

Issues.

Such crap.

All of this was read aloud on those talk shows, and then some gooney psychotherapist came out and told Mags what was wrong with her.

Besides which, Maggy and I formed a bond in third grade when she was the kick-ass new girl who talked back to old Mrs. Burley.

And Mr. Green, or anyone for that matter, calling her Margaret when in fact she was christened Maggy Mae after an old song…Nowhere on her birth certificate is the word, "Margaret." And that word would not describe Mags anyway (I can call her Mags. I've earned the right over all these years. You, and others, cannot.)

In third grade, she was just this dark thing. That's all I can tell you. I was of course that whole blond blue eyes ribbon in her hair kind of nice little girl who laughed at boys' jokes as if I knew what the hell they were talking about. But Mags, she was already taller then the tallest kid, long dark hair that obscured most of her face, what I like to call cigarette lips—big pouty pillows right under her nose. Back in those early days, I thought she looked like *not a nice girl.* She looked like trouble and trash, but I got over it fast. I went out to clap the erasers for Mrs. Burley, and there Mags was, behind the dumpster, smoking a Camel.

"WHAT THE FUCK ARE YOU STARING AT?" SHE ASKED. I had never before heard a girl use the F word. She had a dark voice. Everything about her back in third grade was dark.

I was too scared to say anything. Truth be told, I peed my panties right there. I thought she was going to eat me or something. She just sucked back that cigarette till there was nothing but ash, and eyed me with those dark eyes.

"I asked you a goddamned question," she said.

"I'm…not staring…I'm really not," I said.

She shook her head in disgust. I saw the rest of her face for the first time when she pulled back her hair a little. She had a tattoo on her left cheek, just next to her earlobe. Just a small star. "Like it?" she asked, when she caught me staring.

"Not really," I said. Back then I had a mouse squeak voice. I was pretty much a little nothing who had pretty handwriting and a yes'm attitude. Just a little pleasing machine. But I did not like dark thoughts or tattoos. Yet.

"I like it," Mags said, letting her hair drop. "You're probably stuck up like every other girl here, ain't you?"

I shook my head. "No. I'm not. Really."

"Here," she said, extending her hand, the next cigarette already lit. "Have a smoke."

"I uh no thanks."

"Have a goddamn smoke," she said. She reached out and grabbed my hand. She thrust the cigarette between my fingers. I stared down at it.

"My mother used to smoke," I squeaked.

"It's good for you."

"No it isn't, the Surgeon General said—"

"You believe that government tool? Smoke," she said.

It was a command.

I delicately put the cigarette between my lips. I thought she was going to kill me if I disobeyed her.

"Inhale, come on, inhale," she commanded.

I sucked back the smoke, and coughed, and sucked, and coughed, and pretty soon I was hooked on the damn things, and I still am. One of life's little pleasures. Come to Marlboro Country. Get the Most Out of Life.

Sure, Mags corrupted me thoroughly. By junior year in high school, she'd taught me all about smoking and drinking and why it was important for a boy to have a big one. It took me awhile to figure out what big ones were, but I was happy Mags had warned me ahead of time.

The vodka helped with that, too.

I hid most of it from my mom and dad, who weren't too cool. They were church going types, and basically so was I.

Unfortunately, I was also heavily into sin as both a concept and an action. After church, I'd sneak off down to the alley behind the Meat Market in town, and me and Mags would smoke and have a few beers and then go out and raise hell. I'm sure God in His Heaven didn't give a rat's ass if we got into trouble now and then.

Sin was not new to my family. My mother once cheated on my father with Dr. Van Graaf, my orthodontist. How do I know? Dad was away on business, and Mom and Dr. Van Graaf were upstairs in bed, that's how I know.

She didn't want me to know; in fact, I was supposed to be staying at Mags' for the night.

Truth was, I was really going to spend the night with Billy Alcott in his backyard tent, along with a bottle of

Stoli and a carton of menthols. But Billy was acting like a creep, so I told him I was having my period and he ran like hell.

All boys do, the wimps. His tent sucked, anyway, barely enough room to move your elbows let alone have some teenager on top of you trying to tell you how much he loved you when you knew he didn't give a flyer and had been doing it with Missy Hanscomb three nights before.

But my mother and Billy and Dr. Van Graaf have very little to do with this, my confession.

Yeah, I know, if you saw us on TV or read *People* or maybe that little piece in the *New York Times* or in our local rag, you might know the rest of it. Six kids all lobotomized and hemorrhaging in the middle of Glasgow High School with their signed yearbooks at their feet. Bullets flying. It was something, I'll tell you.

Gramma would've told me, maybe, how to stop it, but she wasn't around by then.

THERE'S ALWAYS MORE TO THIS STUFF THAN MEETS the eye. *60 Minutes* is doing this thing on us in about a month, and I'm sure it will be more lies. I'm really holding out for Barbara Walters for the interview. Her people haven't contacted me yet. I figure when school starts up in the fall, and things like November Sweeps are going on, she will.

Mags thinks Barbara Walters and her people don't give a flyer about two girls from Minnesota who were suspected of mass murder at the end of their junior year.

But I think based on the coverage we've gotten so far, we're worth the Sweeps Month and maybe even a retro thingy in the spring. I would even say we've put our little town in Minnesota on the map, except there was that movie star who did that back in the seventies before he got eaten up by heroin and a nasty car wreck.

I know that once we get Barbara Walters to interview us—and not just one of her *20/20* interviews, but one of those Specials she does that are so good—the record will be set straight. I'm having trouble convincing Mags to wait till then to tell everything, since we really didn't get a chance on the talk show circuit. Too much yelling and screaming and myth-making. My mother didn't even call them talk shows, she called them Freak Shows of the Very Vapid. I kind of like that. Mom has a way with words.

But Oprah and Jerry Springer weren't like that. They all have a lot of heart. They were sweet. Mags was hilarious on them. I was just doing my Pretty Little Nothing act, because I didn't want to let the world know the truth yet. I was the Loyal Best Friend. Mom'd totally freak herself if she knew I was writing down what really happened, but Mags is in trouble over this now, and the truth is, she's just protecting me.

All right, Mom has known all along, but she is really good at denying reality. Even when it slaps her in the face. I wish I could do that.

She's known ever since I was about four. She saw what I did to the cat.

Now, first off, I've never liked cats. Please don't hold that against me. I've just never met one that liked me. They all act like little bitches around me, they don't purr, they don't preen, they just growl and slash at my ankles. So it's no surprise to me that I did the *Fries With That?* thing.

That's what Mags calls it.

When we were in fourth grade and I did it to this one kid, Mags said to me, "Fries with that?" She meant it as a double joke.

First, because at all those hamburger fast food places the guy on the speaker says, "Fries with that?" no matter what the fuck you order.

You could order shit on a stick, and he'd say, "Duh, fries with that?"

That's part of it.

The other part is that Fries word. All its meanings.

But wait, back to the cat when I was little.

Mom said that the cat was hissing at me, as usual. I was sitting on the kitchen floor.

I just stared at the cat long and hard and suddenly like my eyes rolled back into my head and I turned all pale and started speaking in tongues.

Well, Mom is what Mags called a Super Christian, and even though she knows it probably was not her beloved Holy Ghost talking through me, she always likes to think the best. In fact, I think Mom turned to church-going because of the talent, and gramma had it, as it turns out.

After that, Mom said that cat was not right, and would just walk in circles. Which cracks me up to think of a cat walking in circles all the time. And again, for you cat lovers, it's not that I hate cats, it's that they never like me.

I suppose one day I may meet one who likes me, and then I may take cats on a case-by-case basis. Until then, we really have nothing to do with each other whenever possible.

I told Mags about the cat in eighth grade when I knew for sure she was my absolutely best friend of all friends.

We went from smoking a pack a day to three packs a day each by the time we entered high school. The liquor didn't really kick into high gear till junior year.

We hung out in the girls' room a lot, smoking of course and writing nasty things about girls like Alison Gall and some of the other girls of what we called the Canine Corps. All cheerleaders were a little too kissy face for our tastes, even though they had to go down on the filthy football players.

I really shouldn't have hated Alison so much—that's half my problem. I would obsess on girls and boys I hated, and then I would have no control sometimes. I actually had excellent control, up until the beginning of June when we raised the hell to end all hells, but who knew?

Not me or Mags back when we were scratching our Bic pens into the toilet stall wall. "Alison Sucks Donkeys," I read my exquisite poetry aloud while I scratched.

"No, more sophisticated," Mags said in her smoke-scraped throaty voice.

Then, she lifted her Swiss Army knife and scratched, "ALISON'S DICK IS BIGGER THAN JOEY'S."

"That's so fourth grade," I said, grabbing the cigarette from between Mags' lips and stuffing it in my greedy mouth. I sucked back the smoke and whooshed it out through my nostrils. "Besides which, everybody's dick is bigger than Joey's."

Mags laughed. The stall was tiny, but since we're both pretty skinny, it wasn't too bad. The toilet bowl was almost full of our cigarettes butts.

"What is it she ever did to either of us that makes us hate her so much?" Mags asked. "I almost forget."

"She's just so Alison," I said. Suddenly, Mags thrust her hand over my mouth.

She lipped, *Someone just came in.* The cigarette dropped from her mouth into the toilet, pronto.

The girl's bathroom door swung shut, and we heard little mouse steps over to the sink.

I glanced at Mags, who released her hold on my mouth.

We both knew who it was.

Janine Cunligger—and yeah, it was her real name. I could not make up a name that good even if I tried.

JANINE WAS SPOOKY, BUT NOT IN THE SAME WAY THAT Mags is scary. Janine was one of those girls you knew would one day turn psycho on everybody, or else she'd invent the cure for the Common Cold. Maybe she'll end up revolutionizing software or something. She's that kind of girl. Despite the last name Cunligger, she was called Gyro because of her scientific and mathematical bent. Mags nicknamed her this in sixth grade, after Mags got tired of all the boys calling Janine by a not-so-nice revision of her last name. Mags originally called her Gyroscopa,

Goddess of Science Nerds, but eventually this became Gyro until Janine herself used it when she introduced herself to new kids.

Janine was also plug ugly, at least as far as any of us knew. Unlike Mags who had the cool hip urban look of dark hair on dark clothes and dark heart, Janine a.k.a. Gyro had a frizz and thick glasses and Pippi Longstocking legs and was flat as a pancake even at sixteen when the rest of us had pretty much Jiffy Popped to our full bra sizes.

And as Mags and I stood silently in the toilet stall, we heard the saddest most mournful sound coming from the sink where Gyro stood letting water run over her hands.

"Jesus," Mags gasped, closing her eyes.

Gyro was sobbing up a storm, and the running water didn't hide it.

I was the first out of the stall. I stood back a ways from Gyro, because she still was a bit spooky in my opinion. I had never really warmed up to her after I'd been held back a year in Chemistry and she had moved on with Honors.

She saw me in the mirror over the sink. Her headband was askew. Her frizz of hair seemed frizzier.

"You okay?" I asked. I felt Mags' hand on my shoulder, as if trying to pull me back.

Gyro leaned over the sink again, pulling her glasses off. "Yeah, fine. Just got some dirt in my eyes."

"You were crying," I said.

"We heard you," Mags added. "What's up?"

Gyro kept pretending until Mags just went up to her and threw her arms around her. "It's okay," Mags said, "We're not gonna hurt you or anything."

Gyro pulled away, shrugging her off. "Yes you are. You're like all the rest of them."

"The hell we are," Mags said.

"That's right," I volunteered weakly. Truth was, I didn't really care to delve into Gyro's problems. She was one of those girls I didn't want to get to know too well because a) we had nothing in common and b) there was nothing I was going to gain by being friends with her. Now my b) choice may seem cold and unfeeling, but I learned years ago that there's no point in making friends if it doesn't help you in some way.

I don't mean namby-pamby help, I mean, if a friendship doesn't take you to a new level, or open up a different world, or feed you in some way, why have it?

All right, maybe I am a bit cold. I got burned by some of those other girls and boys enough to know that you are lucky if you can make one good friend in your lifetime.

Mags was *that* friend.

But Mags has a better soul than I do.

She managed to wrestle her arms around Gyro's shoulders again. Gyro started crying again. I went and hopped up on the edge of the sink. I brought another cig out from the pack, lit it, puffed, and passed it to Gyro.

Gyro didn't hesitate. She snapped it out of my hand and took a long drag on it. I reached into my fanny pack and brought out some Kleenex for her. Then, I drew the flask out. It was rum and Coke, and not a lot of rum so please don't get the idea I was drunk twenty-four hours a day. Mags is the one with the bar in her locker at school, not me.

"So what's the deal?" I asked.

Gyro sucked back another lungful of smoke. On exhaling, she said, "It's Alison Gall."

I looked at Mags.

"We were just talking about her," I said, with glee.

"What's she done to you?" Mags asked. Mags really has the milk of human kindness in her veins. She looks dark and nasty, and she talks like a whore sometimes, but she really is the kind of person who would save a gnat on the ass of a weasel.

And then, Gyro told us. All of it.

It's not really important what she told us. In fact, I think it would hurt her feelings if she knew that I was writing this, and knew that it probably would get published someday since we're so famous now. But let me put it this way: Alison did something to Gyro that was so terrible, something that is the worst thing one girl can do to another girl. I do not make this stuff up. I

f you're female, you know what that is.

If you're male, you probably don't have a clue.

But when you're sixteen, and a girl, and another girl does to you what Alison Gall did to Gyro, you would feel on the inside like all the joy in life had been extinguished —no, stolen from you by the worst kind of thief. Boys sometimes do this to girls, but they don't have a clue.

Girls sort of accept that boys do this because boys don't understand what it means. Or we just think they're stupid.

But for a girl to do it to another girl is the lowest form of life.

So then and there, the three of us made a pact, Gyro, me and Mags.

We set our plan into motion before Friday, the day of the Prom.

It was easy enough to lure Alison Gall to the old farm off Route 7.

Not that she was exactly a farm-lovin' girl, but we knew that the guy she really wanted to ball was Quent Appenino, the Italian Stallion quarterback who had transferred from some California school when his folks got divorced.

Quent was built, and had good buns and a great smile. If he weren't such a moron when it came to school, I'd have lusted after him, too.

But he was a big pretty guy and since he'd arrived he'd been going steady with Susie Malloy. Quent was a good boy, too, and didn't cheat, and this drove Alison nuts. So what we did was we told Quent that it was Susie's birthday, and we had this card for her.

We wanted him to be the first to personalize and sign it.

So he takes up like half the card, the doofus, and writes, *You know how much I care for you, baby. You + Me=4-Ever.* Then, pretending I'd forgotten the way out to the farm—which Quent's grandfather owned—I asked him to write down directions on this really thin piece of paper. "I want to drive out with my dad this weekend just for fresh air."

Quent really was a moron. He didn't question this at all.

He just wrote out the directions.

Then, Mags who is a genius at this, carefully traced his note about the directions. Again, trying to imitate his handwriting, which she did remarkably well. She scrawled at the bottom: *Before the Prom, 4 p.m. I want you. Quent.*

"She's going to melt," I said.

Gyro nodded. "But what do we do when we get her out there?"

"Don't even worry about it. We do what we do," Mags said, passing another cigarette to Gyro.

Gyro had a bad jones for cigs, it turned out. I discovered that we had that in common.

Okay, now here's where it gets hazy.

Not that the Prom coming up was any big deal to us since we weren't seniors. We didn't have steadies, and I'm not big on wearing a big poofy dress with my hair up like Cinderella. Maybe my third grade pre-Mags self would've been into that crap, but I was more of a let's get drunk and break into the arcade kind of girl by junior year. If I wanted a boy sexually, I didn't need all that filler: just give me the guy. The bad influence of my best friend again.

She always said I was the real bad influence, back when we were little.

It was that fourth grade thing, when Jonathan Rice was on the monkey bars and Mags and I were stepping on his hands as he swung around. Jonathan was, I think, a budding masochist, or else he liked to look up my skirt. Back in fourth grade I wore what Mags still calls the

Betsy-Wetsy outfits where "You looked like one of those American Girl dolls."

But Jonathan grabbed my ankle. I slipped, landing on my tailbone on the cold metal of the monkey bars, which hurt bad enough, but then I lost my balance and fell down into the gravel.

It was the first time I realized you could actually see stars when you slammed into the earth hard enough. I thought my brain had been knocked to my shins.

Now, maybe Jonathan jogged something in my head a little more than it should've been, or maybe what I did to that cat when I was four just got worse the closer I got to puberty.

Or maybe it was just fate.

That was the first day Mags had ever used the term *Fries With That?* About what I can do. I don't do it often, and in fact, I never planned on doing it.

But I almost fried poor little Jonathan Rice right there on the playground during recess. He came over to me, kneeling down to see if I was okay.

And I just went blank. Like the white dot that's left on the TV. when you turn it off sometimes. I went down this winding tunnel in my head. I figured I must be dying or something.

When I came to, Mags described the whole thing to me.

"Damn, it was scary as all hell," she said. "Jonathan was crying about you, and you start showing the whites of your eyes and frothing at the mouth, and breaking out in rashes all over your face. Then your mouth opens wider than I figured it could go, like a largemouth bass screaming or something, and your tongue starts waggling, and then..."

Mags paused here for effect. Her eyes widened.

"Then...all these words I never heard of come out of your mouth, words that are almost like English but aren't quite, and you're shaking, and I break out in goose bumps all over, and Jonathan starts making choking sounds and then I smell what seems to me to be the smell of toast burning in a toaster, and then it doesn't smell like toast but it smells like when the dentist drills in your mouth at a cavity and how it doesn't hurt because of the Novocain but this weird burning smell comes up...And I look at Jonathan and his face is all red and then the color in his eyes just kind of melts into nothing."

THAT WAS THE DESCRIPTION, BUT NOBODY EVER blamed me for what happened to Jonathan Rice.

At first, they called it stress blindness, then shock. But Mags and I knew he just got the *Fries With That?* treatment.

She called him Fried Rice.

One day, when Jonathan Rice was in seventh grade, now at a special school for kids, he took a long walk off a short pier.

I've always felt a little guilty about that.

I asked my mother about it then, and she was cagey, but she finally admitted that my gramma had it.

So I go to the nursing home where gramma lays sputtering through her nostrils, god love her, and I tell her what mom told me.

Gramma had these curious eyes back then, pale blue, covered with a translucent milky color. Her skin was as thin as tracing paper, and you could see all these blue veins under the surface. I loved my grandmother, even though she had to wheeze when she breathed. I snuck her cigarettes, too, and played Hearts with her sometimes for hours.

When I tell her about Jonathan Rice, and then the cat, her eyes fill with tears. Gramma was from Ireland, and she wells up with tears easily, from hearing "I'll Bring You A Daisy A Day," to when she thinks of County Clare and all its green pastures and blue skies. Harp ale does it for her, also.

She reached for my shoulder to steady herself as she rose up on the bed. "You have the evil eye, then," she said, her voice all soft and wispy like cotton candy. "I knew it would show again."

"It's not my eyes," I said. "I speak and other stuff happens, too."

"It's through the eyes," she said. She pointed to the pale blue of her eyes. "Look, you and I have the old blue. Your hair is blond like your daddy's, but you got the old ways in your spirit. They say we're descended from fairies, but we are from the original people of the islands. We have the eyes and we have the talent."

"But I didn't mean to hurt Jonathan." I began crying, still somewhat in my Pretty Little Nothing phase.

"'Evil eye' is what others called it. It's a vision that takes over. It's a reshaper of minds, it's a molder of people's insides." Then, Gramma hugged me close. Her breath was terrible, like a cat's. Her light whiskers scratched my cheek, but her warmth was not to be denied.

I lay there, letting her hold me, the sticky warmth between us, until it grew dark. Before I left, she asked me to learn to focus.

"Through craft," she said. "Talent is nothing but wildness without craft."

"Like witchcraft?" I asked.

"Nothing like that, dearie," Gramma said, her voice going raspy from the long day of cigarette smoking. "The craft of your art. Your art is there, and now you must make it sing."

"I don't know about that."

"But stay away from the dead," she whispered. "It's not meant to be near them."

"Why?"

"Nothing good comes of it when near the dead. Your great-great-grandmother Irene had it, and once, she was at a wake. She thought she heard her dead uncle knocking at his coffin after she'd danced around it a bit."

"Cool," I said.

"Not so cool," Gramma whispered. "Not so cool at all."

She fell asleep soon after, and then a few weeks later, before I could actually ask her how I was to go about perfecting this so-called craft, Gramma died.

The day she died, it felt like someone kicked me in the gut. Death does that to you.

I imagine it didn't feel so wonderful to Gramma, either.

Because I didn't like to think of myself as Evil (I was a God-fearing little Jesus freak back then for the most part, although I was moving closer to my ultimate embrace of hormones and sin as time went on), I dropped the whole Evil Eye phrase. I went with Mags' *Fries With That?* designation.

So, when Mags said to Gyro, the afternoon of the Prom, "Don't worry. We do what we do," I was a little afraid of the *Fries With That?* syndrome coming through.

Mags assured me this was next to impossible. "I mean, it hasn't happened since you were in fourth grade. For all we know, Jonathan Rice just went brain dead right then because of some interior alarm clock."

"Freud said there are no accidents," Gyro cautioned, although she could not possibly have known about what I accidentally did to Jonathan Rice in fourth grade.

WE REPEATED A LOT OF THIS AS WE STOOD OVER POOR Alison Gall, whom we had most heinously trapped at Quent Appenino's grandfather's farm out in the middle of Bumfuck.

Alison wore a cute little yellow pullover that showed her melons to their best advantage and her little tight-ass cheerleader skirt, knee socks, cute little black shoes, and no underwear to speak of.

Need I mention what a shock she had received when she entered the old barn that had yet another forged love note tacked to its door?

Three furies standing around in the semi-dark of the barn, with rope, duct tape, and gun.

Okay, the gun was a last minute thing.

GYRO'S OLDER BROTHER LANCE WAS A COP WANNABE. He was too smart for the local police force, apparently, but still he kept a major stash of Glocks and Smiths & Wessons and big old rifles, none of which Gyro knew much about.

Mags picked out the Glock 17. "I've seen this on TV shows," she said. "At least, I think I've seen this."

"I don't think we need a gun, do we?" I had asked as we stood shivering in Gyro's brother's room, knowing the fearful act we were to perform a few hours down the road.

And then, it was Alison Gall's turn to shiver, which is what I expected when she saw the gun.

Instead, she became the bitch of all bitches.

"What the hell kind of joke is this, you losers?" she asked, and then, looking at the gun, she laughed. "You planning on going to prison for the rest of your lives?"

Mags laughed. She had that great throaty laugh, the kind of laugh that old movie stars have, or old smokers. "Listen, Alison, we're minors, get real. Gyro's dad is a brain surgeon, and Nora's dad is a tax lawyer. Who do you think's going to go to prison?"

"You, trailer trash girl," Alison huffed.

"Shut up," I said.

"Shut up yourself, geek."

"Don't make me bitch slap you," Mags said. She meant

business, particularly after the trailer trash comment. "My dad may not be some big professional, but he's been known to spring a few dudes from prison. I doubt reform school is going to take a major army to overcome."

Alison quieted down. She glanced at me, then at Gyro. "Is this a lesbian thing or something?"

I laughed. "You'll wish when it's over."

"No," Gyro said. "We just want you out of the way until after Prom."

"No way!" Alison shouted, and for a moment I felt sorry for the poor thing.

Alison Gall lived for major social events. She never missed a football party, or a dance, or a chance to show off her cheering skills. She was a debutante in the big cotillion up in St. Paul.

For just a second there, I saw the sad little girl beneath the makeup and the dye job and the "Look How Cute I Am" clothes.

She was just like I was years ago. A Pretty Little Nothing. Trying to make do. Trying to please other people. Dealing with a social structure where girls really had to tread water when the boys around her just got stuff for free.

No wonder she was so nasty to us girls all the time— we were the one group she didn't have to please.

I was about to call the gag off, but this was Gyro's game.

Gyro stepped forward with the rope. After the initial scuffle, we got Alison's hands behind her back.

I only had to hit her once.

By the time the duct tape went over her mouth,

Alison's eyes were red from tears. Mascara ran down her cheeks.

"I should shoot you just for being a cheerleader," Mags said, pointing the gun directly at her forehead.

Alison didn't even flinch. I knew why. She was such a Pretty Little Nothing that she thought death was no more terrifying or hurtful than missing the biggest dance of the year. Maybe this was shallow of her, I don't know.

We all want something out of life, don't we? We all want something, and to someone else, it probably sounds stupid and shallow and empty, but to each of us, it's the shining moment that we can always have at the center of our lives.

And Prom was going to be Alison's shining moment.

Here she was a senior, probably going to the local college next year, if at all, and her entire future life depended upon looking back on high school as that peak, that golden moment.

We were taking that away from her.

Mags must've guessed my shift in sympathies. "Don't forget what she did to Gyro," she said.

I shined my flashlight over at Gyro, fury still in her eyes. She carefully wrapped the remainder of her rope around Alison's ankles.

I shut my flashlight off.

I no longer wanted to look at our captive.

And that's when Gyro rose up and took the gun from Mags' hand and aimed it at the side of Alison Gall's head and shot her at point blank range.

SOMETIMES THERE ARE THINGS YOU DO IN LIFE AND you know when you're doing them that later on you'll hate yourself, or you'll want to go back and erase part of the picture of that moment.

In that millisecond when Gyro fired into Alison's skull, I tried to, at least in my mind, turn the clock back by a minute so I could grab the gun before Gyro could get it.

I know neither Mags nor I had intended to use that gun. It was just a scare tactic. But Gyro, I think, probably had planned Alison's death for at least a week, from at least that moment when she entered the bathroom sobbing, from the moment that we told her that we'd seek a suitable revenge for her humiliation.

Gyro, bullied her entire life, her last name turned into an obscene joke, her hair made fun of, her face, her clothes.

Girls like Alison had done a lot of it.

Maybe even girls like me.

And she rolled all of that into one moment with a gun in a barn and a cheerleader who had pissed her off.

THE SILENCE AFTERWARDS WAS LIKE A ROAR OF locusts in my head.

I thought I heard light bulbs sparking and popping all around us. I thought it was the Fourth of July, from the crashes and booms inside my head.

Alison lay on her side, half her scalp blown off. Part of her face was on the dirt, as if the bullet had unmasked her.

Mags was the first to speak. "Oh, Christ, Gyro."

"Yeah," Gyro nodded, tossing the gun down. "I know. I shouldn't have. But I had to before it went the other way."

"Went the other way?" I asked.

But I knew what she meant.

If you didn't put a bullet in the head of the one who tormented you, you put the bullet in your own head.

It was always either-or when it came to vengeance.

"All right, now, we're fucked," Mags said. "Now we're really fucked." She slapped the side of her face. "Christ, my heart is beating like it's gonna jump out from my chest."

"Funny," Gyro said, almost kindly. "I've never felt this calm. You?"

"I have no idea what I'm feeling," I said.

"As long as she doesn't get the *Fries With That?* feeling, we're fine," Mags managed to joke.

Long after the Prom was over, we sat in that dark barn with the corpse, passing cigarettes around until our packs were empty.

"Gyro," I said, offering her my flask. "You may go to jail for this. Wait, not 'may', 'will'."

Mags waved the last of her cigarette, tracing a red line in the air. "We're accomplices. Or accessories."

"Accessories," Gyro gasped after taking a long swig of my special brew. "But I'm the killer."

"You think she was going to change later?" I asked.

"Huh?"

"Well, I mean, this wasn't her prom dress. I wonder what she was going to wear to the dance."

Gyro gave me a look like I was crazy.

I shrugged. "The one thing I can say for Alison is she had some nice dresses."

"People loved her," Mags whispered, reverentially. "I don't know why, but boys and parents and local business people, and little kids all loved her. Alison Gall, the bitch." Then she laughed. "I can't believe we're sitting here with a cheerleader's body drinking bad rum and Coke from a cheap flask on Prom Night."

"It does lead one to suspect we're insane," I said, drunkenly.

The flask was dry by the next go round.

"Almost insane. If we were insane, we'd probably play with her or something," Gyro said.

"Yuck," I said.

"That is disgusting." Mags shivered. "One thing, though. We need a plan of action now."

Instead, we went swimming.

OUT BACK WAS THAT DUCK POND, EMPTY OF DUCKS AT two a.m., and Mags was the first of us to shed her clothes. She grabbed the old rope swing, and swung out over the middle of the pond before dropping.

The splash was huge. Mags bobbed up laughing. Gyro told me she wasn't in the mood, but I convinced her we should go in because of how filthy and stinky we'd all gotten since she'd shot Alison Gall in the head.

Soon, all three of us were in the pond, splashing and laughing and trying to forget the millisecond of bad judgment when we decided to set any of this in motion in the first place.

In the moonlight, Gyro came up from the water, and both Mags and I gasped.

"What is it? What's wrong?" Gyro asked.

I looked at Mags and then glanced back at Gyro. With her frizz brought down by the water, and her glasses off, and naked so we could see her breasts—

"You are the most beautiful girl in school," I said.

"No kidding. Look at you," Mags asked. "Why hide so much under the frizzy hair and crappy clothes?"

Gyro covered her breasts with her hands. "You're making fun of me."

"No," I said. "I swear, Gyro—"

"Janine," Mags corrected me. "No girl who looks like this could be Gyroscopa. Jesus, Janine, you look a movie star. And you've got those champagne glass breasts."

"And not the fluted kind," I joked.

"You're embarrassing me," Gyro said. "Seriously. Call me Gyro, I don't like being called Janine."

"I can't anymore," Mags said. "No way. Christ, Janine. You're a murderess and a beauty. Surprises galore."

"You may prove popular in prison," I said. It was meant as a joke, but suddenly they both went silent for too many seconds.

"Please," Gyro began sobbing. She swam over to the muddy shore.

~

THERE WAS NOTHING TO DO, OR AT LEAST, WE DIDN'T figure out what the hell we were going to do yet. We sure as shit couldn't go home.

We couldn't just leave Alison's body there in the barn.

We toyed with the idea of pinning the murder on Quent Appenino, because the notes would be in his handwriting.

And he *was* stupid.

But that story would probably have flaws we couldn't figure out.

We thought about saying some strange man did it, but what if some innocent guy matching the description got the chair over this or something?

We still had shreds and scraps of conscience, after all.

Then, 'round about five thirty, just as the first pink rays of June sunlight appeared, Mags slapped me on the shoulder.

"You!" she cried out.

"What the—"

"*Fries With That!*" Mags began dancing around in a circle, her blouse still not buttoned up so her breasts kind of swung out like ripe pears about to fall.

"What's that mean?" Gyro asked.

I shrugged.

Mags clapped her hands together and stood still. "It's her thing. It's like an ability. It's like a magic thingy."

"No it isn't. It's like the evil eye."

"No negative thoughts today," Mags announced boldly. "Now, Nora, you can fry people's brains, right?"

I shrugged again. "Animals, people. Only done it twice that I know of."

"What?" Gyro asked, her beauty still apparent in the early light.

"Okay," Mags said. She paced in a circle around me like some mad professor. "Okay. So! You know how this ability of yours works?"

"Nope," I said. "It's inherited. It's like having a bunion as far as I'm concerned."

"Wait — you can inherit bunions?" Mags asked.

"Like a recessive gene," Gyro volunteered, still with a confused look on her face.

"Exactly, and it's there. It's inside you. It's sleeping, but," Mags stopped pacing and stood almost nose-to-nose with me. Her breath was sour.

Her voice dropped to a whisper. "Ever tried it on a dead girl?"

Gyro probably whined about not understanding us or something, and Mags probably went on with her ravings, but actually the idea burst within me as Mags said that one sentence.

Ever tried it on a dead girl?

Yeah, my gramma's words came back to me then. "*Stay away from the dead.*"

Then I remembered what she'd told me about my great-grandmother. How something had been knocking from inside her uncle's coffin...

BIRDS BEGAN SINGING BEFORE THE LIGHT WAS FULLY up that morning.

We were worried about when the farm folk would

come out to their barn, even though there were no animals to be seen in it, only the basics of farm machinery.

So, we took Alison up, using Mags' sweatshirt to jam her face against her skull. Any little bloody bits, we covered up with straw and dirt. We took her back to her car, and put her in the trunk.

It was a cute little Toyota with leather seats. Alison had been so spoiled in her lifetime. But honestly, if you're going to die young, might as well have had the best of everything.

So Mags and Gyro drove Alison's car and I drove my mother's Buick back to my house.

MY HOUSE WAS THE BIGGEST, AND MY ROOM WAS THE furthest from the front door and the closest to two side doors. We would not be noticed by my parents at all, given that it was Saturday morning, which meant Country Club B.S. for both of them.

They laid Alison on my bed, keeping her bloodied head on Mags' sweatshirt.

Gyro looked at me gravely. "I don't know if I can believe all the stuff she told me in the car, but if you can do anything, it might help."

I looked at Mags. My best friend in the whole world. Better than best. Best of the best. She seemed small and vulnerable now. The way I felt on the inside.

I looked down at poor Alison.

"It's not working," I said after a few minutes.

"How does it work?" Gyro asked.

"I need to get mad at her."

"Stimulus, response," Gyro nodded. "And between stimulus and response there's a pause. In the pause, we decide what the response will be."

"Huh?" Mags asked.

Gyro nodded again to herself. I could practically see the little wheels turning.

Hesitating only a moment, she walked over to me, leaned close, and whispered something in my ear.

The explosion from inside my head seemed to knock me back against the wall. The room began spinning, and I swear—I swear—I saw a fire burst across the wallpaper, ripping and devouring the flower print, until the walls were charred—

And I was there with Alison's corpse, Alison's bloodied corpse, but poison spewed from inside me, and then my vision blackened.

When I awoke, I was on the floor, fever in my head, and Mags kneeling beside me.

"What the fuck did she whisper?" she asked.

I looked at Mags, wondering for a moment where I was and what was going on.

Gyro stood beside the bed, looking down.

"What made you so mad at Alison again?" Mags asked, and then turned to Gyro. "What'd you say to her?"

My mind returned from blankness. "She said...she said..."

I could barely recall the words that Gyro had whispered to me.

"Please...help...oh god," Alison's voice came like a scratched up old cat from the thing on the bed.

How long we all stood in the room, waiting for what was to come, I'm not sure. My memory is spotty on this.

But Alison, her face still sliding off, eventually sat up, and all of us saw what my *Fries With That?* had brought back from the dead:

A bitch that looked like hell.

I DON'T NEED TO GO INTO A LOT OF THE REST.

I'm waiting for the Barbara Walters interview. I want to give an exclusive.

Suffice it to say that we had one week left of school, and Alison Gall was alive again.

No need to go into the surgery that Gyro did using some medical equipment we grabbed from her father's office, or the fact that Alison was there inside her body but not on the surface yet, the way most of us are. Alison was down deep. Somehow I had rewired some circuits in her, while others had been permanently damaged.

She barely said more than squat anymore.

We made up a story for her mother about how we rescued her at the Prom, how she'd fallen down some stairs drunk after coming in with some boy from out of town.

Her now ex-boyfriend believed this, as did most everyone else. Thus the stitches, thus her slowness, thus the fact that while she still performed routine tasks, like getting up in the morning, showering, eating, dressing for school, even cheerleader practice,

Alison Gall was, for all intents and purposes, not all there. I wouldn't exactly use the kind of words you might use for somebody who comes back from the dead and might actually still be somewhat brain dead and might shuffle along, hiding the rotting of their corpse…because Alison kind of was like that, but kind of not, and I don't like name-calling anymore.

Not since it happened.

She was hideous to see, too. Her face, with the tiny threads, her hair a bit lopsided. From the neck down she was still gorgeous, but the meaner boys started calling her a two-bagger hump, "in case the bag falls off her head, you wear one yourself."

Now and then, in the last days of school that year, I would sit across from her, and a little shriek like a seagull makes would come from deep down in her throat.

MAGS AND GYRO AND I DIDN'T TALK MUCH, BUT nodded to each other in the halls every now and then. I smoked in the girl's bathroom sometimes, hoping Mags would come in, but she never did.

Then on the last day of school, Alison Gall — moving in a fumbly daze down the hallway — turned to her ex-boyfriend Joey…and I saw it coming.

I don't know why I didn't think of it before, but I should've.

We all should've wondered what would happen if Alison came back.

What she might be able to do if her brain got *Fries With That?* from death to life.

I saw her pupils go up under her eyelids. I watched in fascination as a strange rash spread across her face. She opened her mouth wider than a scream.

And I knew.

I felt it.

She had it now, too. Whatever I had endowed her with, it had opened up something in her, too. Maybe we all have it within us, and only some of us have it at the surface.

She had *Fries With That?*

SHIT, I THOUGHT. IT'S CONTAGIOUS. SHIT. JUST LIKE *gramma said to me. "Stay away from the dead."*

And now, she did it to Joey. His body began twitching, and the blue of his eyes melted across his face like punctured egg yolks.

Like lightning, it passed around the hall, five other kids, some innocent of past association with Alison, some not so innocent. All shaking and shivering, foaming at the mouths, their eyes rolling up in their heads.

It was contagious. I had passed it on. I was the Typhoid Mary of *Fries with That?*

Five kids, and Mags came down the hall and watched it, too. Others came out, but ran when they saw the jolts and smelled the burning.

Mags turns to me, shaking her head. Not at me, I guess, but at our bad decision. At our bad cover up of Gyro's killing of Alison and us as accomplices in murder.

There was a lot of love in her gaze as she looked at me.

It was either-or, I could tell.

Either it ended right there, or it goes on, and who knows how many brains would fry because I have this little talent inherited from my gramma's side, a little talent that no doctor has figured out yet though god knows they probed and poked inside my head enough these past couple months.

I know what she's going to do, and I'm wondering why she still has it on her.

Why she carries it.

And that's when Mags pulled out the Glock from the inside pocket on her black denim jacket and started firing at all the kids who were fizzling into the Fryer that Alison is beaming at them.

I guess she just didn't want to take it anymore.

Later on, when Mags was taken in, I went to visit her.

"Don't tell them what happened," she whispered. "I'll be out in a couple of years anyway. I'm a teenager. How much can they do?"

"But it's not your fault," I said.

"Look," Mags said. "I'm from the trailers. You and Gyro are Country Club Acres girls. Like Alison. You wouldn't survive what I'm going through right now."

Then, the tears welled in her eyes. "You are my best friend. It's no big deal for me to be here."

We both had a good cry that afternoon.

I felt the same way I did when my gramma had been alive. That kind of warmth for her. There were times when I wanted to hug Mags tight and never let her go. I could watch her face, the way her eyes sink into it, the way her dark hair hangs like a canopy over and around it, I could watch her face for hours. She has this perfect way of being. Even when she's going through hell.

Then I asked her why she had done it. I mean, I knew *why*, really.

I knew that we had started something that wouldn't stop on its own.

But Mags surprised me.

She said, "Because I have wanted to shoot those kids since the third grade when I first met any of them. Fried brains or no."

Mags is probably the boldest person I know.

Bold as they come.

But her boldness is losing its edge. I think jail did that to her.

LATER, ALL THE TALK SHOWS STARTED, AND THEN Mags was let off because Alison had recovered from her wounds.

You can't kill the dead twice, I guess.

Alison was living on some machines and spilled a fake story about someone other than Mags doing the shooting.

Even though it was an obvious lie I was happy to know that Alison had regained her speech a bit more; and I was thrilled that Mags was no longer the prime suspect.

Then, of course, we all found out that Alison somehow escaped the hospital, pulling out all her wires.

THERE'S A RUMOR THAT SHE WROTE SOMETHING IN blood on the hospital wall, about coming after each of us, me, Mags and Gyro, but I'm not going to sit around getting scared over this.

Life is too short.

Alison's probably doing some zombie strip show up in Duluth or something by now.

Gyro has stayed out of the limelight, but occasionally she calls after midnight. Crying, whispering, full of fear of things that might happen.

She's afraid of Alison, but I think Alison probably did what she should've done before we even had decided to abduct her.

Got the hell out of town.

Dead or alive, it's all any of us wants to do.

OF COURSE, *THAT'S* THE TRUE STORY.

Mags is covering for Gyro when she tells it her way.

Her way has me as an insaniac and Gyro as an innocent and Alison Gall as the bitch goddess.

Mags says the truth is that she and I went nuts one day

in school. That she had stolen Gyro's brother's gun. That I laughed while she fired the shots at Alison and the others.

Sometimes, she tells me on the phone that she doesn't really believe the truth anymore.

She told me, "It couldn't happen the way we saw it. It just couldn't. It had to be us, Nora. You and me. Maybe we just got too fucked up in life to know what was really happening around us. I don't know. I'm not smart enough."

Mags lost her courage sometime after all the TV shows and newspapers and *People* magazine. She's still my best friend, and I admire the hell out of her, I really do.

But I wish she'd face the truth.

Yeah, there's more, like what Alison did to humiliate Gyro. And what Gyro whispered in my ear to make me so mad I could focus my *Fries With That?* on poor dead Alison.

I mean, even thinking it again makes me mad enough to spit, but I'm saving it for when Barbara Walters' people call me.

THE MACHINERY OF NIGHT

He thinks:
   Our thoughts make us solid.
   And daylight. Daylight affects our vision so we believe in solids, in mass, in the religion of material and weight.
   But when the night washes over us like a flood, it draws back the veil. Pagans knew this; Buddhists knew this; maybe even some Christians know it, which is why they fear the devil and all his works so much.
   The devil is night. The devil is low definition. The devil is where one ends another begins and all of it a great stream. The devil is darkness. It's a mechanism for seeing without seeing.
   Starlight reveals how fluid we are. How there is no beginning and end. Christ said I am the Alpha and the Omega, but the darkness says there is no beginning and end, there is only world without end, world without definition, world without boundary. How to erase the lines between the boundaries is the thing.

Then he stops thinking. Light, somewhere, light spitting out of the hole in the sky.

The night recedes again, the world hardens. Walls arise, windows, doors, beds, restraints.

"WHO DID THIS?"

"The ones who come in the night."

"Stop that. Who did this? Tell me right now. I mean now. Come on. One of you did this."

"I told you. It doesn't surprise me you don't believe us. You don't believe in much, do you?"

Human feces spread like a post-modern landscape across the green wall.

The words: *I FORGIVE YOU SON* in curlicue shit paint.

Layton glanced at the three of them, knowing that not one man among them would confess. All it meant was more work for him. More cleaning, more scrubbing, all the things he hated about his job.

Meanwhile, the world spun — outside the window, he could see the river as it ran beside the spindly trees, the flooding having subsided three days earlier; the sun through morning mist; the gray doves like a child's paper airplanes floating on the breeze, finally landing on the outer wall, beyond the razor-wired fence.

He wanted to be out there.

He wanted to quit his job that day, but he was still waiting for things to happen — he waited for the other offer from a better hospital, or even a nice administrative position at the cancer society.

Anywhere but here, this place where no one ever seemed to get better, where the depressed remained bleary-eyed, their blood nearly all Thorazine and Prozac at this point; or the criminals, the ones who had done terrible things out there in the world and now were with him, with Layton Conner, behind these walls; and who, after all, were any of them? It was said that even one of the nurses had ended up in a bed down on Ward Six, her mind scrambled because she let them in, she let the patients' world engulf her own until she didn't know there was an Outside.

Look outside when they get to you.

Just for a second.

You need to do this to keep yourself safe.

When they are getting inside you, look out the nearest window for a second, look at your shoes, look at anything that will take your mind away from them for a moment so they won't own you.

He wished he'd had a cigarette on his break. He felt the addiction kicking in, and even with the patch on his arm, it wasn't enough drug to keep him sane in this environment.

He glanced from the window to the three men — Nix, Hopper, and Dreiling, each with his secret history, secret insanity, secret darkness.

He looked beyond the three patients to the far wall where one of them had taken their excrement and had written the words.

Dreiling, who had prettier hair than any of the others

in the ward, shook his locks out and grinned. "It's music," he said, and the interminable humming began; Nix clapped his hands in the air, catching imaginary flies, or perhaps keeping time with Dreiling's annoying tune.

Hopper, who was rather nice in Layton's opinion, gave an 'aw, shucks,' look, shook his head, and whispered something to himself.

"You can't do this anymore," Layton said, easing away from his own frustration. "It's not going to help when Dr. Glover comes in and sees this."

At the mention of the psych director's name, all three shivered slightly as if a ghost had kissed them on the neck right at that moment.

Layton felt a little powerful invoking the name of the dreaded man.

Nix's face broke out in sweaty beads, and he put his hand up to his throat. "I...I can't swallow..."

"Of course you can, now, Nix, come on, take a deep breath," Layton stepped forward, pulling Nix's hand away. "Let go. You can swallow just fine."

"I can't," Nix said somewhat despondently, but in fact, he could. "I hate Dr. Glover. And Dr. Harper. And you nurses."

"Do you ever think she'll stop?" Hopper asked later while Layton guided him back to his own room for the daily dose of meds.

"What's that?"

"She dreams all of it, her and the baby, and the old man, all of them." Hopper whispered, a secret, and Layton nodded as if he knew what the hell the tattooed man was babbling about, and then he gave him the little pink drink from the little white cups, and eventually, Hopper fell asleep on the cot while Layton fastened the restraints to his arms.

"THIS IS NOT EVERYTHING I'M ABOUT," LAYTON SAID to the girl in the bar later, a mug moving swiftly to his lips. He had bored her with his day.

She was cute. She laughed at his jokes; she smiled at the stories of Nix, Hopper, Dr. Glover, Shea, Shaw, and Rogers and the Night Nurse.

It was getting on towards evening, and he had stopped in for a quick drink or two before heading back to his place on Chrome Street. The day had been long, with two major eruptions (as Hansen called them) between inmates.

First — in the showers — what had begun as a fist fight between two very violent individuals escalated to a riot with a dozen patients.

Then, as Layton finished up his shift, he'd heard the screams from Room 47.

He ran down the hall to intervene with Daisy, the Flower girl, when she didn't want to get her sponge bath.

Daisy was sweet, and Layton hated seeing her get hurt, particularly from the techs and nurses on the floor, all of whom seemed to loathe the woman for no apparent reason.

Once he'd calmed her down, she'd gone to her bath fairly easily; he watched while they held her and then he had taken the sponge himself, frothy with soap, and had spread it across her neck and arms and along her back before the female nurse took over.

He felt bad for poor Daisy, but still, she had made him stay an extra two hours — for which he got no pay.

And now, the bar, the beer, and the pretty girl who could not be more than twenty-two; even so she worked hard to exude girlishness.

Her skirt too short, her laugh too tinkly, her eyes much too shadowed. "But the insane, that's who you work with?"

He shrugged. "That's one way of looking at them. They're ordinary people who have had something go wrong. Sometimes, what went wrong is small and nearly unimportant, but it's enough to make them want to attempt suicide. Sometimes, it's a big wrong, and a few of them have murdered or harmed others. Sad thing is, bottom line, they're there to be protected from themselves more than anything."

"Crazy people," she shook her head. "I can't imagine. My mother went crazy during the storms…"

"They were bad," he grinned, noticing that something seemed to be ripening about her right there, in the bar, at nine o'clock in the evening, fertility swept her hair and lifted her breasts and reddened her lips like a Nile goddess. He wanted her. He wanted to touch her.

"When the river flooded, we had to go to my grandfather's place in the hills, and we almost didn't get my mother out in time," she laughed, shaking her head.

He bought her a beer, she sipped it, and he had another one, and it seemed as if he'd just ordered another one when he was in the dark with her, in a small bed, and he was almost inhaling her skin and kissing down and up the smoothness of her.

Even when they made love, he looked beyond her, out the arched window of the bedroom in her mother's house, at the moon casting nets of light across the river, sparkling on its rumbling surface; across from them, up the third hill, the asylum waited to snatch his days.

He smoked three cigarettes afterward, and fell asleep in the crook of her arm.

"I can't offer you coffee," she said. *Angela*. That was her name. Or was it something else?

Out the window: night.

He smiled, almost afraid he would forget her name.

"Mom would throw a fit if she knew you were here. Got to be quiet."

"How old *are* you?"

"Nineteen," she said.

Shit, he thought.

"You?" she asked.

"Twenty-eight."

"When you were ten," she said.

"Back when you were still a baby."

"When you were ten," she repeated, "you found your father crawling on all fours and braying like a mule."

At first it didn't register, and then the memory returned.

"How did you know that?" he gasped.

"You told me last night. Remember? You wept."

"I wept?"

She kissed his cheek as he buttoned his shirt. "I thought it was sweet. It's why you became a nurse.

Remember? Your father attacked you. You had to somehow take care of it all. I can only imagine."

Layton laughed, hugging her. "My god, what was in that beer?"

"Shh," she said, covering his lips with her hand. "I have to get her breakfast and then get ready for class. You need to go."

"What time is it?" He glanced at the clock on the table. It was nearly six; not quite light out. "Damn it."

"A LOT CAN HAPPEN IN TWENTY MINUTES," SHEILA said, her starched blouse looking like white armor covering her starched soul. "In twenty minutes I could've been home in bed already."

"Sorry. I'll come in early tomorrow." Layton took up one of the pens from the cup, and signed his name on the yellow paper next to her hand.

"Well, I'm exhausted," Sheila said. Her eyes would not meet his — typical — and she signed off on her papers, her shift done, passing him the clipboard. "Jones and Marshall are on today, and at nine, Harper comes in to do meds. Glover is over at State for three days. You need to do better on sharps check; I found this."

She drew something from her pocket. Passed it to him.

He glanced at the thing in his hand — a safety pin.

Her voice was gravel and rain. "Nix had it. Don't know how he got it. Said something about some people giving it to him. He's been known to kill with things like that."

"I can imagine," Layton said, trying to keep it light.

Sheila was senior staff and stupid, a terrible combination. She had Doc Ellis's ear, and that meant she could make sure his review bit the dust, no raise, and no promotion to an easier ward.

He grinned. "Thanks for covering for me. Twenty minutes is too much. Had a car issue."

"Oh," Sheila said, her voice now all sleet. "That's twice in six weeks. Better get it into the shop."

After she left — making sure to check his keys for him like he was a baby — he started on the basic rounds with one of the psych techs.

Sharps check, whites check, laundry baskets rolled out as more staffers arrived, coffee in the vending room, twice-told jokes about the boy who grew trees on his back, complaints from Shaw and Rogers about their treatment, a backed up toilet, followed by basic bed check — Rance had the sniffles, and Layton quickly checked his temp only to find a high fever and then, oh shit, the day was screwed.

Harper arrived and began a mini-quarantine to make sure it wasn't anything worse than the flu — six ended up in Rance's room, all with fevers, all beginning to moan about the demons who were scratching at them or their skin falling off, or any number of odd complaints.

Diarrhea on the floor, dripping, spitting, and Layton going between them with juice and toast, just hoping for once they'd all get the plague and die.

When he finally got to Nix's room, he unstrapped him. "I thought Shaw would've done this by now, damn it," Layton said, muttering to himself, but Nix laughed.

"That's the first time you've ever said anything that

made sense, Mr. Conner," Nix said, "and now, if you don't mind, a little privacy?"

Layton nodded and turned his back. He watched the wall, and tried to ignore the pissing sounds coming from the toilet in the corner.

"All done," Nix said.

"Glad to see no writing on the wall today," Layton said, turning.

Nix had a face that was a genetic mix of wise child and prematurely old troll — Layton had never noticed 'til now that Nix had a scar on his chin, or that he was beginning to go bald. His blond hair receded from a point on his crown.

How old was he?

Layton thought he was forty, but he might've been mid-thirties. It was on his chart, but who looked at the charts anymore? Administrative bullshit.

"She finally stopped," Nix said, getting fidgety. His face became stormy — his brows twitched, his lips curled, his skin began wrinkling with nervous spasms.

Needs his meds. "You sleep okay?"

"Not really," Nix giggled, his fingers beginning their familiar snapping.

Where the fuck is Rogers and the med cart?

"Couldn't sleep — "

"At all?" Layton asked.

"The baby kept me up, so I had to wander." Nix said, and then went to the sink and began washing up. He shook like a drunk. Where the hell was the med cart? Layton watched him in the steel mirror. "I went out and had a drink or two and then made friends."

"Oh did you," Layton nodded. He glanced at the open door.

The squeaking whine of the med cart wheels echoed along the green corridor. Somewhere a fly buzzed. Out the window?

He glanced outside, through the bars and glass, past the pavement, the fences, to the river and the valley. God, he wished he could be anywhere but in this room.

Layton went and sat down on the mattress. It was clean, unlike other patients' rooms.

"Another night on the town?"

Nix turned slowly, his face shiny with water. "Yeah. I met someone and we spent the night together."

"Well," Layton grinned. "Not a total loss then."

Stretched his arms out, and hopped up again.

Nix was an easy patient for the most part; violent when he was on the outside, but inside he was pretty much a kitten. Nix never went for the eyes. He spoke sensibly except when he ventured into some delusional chatter.

Layton went to the sink and grabbed a towel for the patient.

Taking the towel, wiping his hands slowly, Nix said, "Not a total loss at all. But then…that baby was still wailing. She hadn't changed him, that's why. She doesn't know how important it is. See, the thing is, she can understand all this movement, this jumble of molecules, but he's just a baby, his mind hasn't quite sorted it out. She thinks because he's a baby he's better at it. I had to change him myself."

"Is that how you got the safety pin?"

"The *what*?" Covering his face in the white towel, Nix's features came through the cloth. Layton shivered slightly.

Something about the towel on the face reminded him of his father's madness. Form without expression. The open mouth without sound.

"Nurse Allen found it, this little pin," Layton grabbed the towel back, rolling it into a ball. "She took it from you. Last night."

"Oh, that," Nix swept a hand in the air. "That night nurse is no good. She's a brick. She finds that and she thinks I'm just plotting to stab her in the neck twenty times with it or plunge it into her heart and extract it. She's crazy."

Layton wanted to add:

It's what you did to two women on the Outside, Nix. Why wouldn't she think you'd use it on her, too?

LAYTON MET ANGELA AGAIN THE FOLLOWING Saturday, they got a little drunk again, ended up down on the muddy bank of the river, found a dry rock, kissed, almost began to make love, but she said she just wasn't in the right mood.

"It's my mother," she said. "She's been giving me hell lately."

"I keep forgetting you're nineteen."

"I turned twenty."

"When?"

"Thursday."

"Happy Birthday."

"I don't care about birthdays or age. Or anything. It's all this proof. It means nothing. If I told you I was twenty seven, you wouldn't really know the difference. It's just revolutions of the earth. Years go by. Gravity pulls. We all buy into it."

Angela reached into her breast pocket and withdrew a pack of cigarettes. She offered him one — he snapped it up — and then sucked one up between her lips, lit it, puffed, and sighed. "All learning is about trapping. Keeps you trapped inside this...vehicle...we call a body. We learn that we're flesh and bone, but somewhere it's all particles. Somehow the particles convince us we're solid. I took molecular biology last semester and barely under- stood a word, but the way I see it, we're all just convincing ourselves that anything we are or see is solid, but it's not. It's confetti. Bits and pieces and then it's all like this river. Look at the river — silt and fish and water and amoebas and all kinds of things, and we call it river, but it's all one thing, and who's really to say that the fish actually moves or if it becomes water and in the next second is fish again only because it was water?"

"Well," he said, nibbling on her ear, "college and beer are doing you a lot of good I see."

"It's hard to swallow some of the bullshit."

"Yeah, tell me about it. It's like being raised Catholic."

"You? Catholic?"

He laughed. "Yeah, you know all that belief shit. Even science is full of its little beliefs, and half the problem is buying into them or not. Just like you said."

"Well," she shrugged, "I believe in a lot of what you'd probably call 'belief shit'."

"I gave up believing in anything I can't see when my father died," he said.

He wanted to laugh and make a joke of this, but he couldn't.

She opened her mouth to speak, but smoke came out.

SHE STUBBED THE CIGARETTE OUT ON THE ROCK.

"My mother is basically dying," Angela began, almost inaudibly.

She said it again a bit louder.

Layton had nothing to add. He wanted to say something wise and kind, but no words came to mind.

"She's dying, and I'm just getting started on life. She's a nightmare at times. I've wished her dead with each surgery. For her own sake. I've wished her gone. Can't imagine having a daughter like me."

She brightened for a second. "Change the subject, quick. I don't want to think about it."

"I had a boring week," he said. "You don't want to hear about it. I'm sorry about…"

"I really mean it. Change the subject. Poor baby. Boredom is worse than dying. Change the subject. Your work, your boyhood, your religious awakening, anything."

"In my job, boredom is good."

"Well, then." She lit another cigarette. "Tell me how it was boring."

"No attacks, no riots, no bizarre rituals involving stray cats, no eyes getting popped out."

"Something to celebrate."

"Along with your birthday."

"Now I feel like it," she said, leaning into him, and he felt her ripen again, as if she wanted him to open her, to be part of her.

The cigarette went into the mud, his hands found their way beneath her blouse, her hands encircled his back.

Nature took over — he found himself making love to her on the rock, in the torn fingernail of light along the banks of the flooded river.

They dozed afterward for just a few minutes; then she said something; he opened his eyes but was still in a half-dream.

"You see? You're in it, too. You think you're outside but you're really in," she said.

When he asked her what she meant by that, she acted as if he'd dreamt the words she'd just said.

IT WAS TWO A.M. WHEN HE WALKED HER HOME, AND kissed her on the forehead.

She looked surprised. "That's it? Fatherly kiss on the old noggin?"

"You took all my passion." He chuckled.

"Ah," she nodded. "Well, I best get some sleep. I have a Physics exam Monday, bright and early."

"Physics? Ouch," Layton grinned. "My worst subject."

"I kind of like it. We have a bizarre professor who talks about string theory and molecular shake-ups and why we can't just go through chairs and things."

"Okay," Layton nodded. "You lost me. I'm just a nurse."

"Don't play dumb," she swatted him playfully. "Hey, wait, before you go, you need to give me something."

"Oh I think I did already."

"Not that, you cad," she said. "Something to show you care."

He reached into his pockets.

"Christ, I've got nothing. No mementos at all. Wait," he brought up a half-roll of *Lifesavers*. "There you go. To save your life with."

He pressed it into her hand, and she giggled and told him that until they met again she would treasure each and every tropical fruit flavor.

"Where did you get those?" Layton asked.

It was a few weeks later and Angela had not been answering his calls and no one answered her door, and now he was at work feeling the worst heartache of his life — and Nix the Needle had a half-roll of tropical fruit *Lifesavers* in his hand.

"You going to take those off me?" Nix asked, tugging at the restraints that held his hands to the bed. "Don't I even have a right to candy?"

"Give it to me," Layton said, plucking the roll from the man's hands. "Where did you get —"

Nix looked up into his eyes, soulfully, and whispered in a soft voice, "She's dying, and I'm just getting started on life. She's a nightmare at times. I've wished her dead with each surgery. For her own sake. I've wished her gone. Can't imagine having a daughter like me. Change the subject, quick. I don't want to think about it."

"I'm afraid for you," Dr. Glover said.

Mid-afternoon, Layton would be off-shift soon. "I'm afraid in a way that I was afraid for Molly Sternberg."

"Please. Molly had a history of —"

"All of us have histories," Glover said. "None of us is immune to this. You work with mentally unstable people — sociopaths as well — and you become enmeshed. You begin to experience a similar dissociation from reality that they also experience. It is not that unusual. It is somewhat expected."

Glover scratched at the side of his head. "Don't worry, Conner, I'm not going to put you away. You haven't identified yourself as insane. But it wouldn't surprise me that you might just need a little distance. When was your last vacation?"

"Three months ago."

"Perhaps this is just one of those things," Glover added.

"Those things? You're a psychiatrist," Layton nodded his head slightly hoping that the doctor would laugh it off.

"Because I'm trained in a way of handling medical issues doesn't mean I have all the answers. Sometimes the unexplainable occurs. Sometimes it's a delusion. Sometimes it happens. I've been here long enough to realize that there's more to the world than has been catalogued in the medical texts. Now, what did Nicholas say?"

"He said exactly what this woman said the previous weekend."

"Precisely?"

"As precisely as I could recall it."

"You could recall it?"

"Christ," Layton said. He stood up. "I'd like a few days off."

"Speak to your supervisor; as far as I'm concerned, take any amount of time you want off. Your job is secure." Glover glanced over to his bookshelf. "You know, Conner, you've been here a few years. You know your ward inside and out. You've seen a lot. You've handled a lot. On the one hand, this could be your mind playing tricks on you."

Glover reached beneath his glasses and rubbed two fingers along the bridge of his nose. He shut his eyes for a moment. "On the *other* hand, sometimes there are things that come through the patients. I'm not even sure what I mean by that."

He took his glasses off. "Without my glasses, you are blurred." He put them back on. "Now I see you clearly. Does that mean that when I see you blurred that you are in fact blurred and that my vision is perfect but your image is in flux?"

"Sir?"

"All I'm saying is, we can't know everything. Assuming that Nicholas Holland said what you heard, perhaps he did know what this woman said to you. Perhaps he made it up and by some strange coincidence, for the first time in his own history, he said the exact words to disturb you.

But I've learned in twenty-eight years as a psychiatrist handling the more extreme cases of human insanity, that —" Glover leaned toward him. "We know nothing of the human mind. We are still in the Dark Ages of psychiatry. We are fumbling. Do you know what Nicholas said to me when he first entered this place? He told me that when the night came, the mechanisms changed, and that while I was eating supper the night before with my wife, he had already seen to it that the pie in the kitchen had fallen to the floor."

Layton, caught up for a moment, asked, "Did it?"

Glover drew back, laughing. "No, of course not. And we hadn't *had* any dessert. It was a complete fabrication. But how was I to know? I didn't even mention it to my wife. I thought it was just a rambling delusion on his part.

"But a year or so later, I attended a dinner party at a colleague's home. Some of the doctors were telling tales out of school. The usual — patients who sat up in the middle of operations, the near-malpractice suits that managed to get cleaned up in some hilarious way, the patients who hallucinated bizarre images — and so I had my glass of wine and told the story about Nicholas claiming to break into the house. I had them rolling mainly because I recalled all the details he added — how he sipped milk from the fridge, how he peed in the sink. And then I mentioned the pie claim, I said, 'and he then told me that he dropped a pie on the kitchen floor just so I wouldn't eat it.'

"And Layton? I saw it in my wife's face, out of the corner of my eye, even then I saw that she had gone white as if something dreadful had come over her. She said nothing at dinner, but on the way home she told me that she had bought a pie at the A&P and warmed it in the oven for a bit before letting it cool on the cutting board by the sink. 'And,' I asked, 'did it fall on the floor?' She told me it had not, but that someone had broken the crust, a man, she thought, because the handprint was big. Handprint? Yes, she said. It scared her because it was nearly perfect, almost as if someone had baked his hand into the crust. She threw it out, not wanting to even think about it. So, you see, perhaps Nicholas knew something. Perhaps he didn't. How could he? I am a man of some education and knowledge of science, Layton, but I have no basic explanation for this — or for you. Except to say: take a few days off and let this go."

AND THEN, ON HIS DAY OFF, LAYTON SAW ANGELA again. It was just after nine at night, and the rain began.

Layton was going to have a late dinner at the *Hong Kong Moon* restaurant when he noticed her walking out of the convenience store with a small bag of groceries.

When he caught up to her at her car, she didn't look happy to see him at all.

He wanted to ask about the Lifesavers, but it seemed trivial and stupid now.

"Oh, hi," she said. "I'm sorry I haven't been around. My mother died. There was a lot to take care of."

"God, I'm sorry."

She got in the little car.

He stood there, the blur of rain on the car window

obscuring her features. He felt the shiver that always came at the end of new love.

And then, she began laughing.

For just a second — was it the rain? His tears? —he thought that it all shimmered.

Not just her, but the rain and the glass and the metal of the car.

IT TOOK LAYTON TWENTY MINUTES TO GET UP THE hill, flash his badge at the guards, nod to the night nurse who seemed surprised to see him, and make his way down the ward.

He found Nix sitting up on his mattress, his hair soaked. Nix glanced up, then back down to his own upturned palms.

"My nerves are all tingly," Nix said.

"Tell me everything," Layton said.

Nix didn't look up from his hands. Then he licked his lips like a hungry child. "You don't know this for sure, Conner, what you're thinking. Whatever it is you're thinking."

"Do you know who Angela is?"

Nix grinned. "I have known many angels."

"*Angela*. She's the one who gave you the Lifesavers."

"I have saved several lives," Nix said.

Layton rushed over and grabbed him by the shoulders, lifting him to his feet.

They stared eye to eye; sweat ran down Nix's face. "What the hell *is* it you do? What is it about the baby crying and the woman and the things that you babble about?"

Nix's grin faded. "It's the machinery. It's how it works. It's how we work. It's how the world changes in the dark, Conner. It's how when light particles are lessened, it's not just about seeing, it's about how in absolute darkness it can change. We can change."

Layton pushed him back down on the bed. "Half an hour ago you were a woman in a car."

"Was I?" Nix asked, almost slyly. "Was I? Well, then, Nurse Conner, you have already begun your journey. Do you remember being inside her, this Angela? How you pushed in, how she opened, how she made those little noises that made you push to greater and greater heights, how she turned twenty on a particular week and how she told you all about her dying mother and how you fell in love and how she broke your heart one night in the rain? Do you remember playing with her body, or asking her to do something that you find in your heart of hearts to be repulsive and lowly but which brings you great pleasure? Do you remember when she told you all her secrets, even the one about her uncle, or the time you both laughed at once over something you seemed to think of at the same time, as if you had so much in common, Nurse Conner, that this might just be the girl for you, this might just be Miss Right and you just might be the luckiest man in the world? And then you told her that awful secret, the dark secret, the one you thought you could trust her with, the one about your father's madness, about how it pushed you to the edge and how one night you…"

Later, when two psych techs pulled him off Nix,

Layton could not remember raising his fists, let alone bringing them down nearly forty times over Nix's head, nor could he remember through the trial that even after he'd begun to break the skin of Nix's face, long after the patient was dead, particles of bone from the patient's jaw and nose had splintered and some had gone, needle-like, into the palm of Layton's hand.

NEARLY A YEAR LATER, LAYTON TRIED TO SIT UP IN bed, but the restraints held him fast.

He wanted to shout for the night nurse, but whom could he trust?

He knew them all, he knew they thought he was one of the many criminally insane, but he knew the staff well, and he didn't understand why they should restrain him when he had only tried to kill himself once, and had botched the job anyway.

It was the whisper of night coming up under the barred window, the last light of day was nearly vanished, and he still felt drowsy from the last med administered at two.

The nights were the worst, because of the people who moved through the dark, who came and went and he watched in horror as they did what had to be done.

Even Nix, even he came through, his face sometimes a bloody tangle, a forest of twisted flesh and bone, sometimes it was just his face, beads of sweat on his forehead, that trollish look, that milky complexion.

The machinery hummed and if he could just believe

strongly enough, he could slip through the restraints and join them, he could go and be anywhere and anyone, but it never seemed to happen.

Some of the other patients came and went; the walls rippled like a flooding river; the air itself became vivid with the movement of nearly invisible molecules as they went like clouds of mosquitoes, forming and splitting apart again.

Layton, in restraints, tried to pray.

His heartbeat raced as he watched a swollen bubble of glass move along the window.

"It's belief," he whispered. "Belief makes it move. It's absolute belief," but it wasn't coming for him, the molecules weren't changing, the mechanism of darkness was not clicking into place.

"Please let me go. Please," he begged, and then, as happened nightly, his voice became louder, sobs and screams.

One of the nurses came by with another med.

As she wiped the sweat from his forehead, he told her how they left nightly, how when the sun went down the machinery of night made it happen and their molecules swirled and how even the two men he had killed in his life, his father and Nix, sometimes came to him and made him do terrible things in the dark.

"And the woman who spoke to the courts? Her name was Angela, but she's really one of the men I killed, only you can't ever really kill anyone, you can't, it's just a rearrangement of molecules and at night they can change again or if they want they can stay as they were that night for a whole day and they can even come to your trial and talk about you and things you told them and how you seemed to be going slowly mad only you never ever went mad, if anything it's complete sanity, it's the kind of sanity that's like the sun at noon all bright and sharp and please don't turn off the light, that's all I ask, when you leave and I get sleepy from the pills, please leave the lights on," his voice softened, and the nurse nodded.

WHEN HE AWOKE LATER — WHEN THE MEDS WERE beginning to wear off — the room was dark and he felt the brush of a thousand particles that whispered with the voice of his father.

THE WOLF

The man and the boy had been tracking the wolf since sunrise, but by the time the moon came up they made camp along the ridge.

"Put your rifle over there," the man told the boy, pointing to a pile of rocks covered with fern. "Always put your rifle as far from you and the fire as possible. Accidents happen when they're too close. We don't sleep with them. The wolf won't attack us. It's sheep he's after, not you. Not me."

The boy at first questioned this, because he liked to have his rifle close to him when he hunted. After a few minutes of consideration, the boy decided that the rancher had hired the man to lead, and he would let him. The boy also had done something he wished he hadn't that afternoon, by shooting at what he thought might be the wolf, but turned out to be a silver fox.

By the fire, after supper, they sat across from each

other. "We might have had him at the bluffs," the man said. "He's smarter than us, I think."

"I didn't mean to shoot at it," the boy said.

"It doesn't matter."

"I thought I saw him."

"Foxes can look like wolves, sometimes. Coyotes, too."

"It was a stupid mistake."

"I don't care. You're young."

"I'm the best hunter for a hundred miles."

"I can tell."

"Mister, maybe they pay you money to hunt wolves, but when I hunt, it's for the love of the sport," the boy said. "I can take anything out fast. Once I target it, it's mine and that's the end of it."

"I'm not here to argue with you, son."

"I'm not your son."

They went silent again. After he had relieved himself in the woods, the man checked their rifles, and then felt for the small gun beneath his jacket. The man returned to the fire and saw that the boy still sat there.

"We need to get up before first light," he said.

"How many wolves you kill?" the boy asked.

"What?"

The boy glared at him in the firelight. "How many?"

"Twenty. Maybe more."

"That's not a lot."

"No," the man said. "It's not."

"When I'm your age, I bet I'll have more than twenty pelts."

"I don't keep souvenirs like scalps," the man said. "You need to sleep closer to the fire. Take your coat and anything in your pack. Cover yourself good. In a few hours, it'll be colder than you can imagine."

"I hunt a lot," the boy said. "I know how cold it gets up here."

The man did not sleep much. Just before dawn, he rose and rekindled the fire and drew an old rusty skillet from his pack. He made breakfast with the meager supplies he'd brought.

The boy awoke to the smells, and after a mug of coffee began laughing.

"You look like crap," the boy said.

They wandered off the main trails that morning.

THE MAN SAW EVIDENCE OF THE WOLF'S PASSING through a route between narrow rocks. There was blood of fresh kill and the rotting smell of a dead animal in the air as they moved further along through the pines. He motioned for the boy to remain still. The man went up along moss-covered rock, through underbrush, and finally came to a cliff's edge overlooking the valley. He glanced out over it to see the distant lake and the dots that were the ranches below. He saw three whitetail deer in a clearing among the trees just above the rocks where he stood.

He sensed the wolf, yet did not see him.

The boy followed him up the trail. When the boy drew close to him, the man whispered, "He knows we're following him. This is a problem now. Yesterday, he didn't know."

The boy remained silent until they had made camp for the night.

"It ain't my fault."

"No one's blaming you."

"You are. You think I scared him off. When I shot my rifle."

The man continued to peel an apple as he leaned back against his pack. "You can't look for blame all the time."

"It was one mistake," the boy said. "I won three hunting trophies before I was fifteen."

The man glanced at him, nodding.

"I bet they paid you a lot of money to do this," the boy said after a minute. "I bet it's a racket you got. You set wolves free down in the valley. Then, eventually, they hire you."

The man laughed at first, but then saw that the boy meant every word. "There would be easier ways to make a living."

"I just can't figure why they'd hire a stranger when we got a lot of hunters in the valley," the boy said. "That's all I meant."

"What did you do makes you special to that town?" the man asked.

The boy wouldn't tell him. He shook his head and said, "I just hunt. That's all. I can hunt and trap and shoot. I win a lot of trophies at the fairground. I can shoot just about anything. Could since I was a boy. First kill was a rabbit when I was ten."

"Jack rabbit?"

"Peter Cottontail," the boy said.

The man said, "What's the last thing you killed?"

The boy didn't answer.

The man said, "First thing I ever killed was a wolf. I was younger than you. You kill a wolf, you start to understand it."

After that, there wasn't much talk around the fire, and the man chuckled to himself when he rolled over to sleep. They had to sleep close beside each other for warmth. The boy's breathing kept him awake for another two hours.

The next day, they went off toward Needle Heights, the bony points of the mountain that crossed into the mountain range leading up north.

The boy asked him what he smelled in the air, and what signs of the wolf he followed, for the boy could not track as well as the man and knew it.

At twilight, the man told him, "I learned from the old mountain men, when I was a boy. There are ways to track wolves. Different from tracking other animals. There was a mountain man, half-Cherokee, half-Scot. He was an old man, and he took me out to hunt wolves back in the days when we all hunted wolves. He told me that a wolf that got a taste for sheep would draw other wolves down to the ranches. You have to kill them before they can get back up to their pack. Usually, it's the young males. You see it with them first. Old wolves, they know not to go in the valleys, to the ranches. The young ones just see sheep and want them. We tracked this wolf for nine days, and when we finally cornered him, he didn't seem like a wolf anymore. He seemed like a man. I felt as if I knew him, just like I know you. I saw his eyes and I could almost tell what he was thinking. He wanted what you might want. Yes, you. What a lot of men want. He wanted a bite of it. A piece of it. He had wiles and instinct. He knew that if he found a pen full of sheep he might eat better than if he spent his time chasing deer or rabbit."

"Wolves are like rabid dogs," the boy said.

"You just never met one yet," the man said. "They're smart. When they feel threatened, they attack. When you hunt a wolf, you don't let him know he's being hunted until you absolutely have to do it. You wait. You have patience.

You let him think you're just part of the scenery. Just another wolf, maybe. This wolf.

He's just looking for the sheep and then a place to hide. When he finds the prize sheep, that's the one he wants. He doesn't want the sickly or the scrawny. He wants the best."

"It's funny we kill 'em, then," the boy said. "'Cause that's the way some people are. Some people I could name. Where I live."

"Wolves know each other," the man said. "When I had that wolf cornered, when I was younger than you, that wolf looked at me and knew I was a wolf, too. He'd met his match. Only I wasn't a wolf until that day. I didn't want to take a bite of anything until that day. You think you're a wolf, son?"

"A wolf? No."

"Some people are sheep. Maybe most people. And a few people in a thousand may be the vigilant dog that guards the sheep. Now and then, there's even a shepherd. But whenever a group of sheep are together, a wolf always comes 'round. You can count on it. That's why I get work. I'm an expert at wolf killing. They know it in towns in this region. Somebody talks to somebody, and they call me in and pay my fee," the man said. "And I track the wolf. I don't make errors. I don't let the wolf know he's being tracked. I usually work alone. I make sure the wolf I kill is the wolf that's causing distress for people. I don't just kill wolves because I can. I find the right wolf and I do my business."

"I think all of them should just be killed. Every wolf. They all eventually will come down to the sheep. That's what I think," the boy said.

"That would be wrong," the man said, looking the boy in the eye. "What if a man killed another man? Should all men be killed because that one man did wrong? Of course not."

"We're talking wolves, not men."

"Some men are wolves," the man said.

WHEN THEY HAD CROSSED INTO THE DEEP FOREST, the man thought for sure the wolf was near. He motioned for the boy to remain silent and at the ready. The man pointed toward the ramble up ahead, overgrown with dead vines.

He gave the signal for the boy to step ahead of him.

The boy raised his rifle up. He stepped slowly between the rocks and trees.

Breaking the silence, the man said, "I was wrong. It's not him."

The boy glanced back at him. His face gleamed bright red with sweat. "How do you know?"

"It's a bitch," the man said. "Heavy with cubs. I don't hunt like that."

The boy moved forward. The man raised his rifle and shot it into the air above the boy's head.

Birds flew out from the underbrush, and the boy turned around in anger.

AT CAMP THAT NIGHT, THE BOY SAID, "YOU DID THAT to scare me."

The man nodded. "We are after one wolf only. We don't shoot any others."

"How do you know she wasn't the wolf?"

"I know the wolf is male. I know its size. I know the color of its coat. And I know its track. This was not the wolf."

"I say kill them all," the boy said.

"You're not a hunter if that's how you feel," the man said. "You may win a hundred trophies, son, but a hunter does not wish to kill them all."

"I hate wolves," the boy said. "I'm tired. I want to go home. The food is awful. Your coffee's awful. I want to be in my bed. At home."

"I know you do," the man said. "You shouldn't have come with me. But here you are. Make the best of it. We'll have him soon." After a moment, the man asked, "Why did you come?"

"I owe it to him. The rancher."

"What do you owe him?"

"I made a mistake once, on his ranch. With him. I

need to make it right."

"Mistakes can be forgiven," the man said. "But it's not good to make them."

The boy's lip turned up into a snarl. "That was a mistake. What you did today. Shooting like that. Warning the wolf. He was probably nearby."

"Everyone makes mistakes."

"I bet when they hired you…"

"They?" the man asked.

"The people in town. The ranchers. I bet when they hired you they thought you'd have this done fast. They sent me to learn from you, I bet. Learn. What I learned so far is you worry about wolves too much."

"I wasn't hired by people. I was hired by a person."

The boy thought about this for a moment, and seemed to chew on it. "The rancher was good to me once, but that changed. Maybe it was the wolf attacking his stock. Maybe it was something else."

"You see him as a rancher. I know him as a man who lost his only daughter."

The boy went silent for several minutes. The man watched him.

Then, the boy said, "Not my fault, either."

"I believe you," the man said.

"I didn't do that to her," the boy said.

"I believe you," the man said. "But he hired me to track this wolf. You came along because he wanted you to know what it meant to track a wolf. That's all."

"She was a good girl," the boy said. "We would've been married if…it doesn't matter. It was an accident."

"I know nothing about her or you," the man said. "I

just know I was hired to track the wolf. You are the local boy who has all the hunting trophies. So you came with me."

"I wanted to help him. Her father. To make up for it," the boy said.

"If it was an accident," the man said, "then there was nothing to make up for."

The man glanced over at the rifles, placed beyond the fire, in a ditch between rocks and a rotting log.

The boy began to get up as if he, too, thought about the rifles.

The man drew out the gun tucked under his coat, and pointed it at the boy. "Stay where you are, son," he said.

"You're not tracking the wolf," the boy said.

The man stood up and moved closer to the boy. He whispered to the boy that he should not be afraid.

The boy looked as if he might turn and run at any minute, but the man's whispers were calming. The man spoke about how everything would be all right.

"I didn't kill her," the boy said. "Her father is crazy. I didn't kill her. She decided to do what she did. I had no part of it. I was hunting with my uncles. She thought I had abandoned her. I would've married her. I would've come back. If I had known. I would have. She was good. She was a wonderful girl. I knew I wanted a girl like that. Any man would. You would've if you had known her. She was like an angel to people. I saw it the minute I laid eyes on her. She was one of the good ones. Not all people are good, are they? But she was. She was a good one."

The man aimed the gun to the side of the boy's head.

"Most people are sheep," the man said. "A few are the

dogs that guard the sheep. Now and then there is a shepherd, but they are rare. But there are always wolves. A wolf
wants to find the best of the sheep and devour it. That is
all a wolf wants to do when it finds sheep. That is all it
can do."

AFTER THE MAN BOUND THE BOY'S HANDS AND LEGS,
he went to get his rifle. He stood several feet back from the
boy, estimating where best to make the killing shot.

THE WICKED

P *oor little Charlie,* the man grinned.

His hands were shaking as he stood there at the edge of the field. All those boys, and Charlie there, standing with his fat little glove on his hand, his scrawny legs poking out from his balloon shorts, his baseball cap askew, his blond hair thrusting out from his cap like straw.

Poor little Charlie. His mother was a lazy drunk. She drove a Buick with the windows blacked out so no one could watch her drink while she stopped at the light.

His father was a workaholic who spent idle hours with the factory girls down at the road houses out on the parkway.

They took a two week vacation together as a family every year, usually to the Caribbean, hiring a local girl to take care of the boy.

All the neighbors knew this, apparently, and felt sad for the boy.

"Always alone," the busybody down the block from them had told the man four weeks before.

Local gossip, told just in passing, in the local market when Charlie walked down the aisles looking for some candles.

"His mother collects candles," the busybody had said. "Poor little Charlie. You know, even on their holidays, his parents have practically nothing to do with him. No wonder he's the way he is."

Charlie was all alone most of the time.

The man had watched Charlie more than just at the house, but also when the boy walked from the bus stop, on Linden Avenue, all the way over to the small yellow house on Backus Street.

The boy dragged his feet sometimes when he walked.

Charlie kept his eyes down, and his hands over his books, which he hugged to his chest like treasured possessions.

The man would sit in his car, and slowly follow the boy as he rounded the corner.

He would see the aura around the boy that begged to be taken.

Once, the man had gotten quite daring, and walked into the empty lot behind Charlie's house.

He'd crouched down at the back fence—an old wooden fence ready to fall down in a slight wind. The nervousness was delightful. If a neighbor caught him, or a passing patrol car, it might be the end for him.

He crouched there for an hour before Charlie came down the steps of his house. Charlie shuffled his feet as he went to the little dirt and gravel area. It was almost a pit, beneath the dying crabapple tree where Charlie liked to play.

The man had carved a small opening in the worn fence with his Swiss Army knife.

Just to watch Charlie play.

All afternoon, Charlie had played by himself. He sat down in the filthy pit, arranging stones in a circle around himself. The flies that always seemed to be seeking him out rose and fell like dust around each of his movements. Then he lit a match, and waved it around. He lit four small candles, no doubt filched from his mother's kitchen without permission.

That was the marvelous things about little boys. They could get up to such innocent mischief.

He watched Charlie for a long time that afternoon as he sat in the pit and watched the candles as they burned. Charlie had held his hands over the flames a bit, and then closed his eyes and hummed even more.

Charlie was a typical victim boy. His imagination took him away from the squalor of his existence.

The man liked that about him. Knew that what he needed to do to Charlie was good for the boy. It wasn't as if Charlie would even care about the pain.

And the money he'd get from bringing the boy in, and taking the photographs: it was good compensation, but not the same as the sensation Charlie would give him.

Murder was, after all, more a feeling than an action.

ON ANOTHER NIGHT, WHILE HE DROVE AROUND THE

neighborhood to get a feel for it, the man saw Charlie up in his bedroom window.

The boy stood, without his shirt on, at the open window. He held his hands straight out into the night. He was humming again, and the man had laughed.

Oh, poor little Charlie. Poor little Charlie who had no friends, whose parents were negligent and terrible, and who only had himself and his sad imagination to comfort him.

Now, Saturday morning, eleven a.m., with the Little League game winding down, it was nearly time.

The man glanced at his watch.

Only ten minutes or so to go.

They were in the last inning of play, and Charlie's team was losing miserably.

Not that Charlie seemed to mind. He stood in the outfield, apparently humming to himself.

The man tried to keep from grinning. He remembered the other little boys, how they begged for death.

Charlie would beg, too.

The man felt the warm sweat along the back of his neck.

Someone, coming up behind him, said, "You're Charlie's dad?"

The man turned.

It was one of the fathers.

The fathers all had the same faces, and he knew why. They had abandoned sensation years ago. They had gotten fat and bald and were terribly nice. They had a glaze of niceness all about them as if they'd been too long in the freezer of nice.

This one wore a black polo shirt and khaki shorts. All the hair that should've been on the top of his head was at the back of his neck. One day when this father got older and wealthier, that hair would crawl up again. He was one of those nonsexual fathers, with the wife who refused, with the pasty morals of one who would not find the thrill elsewhere. He had sad dog eyes. "Put me out of my misery" eyes.

The man nodded. "Yeah. I'm so proud of him."

"I'm Hank Wilson. Billy's dad. That Charlie, he's a… quiet boy," the father said.

The father offered him a cup of coffee, which he accepted so as not to seem out of place. "All the fathers hang out after the game. You should come sit with us."

"Oh, no, really. I like it here. Where I am." Could the father see through him? It didn't seem likely.

"My kid told me that Charlie's real smart." The father said this as a form of compensation for that other thing that hung in the air. *Charlie is not a good Little Leaguer. Charlie's a weakling.* "He told me he did some amazing things with that science project of his."

"Oh?" the man said. "He never brags at home. I had no idea." Sip of coffee. A brief flash of grin. A gentle nod. All to fit in.

The father laughed. "Well, Charlie's probably as modest as he is smart. Billy told me that he made this piece of paper turn into fire and then into a rock. He said even the teacher was amazed. But Charlie told them it was all scientific."

"He's strange," the man said, and then wished he

hadn't. Then, he made a joke of it. "I mean, it's strange, considering how unscientific his mother and I are."

"That's just it. That's just it. I met your wife when she dropped by three weeks back, and she said almost the same thing." The father was searching his face for something. For what? He couldn't figure out.

At first, the man thought that the father was looking for some crack in the mask he was presenting. Then, he knew. The father simply wanted to make sure they saw eye-to-eye.

The crack of the bat — a fly ball — made them both look back at the game.

"Well," the man said. "Charlie is brilliant, isn't he. Young and smart. Not much of an athlete, though."

"Kids can't be good at everything." The father sipped his coffee.

The man sipped his coffee, too. A brief silence.

The man was about to say something so that the father would move away. Maybe say that he had a headache. Maybe that he needed to get something from his car.

Then, the father said, "Your wife told me about the cat."

The man nodded. He was going to go along with this.

"I hope you don't mind my bringing it up. But since I'm a psychologist…"

"Really?" the man said. Could the psychologist see his nervousness? No. He was too good at hiding it.

"Yes. So when I spoke to your wife…"

"Oh, now I remember," the man nodded. "Yes. Yes. She told me she spoke to you…about it."

"Oh, good. I didn't want to be breaking a confidence.

But most of the other kids know about it anyway. I just didn't want to cause problems at home."

"No," the man grinned, wishing he were anywhere but standing at the outer edge of the park, talking to Billy Wilson's father. "No secrets between us. We try and keep up with what's going on with Charlie. That cat…"

"Well, it scared the other kids. I'm sure you talked to Mrs. Reilly yourself."

The man tried to place the name. Mrs. Reilly. The owner of the cat? Mrs. Reilly, the school teacher? Mrs. Reilly, the mother of one of the other boys? He sipped the last of the coffee. He peered into the coffee residue at the bottom of the cup.

"I've been meaning to," he said.

"Well, I guess since it's summer, it can wait. Frankly, I'm surprised about how she reacted herself. It seemed rather unprofessional."

"Women," the man said, hoping the father had a sense of humor.

The father gave him an odd look.

He can see through me.

He knows what I'm thinking.

But the father chuckled. "I wouldn't say that. She's a good teacher, too. But I guess she just reached the boiling point with the cat. It was a neighbor's?"

The man nodded.

"Well, I'm just happy to hear your wife got him some help. A counselor over in the city, I guess."

The man nodded.

"I don't mean to get into it here, but it does explain a bit why the other kids are a bit…shy…of being around

Charlie." When the father said this, the man glanced out at the playing field.

Charlie stood off by himself, his face turned up to the sun. His baseball cap had fallen off, and his blond straw hair seemed longer than usual.

He shut his eyes. He whispered something as if he were wishing to be somewhere else. The man knew about this, because he'd seen other little boys do it when they wanted to be somewhere else.

They held their heads back, closed their eyes, and whispered.

Or prayed.

But now the man noticed the other boys. They played the game, paying little attention to Charlie.

As he watched the boys move around, trying to catch a fly ball or running to change position, he noticed something that he'd missed before, in every single game.

Yet it had been there.

It had happened since late spring when the Little League started up.

It wasn't that they just didn't like Charlie, or that they made fun of him.

In all the months he'd spent watching Charlie, picking him out, he'd never seen the other kids interact in any way at all with the boy.

On the field, it was as if there were an invisible barrier around Charlie, a horseshoe shaped magnetic field that the other boys moved around, without ever getting close to Charlie.

Without ever coming within a certain number of feet of him.

THE FATHER TAPPED HIS SHOULDER. "I'M SURE IT WAS a one time thing. I'm sure it's not one of those worst-case scenarios where he'll be scarred for life."

The man kept his eyes on the boys as they played the game around Charlie. "I never noticed."

"Huh?"

"I never noticed how the other boys were shy around him. I thought it was the other way around."

"I guess it was...before. But something changed last year. Your wife said it was on your vacation to the islands. The Caribbean. She said..." The father patted him on the shoulder. "Oh, she just said something about how you two hired that babysitter. That native woman. To watch him. And how she taught him all kinds of crazy things."

He didn't like men's hands on him. It made him squirm. He took a step forward to be out of patting reach.

"My wife didn't tell me. Oh, wait. Yes, that island woman. I can't recall her name," the man said. He kept his eyes on Charlie who nodded his head side to side. "My wife doesn't always tell me everything about this kind of problem. And of course, Charlie doesn't."

"We dads are always the last to know," the father said. "Well, when Charlie killed the cat," and the man was glad he hadn't turned back to face the father, because this reve-lation nearly made him choke, and his eyes widened, "your wife told me that it was an accident. I buy that. I really do. Accidents happen. It's not good to leave little kids with animals. And hell, Billy killed a bird with his slingshot once and we were none too happy about that.

But kids do these things, right? But for Charlie to cut out its heart and bring it into school. Well, you know the rest. Mrs. Reilly got ferocious and ended up slapping him too hard."

"Oh, right," the man said, as if he were recollecting. "The bruise."

"I'm sure the school district'll fire her over it eventually. But Billy told me Charlie did this thing after she slapped him. And he made the lights go off in the classroom."

"Made the lights go off?"

But the father kept talking, "And then made them flicker on and off. And Mrs. Reilly started screaming, and Charlie started saying something over and over. Some kind of nursery rhyme. And Billy said Judy Goffman tried to get out, but the door wouldn't open. And then Charlie made Mrs. Reilly eat the cat's heart right in front of the other kids." The father was silent for a moment. "Your wife didn't tell you?"

The man shrugged. "Our marriage has its ups and downs. You know. She protects Charlie a lot. Too much."

"Sure," the father said.

The man could detect that edge in the father's voice, as if maybe he suspected something wasn't quite right.

"Well, then Charlie, well, I know boys, and I understand these things, he apparently shows the other boys something. Only Billy won't tell me what it is. I'm sure it's nothing much. Maybe that dead cat, huh? Billy said something about not being able to tell, or else he'd get killed."

"What happened to the teacher?" The man tried to

hide his nervousness. It was no longer pleasurable. It felt like insects stinging him.

"I told you, the school district will probably fire her. You can't hit kids. Not these days. Well, they'll wait until she's better."

"Better?"

"She was in an unfortunate accident early in the summer. But when she's better…"

"What is it he showed the other kids?"

"That's the big question."

The man was getting a headache.

The boys shouted from the field.

The father said, "Oh, gosh, the game's over. Give me a call if you need some help."

The father handed him his business card.

The man curled it up in a small paper ball and dropped it on the ground once the father had returned to the group of other fathers.

Charlie stayed in the outfield, raising his hands up to the sky as if he had won or lost the game all by himself.

When the field was clear, Charlie walked by himself, dragging his feet as he went, heading to Green Street.

The man picked up his backpack. He reached inside it, digging around the soup cans and rope for the stun gun.

When Charlie neared, he said, "Hi Charlie."

Charlie glanced up. "Hi. Who're you?"

"Your mom sent me."

Charlie screwed up his face slightly. He squinted. "She did? My mom?"

The man nodded.

WHEN THEY GOT TO HIS CAR, THE MAN TOLD HIM about what was in the trunk of the car.

He always did this with boys. It was the simplest thing.

With girls, you had to show them something. Usually something pretty. Girls were harder because they usually wouldn't come near the car.

With boys, it was easy.

"Real firecrackers?" Charlie asked, his eyes brightening.

"Yeah, Roman candles, black cats, all kinds of things." He thrust the key into the trunk, twisting it.

The trunk popped open.

"Aren't they against the law?" Charlie's voice was like innocence with just a spark of corruption. Boys were like that.

"Not around Fourth of July time," the man said.

"Fourth of July happened already." Charlie peered into the dark trunk. There was a blanket, two small pillows, and rope.

"Where are they?" he asked.

"Under the blanket."

As Charlie reached for the blanket, the man brought the stun gun down and pressed it against the small of the boy's back.

THE MAN GLANCED ABOUT AS THE CRACKLING SOUND went off.

The suburban streets seemed empty and painted with sunshine.

He only had a minute or less.

THE FATHERS AND SONS WERE OFF IN THE LOT ON THE far side of the park celebrating both victory and defeat as the man dumped Charlie into the trunk.

From his backpack, he withdrew the duct tape. He measured off a bit of it, and taped it over Charlie's mouth. Then he brought out a length of rope from the backpack and tied the boy's arms behind his back. Then his legs. Then he put the pillows under the boy's head.

Shut the trunk.

The sweat on his forehead was thick.

He stared at the trunk.

"Damn it," he whispered.

IN HIS MIND, HE TRIED TO REMEMBER WHAT HE'D done with the car keys. *Unlocked the trunk. Stunned the boy. Dumped the boy in. Reached for the duct tape*

Set the keys on the blanket.

"Damn it to hell," he whispered.

He glanced down the block. A teenager rode his bike

slowly by. A flock of sparrows flew overhead, chattering as they vanished into an oak tree's branches, thick with summer green.

He brought out his Swiss Army knife and jimmied the lock.

The blade broke off.

The father who had spoken to him, drove slowly alongside him in his Cadillac. He lowered his window. "Where's Charlie?"

The man shrugged. "He wanted to walk home. You know kids."

"Got problems?"

The man laughed, but it was a fake jittery laugh. *Don't give yourself away.* "I locked them in the trunk. My keys. Stupid me."

"Want me to call a locksmith?"

The man waved him away. "No, but thanks! I have an extra set at home. I'll just walk over and get it myself. Probably catch up with my kid."

"Sounds good," the father said, and then drove off.

"Damn it all to Hell," the man muttered.

He went and sat in the front seat of the car. He glanced about, looking for some instrument, something, anything that might jimmy the trunk open.

He looked at himself in the rearview mirror. Looked like hell. He looked like a junkie dying for his fix, unable to get it.

His fix was in the trunk.

A patrol car drove up alongside him, stopping. It was that kind of neighborhood. Patrol cars were always around. He'd noticed that. It had been an acceptable risk, but now it was unacceptable.

Completely unacceptable.

He picked this place to scope out a kid because it was just this kind of neighborhood that was easiest to hit. It seemed safe.

In the world, there was no "safe."

A cop, big and burly, strutting as if he owned the block and everything in it, got out of the car, and tapped on his window.

THE MAN ROLLED THE CAR WINDOW DOWN.

The cop leaned in. "Hank Wilson told me you were having some car trouble."

"Hank Wilson?"

"Billy's dad," the cop said. "You're Charlie's dad, right? I've known little Charlie since he started school. Wild kid." The cop flashed a funny look. The guy talked a mile a minute. "I've known him since he was five and almost ran in front of my car. Almost gave me a heart attack."

"Thanks. Everything's fine. I just locked my keys in the trunk."

"Can't you just pop it open from inside?" the cop asked, peering through the window.

"Wish I could. Nothing works right in this old pile of junk," the man said.

"You sure?"

The man offered up a blank stare. "Don't you think I would've done that already?"

The cop shrugged. "Trying to help. Well, jeez, Charlie's dad. What must that be like?"

The man felt sweat break out on the back of his neck. "Yeah, he's a handful."

"That time we caught him with that baby. Remember that? I know he didn't know what he was doing. Kids never think about death like it really is. I got worried we were gonna have a pan of baby soup on our hands, know what I mean? Just a joke. Glad he didn't really hurt that baby. There'da been hell to pay. Hey, I can help you with that," the cop said.

He went back to his car, and returned with a long thin bar. "Come on, I'll show you how to use it."

The man got out of the car and leaned against the door. He wasn't sure if his heart was still beating. He heard a clanging noise in the back of his head.

"Here, it's easy, done this a million times," the cop said.

THE MAN WALKED TO THE BACK OF THE CAR.

The cop took the long slender metal bar and pressed it into the lock. "This isn't going to be wonderful for your lock, but I assume you were going to have to get a locksmith anyway?"

"No, really," the man said, touching the cop's arm. "I have an extra set of keys at home."

"Oh," the cop said, retracting the instrument. "Okay. You want me to give you a ride?"

The man glanced at the trunk. Charlie would be awake by now.

"It's a nice day. I don't mind the walk," the man said.

"You sure? I don't mind," the cop said.

"I need the exercise."

The cop nodded. "Don't we all. Well, good to meet you, Mister… "

The man tried to remember Charlie's last name.

Charlie Jones.

Charlie Howard.

Charlie Randel.

Charlie…

"Carter. Mike Carter."

"Mike Carter," the cop said thoughtfully.

The man wondered if the cop knew Charlie's father's first name.

"I knew a Mike Carter back in high school. You never went to…"

"I grew up in the South," the man said.

"Oh," the cop grinned. "Well, good to meet you, sir. That Charlie of yours is something. I know he's a big joker, but man I've had to rescue more kids and dogs from his clutches. He'll grow up to be something, he sure will."

THE COP WAITED BY THE CAR, WRITING SOMETHING up in his log book, which frightened the man a bit, but it was too late. It's not like he could go back and erase this day, this day that had begun so perfectly.

All the man needed to do was walk around the corner to the drugstore, buy a screwdriver and do some major damage to the trunk of his car. Then, tie it shut, and drive back to his place.

He would take Charlie down into the cellar, where no one ever heard the screams, and then he could go to work on him and set up the cameras to take the pictures.

The man walked down Green Street, remembering that there was a convenience store just a block or two over.

The heat of the day was getting to him, and he wished he had planned for such possible mistakes with an extra set of keys, but he had been too eager.

That was always his problem.

He was too eager to get on with it. He had always been overly cautious before, but he'd been younger then, and now, he was getting sloppy.

He had thought Charlie was such a perfect target, and everything had seemed as if it pointed to this day, but maybe he was wrong.

Still, he got an adrenaline high, knowing that Charlie was in that trunk and that he had passed himself off as the boy's father—the ultimate thrill—knowing that a cop had almost opened that trunk.

HE FOUND A SMALL SCREWDRIVER DOWN THE SECOND aisle of the convenience store, and slipped it into his back pocket.

Part of the thrill was shoplifting. It aroused him a bit too, watching the young woman at the counter who watched him. She knew he was up to something, but she had missed that second—no, that millisecond—when he'd stolen the screwdriver.

It took him ten minutes to get back to the park, and at first he thought he was on the wrong street.

Then, he saw the police car.

THE COP DROVE UP BESIDE HIM AT THE SIDEWALK. "Sorry, Mike. I called your wife."

"My…wife," the man said.

"Yeah I figured I'd save you the trip home, but she said she didn't have any extra sets of keys."

"My wife said that?" the man asked. He felt something clutch at his throat.

The cop nodded. "She told me to tow it. She told me you had about twenty outstanding parking tickets and two speeding tickets and your license was suspended." The cop shrugged. "I had to follow up. Dispatch hasn't confirmed, but your wife swore up and down on a stack of Bibles. She sounded a little funny, too, so maybe you better get home."

"My *wife*," the man repeated again as if he could not believe any of it.

"Look, I'm sorry. But you're lucky the Sheriff hasn't sent someone out to arrest you yet." The cop paused, while the man took all this in. "One other thing, Mike. You got one nasty old lady."

"My wife lied," the man said, stunned.

"Well, maybe she did, but I can't take that chance. If you don't have tickets, I'll go down personally with you and get that car. But until our computers come back up at Dispatch, I'm going to assume for the good of my job that she may be telling the truth. Seems to me, Mike, I remember someone down at the office mentioning those tickets when I had to go talk to Charlie about how not to hurt little babies. Seems to me."

"Yes, now I remember. Yes, the tickets." The man felt his mouth go dry. "Where was it towed?"

"Impounded, Mike. You can't get it back today. On Monday, go down and pay your fines and it's all yours."

The man watched the police car as it slowly drove on down the road.

The cop glanced in his side view mirror and looked back.

All right. All right. Enough.

He could get it. There's a way to get it. To get the boy. To get in the trunk and get the boy out of the trunk and then get the boy somewhere else. The boy would have to be killed right away. The fun was out of it now. The fun was definitely out the door.

But it could be fixed. It could be fixed and then it would be all right.

THE MAN HAD NO FRIENDS. HE HAD BUSINESS associates, but they never liked to be called in times of trouble. He had his parents, but they didn't really like to hear from him either. He was very much a loner. He walked across the park and sat in the bleachers as the afternoon wore on, wondering how he would get to the car, and ultimately, to Charlie.

When it came to him, it was like a pinprick at the back of his skull.

He would just leave Charlie there.

The old car would be in the lot for at least a month before anyone would decide to do anything about it.

In a month, he'd be in some other country.

He could create a new identity. Sure, they might find the other kids buried beneath the house, but that would be all right. He would already be someone else, somewhere else.

It seemed like a plan.

The more he went over it, the better it sounded.

It was either that or suicide, and he hated the thought of not being on earth anymore. He wasn't even sure that it would serve anything to kill himself. And Mexico was nice. He heard good things about Puerto Vallarta. Even Costa Rica was supposed to be lovely. He could just get a house on the edge of a beach and be free.

He had lots of money.

Then he remembered.

The money was in the cellar of his house.

His house was fifteen miles away.

He glanced at his backpack, sitting beneath the tree where he'd left it that afternoon.

He kept almost everything he needed with him, except the cash.

One could not be too careful.

It was nearly seven at night, still fairly light out, when he began the walk home. By one a.m., he arrived at the small house at the end of the cul-de-sac. The lights were off, but the front window seemed to reflect some yellow light from inside.

The man was usually very good about turning lights off when they were unused, but he was getting sloppy, he knew. As he stepped up to the door, he remembered that he had no key.

Of course you have no key, you fool. You locked it in the trunk with poor little Charlie.

He thought it again, Poor Little Charlie.

The boy had been doomed from the start of his life. The misfit of that little boring suburb and those boring people. He was off in his own world half the time anyway. The trunk would not be a big change for him.

Poor Charlie.

Humming his tunes, whispering his prayers, cutting the hearts out of dead cats.

That last bit was a strange sort of thing. Even as a child himself, the man had never cut hearts out of anything he'd killed.

It was too intricate.

Too *primitive.*

He preferred the torture and the pictures, but not hearts. Nothing so…so…*visceral.*

Poor crazy little misfit Charlie.

The man took the screwdriver and jammed it against the door. The old wood crackled and gave, and after a few moments, the door flew open.

He went inside, flicking on the overhead lights.

THE PLACE WAS EMPTY OF ALL THINGS.

He hated cluttered homes. He liked sparse. He liked clearings, not thickets.

There, on the bare living room floor, a little boy sat in a circle of small stones and candles. Red and white chalk markings of foreign symbols were all over the floor.

A ram's skull in the center of the circle, at the boy's feet.

Circling in and around the flames, houseflies, as if they'd been trapped by the dozens in the house all day.

Charlie had his hands up in the air, his legs crossed in front of him, his shirt off. He wore only his shorts. His skin was covered with painted symbols. Paint covered his face, one half, blood red, the other, bone white.

Charlie looked up at him.

"You left me to die."

The man grasped the wall to steady himself. "How did you…"

"You put me in that trunk and left me to die. By the power of the Loa, and Chango, my guardian, I send to you all that you were gonna do to me."

The overhead light began flickering on and off.

Charlie grinned. His voice changed, as if he'd swallowed something distasteful. "We're going to spend the night here, just you and me. That's what you want, huh?"

"How?" was all the man could say, and as he stood there, some gut level instinct told him to run.

When he turned, the door slammed shut right in front of his face. He tried the knob. The door was locked.

"Poor man," Charlie said. "Poor little misfit man."

The man turned around to face the boy.

I'll kill him. I'll kill the little creep.

Charlie's lips moved but made no sound. The candle flames rose up like spears, and a smell of sulfur permeated the room.

A growling, as of some panther, came from back near the dining room, but the man could not see for all the smoke and fire.

Then all the lights went out.

The man grew faint, unable to breathe, and felt his knees buckling under him just as he lost consciousness.

WHEN THE MAN AWOKE, HE FOUND BREATHING difficult.

The tape over his mouth prevented him from screaming, but he tried anyway.

He guessed where he was. He smelled gasoline and oil and the way trunks of cars smelled. He didn't know how the little boy had done it.

Something else was in the dark place with him. He sensed it there.

It began to growl after the second day.

Or was it a hum?

That was it.

A little boy humming.

AFTER TWO MONTHS, A NICE FAMILY BOUGHT THE old rundown car at an auction the town had twice a year.

One of their neighbors, a little boy named Charlie Carter dropped by and gave them an extra set of keys that he swore he found in the park down the street.

The new owner of the car didn't believe the little boy, but Charlie convinced him to go out and try it on the trunk, which — up until that morning — had remained unopened.

I t began as a routine call about an old drunk out at the trash cans.

Paul was new to the uniform, having only seen a couple of drug busts of the non-violent variety and one DUI.

It was that kind of town. One murder in the past six years, and one cop killed in the line of duty since 1957. He and his little sister had lived there five years, and picked it because it was fairly quiet and calm, a good hospital, good visiting nurses' association, and no one to remember them from nine years before. He had been a security guard back in St. Chappelle right after college, but it had been his dream to be a cop, and now he was, and it was good, most nights.

Most nights, he and his partner just trolled the streets for small-time hookers and signs of domestic violence.

Sometimes they arrived too late at a jumper out on the Pawtuxet Bridge. Sometimes, they watched the jump.

Paul couldn't shake the vision in his mind of the kid who had jumped two weeks back. *Damn lemmings, some of these kids. Just wanting to get out of town so bad they couldn't wait for the bus.*

"Some guy's over in front of the Swan Street apartments knocking over cans and covered with blood," the dispatcher said.

"Christ," Paul muttered. "Swan Street. Why does everything seem to happen over there?"

He glanced at his watch. Nearly midnight.

His partner, Beth, sighed and shook her head when the call came from dispatch.

"I bet I know this guy," she said, "Jesus, I bet it's this old clown."

She turned left at Wilcox, and took two quick rights until they were on Canal Road.

The night fairly steamed with humidity, and the sky threatened more rain.

Paul wiped sweat from the back of his neck.

"He used to be with the circus, a real carny-type." As she spoke, Beth managed to reach across the dash, grab a cigarette from the pack, thrust it between her lips and punch in the lighter while still keeping her eye on the road. "He spends half the year God knows where and then comes back here in the summer. We had to ship him out twice last year."

"What a night," Paul said, barely hiding disgust in his voice.

The flat-topped brick buildings, dim blue windows, dark alleys of downtown passed by as he looked out the window.

The streets were dead.

When Beth pulled the patrol car to the curb, Paul saw him.

A fringe of gray hair around a shiny bald scalp, the checkered shirttail flapping, the saggy brown pants halfway down his butt. The guy stood beneath the street-lamp, his hands over his crotch.

"He jerking off or what?" Beth asked, snorting.

"Poor old bastard," Paul said. "Can we get him to the station?"

"Easy," she said, "you just tell him we're taking him for some free drinks."

As she opened her door, she shouted, "Hey! Fazzo! It's your friend!"

The old man turned, letting go of his crotch. He hadn't been masturbating; but a dark stain grew where he'd touched. He cried out, "Friends? My friends!"

He opened his arms as if to embrace the very darkness beyond the streetlamp.

Paul got out, too, and jogged over to him. "Buddy, what you up to tonight?"

Looking at his uniform, the guy said, "I don't got nothing against cops. Believe you me. Cops are gold in my book."

Paul turned to Beth, whispering, "His breath. Jesus."

The guy said, "I just been having a drink."

"Or two," Beth said. "Look, Fazzo…"

"Fazzo the Fabulous," the guy said. "The greatest magician in the tri-state area."

"We got to take you to another bar."

"You buying?" he asked her.

"Yeah sure. You got a place up here?" Beth nodded towards the flophouse apartments beyond the streetlamp.

Fazzo nodded. "Renting it for thirty five years. Number 265."

Paul shined his flashlight all over Fazzo. "I don't see any blood on him."

"It's the piss," Beth whispered. "Someone reported it as blood. It happens sometimes. Poor old guy."

Beth escorted Fazzo to the car. She turned and nodded towards Paul; he took the signal. He went over to the back staircase. The door was open. He walked inside. The carpeting was damp and stank of mildew.

A junkie sat six steps up, skinny to the bone, leaning against the peeling wallpaper, muttering some junkie incantation.

Paul stepped around him.

The hallway above was narrow, its paint all but stripped off by time. The smell of curry; someone was cooking, and it permeated the hall.

When he got to 265, he knocked. The door was already ajar, and his fist opened it on the first knock.

There was a light somewhere at the back of the apartment.

Paul called out to see if anyone was there. He gagged when he inhaled the fetid air.

All he could see were shadows and shapes, as if the old guy's furniture had been swathed in drop cloths.

He felt along the wall for the light switch. When he found it, he turned on the light. It was a twenty-five watt bulb, which fizzled to life from the center of the living room ceiling. Its light barely illuminated the ceiling itself.

The chairs and couch in the room were covered with old newspapers, some of them damp from urine. The old man hadn't even bothered to make it to the bathroom anymore. There was human excrement behind the couch. Empty whiskey bottles along the floor in front of the television set.

Paul found it hard to ignore the stench of the place.

Beth arrived at that point. "I got him cuffed, not that he needs it. He fell asleep as soon as I sat him down in the car. Jesus!" She covered her mouth and nose. "I thought he'd been living on the street."

Her eyes widened as she took in the other sights.

"Look at this," Paul pointed to the window, shining his flashlight across it.

It was black with dead flies, two or three layers thick.

He continued to the kitchen. "Should I open the fridge, you think?"

"Sure," Beth said. "Looks like Fazzo the Fabulous is going to end up in state hospital for awhile. What the hell?" She picked something up off a shelf and held it up. "Paul, look at this."

In her hands, a wig with long, thin hair. "You think Fazzo steps out on Saturday night in pearls and pumps?"

Paul shook his head, and turned back to the refrigerator. He opened the door, slowly. A blue light within it came on. The refrigerator was stacked three trays high with old meat—clotted steaks, green hamburger, what looked like a roast with a fine coating of mold on it. "Shit," he said, noticing the dead flies encrusted on the shinier cuts of meat. "This guy's lost it. He's not just a drunk. He needs serious help."

Beth walked into the bathroom, and started laughing.

"What's up?" he asked, moving around the boxes in the kitchen. Paul glanced to the open door.

The bathroom light was bright.

"It's clean in here. It's so clean you can eat off it. It must be the one room he never goes in." Beth leaned through the open doorway and gestured for Paul to come around the corner. "This is amazing."

Paul almost tripped over a long-dead plant as he reached her.

THE BATHROOM MIRROR WAS SPARKLING, AS WAS THE toilet, the pink tiles. Blue and pink guest soap were laid out in fake seashells on either side of the brass spigots of the faucet.

Written in lipstick on the mirror: a phone number.

For a second, he thought he saw something small and green skitter across the shiny tiles and dive behind the shower curtain. A lizard?

Paul went to pull the shower curtain aside, and that's when he found the woman's torso.

PAUL WASHED HIS FACE SIX TIMES THAT NIGHT AT THE station. He wished he hadn't found the torso. It was the sort of image he had only seen in forensics textbooks, never in living color, never that muddy rainbow effect, never all the snakey turns and twists.

He had to put it out of his mind. He didn't want to think about what was left of the woman in the tub.

He had not seen her face, and he was glad. She wasn't entirely human to him without a face.

Her name was Shirley. Fazzo the Fabulous told him. "Shirley Chastain. She was from the Clearwater District. She ran a dry cleaners with her mother. I thought she was a nice sort of girl right up until I cut her. I dug deep in her. She had a gut like a wet velvet curtain, thick, but smooth, smooth, smooth. She had a funny laugh. A tinkly bell kind of laugh." He had sobered up and was sitting in county jail. Paul stood outside his cell with the county coroner, who took notes as Fazzo spoke. "She had excellent taste in shoes, but no real sense of style. Her skin was like sponge cake."

"You eat her skin?" The coroner asked.

Fazzo laughed. "Hell, no. I mean it *felt* like sponge cake. The way sponge cake used to be, like foam, like perfect foam when you pull it apart." He kneaded the air with his fingers. "I'm not a freakin' cannibal."

Paul asked, "You were a clown or something? Back in your circus days, I mean?"

"No, sir. I wasn't anything like that. I was the world's greatest magician. You know, a great magician — one of the best ever — told me, when I was a kid, he said, 'Fazzo, you're gonna be the biggest, you got what it takes.' Didn't mean shit, but my oh my it sure did feel good to hear it from him."

"I guess you must've been something," Paul said.

Fazzo glanced from the coroner to Paul. "Why you here, kid? You busted me. What are you gawking for?"

"I don't know," Paul said. "You kind of remind me of
my dad I guess." It was a joke; Paul glanced at the coroner,
and then back at Fazzo. Last time Paul saw his dad, his
dad's face was split open from the impact of the crash.

"Shit," the old guy dismissed this with a wave. "I know
all about your old man, kid. It's like tattoos on your body.
Everybody's story is on their body. Dad and Mom in car
wreck, but you were driving. Little sister, too, thrown out
of the car. I see it all, kid. You got a secret don't you? That's
right, I can see it plain as day. You should never have gone
in 265, cause you're the type it wants. You're here because
you got caught."

"*I* got caught?"

"You went in 265 and you got caught. I pass it to you,
kid. You get the door prize."

"You're some sick puppy," Paul said, turning away.

Fazzo shouted after him, "Don't ever go back there,
kid. You can always get caught and get away. Just like a
fish on the hook. Just don't fight it. That always reels 'em
in!" Paul glanced back at Fazzo. The old man's eyes became
slivers. "It's magic, kid. Real magic. Not the kind on stage
or the kind in storybooks, but the real kind. It costs life
sometimes to make magic. You're already caught, though.
Don't go back there. Next time, it's you." Then Fazzo
closed his eyes, and began humming to himself as if to
block out some other noise.

It sickened Paul further, thinking what a waste of a
life. What a waste of a damned life, not just the dead
woman, but this old clown. Paul said, "Why'd you do it?"

Fazzo stopped his humming. He pointed his finger at
Paul and said, "I was like you, kid. I didn't believe in

anything. That's why it gets you. You believe in something, it can't get you. You don't believe, and it knows you got an empty space in your heart just waiting to be filled. You believe in heaven, kid?"

Paul remained silent.

"It's gonna get you, then, kid. You got to believe in heaven if you want to get out of 265."

Then, Fazzo told his story. Paul would've left, but Fazzo had a way of talking that hooked you. Paul leaned against the wall, thinking he'd take off any minute, but he listened.

"I was famous, kid, sure, back before you were born, and I toured with the Seven Stars of Atlantis Circus, doing some sideshow crap like sword-swallowing and fire-eating before I got the brilliant idea to start bringing up pretty girls to saw in half or make disappear. This was way back when, kid, and there wasn't a lot of entertainment in towns with names like Wolf Creek or Cedar Bend or Silk Hope. The Seven Stars was the best they got, and I turned my act into a showcase.

"I was hot, kid. I blew in like a Nor'easter and blew up like a firecracker. Imagine these hands—these hands—as I directed the greatest magic show in the tri-state area, the illusions, kid, the tricks of the trade, the boxes with trap-doors that opened below the stage, the nights of shooting stars as I exploded one girl-filled cage after another. They turned into white doves flying out across the stunned faces of children and middle-aged women and old men who had lost their dreams but found them inside the tent. Found them in my magic show! It was colossal, stupendous, magnificent!

"I gave them a night of fucking heaven, kid. We turned a dog into a great woolly mammoth, we turned a horse into a unicorn, we turned a heron into a boy and then into a lizard, all within twenty minutes, and then when it was all done, the boy became rabbit and I handed it to some thrilled little girl in the audience to take home for a pet or for supper.

"Once, traveling during a rainy spring, the whole troupe got caught in mud. I used my knowledge of traps and springs to get us all out of there—and was rewarded with becoming the Master of Ceremonies. It was practically religious, kid, and I was the high priest!

"But the problem was, at least for me, that I believed in none of it. I could not swallow my own lies. The magic was a fake. I knew where the animals were hid away to be sprung up, and the little boy, bounced down into a pile of sawdust while a snowy egret took his place, or an iguana popped up wearing a shirt just like the one the boy had on. The boy could take it, he was good. Best assistant I ever had. The woman, too, she was great—saw her in half and she screamed like she was giving birth right on the table—not a beauty except in the legs. She had legs that went right on up to her chin.

"When she got hit by the bus in Memphis, everything changed for me, and I didn't want to do the act again. Joey wanted to keep going, but I told him we were finished. I loved that kid. So, we quit the act, and I went to do a little entertaining in clubs, mostly strip joints. Tell a couple jokes, do a few tricks with feather fans. Voila! Naked girls appear from behind my cape! It was not the grandeur of the carnival, but it paid the rent, and Joey had a roof over his head and we both had food in our mouths.

"One month I was a little late on the rent, and we got thrown out. That's when I came here, and we got the little place on Swan Street. Well, we didn't get it, it got us.

"But it got you, too, didn't it, kid? It wasn't just you walking in to 265, it was that you been preparing your whole life for 265. That other cop, she lives in another world already, 265 couldn't grab her. But it could grab you, and it did, huh.

"I knew as soon as I saw you under the streetlamp.

"I recognized you from before.

"You remember before?

"Hey, you want to know why I killed that woman? You really want to know?

"Watch both my hands when I tell you. Remember, I'm a born prestidigitator.

"Here's why: sometimes, you get caught in the doorway.

"Sometimes, when the door comes down, someone doesn't get all the way out.

"You want to find the other half of her body?

"It's in 265.

"Only no one's gonna find it but you, kid.

"You're a member of the club."

PAUL WAS OFF-SHIFT AT 2, AND WENT TO GRAB A BEER

at the Salty Dog minutes before it closed. Jacko and Ronny got there ahead of him and bought the first round.

"Hell," Paul said. "It was like he sawed her in two."

"He saw her in two? What's that mean?" Jacko asked. He was already drunk.

"No, he sawed her in two. He was a magician. A real loser," Paul shook his head, shivering. "You should've seen it."

Jacko turned to Ronny, winking. "He saw her sawed and we should've seen it."

"Cut it out. It was…unimaginable."

Ronny tipped his glass. "Here's to you, Paulie boy. You got your first glimpse of the real world. It ain't pretty."

Jacko guzzled his beer, coughing when he came up for air. "Yeah, I remember my first torso. Man, it was hacked bad."

"I thought nothing like that happened around here," Paul said. "I thought this was a quiet town."

Jacko laughed, slapping him on the back. "It doesn't happen much, kid. But it always happens once. You got to see hell at least once when you work this job."

Paul took a sip of beer. It tasted sour. He set the mug down. "He called it heaven." But was that really what Fazzo the Fabulous had said? Heaven? Or had he said you had to believe in heaven for 265 to not touch you?

Jacko said, "Christ, forget about it Paulie. Hey, how's that little Marie?"

Paul inhaled the smoke of the bar, like he needed something more inside him than the thought of 265. "She's okay."

~

WHEN HE GOT HOME TO THEIR LITTLE PLACE ON Grove, with the front porch light on, he saw her silhouette in the window.

He unlocked the door, noticing that the stone step had gotten scummy from damp and moss.

After he stepped inside, he glanced over to where his sister sat in the semi-dark.

"Hey, Marie," he said.

"I couldn't get the TV to work."

"Sorry, kid," he said, trying not to show exhaustion. "I'll get it fixed tomorrow. You should be asleep."

"I should be," she said.

"How was Mrs. Jackson?"

"Her usual," Marie said.

"How's the pain?"

She didn't answer.

Paul went over and kissed his little sister on the fore-head. "I need to go to bed. You should, too."

"I hate what you did to me," she whispered.

She said this more than he cared to remember.

"I hate it, too," he said. Trying not to remember why she could say it in the first place. "You keep your oxygen on all day?"

She may have nodded; he couldn't tell in the dim light.

"I hate what I did to myself," she whispered, but he wasn't sure. She may have said, "I hate what I do to myself." Or, "I hate what I want to do to myself." It was late. He'd had a couple of beers. She had whispered.

The three possibilities of what she said played through his mind every now and then, and in the next few days (staying up late, staring at the ceiling, hearing the hum of the machines that helped keep his beautiful sister alive) he was sure she'd said the last thing.

I hate what I want to do to myself.

THE CLEAN UP CREW HAD BEEN THROUGH, photographers got their pictures, the apartment was cordoned off.

Paul stood in the doorway, giving a brief nod to one of the detectives.

He glanced around the apartment; it was trashed.

The bathroom light seeped like pink liquid from under the door.

He didn't go in.

He didn't want to.

He didn't want to think about the torso or the magician or even the lizard he'd seen scuttle into the bathtub.

But it was all he thought about for the next six months.

ON HIS NIGHTS OFF, HE'D SIT IN THE LIVING ROOM with Marie and watch television. Marie loved television, and besides her books and magazines, it was the only thing that got her out of herself.

"I saw a great movie last night," she told him.

He glanced over.

The small thin plastic tubing of the oxygen hung from beneath her nostrils, hooked up to the wide machine with blinking lights. The braces on her arms connected to a brace around her torso that nearly made her look robotic.

Still, she looked like Marie under all the metal and wire and tubing.

Pretty. Blond hair cut short. Her eyes bright, occasionally.

Sometimes, he thought, she was happy.

"Yeah?" he said. "Which one?"

"I can't remember the name. It was amazing. A man and woman so in love, but they were divided by time and space. But he wanted her so badly. He sacrificed his life for her. But they had this one...moment. I cried like an idiot."

"You should be watching happy movies," Paul said, somewhat cheerfully.

"Happy or sad doesn't matter," Marie said. "That's where you mix things up too much. Happy and sad are symptoms. It's the thing about movies and books. It's that glimpse of heaven. No one loves anyone like they do in movies and books. No one hurts as wonderfully. I saw this other movie about a woman in a car wreck — just like ours — and she couldn't move from the neck down. Her family spurned her. A friend had to take care of her. She thought of killing herself. Then, the house caught on fire. She had to crawl outside. A little boy helped her. The little boy couldn't talk, and they became friends. But she'd lost everything.."

"I don't like things that make you sad," he said.

"This," Marie nodded to the machines and the walls. "This makes me sad. The stories get me out of this. They get me into heaven. Even if it's only for a few minutes, it's enough. You want to know why people cry at movies even when the movie is happy? I've thought about this a lot. It's because life is never that good. They know that when the screen goes dark, they have to go back to the life off-screen where nothing is as good. People who have cancer in movies have moments of heaven. People who have cancer in real life just have cancer. People in car wrecks in movies and stories get heaven. In real life..."

"So you feel like you're in heaven when you read a story?"

She nodded. "Or see a good movie. Not the whole movie, just a few minutes. But a few minutes of heaven is better than no heaven at all." She closed her eyes for a moment. "You know what I dream of at night?"

"No machines?" he said.

She shook her head. "No. I dream that everything is exactly like it is, only it's absolutely wonderful. Then, I wake up."

"Some dream," he said.

"Paul," she said as if just realizing something important. "I know why people kill themselves. It isn't because they hate anyone. It isn't because they want to escape. It's because they think there's no heaven. Why go on if there's no heaven to get to?"

PAUL WENT TO SEE FAZZO THE FABULOUS ON DEATH

Row. Fazzo had gained some weight in prison, and looked healthier.

"I have to know something," Paul said.

"Yeah, kid?" Fazzo looked at him carefully. "You want to know all about 265, don't you? You been there since I got arrested?"

Paul nodded. Then, as if this were a revelation, he said, "You're sober."

"I have to be in here. No choice. The twelve step program of incarceration…Let me tell you, 265 is a living breathing thing. It's not getting rented out any time soon, either. It waits for the one it marked. You're it, kid. It's waiting for you, and you know it. And there's no use resisting its charms."

"Why did you kill that woman?"

"The forty million dollar question, kid. The forty million dollar question."

"Forget it then."

"Okay, you look like a decent kid. I'll tell you. She was a sweet girl, but she wanted too much heaven. She and me both. Life's job is not to give you too much heaven. But she got a taste for it, just like I did. You get addicted to it. So," Fazzo gestured with his hands in a sawing motion. "She got in but the door came down. I mean, I know I cut into her, using my hands. I know that. Only I wasn't trying to cut into her. I liked her. She was sweet. I was trying to keep it from slamming down so hard on her. They thought I was insane at first, and were going to put me in one of those hospitals. But all the doctors pretty much confirmed that my marbles were around. Only all that boozing I did made me sound nuts."

Fazzo leaned over. "You got someone you love, kid?"

Paul shrugged. "I got my little sister. She's it."

"No other family?"

"I got cousins out of state. Why?"

"No folks?"

Paul shook his head.

"Okay, now it's clear why 265 chose you, kid. You're like me, practically no strings, right? But one beloved in your life. Me, I had Joey."

Paul grimaced.

"Hey!" Fazzo flared up. "It wasn't like that! Joey was a kid whose family threw him out with the garbage. I gave him shelter, and that was it. Wasn't nothing funny about it. Sick thing to think." Then, after a minute he calmed. "I gave Joey what was in 265 and everything was good for awhile. Joey, he had some problems."

"Like what?"

Fazzo shrugged. "We all got problems. Joey, he had leukemia. He was gonna die." Then it was as if a light blinked on in the old man's eyes. "You know about Joey, don't you? It touched you in there, and it let you know about him. Am I right? When it touches you, it lets you know about who's there and who's not, and maybe about who's coming soon. You know about Joey?"

Paul shook his head.

Fazzo seemed disappointed. "Sometimes I think it was all an illusion, like my bag of tricks. In here, all these bricks and bars and grays. Sometimes I forget what it was like to go through the door."

"What happened to Joey?"

"He's still there. I put him there."

"You killed him?"

"Holy shit, kid, you think I'd kill a little boy I loved as if he were my own son? I told you, I put him there, through 265. He's okay there. They treat him decent."

"He's not in the apartment," Paul said, as if trying to grasp something.

"You want me to spell it out for you, kid? 265 is the door to Heaven. You don't have to believe me, and it ain't the Heaven from Jesus Loves Me Yes I Know. It's a better Heaven than that. It's the Heaven to beat all Heavens." Fazzo spat at the glass that separated them. "You come here with questions like a damn reporter and you don't want answers. You want answers you go into that place. You won't like what you find, but it's too late for you. 265 is yours, kid. Go get it. And whoever it is you love, if it's that sister of yours, make sure she gets in it. Make sure she gets Heaven. Maybe that's what it's all about. Maybe for someone to get Heaven, someone else has to get Hell."

"Like that woman?"

Fazzo did not say a word. He closed his eyes and began humming.

Startled, he opened his eyes again and said, "Kid! You got to get home now!"

"What?"

"Now!" Fazzo shouted and smashed his fist against the glass.

The guard standing in the corner behind him rushed up to him, grabbing him by the wrists. "Kid, it's your sister it wants, not you. You got caught, but it's your sister it wants. And there's only one way to get into heaven! Only one way, kid! Go get her now!"

PAUL DIDN'T RUSH HOME.

He didn't like giving Fazzo the benefit of the doubt. He'd be on shift in another hour, and usually he spent this time by catching a burger and a Coke before going into the station.

He drove the murky streets as the sun lowered behind the stacks of castle-like apartment buildings on Third Street.

It looked as if it would rain in a few minutes.

Trash lay in heaps around the alleys, and he saw the faces of the walking wounded along the stretch of boulevards that were Sunday afternoon empty.

He passed the apartments on Swan Street, doing his best not to glance up to the second floor.

265.

No one would live there, not after a woman's torso was found in the bathtub.

Even squatters would stay away.

Paul drove home. He just wanted to see if she was watching her movies or reading.

He didn't believe Fazzo.

IN THE LIVING ROOM, THE TELEVISION WAS ON, BUT without sound.

Soft music played from the bathroom.

Paul knocked on the bathroom door. "Marie?"

After four knocks, he opened it.

The machines were off.

She lay in the tub of red water. On her back. Her face beneath the water's surface like a picture he'd seen once, when they'd both been children, of a mermaid in a lake.

Scratched crudely on the tile with the edge of the scissors she'd used to cut herself free from life, the words:

I don't believe in Heaven.

IT WAS ONLY YEARS LATER, WHEN PAUL SAW THE ITEM in the papers about Fazzo the Fabulous finally getting the chair, after years of living on Death Row, that he thought about 265 again.

He heard, too, that the apartments on Swan Street were being torn down within a week of Fazzo's execution.

Paul had led what he would've called a quiet life. He'd been on the force for fifteen years, and the town had not erupted in anything more than the occasional domestic battle or crack house fire.

He kept Marie's machines in his apartment, and often watched television in the living room feeling as if he were less alone.

But one evening, he went down there, down to Swan Street, down the rows of slums and squats where the city had turned off even the streetlamps.

Standing in front of the old apartments, he glanced at the windows of 265. The boards had come out, and the windows were empty sockets in the face of brick.

He carefully walked up the half-burnt staircase, around the rubble of bricks and pulpy cardboard, stepping over the fallen boards with the nails sticking straight up.

The apartment no longer had a door. When he went inside, the place had been stripped of all appliance.

The stink of urine and feces permeated the apartment, and he saw the residue of countless squatters who had spent nights within the walls of 265.

Graffiti covered half the wall by the bathroom, all of it spray-painted cuss words, kids' names, lovers' names...

Scrawled in blue across the doorway to the bathroom, the words:

THE SEVEN STARS

The bathroom had been less worked-over. The shower curtain had been torn down, as had the medicine cabinet. But the toilet, cracked and brown, still remained, as did the bathtub and shower nozzle.

Paul closed his eyes, remembering the woman's bloody torso in the tub.

Remembering *Marie in the pink water.*

When he opened his eyes, he said, "All right. You have me. You took Marie. What is it you want?"

He sat on the edge of the tub, waiting for something. He laughed to himself, thinking of how stupid this was, how he was old enough to know better...how Fazzo the Fabulous had butchered some woman up here, and that was all. How Marie had killed herself at their home, and that was all.

There was no Heaven.

He laughed to himself. Reached in his pocket and drew out a pack of cigarettes. Lit one up, and inhaled.

Sometime, just after midnight, he heard the humming

of the flies, and the drip drop of rusty water as it splashed into the tub.

In a moment, he saw the light come up, from the edge of the forest, near the great tree, and two iguanas scuttled across the moss-covered rocks. It came in flashes at first, as if the skin of the world were being stripped away layer by layer, until the white bone of life came through, and then the green of a deep wood. The boy was there, and Paul recognized him without ever having seen his picture.

"You've finally come to join us, then," the boy said. "Marie told me all about you."

"Marie? Is she here?" Paul's tongue dried in his mouth, knowing that this was pure hallucination, but wanting it to be true.

The boy—and it was Joey, Fazzo's friend—nodded, holding his hand out.

The world had turned liquid around him, and for a moment he felt he focused a camera lens in his mind, as the world solidified again.

The great white birds stood like sentries off at some distance. A deer in the wood glanced up at the new intruder. He saw something else, like a veil, through which he could see another person.

Someone watched him from the other side of the gossamer fabric.

Lightning flashed across the green sky. A face emerged in the forest—from the trees and the fern and the birds and the lizards. A face that was neither kind nor cruel.

And then, he saw her — Marie — running to him so fast it took his breath away. She was still twenty, but she had none of the deformities of body, and the machines no longer purred beside her. "Paul! You've come! I knew you would!"

She grabbed his hand, squeezing it. "I've waited forever for you, you should've come earlier."

Joey nodded. "See? I told you he'd come eventually."

Paul grabbed his sister in his arms, pressing as close to her as he could. Tears burst from his eyes, and he felt the warmth of her skin, the smell of her hair, the smell of her —the fragrance of his beautiful, vibrant sister. He no longer cared what illusion had produced this, he did not ever want to let go of her.

But she pulled back, finally. "Paul, you're crying. Don't." She reached up and touched the edge of his cheek.

"I thought I'd never see you again," he said.

"Yes, you did," Marie said. "You believed in 265 all along. They told me you did. They knew you did."

"Who are they?" he asked.

Marie glanced at Joey. "I can't tell you."

"No names," Joey whispered a warning.

The rain splintered through the forest cover like slivers of glass, all around them, and the puddles that formed were small mirror shards reflecting the sky.

Marie grasped Paul's hand.

He could not get over her warmth. "How…how did you get here?"

She put a finger to her lips. "Shh. Isn't it enough that we're here now, together?"

Paul nodded his head.

"It won't last long," Marie said, curiously looking up at the glassy rain as it poured around them.

"The rain?" he asked, feeling that this was better than

any heaven he could imagine. This was the Heaven of all heavens.

"No. Not the rain. I mean about you being here, that's what won't last. Each time is only a glimpse. Like striking a match, it only burns for a short while."

"I don't understand," Paul said.

When Marie looked up at him all he felt was joy. He had never remembered feeling so alive, so much part of the world, so warm with love.

Again, his eyes blurred with tears.

"It's only a glimpse," she whispered. "Each time. When Fazzo was executed, he was the sacrifice. But they need another one. This time, they want the sacrifice to be here, on the threshold. It works longer that way. Just one. Each time. For you to be here."

Her mood changed, as she smiled like a child on her birthday. "Oh, but Paul, it's so wonderful to see you. Next time you come I'll show you the rivers of gold, and the way the trees whisper the secret of immortality. The birds can guide us across the fire mountains. And I have friends here, too, I want you to meet."

"I don't understand," Paul whispered, but the rain began coming down harder, and a glass wall of rain turned shiny and then melted, as he felt her hand grab for him through the glass.

He was sitting in the darkness of the bathroom at 265, a young woman's hand in his, cut off at the wrist because the door had come down too hard, too soon.

～

For Paul, the hardest one was the first one.

He found her down in Brickton, near the factories. She was not pretty, and looked to him to be at the end of her days from drugs and too many men and too many pimps beating her up. She had burn marks on her arms, and when she got into his car, he thought: I won't be doing anything too awful. Not too awful. It'll be like putting an animal out of its misery.

"You a cop?" she asked.

"No way. I'm just a very desperate guy."

He told her he knew this place, an old apartment, not real pretty, but it was private and it got him off.

When they reached Swan Street, she laughed. "I been in these apartments before. Christ, they look better now than I remember them."

He nodded. "Will you be impressed if I tell you I own them?"

"Really? Wow. You must be loaded."

Paul shrugged. "They went for cheap. The city was going to tear them down. I got that blocked, bought them, fixed them up a bit."

"Looks empty to me."

"I only just started getting them ready for tenants," he said.

They went upstairs.

Inside the apartment, he offered her a drink.

"All right," she said.

"Need to use the bathroom?" he asked, opening the freezer door to pull out the ice tray.

"If you don't mind," she said.

"Go ahead. Take a shower if you feel like it."

"Well, you're buying," the woman said.

When he heard the bathroom door close, Paul took the key from the dresser.

STANDING IN FRONT OF THE BATHROOM DOOR, HE waited until he heard the shower turn on.

He checked his watch.

It was two minutes to midnight.

From the shower, she shouted, "Honey? You mind bringing my drink in and scrubbing my back?"

He opened the bathroom door.

Steam poured from under the shower curtain.

Once inside, he turned and locked the door.

He put the key in his breast pocket.

"That you?" she asked.

"Yeah," Paul said. "I'll join you in just a few seconds."

He crouched down.

Beneath the sink, a large wooden box.

Opening it, he lifted the cloth within.

He grabbed the hand-ax that lay there, and then closed the box.

PAUL SET THE SMALL AX ON TOP OF THE SINK.

He unbuttoned his shirt, and took it off. He hung it on the hook by the door.

Then, he stepped out of his shoes. Undid his belt, and let his trousers fall to the floor.

"Baby?" she asked.

"In a minute," he said. "We'll have some fun."

He pulled off his socks and then his briefs.

Grabbed the hand-ax.

Looked at himself naked in the mirror, ax in fist.

For a second, the glass flashed like lightning, and he saw Marie's face there.

A glimpse.

Then, he pulled back the shower curtain and began opening the door to Heaven.

ICE PALACE

I once helped murder a boy when I was nineteen. Only we didn't think of ourselves as boys back then.

It was in college, at a university in the mountains of Virginia, when the snow had piled up and the parties were in full swing.

I lived with my brothers—we weren't blood relations except through the college fraternity system.

It was February, and certain aspects of fraternity hazing were not yet complete. It was always in the harshest part of the season that the sadistic rituals took place on campus, from paddling to raiding to a particularly cruel torture called Ice Palace.

I was just buttoning up my shirt, about to start shaving, when Nate Wick, known as the Wicked Wick or the Flaccid Wick, grabbed me by the collar and slammed me against the wall; the whole world shook and I cussed him out something fierce; his face was all scrunched up like he was about to cry. He had hair growing from his ears even at twenty-one, and fat cheeks like a cherub gone to seed. I socked him in the jaw, 'cause he could be crazy sometimes, even if he *was* my fraternity brother. He took the blow pretty good, and my fist ached like a son of a bitch, and he dropped on my bed, right on the wet towel, so it made a smack kind of sound, and if he hadn't been naked I'd have grabbed *him* by *his* collar and heave-hoed him right onto the balcony, where it was twenty below and iced smooth.

"Damn it, Wick," I said, "you drive me, you know that? You drive me, Christ."

"Drive you what? Nuts?"

"You just drive me, that's all," I said, finally catching my breath.

Nate said, slyly, "I know what you want, Underdog. I know what you want." I felt my face going red. Something disturbed me about his comment.

"What the jizz you shittin'?" Stan, ever the poet, said from the doorway to my room. Stan was naked, too, which was pretty much how the guys went around on a Saturday morning in February when the nearest open road to the girls' college was ten miles away.

It was funny, being as generally modest as I was, how I'd got used to all this flaunted nakedness in the ice-cold mornings. Myself, I never got out of the showers except with a big blue towel around my waist, and never left my room except with a shirt and khakis on.

Nate began laughing, and I figured given his jugface that I hadn't even caused him a moment's pain; but I was still mad 'cause I hated being surprised like that.

Everything in that frat house was a surprise attack, especially on Big Weekends.

Nate was on edge on account of his girl might not be making it down for Fancy Dress, so there was a chance he might be the dateless wonder.

Nate said, "Look, Underdog, we got the pledges coming over for Ice Palace, and you look like a queer from Lynchburg."

"If that's what you think, jerk-off, then you better not lie naked on my bed too long with that come-hither look on your face," I said.

I went back to shaving in the bowl I'd put beneath the mirror in my room for privacy; it saved me from running to the communal and much-pissed-upon bathroom every time I needed to shave or wash.

Stan said, "Fuck the fuck it very."

It was a line he said often, sober or drunk, and I couldn't figure it out for the life of me. He had patches of hair up and down his body, armpits to knees, like he had some ape pattern baldness problem. "I can't wait for tonight, girls, I'm gonna get me some fine pussy, *fine* pussy."

"Underdog," Nate addressed me in his usual manner, "the Hose Queen's coming down tonight. You want to get laid?"

"No thanks, and get out of here, willya?"

This particular winter semester, in my second year, Nate, who was my big brother in the House, wanted me to learn how to be a man as only Nate knew how.

It wasn't enough that I was flunking Physics for Poets because of the midweek grain parties, nor that I had no interest in cow punching or whore hopping.

Nate was a wild man and rich redneck from Alabama,

and his life was something to marvel at. He had learned the ropes of human sexuality at twelve from his babysitter; at seventeen, he'd saved an entire boatload of immigrants off the coast of Bermuda — losing three toes in the process.

He *knew* life, how to live it, which paths to go down, when and where to get a hard-on and what to do about it — and with whom. The bizarre part was, he was an honors student, his old man ran one of the growing tobacco companies, and he never, *ever* had a hangover.

Somebody stuck a condom in the scrambled eggs that morning, a typical frat joke, so I passed on breakfast and headed up to the Hill to do some studying on campus.

I didn't have a date for the Fancy Dress Ball that night, even though I'd bought two tickets well in advance thinking this girl I knew from high school, Colleen, might want to go, or maybe I'd meet someone else last minute. But Colleen was not to be wooed down to what she called the "last bastion of the old South."

I called three girls I knew "down the road," but each had had a date since October. One of them was kind enough to say she could set me up with this really homely girl who majored in Chemistry. I passed, and figured I'd get some studying done for once, and let them all go to hell. I was determined to spend the day studying, not scrounging for dates or hazing freshmen.

But Nate was not one to give up easily in his quest to keep me from doing anything productive. He hunted me down on campus, shut my American history book for me, sat on the edge of my desk, and said, "You missed Ice Palace."

"Big deal. Jesus H., quit following me around like some kind of retriever."

"Jonno told a good one. Got us laughing right off. Bug Boy practically froze to death, we had to let him off after about half an hour, just 'cause we were getting bored watching his lips turn purple. Only one part left."

I groaned. "Yeah, yeah, the crowning of the King. It's like being with Nazis in kindergarten."

"Hey, it takes a special kind of guy to be King of the Palace." Nate Wick had a snarly way of talking that was both seductive and distancing, as if he were an untamed dog waiting for the right master. "Ice Palace is almost as good as fish dunking."

"I hate the whole thing. Ice Palace could make one of them sick."

"You liked it well enough last year."

"Well, I was drunk last year. I liked lots of things then."

"Well, piss on you, Underdog. Sometimes I wish the old you would come back, the one that would stay out all night and really howl." But his mood changed again. "We're gonna kidnap Lewis," he said, like he was planning out the day in his head. He grinned so bright I thought the sun had come out from the gray sky outside the window.

"When?"

"This afternoon. Few hours."

"Shit," I said. "Jesus, of all days. He's your King? Christ, Wick, that poor son of a bitch won't last three hours in the cold. He's got bronchial asthma, he'll come down with something." The truth was, I was protective of Stewart Lewis, who didn't even have the hapless luck to be a brain, for he was skinny and homely and not too bright; if he hadn't been a legacy, he would've gotten blackballed by sixty percent of the House. But his old man was a major brother back in his day, so the frat had no choice, because it was in the charter to take legacies no matter what. I had known Stewart Lewis back at St. Sebastian's, the Episcopal school I'd gone to before college. Lewis was always a weenie, always sick, always a mama's boy, always something not so good.

Nate dismissed Lewis with a snap, and then a slap on the desk. "He's a Spam, don't worry about him. We're gonna take him to Crawford's Dump, stick him in the snow, pay Donkeyman to watch him, tie him up, nothing bad. We won't leave him there all night, you fiend. Just a couple of hours, and then I'll go get him in time for Fancy Dress. I doubt he's got a date, though. He's such a Spam. Maybe we'll write on him. The usual. Scare the kid a little. Just a shit speck. He'll get to wear his Jockeys, whatta you want? Whatta you want?"

"You always sound homo to me when you talk about it," I said, hoping to get him angry. I was only a sophomore, but I'd hated hazing so much from the year before —I'd been too blotto to protest much—that I felt very protective of the poor freshmen pledges who went along with any idiotic torture that seniors like Nate devised.

"Maybe I am homo, Underdog. Wanta suck it to find out?" Here he whipped out his thing, which was not the most unusual sight between frat brothers, and was, perhaps, a big reason why we were all so homophobic.

Then he put it back in his trousers, zipped up, and said, "You gonna go tonight?"

"Why? You want to buy my ticket?"

"Just wondering. I'm not always as insensitive as I seem, buttface."

It started to snow again, and the wind picked up outside, whistling around the old brick and columns along the colonnade; feather flakes seesawed beyond the beveled glass of the windows. It was an ancient campus, from the 1700s, all columns and Greek Parthenon-types and mountain vistas, and I wished I was somewhere, anywhere, else.

"Look," Nate said, "Helen's coming up from Hollins. She likes you. She said she wants to see you." Helen was his girl friend, a pretty girl who, for some reason, idolized Nate, possibly because she was more unbalanced than she seemed—there was a hint of this in her Sylvia Plath-like scribblings. I thought she was too good for him.

"That's nice," I said. "Look, Nate, I don't want Lewis to go to Ice Palace. He'll get sick. If Dean Trask hears about it, we could get shut down. Think about that. I mean, a half hour of Ice Palace is one thing, but three or four hours, and it's snowing…it's not that funny."

Nate laughed, drumming his fists into the desk. I'd seen him pummel a stray dog like that once, just because the dog was in his way.

That was how he used his fists most of the time.

He said, "I think it's a goddamn laugh riot."

I avoided the frat house until six, when hunger got the best of me. I was wary of most of my brothers, because I wasn't good at taking any kind of teasing, and that seemed to be their primary business in college.

When I entered the foyer, I smelled the steaks—it was a special night, Fancy Dress Ball and all that, and so our cook was doing it up good, steak and asparagus and biscuits and potatoes and fruit and apple pie.

Most of the brothers had taken their dates out to dinner, but the poorer among us sat at the long tables, not yet dressed in black tie, with dates astride hard-backed chairs. Plain girls, too, for the most part, until, upstairs, in a guarded bathroom, they would make up and spray, Vaseline their teeth for smiles and for other, more urgent desires, later; spruced with expensive, oversize gowns, transforming from ordinary faces and bodies to creatures of unconscionable beauty, perhaps gaudy in the garish light of the upstairs bathroom, but almost mythic, the Woman in All Her Glorious Aspects, in the dimmed, squinting light over at the student center, where the dance would take place.

Nate called out, "Underdog!"

He was at the last table, with Helen at his side. She looked up briefly, and then down at her plate again — a flash of curiosity about me, about what I'd been up to since summer.

She was skinny—looked like she had starved herself for this one night—and she'd greased her hair back around her ears with some sort of conditioner.

I went over and took a chair, grabbed some slop, and lopped it on my plate. "Helen," I said.

"Hey, Charlie," she said sweetly, her accent growing more Southern with each year she spent in Virginia. She did not look up from her plate; it was obvious she hadn't eaten.

Nate lip-farted. "Call him Underdog. Humble but lovable."

I smiled at Nate. "Things go okay with Lewis?"

Nate winked. "Fine, fine."

"He around?"

"Yeah. I don't know. I guess he was upset."

I wasn't sure whether to believe Nate or not, but Helen must've detected my doubt. She said, "He said he was going to a movie. He was very upset. Y'all are so dang insensitive. It's what I hate, absolutely hate, about y'all being in a fraternity and all."

"Helen's on the rag," Nate half-whispered, loud enough for all six tables to hear.

I looked to Helen, and reached my hand across to touch hers because I felt so bad for her at that moment, stuck with Nate,

Nate who bragged about doing her on his water bed, about muff-diving her in the backseat of her father's Continental, taking her every which way but loose up in the carillon tower of chapel when she didn't want it but loved it anyway.

I didn't know Helen well, but I wanted to touch her more than anything.

Helen glanced up at me, her eyes dry.

Nate was clanking his fork on the side of his plate. He was always jealous when it came to Helen, and he must've seen the way she looked at me.

"Why don't you just fuck her?" he asked, shoving himself away from the table, his chair falling backward.

He was drunk; so that was it. He stomped across the room, and went upstairs.

Helen said, "I hate him."

"Nah," I said, "he's a jerk sometimes. But he has his good side."

Helen laughed. "No, he doesn't. I don't know why I'm even here."

She shut her eyes, her face taut, hands clenched in fists. "Because I'm a good girl. Because I do what I'm told."

She said it like it was taking her medicine, an antidote to some other, more profound venom. "I'm not really a very good girl. Will you go with me tonight? I don't want to go with him. I'd rather die, frankly. He brings out the worst in me."

THERE ARE CERTAIN HUMILIATIONS WE WILL withstand when we are young, if it means that we can become part of something bigger than just ourselves, by ourselves. This notion upheld all the tortures of hazing.

Ice Palace was a peculiar ritual, in which a tunnel at least the length of a man's body was dug out in the snow. The pledges had to dig it, for they were virtual slaves to the upperclassmen. Then, one at a time, the pledges were stripped down to their underwear. Each was then hosed down with water, and sent into the tunnel, which was now deemed the Ice Palace. The pledge had to sit back in the freezing ice and tell a joke until every upperclassman present laughed.

When I endured Ice Palace, I got them cracking up within ten minutes; but I was good with jokes. There had even been something of a respite from the outer world when I had crawled into that ice cave, shivering for sure, but also experiencing a strange pleasure, as if I were protected in a way I didn't quite understand. Some pledges could not tell a joke to save their lives, however, and so it could be a painful, if not simply a chilling, experience. This was one of the least pleasant aspects of hazing. The other rituals (egg yolk passing from mouth to mouth, or fish dunking in a toilet) were disgusting, but essentially harmless. Even paddling was child's play, with the only casualty being a sore butt for a few days.

But Ice Palace…

I thought of Stewart Lewis, with his taped-up glasses on his beaky nose, his small peapod eyes, that squirmy way he had of moving as if he had worms or something, and of the humiliation of the whole ritual, particularly of being chosen to be the King of Ice Palace, as he had been. King of Ice Palace: the honor at the shit end of life's stick, the pledge chosen basically because he was commonly known as the Spam, the Nerd, the Loser, the Meat. There was always one pledge that fit this bill—almost as if, each year, the brothers decided to admit someone they could torture, someone who was so desperate to be accepted that he would take it.

The King's hands and feet were roped together, and he was to be sealed up in Ice Palace until someone came to get him out. Cold water was hosed over the entire tunnel in order to truly give it a thick layer of ice. Then, after a set period of time, the Brother High Alpha, which in our case was Nate, would break open the door to Ice Palace.

The King would come forth from his white chamber,

freezing and cursing, yet somehow stronger, and more part of the group than he could ever be through ordinary means. If the chosen one tried to get out early, there was Donkeyman, the local wino.

He was as scary as any nightmare, his face elongated, his ears out and pointy like a mule's, only three teeth in his head, and barely a nose at all, just two flared nostrils exhaling frosty clouds of carbon dioxide. The freshmen weren't familiar enough with the university to have seen Donkeyman yet, for Donkeyman was a creature of alleyways and Dumpsters.

He was perfectly harmless, but he looked like a demon lover of donkeys.

Ice Palace was a fraternity secret and, by all accounts, illegal, at least as far as the college went. If it had been known that it was an ongoing ritual, the entire fraternity system, which was then enjoying a rebirth in popularity, would have been shut down.

There was a story that back in the late fifties a boy had died in Ice Palace.

"THAT'S THE BOY," HELEN WHISPERED IN MY EAR. WE were slow dancing, off the dance floor. She had abandoned Nate to his drunken fury earlier in the evening. Because I owned my own tux, she grabbed me and we'd gone to the Student Center and the Fancy Dress Ball before I could protest much.

I felt a little guilty for snaking my big brother's date,

but she was pretty, and he was acting like an asshole, anyway.

I glanced up from her shoulder, for I had been watching the bone there, beneath the skin, so delicate, so feminine. Smelling her, too, like jasmine with the snow just on the other side of the walls, and here, there were flowers and sandalwood. "Huh?" I asked.

"That boy," she said, dreamily, "the one they put in the snow."

We stopped dancing, and I turned around to look at Stewart Lewis. "I didn't know he was going to be—" I said, but then, there was no Stewart.

Just Stan the Man, who came over and slapped me on the back. "Fuck the fuck it very," he said, his breath stinking of whiskey. "So, Underdoggie, you got Nate's squeeze, bravo, good job, didn't deserve her, the Flaccid Wick didn't, my god, this wine tastes like cow jism." His eyes barely registered either of us; his date, Marlene, stood off to the side, avoiding just about everyone.

"Stan wasn't Ice Palace King," I told Helen. "Is that who you saw in Ice Palace?"

"I didn't see him." Helen turned away from me, waving to a friend. "Nate told me it was him. Isn't that Stewart?" and then, to Stan, "Aren't you Stewart Lewis?"

"The Spamster?" Stan guffawed. "Lawdy, no, Miss Scarlett, I don't know nothing about birthin' no babies."

"He's too drunk to make sense," I said. "Nate told you?"

Helen shrugged. "I thought this guy was Stewart. You boys all look alike with your khakis and down jackets. Are you sure you're not Stewart?"

Stan grinned, but wobbled back to Marlene, who apparently scolded him for something.

"Jesus, I wonder if he ever let Lewis out," I said. "Look, Helen, you wait here, I'll be back in a while."

"Charlie," Helen said, not even startled. "Charlie."

"What?" I snapped, and then blurted, "My god. My god. It'll kill Lewis. It'll kill him."

I left her there, and ran through the make-out room just beyond the dance floor, out through the French doors, down the icy steps, almost slipping on the concrete pavement. The town was a small one, almost a town in miniature, and I didn't own a car. It would be a ten minute jog down Stonewall Drive to get to the House, and to Nate, if he was still there.

The night was a furious one. The wind picked up, and the temperature dropped at least twenty degrees.

I was a decent runner then, but I'd had two beers, and this, with the wind, seemed to slow all motion down by half. I felt like an hour had passed before I arrived at the back entrance to the frat house.

The lights were off in the kitchen; I flicked them up. The place was a mess, like a child's giant toy box overturned, but this was usual. What was unusual were the marks on the wall, as if someone had tried finger painting with bacon grease—which there was plenty of around, for it was stored and used in another hazing ritual.

"Nate! Wick! Where the fuck are you?" I took the stairs two at a time, and came to his room on the second floor.

He lay in bed, with the light on. He was wearing his tux. He opened his eyes. "Underdog."

"Where's Lewis?"

"Lewis? Who the fuck cares? That human spittoon. You stole my girl, Underdog. You stole my girl." He rolled over, away from me, facing the wall. "You stole my girl. But fuck it. Like Stan says, fuck the fuck it very."

I couldn't believe that even Nate would leave Lewis in Ice Palace for the eight hours he would've been in it by now. I almost laughed at myself for worrying. I caught my breath, my hands on my knees, bent over slightly. I looked at the poster of the naked girl with the snake that Nate had on his wall. She was some movie actress, I don't remember who, but her belly seemed to meet the boa constrictor in an almost motherly caress. "Whew, Nate. Whoa, boy. You almost had me going. You know, you miserable—you know I ran all the way down here from Fancy Dress, just to...just to—"

"He's still in it." He didn't turn to face me, but his voice was smug. "And I'm the only one who knows where he is."

"You're joking."

"I'm joking, but the joke's on Lewis. Or should I say, you can now find Spam in the freezer section of your local supermarket."

I went over and grabbed him by the back of his collar and hauled him off the bed. When he turned to face me, I slapped his face four times. "Where is he?"

Calmly, Nate said, "What the hell do you care?" There were tears in his eyes. "What the hell do you care? It might as well be me in there, for all any of you care. Why don't you like me, Underdog? Why?" His tears were both a shock and a revelation to me: He was only a nine-year-old in a twenty-one-year-old's body, the jugface was a mask, the rough talk, a cover, the attitude, a sham.

And I said what I felt, although I regretted it within the hour.

I said, "Because you're not even human."

WE TOOK HIS CAR, BUT I DROVE.

"You said you were doing Ice Palace at Crawford's Dump," I said, "so we'll go there first. You better hope to god Lewis had the sense to break out of there."

"I don't know," he said, a singsong to his voice. "I gave Donkeyman some Chivas to do double duty. I told him to hit Spam on the head with the shovel if he tried to get out. We hosed it down pretty good. Twenty below. Nice thick ice. Ice you could skate on. Ice Palazzo." Nate was still crying, bawling like a baby, and singing; he had cracked; he was drunk; he kept trying to grab the wheel while I was driving.

Crawford's Dump was the old graveyard just outside town, but there were few markers, and even fewer showed through the heavy snow. I skidded the Volkswagen to a stop on the slick shoulder of the potholed, salt-strewn road, and left the headlights on. We tromped in our tuxes through the Styrofoam crunch of snow, and each time Nate tried to pull away I socked him in the shoulder and cussed him out. The snow and a clouded moon provided a soft light, making the dumping ground of the dead romantic, beautiful, sublime. Even Nate, when I spat my fury at him, looked beautiful, too, with the tears streaming, and his eyes always on me. The dump descended into a small valley, where the entire cemetery spread out all around us.

"Where?"

Nate shrugged. His tears ceased. The wind, too, died, but we heard it howling around us, up the hill. Trucks out on the interstate blew their horns, one to another, and even the music from the Fancy Dress Ball, playing "The Swing," could be made out.

"Where, Nate? Tell me."

"Wherever Donkeyman is. You stole my girl, Underdog."

"Look, asshole, Lewis is going to die. You hear me? You will have murdered a human being. Don't you get it? You tell me where that stupid Ice Palace is, or I will kill you with my bare hands."

Nate blinked twice. "Suck my dick."

I got a good clear shot at his jaw, my second in one day, and then a knee in the groin before he swung back; he only clipped me, but I was off balance, and fell into the snow.

I thought for a second—just a second—I felt a gentle tugging.

There, in the snow.

Like a soft mitten, pulling me down.

Nate jumped on top of me, spitting all over my face as he spoke. "You are my best friend, Underdog, you are my best friend in the world. Who the fuck cares about Lewis? Are you in love with him or something? Are you? Is that all you want? Lewis? Why are you doing this to me?" He began boxing my ears with snow, until I felt them go numb; I tried to heave him off me, but Nate was heavy; I felt that gentle tugging again. Soft. Like kittens on my back.

And then, something I had always known would happen, did happen. I just had never had a clue as to the form it would take.

Nate Wick kissed me on the lips as warmly and sweetly as any lover ever had.

SOMETHING CLICKED FOR ME THEN, AND FOR THE longest minute in the world, I shut my eyes and just felt the warmth of those lips, and the even tempo of my own breathing through my nostrils.

I was somewhere else, and the cold of the snow was almost burning now, like a bed of warm coals against my tuxedo. His hands remained around my ears, and the sound of distant music, and trucks, too—their own music —voices up on the hillside, passersby to whom we were invisible. The whiteness of snow, the indigo sky, all there, but without me seeing or hearing.

His lips were rough and chapped, and I felt my own lips opening like a purse that had been kept too long shut; his upper lip grazed my teeth. His breath was a caustic brewery, but I held each one for as long as I could. I hated this boy, this man, so much; I hated him, and yet tied like this, together, unnaturally if we were to believe those who ran the world, we were perverse brothers, children playing. The blood rushed to my face, an unbearable burning sensation. I opened my eyes; his remained closed. I kissed a corner of his lips, and then the other.

He made a deep noise, a churning machine somewhere within his gut, or igniting along his spine, as he rose and fell again, softly, like the tugging I felt in the rabbit-fur snow beneath my back. The knob of desire, or prick, or dick, or wang, whatever we had called it through all the shared moments of college life, pressed from his pants against mine. I shivered as much from embarrassment as from lust; but there was no one around, you see, no one within miles. I remembered him in the showers, soaping his underarms like he was scrubbing a saddle, tender and quick and then sandpapering at the last; the tumescence he had, which I noticed only peripherally. I hated him. I hated him.

He pressed the side of his face against mine, and it was like holding someone for the first time, this boy, this innocent, angry, drunken boy. I wrapped my arms around him. "I love you," he whispered, and even though I smelled the alcohol, I sighed.

He said, "Lewis was nothing. He was nothing."

And then my mind came back to me, through this physical revelation, through this lightning-swift understanding of all I had done before in my life, as well as much of what Nate himself had done.

Lewis.

Stewart Lewis. The freshman that Nate Wick had chosen as King of Ice Palace.

"You fucked Lewis," I said. "You fucked him and then you buried him. Get the fuck off me!" I shoved hard, and he rolled back.

"No," he said, rather meekly, not breaking eye contact with me. "I didn't. He wouldn't let me. He...he didn't want me."

I would've liked to have died right there, my secret self that I had worked so hard to hide buried forever in snow, but I was worried about Lewis. The kiss had made me forget him, briefly, but the reality of who and what Nate Wick was came back to me, a sour taste in the back of my throat. "Get up, get up."

I stood, kicking him in the side.

He gazed forlornly up at the moon, which had swept off its clouds. The lover's moon, I thought, the horny poking male moon, the prick of light, the howling desire of man's madness.

I felt dirty, and picked up fresh snow and rubbed it on my face, my lips, to get that awful taste of *him* off me.

"It's so white," Nate said, packing a snowball, which he threw at me as I wandered the valley.

AT LAST, I SAW A SOLITARY FIGURE, A MINUTE MAN standing guard: the illustrious Donkeyman, his shovel stuck firmly into a heap of snow. He was the whitest man I had ever seen, and even at night, he seemed to glow in the dark.

His chin stretched downward like putty, the ears demonic; blubbery lips, nostrils drippy with snot. He grinned, and brayed some greeting—the bottle of Chivas Regal lay empty beside him, along with several piss stains at his feet.

"Preppy boy, how you doin'?" he asked congenially, waving the flashlight that he held tight in his gloved left hand.

He wore a deerstalker hat and an oversized tan duster around his shoulders — one that a frat brother had no doubt loaned him for the night. "King a Ice Palace in there. I done my job. You got another bottle?"

I took the shovel up and asked, "Where?"

"I said, you got another bottle? Done my job. Icy Palace, nobody goes in, nobody goes out."

I threatened him with the shovel, until he pointed out the mound, not three feet away. I tapped it with the edge of the shovel. Hard as a rock. The ice of its outer layer gleamed, for Donkeyman shone his flashlight upon it.

"Lewis?" I shouted. "Lewis!"

I listened, but heard only the giggling of Donkeyman as he lit a cigarette and puckered his lips at the first puff.

"King a Icy Palace ain't been talkin' since about six, seven. Done a good damn job. Best. You boys know it, too." He spat in the snow.

I took the shovel up, down, up, down. The blade struck the outer edge of the Ice Palace. It was like breaking rocks in two.

The ice finally creaked and cracked where I struck down.

I LOOKED THROUGH THE OPENING I HAD DUG. NATE was already there at my side, perhaps sobering up a bit, because he seemed nervous and worried. Donkeyman patted me on the back now and again in my labor, cheering me on. We were some crew.

"Lewis? Stewart!" I shouted into the tunnel.

Silence.

"I only had him make it maybe six feet in," Nate said, with some regret.

I grabbed Donkeyman's flashlight, and shone it into Ice Palace. The tunnel in the ice and snow did go about six feet or so, but then there seemed to be a twist. Handprints in the ice, too, along the shiny white and silver walls. There were the ropes. "He got out," I said, almost relieved. "He got out."

"He got out," Nate said, solemnly.

"Thank god, thank you god for saving Lewis's life." I stood, leaning against the shovel.

Donkeyman said, "He got out?"

"Underdog," Nate said.

"Thank god, you better thank god, Wick, because if he had died in there…well, you are one lucky SOB."

Nate looked stunned. "He didn't get out, Charlie." Finally, for the first time in his life, calling me by my real name.

"What do you mean?"

"I mean what I said. He didn't get out."

"He must've. See for yourself." I showed him the tunnel, and swirled the flashlight around to show the shape of the curve, to the left, barely visible. "He got loose and dug around that way. The lucky bastard must've gone for about six more feet or something, and then tunneled up."

"He didn't get out," Nate repeated. He shoved me aside, and crawled into Ice Palace.

I watched him shimmy through the thin tunnel, blocking my light.

"Nate, get out of there," I called after him.

I heard his words echo through Ice Palace: "I'm telling you, he didn't get out. I put him here, Charlie, I put him here, so I should know."

"What's he mean by that?" I asked Donkeyman, as if he would have a coherent answer.

Donkeyman scratched his scalp beneath his cap and said, "Don't know. The boy already got Icy Palaced."

I crawled in a ways, shining the flashlight first up ahead, and then to the frozen walls. I saw Lewis's hand prints, as if he'd pressed against the snow to try and push his way out. He must've realized that this end of the tunnel would be iced over from the water that Nate would toss over it.

So Lewis—you smart dog—you figured on digging some more, I thought, *you miserable lucky nerd!* Nate turned left, at the twist in the tunnel.

I noticed a certain indentation in the inner wall.

A word?

I held the flashlight at an angle to make them out.

RESUR

Then, a hint of red. A bit of fingernail. Lewis had cut his fingers in the stiff snow. He had stopped writing.

"Nate?" I called, but there was no answer, so I shuffled on my hands and knees, my back low but still pressing the ceiling, to catch up with him.

I turned the corner to the left, and stopped, for something was different.

I shone the flashlight all around.

I couldn't see Nate at all, anywhere; the tunnel seemed to descend at the turn, rather than do the logical thing, which was to move forward and up. If Lewis were to escape, surely he would've tried to push *up*?

"Nate?" I cried through what now seemed an eternal tunnel of ice. "Nate!"

My voice echoed.

There were other hand prints there, in the ice, none of them the same. All were smeared, and some seemed impossibly thin; in one indentation, I saw what might've been a silken patch of the thinnest skin. I began to back up, to get out of the tunnel. As I reversed as far as I could, I turned a bit, shining the flashlight back toward the entrance.

It was once again sealed.

"Donkeyman!" I shouted. "Donkeyman!"

I thought I heard him laughing, but perhaps it was not on the outside, but within this chamber, this tapeworm that had no end. This chamber of ice. I slammed my fist into the ceiling, but succeeded only in skinning my knuckles. Somehow, Donkeyman had sealed us in there again. I moved forward, the only place to go, past the hieroglyphs of hands and the sides of smooth bony faces, a thread of skin here, a spray of torn hair under my knees. The tunnel descended and then widened, so I could move about a bit more; there was less air here, and what there was of it began to stink like sewage.

And then something grabbed me by the wrist, and

shook the flashlight out of my hand. It rolled to the side, shining its light against the wall, casting gray-white-yellow shadow.

I was in a room with others.

Nate whispered, "I killed him, Charlie. I killed Lewis."

I was too numb to be shocked by what seemed inevitable, for I'd had a feeling from the beginning of the day that Nate would kill Stewart Lewis.

Nate leaned over and kissed me gently on the cheek, then my right ear. Something moved in front of us. "I love you, Charlie. I'm scared. I mean, I'm really scared. I never been this scared." His face shuddered, and I drew away from his caress.

I leaned forward, picking up the flashlight, and shot its beam directly in front of us.

"Oh god," Nate said.

It was Stewart Lewis, hunched in a wider chamber, his white Oxford shirt torn and bloody, with red and black slices through the skin of his chest. His khakis were muddy and soaked.

I had never seen him without his glasses, but he seemed handsomer, with his hair slicked back, and a pale cast to his face. Around him, others, young men all, young and decayed, slashes along their arms, or blue flesh as if their blood were frozen, half-naked, tendons dangling from some, others as beautiful as if they were alive, and in some respects I knew they were, and in some respects they had not lived in a very long time.

Nate said, "King of Ice Palace."

Lewis grinned, naughtily, and leaned into us, until his lips were practically an inch from my face. "Pleasures beyond life, Charlie, beyond the snow. The warmth of life, the sun within the flesh."

Lewis turned his face toward Nate, who clung to my sleeve. "One of you," he said, his voice the same hopeless soprano of an undeveloped choirboy, but the face, full of fierce authority, his lips drawn back, his eyes ice ice ice. "One of you," he said, "is mine."

Nate let go of my arm, recoiling from me, and said, "Him. Charlie. You can fuck him. You can do whatever you want to him."

"Oh, Nate," Lewis said, "you wanted me, in the woods, you held the knife to my throat because you wanted me."

"I'm not like that," Nate said, pressing himself back against the wall. "He is. Charlie's like that. It was because you wanted me to do it. That was all. I have a girl friend. *Charlie*, tell him about Helen. *Tell him.*"

"You miserable—" I said, pushing at him. And then I turned to Stewart Lewis. "Lewis, what happened, what... what...are you?"

"King of Ice Palace, Charlie, just the way Nate wanted me. Frozen, consenting, helpless. Nate, give me your tongue, give me your wet sweet tongue, give me the fire of your breath, give me the secret you." Lewis leaned into Nate, and I moved to the side, but could not get too far from them. Lewis and Nate had locked mouths, and I heard a gurgling, but not of terror or pain. It turned into a tender moan, like a kitten searching for its mother's milk. I watched in the white chamber as color returned to Nate's pale face, for this love was being passed between them, this frozen and glorious and fearful love.

All the young and dead men in the chamber watched as Nate pushed himself against the wall as if trying to break out of there. His hand traced a line along the shiny wall, gripping, becoming a clench of delight as Lewis leaned forward into him. Stewart Lewis was only newly resurrected, but it made me think how beautiful physical love could be, between two people, a doorway between two separate entities, that submission on both parts, that surrender to the warmth and the gasps of physical contact.

I knew then why men enjoyed watching the sexual act almost as much as participating in it:

Because it is a celebration of the perverse, no matter the context—the thrusting buttocks, the muscular legs tight and kicking as if in combat, the slobbering mouth, the exquisite beauty of lost consciousness.

That can happen to me, yes, and that, too, you think when you watch one enter the other, one clasp his hands around the other's shuddering flesh.

I loved Nate Wick, and I loved Stewart Lewis, and I loved the boys who had died, for the ritual of the ice had been known since before I came into the world.

All of them, crowned for a season through years of winter, Kings of Ice Palace.

LEAVING ICE PALACE, WHILE DIFFICULT, IS NOT impossible, for the King is not a tyrant, neither is his court a prison. Nate never followed me out to the other side when the morning broke, but I think he was safer in there.

I did not run from that place, but departed after having left my own hand prints along its white walls.

I helped murder a boy once, or perhaps he had just become a man that night and did not want to return to the warming climates. He was my brother, although he was no blood relation. I do not believe that he is, in any real sense, dead, although his family has given up on him, as has his girl friend, Helen.

Ice Palace: I do not wish to live there, not yet, although I venture into its white, secret chamber often on dark winter nights.

It is a secret chamber, Ice Palace.

But, even so, it is never as cold or as lonely as my days in the world above.

WHY MY DOLL IS EVIL

A POEM

She came from Japan
    In 1963
    My father, on business, saw her in a shop window
    With her fan and her obi
    And her curious smile
    She stood on a chest of drawers

I COULD NOT SLEEP SOME NIGHTS
    Looking at that placid face,
    So shiny and white in the nightlight's halo.
    She beckons and repels with her gently curved hand.
    Her lips move at night,
    But she has no voice.

THINGS HAPPEN IN HOUSES
    Where families live.

SHE WATCHED,
     And I watched her watch.
     She smiled as it happened,
     Held her fan close,
     But her gaze told me nothing.
     I watched her lips move,
     But she remained silent
     While it happened.

NOW, IN THE ATTIC,
     She rests,
     For she knows more than she can say.
     Her black hair is ragged,
     Her obi torn,
     Her perfect feet, tucked into wooden sandals,
     Arthritic at her age.
     But she smiles,
     Holds her fan just so,
     Without voice,
     Reminds me of things that happened
     In families,
     While she stood
     Watch.

THE FIVE

The wall was up against the carport, and Naomi, who was just beginning the gangly phase, stretched out across it like she was trying to climb up the side of the house to the roof.

She heard the sound first.

She knew about the cat, the wild one that lived out in the Wash. Somehow, it had survived the pack of coyotes that roamed there, and she had thought she saw it come near the house a few times before. But there was no mistaking the mewling sounds of kittens, and so she presented the problem to her father.

"They'll die in there."

"No," he said. "The mother cat knows what she's doing. She's got the kittens there so the coyotes won't get them. When they're old enough, she'll bring them out. They're animals, Nomy, they go by instinct and nature. The mother cat knows best. The wall's sturdy enough, too. Walls are good, safe places from predators."

"What's a predator?"

"Anything that's a threat. Anything that might eat a cat."

"Like a coyote?"

"Exactly."

"Where's the father cat?"

"At work."

He showed Naomi where the weak part of the wall was, and how to press her ear up against it with a glass. Her eyes went wide and squinty, alternately, and she accidentally dropped the glass, which broke.

"You'll have to clean that up," he said.

Naomi — barefoot — stepped carefully around the chips of glass as she went to fetch the broom.

She took a few swipes at the broken glass and leaned against the wall again.

Her father was, by this time, just starting up the lawn mower in the side yard. She wanted to ask him more about the cat, but he was preoccupied, and since (she'd been warned) this was one of his few days off for the summer, she decided not to bother him.

She went indoors and told her mother about the cat and the kittens and her mother was more concerned. Her mother was much more sentimental about animals than her father, and went outside with her immediately to examine the wall.

"There's the hole near the drainpipe. I don't know how she did it, but she squeezed in there. Good for her. She protected her children." Naomi's mother pointed up to beneath the eaves, where the pipe only partially covered a hole that her father had put into the wall accidentally when he was repairing the roof.

"I've seen her before," Naomi said. "The mother cat. She watches gophers over in the field. She's very tough looking. My father says she's doing it because of instinct."

Her mother looked from Naomi over to her husband, mowing. "It's his day off and he mows. We see him at breakfast and before bed, and on his day off he mows."

"It's his instinct," Naomi said. The air was smoky with lawn mower exhaust and fresh-cut grass; motes of dust and dandelion fluff sprayed across the yellow day.

SHE THOUGHT ABOUT THE KITTENS ALL AFTERNOON, and wondered how many there were.

"I think several," her mother told her. "Maybe five."

"Why don't people have babies all at once like that?"

Her mother laughed, "Some do. They're crazy. Trust me, when you're ready to have children, you won't want several at once."

"I can't wait to have babies," Naomi said. "When I have babies, I'll protect them just like the Mom cat."

"You're much too young to think that."

"You had me when you were eighteen."

"So, you have nine more years to go and you need to pick up a husband along the way."

Her father, who had been listening to all this even while he read the paper, said, "I don't think it's right to encourage her, Jean."

Her mother glanced at her father, and then back at Naomi.

The living room was all done in blues, and Naomi sometimes felt it was a vast sea, and she was floating on a cushion, and her parents were miles away, underwater.

Her father, his voice bubbling and indistinct, said something about something or other that they'd told her before about something to do with something, but Naomi had known when to block him out, when to put him beneath the waves.

NAOMI CLIMBED THE DRAINPIPE JUST AFTER DINNER, with a flashlight held in her mouth making her feel like she would throw up any second.

She grasped one edge of roof, and cut her fingers on the sharp metal of the pipe, and lodged her left foot in the space between the pipe and the wall. She directed the flashlight down the hole, and saw a pair of fierce red eyes, and movement.

Nothing more than that.

The eyes scared her a bit, and she tried to pull her foot free so she could shimmy down, but her foot was caught.

The mother cat moved up into the hole until its face was right near hers. Naomi heard a low growl, which didn't sound like a cat at all. She dropped the flashlight, and felt a claw swipe across her face.

She managed to get her foot free, and dropped five feet to the ground, landing on her rear. She felt a sharp pain in her legs.

Her mother came outside at the noise, and ran to get her.

"*Naomi*," her mother gasped. "What in god's name are you doing?"

She rushed to Naomi, lifting her up.

"My leg." It hurt so much she didn't want to move at all, but her mother carried her into the light of the carport. She was trailing blood. It didn't spurt out like she thought it might, but just came in drips and drabs like the rain when it was spitting.

"It's glass," her mother said. She removed it; Naomi didn't have time to cry out. Tears were seeping from her eyes. The pain in her leg, just along the calf, was burning.

Her father had heard the shouting, and he came out, too. He was in white boxer shorts and a faded gray T-shirt. He said, "what's going on here?"

"She cut herself," her mother said.

"I told her to sweep up the glass," he said, and then turned to her, and more softly said, "didn't I tell you to clean up the broken glass, Nomy?"

Naomi could barely see him for her tears. She looked from one to the other, and then back, but it was all a blur.

"We've got to take her to the emergency room."

Her father said, "yeah, and who's coming up with the three hundred bucks?"

"Insurance."

"Canceled."

Her mother said nothing.

"We can sew it up here, can't we?"

Her mother seemed about to say something. Almost a sound came out of her mouth. Then, after a moment, she said, "I guess I could. Jesus, Dan. What if this were worse?"

"It's just a cut. It's only glass. You know how to put in stitches."

Her mother asked her, "sweetie, is that all right with you?"

"If it's what my father wants," she said.

Her father said, "she always calls me that. Isn't that strange? 'My father'. Why is she like this?"

Her mother ignored him. She felt the warmth of her mother's hand on her damp cheek. "It's okay to cry when things hurt."

"She never looks me in the eye, either. You ever notice that? You're Mommy, but I get 'my father'. Christ." Her father said something else, but even the sounds were starting to blur because Naomi thought she heard the kittens mewling in the wall, just the other side, and they were getting louder and louder.

Even later, when her mother took out her sewing kit and told her it wouldn't hurt as much as it looked like, even then, she thought she heard them.

THE STITCHES CAME OUT A WEEK LATER, AND although there was a broad white scar, it wasn't so bad. She could still jump rope, although she felt a gentle tugging. She hadn't been outside much; she'd got a fever, which, according to her mother, was from an infection in her leg. But all she'd had to do was lie around and watch old *I Love Lucy* shows, and eat Saltines and guzzle cola. Not the worst thing, she figured. As soon as she was able, she went out to check on the kittens.

She had a can of tuna with her; she knew cats loved it, and her mother would never miss it. She set up the step ladder, and climbed up.

But the hole was no longer there.

It had been sealed up. White plaster was spread across it.

She asked her mother about it.

"They got old enough to leave," her mother said, "and so the Mom cat took them back out to the field to hunt mice."

"What about the coyotes?"

"Wild cats are usually smarter than coyotes. Really, honey. They're fine."

Although she wasn't ever supposed to go into the field that adjoined her father's property, Naomi untangled her way through the blackberry and boysenberry vines, and went anyway.

The grass in the field was high and yellow; foxtails shot out at her and embedded themselves in her socks. She picked them out carefully. There was an old rusted out tractor in the middle of the field, and she found several small stiff balloons near it, and a pipe made completely of brass.

She kept searching through the grass. Something moved along the mound where the grass grew thickest.

A great tree, dead from lightning, stood guardian of this spot. A peregrine falcon sat at its highest point.

She looked up and down, and all around, which was something she'd once heard about.

The grass quivered. The falcon flew off across the field and glided above the orange groves.

She saw two ears rise slowly above the grass.

A coyote crouched four feet away from her. Its yellow-brown head came into view. It was beautiful.

She stood still for several seconds.

She had never seen a coyote this close.

And then, the animal turned and ran off down the field, towards the Wash.

Naomi had been holding her breath the whole time, not realizing it.

The sun was up and boiling, and she looked back across to her house. It seemed too far away. She sat down in the grass for a minute, feeling the leftover heat of fever break across her forehead. She cupped her hands together like she was praying, and rested her head against them. She whispered into the dry earth, "Don't let anything hurt the kittens."

When she awoke, the sun was all the way across the sky. Ants crawled across her hands; some were in her hair. She had to brush them out. She felt like she'd been sleeping for years, it had been that peaceful. Her mother was calling to her from the back yard. She stood, brushed dirt and insects from her, and ran in the direction of the familiar voice. She jumped around the thorny vines, but her leg started to hurt again, so she ended up limping her way up the driveway. She went along the side of the carport to get to the back gate, when something leapt out in front of her.

It was the mother cat. Snarling.

Naomi froze.

The mother cat watched her.

Naomi looked around for the kittens but saw none.

And then she heard them.

She followed the sound.

Pressed her ear against the carport wall.

She heard them.

Inside the wall.

The five.

WHEN HER FATHER GOT HOME FROM WORK, HE WENT in and sat in front of the television to watch the ten o'clock news. Naomi was supposed to be getting ready for bed, but she had been pressing herself up against the wall in the living room, because she thought she heard something moving behind it.

She wandered into the den, following the sounds.

Her father glanced over, then back to the television.

The noise in the wall seemed to stop at the entrance to the den.

Naomi leaned against the door. "You didn't take the kittens out, did you?"

He looked at her. His eyes seemed to be sunken into the shriveled skin around them; his eyeglasses magnified them until she felt he was staring right through her.

"Nomy?" he asked.

"You left them in the wall."

He grinned. "Don't be silly. I took them out. All five. Set them down. The mother carried them into the vines. Don't be silly."

"I heard them. I saw the big cat. She was angry."

"Don't be silly," he said, more firmly. He took his glasses off.

She realized that she was alone in the room with him, and she didn't like it. She never liked being alone with him. Not inside the house.

She ran down the hall to her mother's room. Her mother lay in bed, reading a book. She set it down.

Naomi climbed up on the bed. "Mommy, I have a question."

Her mother patted a space beside her. Naomi scooted closer. She lay down, resting her head on her mother's arm.

"It's about the kittens in the wall."

Naomi looked up at the ceiling, which was all white, and thought she saw clouds moving across it, almost forming a face.

"What I want to know," she said, "is, did the cat take the kittens out before he covered the hole?"

Her mother said, "why?"

"I heard the kittens earlier."

"Before dinner?"

Naomi nodded. The cloud face in the ceiling melted away.

"You didn't tell me you heard them."

"I was really angry. I thought you lied to me."

"I wouldn't lie to you."

"I asked my father, and he said I was being silly."

"Well, it's not silly if you thought you heard them. But you must've imagined it. I saw them leave. With the Mom cat."

"I saw her, too. She looked angry. She looked like she was mad at me for letting her babies get put in the wall like that."

"Oh," her mother said, stroking her fine, dark hair, "cats don't think things like that. She was probably just asking for milk. Maybe she's getting tamer. Maybe one day she and all the kittens, grown up, will come back because you were so nice to them."

"I was sure I heard them."

"Maybe you wanted to hear them."

Naomi was fairly confused, but had never known her mother to lie.

Her mother said, "you got sunburned today."

"I saw a coyote in the field."

"You went in the field?"

"I was looking for the kittens."

"Oh, you. Don't tell your father."

IN THE MORNING, SHE RETURNED TO THE CARPORT wall. She pressed a drinking glass to it, and then applied her ear.

Nothing.

No sound.

She tapped on the wall with her fingers.

No sound.

And then...*something.*

Almost nothing.

Almost a whine.

And then, as if a dam had burst, the screaming, shrieking of small kittens, and the sound of frantic clawing.

She almost dropped the glass, but remembering her leg, she caught it in time. *I wouldn't lie to you,* she heard her mother say, a memory.

I wouldn't lie to you.

She put the glass up to the wall.

Nothing.

Silence.

Sound of her own heart, beating rapidly.

THAT NIGHT, SHE LAY IN BED, UNABLE TO SLEEP. IN the daylight, she would be all right, but at night she had to stay up because of things in the dark. She thought she had forgotten how to breathe; then realized, she was still inhaling and exhaling.

About one in the morning, her door opened.

Someone stood there, so she had to close her eyes.

She counted her breaths, and hoped it wouldn't be him.

She felt the kiss on her forehead.

That, and the touching her on the outside of the blanket, was all he ever did, the nighttime father, but it was enough to make her wish she were dead and wonder where her mother was to protect her.

But as she lay there, she heard them again.

The kittens.

Mewling sweetly, for tuna or milk.

They had traveled to find her, through the small spaces within the walls, to find her and tell her they were all right.

She fell asleep before the door opened again, listening to them, wondering if they were happy, if they were catching the mice that she knew occasionally crawled into other holes and vents and cracks. The five were still there, her kittens, her kittens, and she knew it would turn out fine now.

"What's wrong with her?"

"Well, Dan, if we'd taken her to the hospital instead of letting the infection go like that…"

"And somebody would've accused us of child abuse. That's all that ever happens anymore. And it's not some infection, Jean. Look at her. Why is she doing that?"

"I think she's sick. Her fever's back."

"What's gotten into her?"

Naomi heard them, but paid no attention, because the kittens were getting louder. They were three months old now, and they sounded more like cats. They played there, behind the diamond shaped wallpaper in the kitchen, just behind the toaster. One had caught a mouse or something, and they were playing with it—she could hear the frightened squeaks. She pressed the palms of her hands against the wallpaper, trying to open up the wall, but no matter how much she pressed, nothing gave.

Her father said, "she shouldn't be crawling around like that. She looks like an animal."

"Sweetie," her mother said, stroking her hair. "don't You think you need to get back in bed?"

She glanced up at her mother, "I love them," she said, unable to control an enormous smile, "I love them so much, Mommy."

Her mother wasn't look at her. She said, "I'm taking her to a doctor right now."

"Hello, Naomi." The doctor was bald and sweet looking, like a grandfather.

"Hello," she replied.

"That leg's healing okay. Looks like whoever stitched it, did it right."

"Mommy did it. She used to be a nurse."

"I know. She used to work with me. Did you know that?"

No reply.

"What seems to be the problem?" he asked. He put the stethoscope against her chest. She breathed in and out. Then, a funny looking thermometer, which he called a "gun," went in her ear. Lights in her eyes. A tongue depressor slipped to the back of her throat almost gagging her.

"I don't know," she said, finally.

"Your Mommy's really worried."

"I don't know why."

"She says you listen to the walls."

Naomi shook her head. "Not the walls. The five."

"Five what?"

"Kittens. Each of them know me. I love them so much."

"How did the kittens get there?"

She looked at him, unsure if she should trust him. "I can't tell you."

"All right, then."

He gave her a shot in the arm, which she didn't feel at all. She thought that was strange, so she told him.

"Not at all?"

"I didn't even feel it."

He put his hand under his chin. Then he reached to her arm and pinched.

"Did you feel that?"

She shook her head.

Then, he went over to a counter on the other side of the room. He returned with a plastic bottle. He took the lid off and held it under her nose. "Smell this."

She sniffed.

"Sniff again," he said.

She sniffed hard.

"What does it smell like?"

"I dunno. Water, maybe?"

He was trying to smile at her response, she could tell, but couldn't quite do it. "Is there anything you want to tell me?" he asked.

"About what?"

"Anything. Your Mommy or Daddy. How you feel about things."

She thought a minute, "nope."

And that was it, he took her out to the waiting area where her mother was sitting. Then, she was asked to sit and wait while her mother had a checkup, too.

On the way home, in the car, her mother was in a mood. "Are you playing games?"

Shook her head.

"Well, I think you are. Are you trying to destroy this family? Because if you are, young lady, if you are..." Her mother's hands were shaking so hard, she had to pull the car over to the side of the road.

Naomi began to say something, but she saw that her mother wasn't listening, so she shut her mouth.

And as her mother started lecturing her, Naomi realized that she could barely hear a word her mother said.

THE NIGHTS WERE PEACEFUL. SHE COULD PRESS HER ear against the wall, and hear them, playing and hunting and crawling around one another. She kept trying to think up good names for them, but each time she came up with something, she forgot which was which.

Then, when the bedroom door opened—which didn't happen very often anymore—she listened to the cats (for they had grown in size), and sometimes, if she closed her eyes really tight, she could almost imagine what they looked like. All gray tabbies like their mother, of course, but one with a little bit of white in a star pattern on its chest, and two of them had green eyes, while the rest had blue.

One had gotten very fat from all the mice and roaches it had devoured over the past weeks, and another seemed all skin and bones; and yet, not deprived at all.

ONE DAY, A WOMAN IN A SUIT CAME BY.

She had some manila files in her hand. Naomi's mother and father were very tense.

The woman asked several questions, mainly to her parents, but Naomi was listening for the sound of the five.

"Naomi?" her father said. "Answer the lady, please."

Naomi looked up; her father's voice had gotten really small, like it was caught in a jar somewhere and couldn't get out. She looked at the lady, and then to her mother. Her mother's forehead held beads of sweat.

"Yes, ma'am." She looked back to the lady.

"How are you feeling, dear?"

Naomi said, "fine."

"You were sick for awhile."

Naomi nodded. "I'm better now. It was the flu."

"Have you had a good summer vacation?"

Naomi cocked her head to the side; she squinted her eyes. "Can you hear them?"

The lady said, "who?"

"All of them. They just caught something. Maybe a mouse. Maybe a sparrow got in. I thought I heard one. Do you think that's possible?"

AFTER THE LADY LEFT, HER FATHER EXPLODED WITH rage. "I am so sick and tired of you running our lives like this!"

Who was he talking to? Naomi heard the runt of the litter tearing at the bird's wings, feathers flying. The five could be brutal, sometimes.

They stalked their prey like lions, and brought a bird or mouse down quickly, but then played with it until the small creature died of fear more than anything.

Something beautiful about taking something so small and playing with it.

"There are no fucking cats in the fucking walls," her father's voice intruded.

He came over to her; lifted her up from under her arms. "I am going to tell you what happened to those kittens, right now," he said.

Her mother said, "Jesus, Dan, you're going to hurt her like that," but the voices rushed beneath some invisible glass, caught, silent.

Her father began screaming something—she knew by the movements of his mouth—but all she heard was the one she was calling Scamp tussle over the sparrow's head.

Yowler tore at the beak with her claws, but lost most of the skull, which Scamp took down in one gulp.

Hugo ignored them—he was not one to join in when food was being torn apart—he preferred to lick the bones clean later, after the carcass was stripped.

"I'm going to show you once and for all," her father's

voice came back, and she was being dragged out the back-door, around to the carport wall.

He dropped her to the ground, and went around the wall, into the carport.

She heard Fiona whisper something to Zelda about some centipedes that she had trapped in a spider web behind the wall at the back of the refrigerator.

Her father came back around the corner with a large hammer.

"You just watch what you see," he said, and slammed the hammer into the wall, down where the kittens had once been born.

Back and forth, he worked the hammer, chips of wall flew up, and beneath them, chicken wire, and there, in a small mound, surrounded with bits of cloth and news-paper were small dried things.

"See?" her father said, poking at them with his hammer. From one, a dozen wriggling gray-white maggots emerged.

"Do you fucking see them?" He shouted, his voice receding again.

She looked at them, all stiff and bony and withered like apricots.

Her heart was beating fast. She felt something wet came up her throat. Lights flickered.

Were they the bodies of the mice that the five had caught, in storage for future meals?

And then she thought she was going to faint. She saw pinpricks of darkness play along the edge of her vision, and then an eclipse came over the sun.

The world faded; her father faded; and she reached her

hand into the new hole in the wall, and pressed her head through, too.

Her whole body seemed to move forward, and she saw pipes and wires and dust as she went.

"I can hear her," her mother said, "I think she made a noise."

Her father said nothing.

After a minute: "For three days, she does her weird, unintelligible sounds, and now she snarls her upper lip and you think she's on the road to recovery."

"She said something. Honey? Are you trying to say something?"

But Naomi didn't care to speak with them at the moment.

She held Hugo in her lap, stroking him carefully, carefully, because he didn't like his fur ruffled. Scamp was playing with the ball of thread; the others slept, piled together.

"Look at her," her father said.

"Sweetie?" her mother said, beyond the wall. "Are you trying to talk? Is there something you want to say?"

"You think holding her is going to help?" her father said. "You think she's ever going to get better if you coddle her like that? All that rocking back and forth. She knows what she's doing. She's not stupid."

Zelda rolled on her back and stretched out, a great yawn escaping her jaws. Her whiskers brushed against Naomi's ankle. It tickled.

"Sweetie?" her mother asked.

"She's just doing this," her father said. "It's all for attention. And look at you, giving it to her. She's just doing this to hurt us."

"No, look at her lips. She's trying to say something. Look, Dan. My god, she's trying to talk. Oh, sweetie, Nomy, baby, tell Mommy what's wrong. Are you okay? Baby?"

On the other side of the wall, Naomi pressed her face into the dust-covered fur and listened to the purring, the gentle and steady hum beneath the skin that was like a lullaby. It was warm there, with the five, with the walls around them.

Her father said, "my god, she's starting in again."

"Shut up, Dan. Let her."

"I can't stand this. How can you sit there and cradle her and not scream out loud when she does this?"

"Maybe I care about her," her mother said.

Naomi mewled and rocked and mewled and rocked, safe from predators, safe in the wall.

She watched as one of the cats sat up, her hackles rising, hunting some creature that had the misfortune of entering this most secret and wonderful domain.

THE DARK GAME

Once, I saw a painting in a gallery that depicted a man's hands, bound together.

Its title:

"Victory is Freedom of Mind and Body."

I believe that is true. I would go further and say that victory is freedom of mind *from* body.

Separation from the thing that imprisons us.

Flight.

Perhaps freedom from life itself.

That is victory.

Life is brutal.

It's like this whip and these ropes. It hurts. It scars. But we must take it.

We must find some pleasure and solace within this terrible lashing.

You want to hear it all? You want me to tell you how it went, in the prison camp? Why I like the ropes?

You want to play the game with me?

First let me tell you this:

Youth is something you put in a drawer somewhere.

You lose the thought of it behind socks and letters and medals and old passport photos and keys that no longer fit locks.

You wear it when you're of the right age, and you do things that you ought not to, and then as you gain perspective with age, you put it away, and you close the drawer.

And you lock it.

Then, you live the life you've built toward, and no one needs to see what's in that drawer.

A secret is something to be hidden.

If is hidden well enough, it never becomes a fact. It is just something that is not there when you go to look for it. It is the thing missing, but the thing that is not missed.

That's how I feel.

That is why I don't revisit those times, often.

The camp.

Or the motel room.

The smokehouse.

But since you have me here, like this, I'll tell you.

Maybe you'll leave after that. Maybe you won't want to stay here once you know about me.

BEFORE THE WAR, I WAS IN A MOTEL ROOM WITH A girl I met outside the base.

For fun she tied me up and when she did it, I went someplace else in my head. My hands tied, my feet bound. I remember she smelled like orange blossoms, and she enjoyed tightening the thin ropes around my hands.

But my mind was just gone – drifting upward into darkness, into another place. Back to Burnley Island, I guess, and that's where I've always ended up – *my memories, my family, my home.*

I was just not there anymore. The game had taken me over.

It had become automatic for me.

It was second nature.

In the war, things got worse for me.

The game got worse.

But it wasn't so bad when I was a kid.

Early memory:

Winter.

Bitter cold.

Wind whistling around me, boxing my ears, as I trudged through three feet of snow to get out to the smokehouse.

I was ten, perhaps. Heavy with a burden.

It was the dog I'd had since he was a foundling of two or three years old, and I was too young to remember bringing him home from a walk in the woods.

He was dying now, of some undiagnosed malady. In those days, you didn't take the dog to the vet when it was its time.

You took him someplace and you shot him.

And this freezing February day, that was what I was to do.

My father marched behind me. I could not bring myself to turn and look over my shoulder to see how he kept pace. I was weeping, and it would be the first and last time I would weep for years.

I held my dog – a small mutt, no bigger than my arms could carry – and he looked up at me as if he understood that something not wonderful was to come.

At the smokehouse I stopped and prayed. I wished that God would intervene, just this once.

I would trade, I promised God, my life for this dog's. I would do anything God wanted me to do if he would just take a minute and breathe new life into my dog's body. I would build a chapel.

No, I would build a *cathedral*.

The snow bit at my cheeks and nose.

MY DOG, WHOSE NAME WAS MAC, WHIMPERED AND groaned.

"Go on, son," my father said.

He called me "son" more than he ever used "Gordie" or "Gordon."

Sometimes I thought he wasn't sure of my name. That I was just another son to him. Another child to deal with before I became a man.

I reached up, and opened the door to the smokehouse. I barely kept my balance, for the dog had grown too heavy for me.

My father lit the lantern inside the building – the

smokehouse was old-fashioned, and my mother felt it was a fire hazard, but my father insisted on using it.

A yellow flickering light filled the small room.

After I set Mac down on some straw, I kissed him on the muzzle and kept my prayers going – my deals with God to change this, somehow.

Then, my father handed me the pistol and told me to get it over with quickly.

"Misery is terrible. That animal is in misery. When you brought him home, you promised to take care of him. That is a commitment. This is a way to take care of him, so he won't be in any more pain. You can stop his pain. He won't get better, son. He won't."

"I can't," I said.

"You have to. You promised. You promised me. And you promised that dog when you brought him home. He has had a good life here. But now he's sick. And he needs to be taken care of."

I looked at my dog's face and saw the terribleness of all existence in his eyes. In his shivering form.

And that is when I learned about how life doesn't matter at all.

Not one bit.

It is a misery. A wretchedness foisted on us by a God who turns His back on all.

We live on a planet of ice, and the only thing we human beings can do is endure it and try to make sure that we don't add to the misery too much.

~

HERE IS MY LIFE:

I was born on Burnley Island, in a house called Hawthorn, and I grew up in a family called Raglan that had a history on that island.

We were shepherding people, I'm told, originally. We came with Welsh and Scots and English in our blood, and we were dark and swarthy, as I am, a perfect descendant of the Raglan clan.

My father was a brute, and I don't say that lightly. He was a man more likely to lash with a belt or a switch than to scold with words. He was quick to judge, and hot tempered, and I suppose I joined the army to get away from him more than anything else.

I went off to see the world and fight the good fight, and found myself one dawn in the heat of a jungle, in the boredom of a company that was lost, our communications screwed beyond all measure, and I had a "fuck all" attitude toward the war and the jungle.

I was nineteen, and the last place I wanted to be was in that miasma of heat, humidity and the stink of swamp.

And then, before much time had passed, the enemy got us.

No need to go into specifics.

It was ugly.

There were a dozen of us originally, but by the time I regained consciousness, tied like a pig to a stick, there were only eight or so – counting me and my buddy, Gup (short for Guppy, which was a kinder name than his original nickname, which was Shrimp), Davy, who seemed too young to be a soldier, a man I had no liking for (named Larry Pastor), and Stoddard.

I knew what to do if captured – name, rank, serial number, and nothing else.

The truth was, I was scared spitless and we'd all heard the stories of the POWs and how no Geneva Convention was going to stop our enemy from torturing us and then dropping us in some mosquito breeding ground, dead, when it was all over.

None of us was commander.

We were just soldiers, and we had no valuable information at all, and no reason for a negotiation with our commanders.

But hope is the last thing to go, and so we had it.

I had it, and Gup had it, although Stoddard had already told me that he knew he'd die in the jungle and he didn't give a damn because his girl was already pregnant by some other guy and his folks had disowned him for some reason he wouldn't say, and what the fuck was the point?

That was his attitude, and even though I felt we lived on Ice Planet and life was a hurdle into chaos, I still hoped.

For the best. For life.

For good to come out of bad.

I woke up later on, pain running through my arms and legs like they'd had nails driven into them. I crouched in a dark hole in the ground that smelled like feces and had just a grate at the top so I could see a little of the sky.

Luckily, I still had a pack of gum on me – I kept it in this small pouch at the back inside of my skivvies that my mother had sewn for me to hide money.

Instead, I hid Wrigley's gum, and I took a sliver of a piece and began chewing it just to feel as if I were still an

American and that things mattered even if I was in a hole in the ground.

I WAS A LITTLE BOY WHEN MY MOTHER TAUGHT ME the game, only it wasn't really a game the way she told me about it. It was a way to get calm and to try and get through pain. I guess I was probably four when she taught me it.

She said my grandmother had taught her, and that her grandfather knew about it, too.

It was like make believe, but when I had scarlet fever as a kid, I really needed something to help me get through it. I was sure I was going to die, even though I didn't know what death was at four.

But scarlet fever gave me an inkling.

I WAS FEVERISH AND DELUSIONAL, AND I REMEMBER being wrapped in blankets and taken in the car to Dr. Winding over in Palmerston, and lying naked on his ice cold metal table while his nurse drew out the longest needle I had ever seen in my life and they told me it wouldn't hurt, but I screamed and screamed and my mother and father had to hold me down while that needle went into my butt.

Even though I still had fever, it wasn't quite so bad. But my butt stung, and, wrapped in blankets on the way home, I was in my mother's arms, a baby again. She whispered to me to try the game, that's what she called it.

I named it the Dark Game later on. When it got to me.

At home, in my room, she sat beside my bed and told me to close my eyes despite my moans and groans, and she told me to take her hand. But I couldn't close my eyes. I kept opening them.

Finally she took a handkerchief and put it over my eyes like a blindfold. She began the rhyme. I said it along with her in a singsong kind of voice.

After a bit, she and I were somewhere else, in the woods, in darkness, and I could not feel the pain or the fever at all.

She told me that it was a way the mind worked that was like magic, that it got you out of yourself and out of where you were.

When I began to teach my friends how to do it as a kid, she pulled me aside and told me that I should keep it to myself.

"Why?" I asked.

"Because it can be bad, too. It's important to stay in the world. To not delve into that too much. If you need God, there's church. If you need friends, don't go off into your head too much."

But I didn't understand what she meant then, and I'm not sure I do now.

Or maybe I do and I just don't want to look at it.

"It's a daylight game," she said. "Between you and me. It's a Raglan game. It's just to make things easier when they're rough."

I played it, all by myself, my eyes closed, that wintry day in the smokehouse when I shot my dog, too.

I played it in that hole in the middle of the jungle without a hope in hell of getting out of there alive.

THE FIRST DAY AND NIGHT, THEY WATCHED ME.

'*They*' being the enemy.

I don't want to call them what we called them back then. It was racist. It was nasty. It was a nasty place to be. I hated their guts.

They were Enemy.

They were *They*.

We were *Us*.

My boys – that's how I thought of Gup and Stoddard and Davy – screamed at night. I heard them clearly. I'm pretty sure Stoddard died right away.

That's what I heard, anyway.

I could picture him working hard to piss off the Enemy, even if his nuts were being nailed to the wall. Gup might hang in there. Davy, I worried most about. He was practically just a kid.

I began to discover my darkness in my dirty pit of a bedroom. I began to feel my environment.

I guess I was about twenty feet down. Some kind of well.

Maybe it had been dug up for water.

Or prisoners. I don't know. It was deep but not wide.

I had just enough room to sit with my knees nearly touching my chest. It was dirt and rock, and they lowered water down after midnight, just a cup on a string. Half the water had dropped out of the cup by the time it reached me.

Not even a cup, I discovered. A turtle shell. Drank out of it because I was damn thirsty, and I soon discovered that if I didn't drink out of it fast, they yanked it back up.

They.

Sons of bitches.

I stared up through the grate, trying to see the stars or at least something that meant the hole was not just an o in the earth that had no beginning and no end.

MEMORY:

Back to Texas, back to the night I got tied up, back when I was barely more than a kid and out on an adventure.

The girl who tied me up was named Genie, and she could be had in that sunbaked Texas town for less than twenty bucks.

I was too young to be sure what I could do with a girl like that – I had left my sheltered island a virgin of eighteen, and knew that I would have six months or so before getting my orders overseas into the heart of the war.

I didn't want to die a virgin; and I doubt there has been a virgin in existence that wanted to die in that state, untouched by another.

So, when my buddies and me went out to the local rat bar called *The Swinging Star*, playing pool and chugging too many beers, I let down my guard a bit when one of my friends, named Harry Hoakes, slapped me on the back and whispered in my ear with his sour mash breath that he and a couple of the guys were going down to Red Town, a part of the desert where the whores were cheap and fast and you could buy a few for a good deal less than a week's pay.

I look back with shame, of course, upon this youthful episode in my life.

I do not proudly admit that my first experience with a woman was at the hands of a seasoned pro of twenty-six, but it is what it is – or, it was what it was. I was drunk, stupid, pretty sure I was going to die in some distant jungle, so I went with my *compadres* out in a truck that some townie drove – no doubt the pimp for the Red Town girls.

We unloaded outside yet another bar, and went in, and there they were, like glittery fool's gold, or broken glass mistaken for diamonds on a moonlit highway.

Harry Hoakes looked like a movie star and was from L.A. and had this air of magic around him, no matter what he did.

He died in the war, within a year. I heard he stepped on a mine and it just ripped him up.

But that night, he was completely on and alive like lightning – all around you and illuminating the dark.

This landscape was alien to me – slovenly, lazily pretty girls who looked the way whores are supposed to, not quite unhappy yet with their situation, not quite sure of how they landed in that desert canyon, not quite hardened to the way their lives would surely go.

When you're eighteen and in the army, whores don't seem sad or needy or even lesser.

They seem like angels who don't ask for the reasons of your interest. They know you want them, and they're perfectly fine with that.

Harry Hoakes introduced me to the girls like they were his sisters. The one who sidled up to me was Genie.

"I'm like that old movie star, Gene Tierney. From *Laura*. You ever see *Laura*? It's a beautiful movie. I'm gonna be a movie star someday. I *am*."

She was a big brunette with big teeth, from the Midwest, she said, a farm girl who wanted adventure, and intended to wind up in Hollywood in a couple of months – some producer had discovered her already and she was just waiting to hear from him, she told me all of it so fast it made me laugh.

Then, she asked me what I wanted to do.

WE GOT A BOTTLE OF JACK DANIELS AND WENT BACK to the motel and plunked down the few bucks for a two-hour stay.

After that, she brought out those ropes from some little overnight bag she lugged around with her.

She told me that since I was a virgin, she wanted to make sure I didn't do any of the work.

That's what she called it, and I guess it was her work.

But when the ropes went on, I went off somewhere.

I was no longer in a rundown motel with a big toothed girl, but back on Burnley Island.

IT WAS WINTER (AS MY MEMORIES OF THAT NEW
England island often were) and my father tied me up to
the post that sat at the center of the smokehouse.

He told me I had been bad to do what I had done,
and that he had to teach me a lesson.

I was, perhaps, fourteen, my shirt had been torn off
my back, and I felt the sting of his cat – a cat-o-nine-tails
that he kept to discourage my brothers and me from doing
the bad things we often did.

But in my Dark Game memory, I didn't feel pain from
the stings – I felt myself glowing, becoming a powerful
creature beneath the lashes.

I felt as if I were commanding my father to whip me,
to torment me with the bad things I'd been doing. I felt as
if I were a god, and he were merely my servant.

And soon, in the Dark Game, it was my father with
his shirt torn, tied to the post, and I had the whip, and I
was lashing at him and telling him that he was a bad,
bad man.

When I opened my eyes, the game done, I found that
I was tied to that bed in the motel in Texas. Outside, the
sound of trucks going by.

In a corner of the room, a woman sprawled, a crumpled rag doll, her face bloodied.

HARRY HOAKES CAME A-KNOCKING AT THE MOTEL

room door. I was tied up in Room 13, which made it lucky, I guess.

He was drunk from his own bottle of Jack Daniels, and he nearly busted down the door to get to me.

Inside, he looked at me, tied up and naked on the dirty bed, and then at Genie, her big teeth all but knocked out, lying in a corner, her eyes wide.

He stared at me, then at her.

"I passed out," I said.

"Jesus H." He scratched his head, dropping his nearly empty bottle. His fly was open from his time with his girl. He was too drunk to process everything. "What the hell?"

"I don't know. I passed out. We didn't even do anything."

"Must've been her pimp," he said.

"She's got a pimp?"

"What, you think she's a nice girl from Iowa?"

"Maybe she's not dead," I said.

"If she's not dead, then she's the greatest actress in the world. Because she's dead like I ever saw dead."

"She thought she was going to be like Gene Tierney."

"Who?"

"That pretty actress with the overbite. In *Laura*. You ever see *Laura*?"

He looked at me kind of funny, and then shook his head. "We are up the legendary creek, my friend. You got a dead whore in your room, and you're…well, naked as a jaybird tied up." Then, he let out a laugh. "Christ, you could not have made this up if you wanted to."

"Help me out of these ropes," I said. "Houdini I ain't."

IN THE HOLE, IN THE PRISON, THE ENEMY WOULD sometimes stand over the grate and spit.

They did this a lot, and now and then, they'd take a leak down on me. I'd hear *them* laughing up above.

This might've been happened over a few days or a few weeks. I barely saw the sun in that time, because the grate got covered by a board during the day. They didn't want me to get that Vitamin D from the few rays of the sun, I guess. It was like living in a cave, and time seemed to evaporate.

I lived in endless night.

They'd get me out of there sometimes, too. Usually when it was dark.

They'd send a rope down, and I was to bind my hands to it and they'd pull me up.

Why did I go?

They fed me during those times. Fed me much better than if I stayed in the hole and ignored the rope.

They brought me up and gave me fish or frog or some kind of large maggot cooked with thick flat leaves around it that didn't taste half-bad to a starving guy.

They pretended to be friendly, and the one who spoke English, who I called Harry Hoax after my friend from Texas, because he sounded a little like the real Harry Hoakes, he made light jokes with me about my situation that actually were pretty funny.

So my new friend Hoax took me aside into the mud-brown cell where I'd get the sumptuous feast, and he told me that he was my only friend.

"Your men already betrayed you," Hoax said. "They have told the commander everything. The position of other companies. The plans of the General."

I looked at him, grinning. "I bet they have. Good for them."

"Yes," Hoax said. "It is good. How are you feeling? I see sores on your shoulder."

"I'm fine."

"You seem in good spirits. Are you praying to your god?"

"God has more important things to worry about than me."

"I bet you are thirsty."

"Somewhat."

"Good. We have some pure water for you. And even a small cup of wine. Specially for you."

"To what do I owe this sudden bout of hospitality?"

"We are not primitive people. We may live and fight among the trees and swamps, but we have a sense of culture. You are important to us. We want you happy and healthy."

"That's why you put me in a hole in the ground."

"War is evil. I know that. We know that."

"Am I talking to 'I' or 'We'?"

He laughed.

"Very good. Here," he said, glancing at the doorway.

A young attractive woman entered, a wooden tray in her hands. On the tray, a small porcelain cup, and beside it some palm leaves. Atop the leaves, more of the fried grub I'd had before, and then what looked like a rabbit's leg, also cooked.

After setting this down in front of me, she left and returned moments later with a jug of water.

"You see? We treat you well," Hoax said. "All we ask is that you tell us a few things. They are minor, unimportant questions, really."

"I thought my friends told all. I certainly don't know more than they do," I said.

Suddenly, I heard a wail from one of the other cells.

I tried to place the voice as one of my team, but I could not. I wasn't even sure it was human.

Hoax closed his eyes for a moment as if he didn't enjoy the sound, either. Then, he nodded to the girl with the jug. She rose and poured water into the cup.

I brought the cup to my lips and drank too fast. She refilled the cup; while I sat there with Hoax, she made sure I always had water.

"There is a small bit of opium in the water," he said, softly. "You have pain, and it will help with it."

"You're drugging me?"

He sighed. "I feel bad for the state you're in. It is just a distillation of the poppy. Not enough to make you crave it. Just enough to ease any physical torment you might be feeling."

After a moment, I nodded. "That's kind of you."

"You are different from the others," he said. "You are not like other Americans, Gordon. You have a deeper quality. We do not want to hurt you. We want to bring you into realignment with truth."

"Ah," I said, feeling a bit blurred around the edges. I assumed this was the opium.

Hoax began the routine questioning that had been

done before, and I gave him the standard answer, which was no answer at all.

At the end of this, my meal finished, he sighed.

He told me that he wished me no harm but that the war would end with their victory and our defeat and that all my pain would be for nothing.

"Perhaps," I told him. "Or perhaps not."

Two interrogators came in. I recognized in their eyes the sadism I'd seen before. These were pleasure torturers.

I would be their toy for the night.

Hoax left the cell looking a little sad.

The interrogators bound my hands and ankles, and began to play a game that I believe is called, in torturing circles, the Thousand Scratches.

But it didn't matter what they did to my body.

I closed my eyes, and I could begin the rhyme I'd learned as a child:

Oranges and lemons say the bells of St. Clement's.

And then, my mind eroded into darkness:

I returned to the smokehouse, tied to the post, with my father's cat-o-nine-tails snapping hard at my scarred shoulders.

MY FATHER AND I HAD GOOD MOMENTS, TOO.

He took me hunting and fishing. We spent idle summer Sundays out on a skiff that he'd borrowed from a friend down in the harbor, and he told me of his abiding love for the sea.

He took me on his occasional deep sea fishing voyages,

and he brought me closer to him when my sister Nora drowned off the island, coming home from the mainland on a small boat when a storm hit.

My father pulled me aside and wept with me, the closest he'd ever come to showing genuine softness and true compassion.

If I felt something other than love for him, it was no doubt honor.

I hated him for the whippings, but I knew that some demon drove him to it. I was willing to take it for the building of my character.

Perhaps these days, people might call the police if a boy were being whipped by his father. But in those times, not long ago, it was considered nobody's business outside of the family's own concern.

My father's demons were many, but he seemed to have an overzealous Christian sense of the Devil and of Angels and of saving his children from the Burning Fires of Hell.

He'd shout at me, while he whipped, that this hurt him more than it hurt me, and that angels and Jesus wept as the lash ripped against my skin but that if I were to go to heaven, I must repent of my sinful ways, of the bad things I had done, and I must turn to Jesus and to God's grace and His iron will.

I was, he told me, of the Devil.

~

OH, THE BAD THINGS I'D DONE, THEY WERE TRULY bad, I suppose.

I smoked a bit, and I drank sometimes when I was far too young to drink liquor.

Once, I tried to set fire to the smokehouse, but only managed to burn most of the field nearby and many of the small thorny trees.

He had also caught me in the woods, in a way that a boy doesn't want to be caught, and that was part of my sin.

I deserved the whippings, and took them, playing the game to get through them, and then would spend a feverish night with my grandmother's salve all over my back to help speed the healing.

I honored and respected my father, even then, and I also thought of ways I might kill him someday.

But I never did.

ONCE I AWOKE FROM THE GAME, AFTER THE interrogators – my impersonal demons – had left their scratches all over my too-thin body.

They returned me to my pit, to my dark filthy bed.

Sometime later – days, perhaps – I was brought out again.

This time, Hoax was not happy with me. It seemed that my comrades had not said as much as they'd wanted. It seemed that none of us was behaving.

This time, I was to have a night of theater, he told me.

"Might I have a bit of that opium water?" I asked. I might've begged. I liked the stuff and I wanted to make my time in this Hell as pleasant as possible.

"Perhaps after," he said, rather sadly.

I was brought into a cell lit by the wavering flame of a candle.

In a corner, my buddy Davy

Sweet little Davy.

His eyes, swollen from beatings.

Jaw, cracked.

A festering wound on his scrawny arm.

Ropes again. This time, on his wrists and ankles.

Four men held the ends of the rope.

"This is a play we call the Tug of War," Hoax told me.

Then, he began asking me questions.

Tears came to my eyes, but I had nothing to tell them.

The men tugged at the ropes and I heard Davy's bones pop, one by one, as they pulled, and his jaw dropped open, slack, but he was still alive.

Until one of the men drew what seemed to be the forearm right out of Davy's skin.

Oh, but the game kicked in again, you see, at that point, and I missed most of the evening's entertainment by flying off to Burnley Island, by going somewhere I would be punished for my sins, but they were *my* sins alone and it was *my* punishment and no one else's.

WHEN I CAME OUT OF THE GAME, I WAS SHORT A finger and had no memory of it being taken or of the burning metal that had cauterized it to keep it from bleeding.

Hoax, however, told me the next time I was hauled up that I was a man of iron.

"You didn't make a sound. You seemed…"

"To be someplace else," I said.

He nodded. "Where did you go? The one you call Axeman was using a dull small scissor to cut off your finger. Why didn't you flinch?"

"Magic," I told him. "What's on the menu for tonight?"

"Menu?"

"Bugs? Rats? Frogs?"

"Oh," he said, smiling. "Supper. Well, tonight, we have a special treat. Tongue."

"Cow?"

"Pig. But it's very good. Wild pig makes a wonderful dish."

When I was finished with supper – and it truly was sumptuous compared to my previous ones – they brought another from my company, the scrappy little guy we called Gup.

As with the previous show with Davy, he had obviously been beaten, and perhaps his left leg was broken, also, for he hobbled in and nearly collapsed when the interrogators let go of his arms.

"Your friend cannot speak," Hoax whispered in my ear, like a mosquito circling. "He has, unfortunately, just this afternoon, lost his tongue under the Axeman's blade."

Now, Hoax didn't say that the tongue I had just eaten was my buddy's.

He didn't have to.

Maybe it was, and maybe it wasn't.

But he obviously wanted to give me that message, no matter what the truth of it might be.

I DIDN'T EAT FOR A FEW DAYS MORE, BUT FINALLY, pulled out of the hole again, I gobbled down the food they brought me – a stew made from strips of meat and leaves that tasted terrible but completely satisfied the gnawing in my gut.

Again, Gup was brought out, this time missing both hands, cauterized and bandaged at the wrist.

"His hands fell like leaves from a dying tree," Hoax told me.

"Very poetic," I said, trying to keep my mind from thinking about Gup and the Axeman too much, and forcing myself to keep out of drifting into the Dark Game.

To remain in the moment.

"Have you ever tasted human flesh?" Hoax asked.

I looked at poor Gup's face.

I wished him to die right there. I prayed to God. I prayed to the Devil. I prayed to the Queen of Heaven, Mary, the Mother of God, *Blessed is the Fruit of her Womb, Jesus.*

I prayed that his spirit would be pulled from his body before another night passed.

This entertainment of Hoax's went on for several nights, but each time I refused to answer his questions.

I WILL ADMIT WITH NOTHING BUT SHAME THAT I
began to crave the meals brought to me, and I convinced
myself – no doubt for survival's sake – that this was *not* the
body of Gup that I slowly consumed, sliced from him day
after day and cooked up with spices and aromatic flowers
to make dishes that I began to love.

This was simply meat that had been taken from the
body of pigs and rats and snakes and lizards and frogs and
fish and other creatures of this Enemy's country.

This, a steamy bowl before me, did not hold Gup's
foot, sliced into slivers, swimming in fragrant soup.

This was *not* a bit of flayed skin from Gup's buttocks,
wrapped within an elephant ear palm leaf that had been
buttered and baked into a moist but crunchy crust.

Yet, nightly, Gup was there, before me.

Soon an eye was gone, then his nose, his ears, toes and
left foot, his lips sliced off, until I saw him no longer as a
man at all, as a friend, as a former buddy, as one of
the team.

I saw him as the supplier of my life.

IN A DREAM, IN THE HOLE, I HAD A VISION OF THE
great snake of life, devouring its own tail.

Life eats life, the image of the snake seemed to tell me.
Life devours itself. You are part of this, and so is Gup. The
snake is the whip in my father's hand. The whip is in my
hand and reaches from my bloodied back to whip my
father's hand. The torturer and the tortured are each
playing a part and cannot be without the other.

I awoke from this dream and knew then that life was neither beautiful nor perfect nor magical.

Life was simply the gutter of heaven, the place where offal and waste stagnated, encircled with pestilence.

I BEGAN TO LOVE MY SUPPERS WITH HOAX.

Even when the Axeman came to me, a razor in his hand, and my mind shooting off to the game, I began to enjoy my contact with these cosmic barbarians and I looked forward to whatever they had in store.

I had forgotten my army, my country, and my friends.

There was only my hole and my cell, and my smoke-house back on my beloved home island.

It was the whole universe, and I could not tell whether it was heaven or hell.

Then, coming from the Dark Game out into the cell again, it was pain in my crotch that had me screaming, yet I felt distant from the scream.

I felt I could measure the scream and how it flew along the cell walls, bouncing up and down and back again.

They took another one of my fingers, but worse, one of my nuts was felled that night.

The Axeman had done it with his little razor.

I hadn't answered the questions and they had taken my left ball after slicing off my next finger down from my already-torn-off pinkie.

When I came around, I was in the cell, screaming, and one of my guys – Larry Pastor – sat across from me, watching me, his face trembling as if with an impending storm of sobs.

I had become the new entertainment for someone else now.

I was the star of the show.

≈

THE NEXT NIGHT, I HAD THE BEST SUPPER YET, WITH Larry staring at me from across the room, his face a grimace.

What was I eating? My finger? My testicle? Or simply some special sliced rat over a bed of eel-leaves?

"It's all right," I told him. "It tastes good. It really does."

≈

I WASN'T SURE WHAT I ATE MOST NIGHTS, BUT THE strangest thing of all was that I had begun gaining weight.

I still drank a bit of the opium water – Hoax would bring in barely a thimbleful. I guess he wanted to keep me pliable yet sober enough when necessary.

I attributed my gain in bulk to a combination of the fatty meat they fed me, as well as sitting in a hole in the ground for days on end.

Hoax commented on my healthy look and I could see it in Larry Pastor's eyes – while he got thinner and thinner, no doubt refusing to eat any meat offered him, I was beginning to pack on the pounds.

Truth was, I felt better.

I felt as if my mind had adjusted to the hole and the cell.

I began to realize that, contrary to what Hoax might've thought, I never even felt I was going to escape. I just refused to tell Hoax or his beloved Axeman any military plans or secrets because I knew that once I told, I was as good as dead.

The meals would stop.

They'd leave me in the hole and either forget about me completely, or fill it in with dirt and rocks.

I began to see my imprisonment as a kind of luxury hotel – a fancy five-star place.

I lived inside my head a lot, believing that I went on adventures when I was in the hole. I used the Dark Game to get out – I began to see the world again.

Within one of these visions, I existed in Paris, briefly, for a moonlit walk along the Seine with a beautiful girl who reminded me of a teacher I'd once had a crush on.

I ate a delicious breakfast on the Champs-Élysées, buttered almond croissant and a demitasse of espresso while watching traffic as it headed toward the *Arc de Triomphe.*

Another voyage out, I sat upon a striped blanket along the white-sanded beach of some tropical island, surrounded by bare breasted beauties. I feasted on juicy mango and velvet coconut milk, feeling warm breezes as

the shadows of palm trees cast thin lines along the pumice-
strewn sand.

IN THE CELL, I'D GO TO BURNLEY ISLAND, TO A
moment in the past; but in the hole, I'd be somewhere
magnificent, off on some adventure that was like a wish
fulfillment of my boyhood.

Perhaps this saved me.

Perhaps it damned me.

IN MY RARE MOMENTS OF LUCIDITY, I'D TRY TO STAY
grounded by chewing on a small bit of the Wrigley's gum
– the little I had left. A tiny infinitesimal piece. It
reminded me of who I was, where I was, why I was there.

I began to talk to Hoax, without even knowing that I
might be giving away secrets.

I told him all kinds of things. Not military secrets. Just
about my life.

About my nocturnal adventures.

Hoax became my best friend, and I suppose months
passed.

Other soldiers were captured. Sometimes I saw their
faces, and now and then I recognized them.

But they were part of the *Show* now. I watched the
Show, or they watched me in their version of the Show.

But Hoax didn't let the Axeman cut from me again.

MY PERFORMANCES FOR THE HORROR OF THE NEW recruits tended to be drawn from the contortionist's trade. My limbs were pummeled and pulled and twisted.

I felt none of it, off in my game.

I was valuable. I began telling more here and there. Nothing important, of course, but I'd become quite a good storyteller as I packed on the pounds from my substantial meals.

My tales of wonder and awe for my host, the polite Mr. Hoax, were about life outside of the jungle. He loved these adventures into other worlds. He had studied the works of Shakespeare, so now and then we'd talk about *Macbeth* or about *Othello*, and I told him about *Moby Dick* and how my island was somewhat like Nantucket and had been part of the whaling trade in a bygone era.

He loved American movies, too, so we chattered about them at some length. He offered up critiques that were quite well-thought-out about how Americans approached movies as opposed to other cultures. He also enjoyed discussing famous wars, and warriors of the ancient world.

These conversations often went on during the torture of another countryman of mine, usually roughly my age, once handsome, once with dreams and a sense of goodness of the world, all of them still having some meat on their bones.

I watched a man weep as the Axeman sliced off both of his ears, and then held them high for me as if ready to toss them to a trained seal.

I am ashamed to admit that, deluded and not as sane

as I should've been, I clapped for this performance because I thought it was some kind of special effects magic.

The Axeman was good at his job.

I had no idea what Hoax had in store for me, but soon enough, he brought me into a lower level of Hell with him.

HERE'S THE THING ABOUT THE DARK GAME:

By itself, it's simply a mind trick. It's a way to open doors inside you and to escape.

Pain. Hurt. Sorrow.

That's all it is.

But in that prison camp, with the techniques they taught purely by trying them on me, I learned how to add another level to the game.

How to make it go deeper.

And when it did, something truly magnificent came of it.

"BRAINWASHING."

It sounds like some medical experiment.

But it's really simple.

You just put the subject in a position of separation from every sensory detail.

And then you go to work on him.

I had been prepared for it, in my training.

But I guess you're never really prepared for this kind of

thing, not after months in a hole in the ground, not after watching your friends get their noses and eyes and ears and hands cut off in front of you.

Not after they feed you what might be your left ball.

HOAX HAD ME BOUND UP, HANDS IN FRONT OF ME, but tied to another rope that went to my ankles.

They positioned me, standing, in the middle of a cell.

Plugged a fan into the wall. I guessed this was to help block out any noise beyond the cell wall.

Then, each wall was covered with a dark cloth to block out even the cracks of light that might come in.

Additionally, Hoax tied a blindfold around my eyes.

Plunged into absolute darkness, I felt Hoax touch my hands.

"You are going to be here for several hours," he said. "You are not going to touch the wall. Or sit down. Or fall. Should you fall, you will be strung up so that you are dangling from the ceiling with a stick thrust between your arms to keep you balanced.

"So, do not fall, that is my advice, my friend. You are to keep silent. If you cannot keep silent, our mutual friend Axeman will cut out your tongue and sew your lips together. Understood?

"This is for your betterment. We find that you are truly a patriot to the world, to freedom, and to honor. We want you to realign yourself with nature and man's true calling, instead of with this monster you have served in America. You have been deluded by your country, and we intend to help you recover. You are special to us, and to me, Gordon. You are worth realigning. I consider you my friend."

These were the last words I heard for many hours, during which my bones ached, my bowels let loose without my being able to control them.

After awhile, I felt as if I were floating.

The sound of the fan – a buzzing like a thousand black flies – seemed to take over my mind, as if it were what my brain generated: the noise of a cosmic buzzing.

Somewhere beneath it, after awhile, I heard Hoax's voice again, only I could not make out what he was saying.

I was fairly certain, however, that he existed inside my head, washing my brains the way he might wash his hands with a feminine delicacy, planting ideas and truths known only to the Enemy, trying to make me over into one of his house servants.

I went into the Dark Game.

I heard Hoax clearly inside the game itself. I understood how this brainwashing could serve the Dark Game – and how it could help me survive.

GETTING INTO YOUR BRAIN ISN'T THE PROBLEM WITH brainwashing. Anyone with a good mental crowbar can unlock that mush of gray matter.

It's making your mind separate from your body so completely that your body becomes a servant to someone else's mind.

That is the goal of brainwashing.

They are not cleansing the brain. They are turning it off, and switching on another brain, imprinting another set of memories and values and thoughts so that your past is no longer there.

It is wiped out, but not so completely – you think you are the same person. But someone else has invaded you.

The Other. The one who has turned off one switch has juiced you from another one.

And you are that person's mind now. You are that person's imagination.

That is what I learned. That is how I began to understand that the Dark Game was not just for one to go off on flights of fancy. To protect you from some pain of life.

It could be changed, using this brainwashing.

It could become a way to turn a switch in another – to implant your own mind into another's mind, so that he no longer had his own perception but might, at least briefly, have yours.

I knew there was a way I could use this on Hoax.

On the Axeman.

I felt sure there was a way I could put the Dark Game into them so that I might escape.

THEY TOLD ME LATER THAT I STOOD THERE FOR twenty hours.

They told me later that I had been realigned.

But I had not been.

The Dark Game had saved me. It had protected me. It

had kept me from letting their words and thoughts press into my gray matter.

When they brought me out into the sunlight – for the first time in many months – they rejoiced and called me *Comrade* and *Friend* and *Healed One.*

But, on the inside, I had already begun planning how I would destroy them, set their camp on fire, and sow the ashes with salt so that those demons might never rise again.

BUT I'VE GOT TO PULL YOU BACK TO THAT NIGHT when I was young and in a bad part of some Texas town.

Remember?

Me, tied to the bed, the dead woman on the floor and the real Harry Hoakes, my buddy, my pal, untying me, his breath all whiskey and perfume absorbed from his girl for the night.

"She thought she was going to be like Gene Tierney," I said, and then, "Jesus, I'm going to end up in jail for this."

"Or you'll be in the jungle. In the goddamned war. Which do you want?"

"I choose the goddamned war."

Harry grinned, slightly, despite everything. "You didn't do it. You were tied up. I'm a witness to that."

I got up and got dressed as fast as I could, tripping over my trousers as I yanked them up.

"You let her tie you up?" He laughed.

I shot him a glance that shut him up.

"What are we going to do?" He said.

"We ain't gonna get caught, that's for damn sure," I said.

Next thing I remember, we're dragging that body out to Harry's car, and we plop her in the trunk.

I looked at her once, in that fizzling little light of the trunk, before we shut it down on her.

Her face.

She was somewhere else.

That's what Death is, I thought. It's going into the Dark Game for good.

I had no feeling for her. She was no longer there.

But the drive out to the mesa, thirty miles away from Red Town, the whole way I kept wondering how she had been murdered, and why I woke up from the Dark Game with the strange feeling of pleasure in my loins as if I had truly lost my virginity that night.

But that remains a Mystery with a capital M.

Part of me has felt all these years that I had untied myself, had beaten her to death, and then had somehow wrapped myself up in the ropes again.

Houdini, after all.

WE BURIED HER IN A DESOLATE SPOT, SO DEEP THAT the coyotes and scavengers wouldn't be able to dig her up.

I heard, years later, that Red Town eventually flourished and became more than a saloon and whorehouse railroad stop. It expanded out into the mesa.

I think that at some point a shopping mall was built

near that grave of the girl who thought she looked like Gene Tierney and kept a rope in her overnight bag.

HARRY SAID TO ME, AT FOUR THAT MORNING, DRIVING back to base, "No matter what happens, we can't ever say we met her. Or were even there. The other girls won't tell. They don't like cops. But you and I have to be clear on this. We were never there."

"Where?" I asked, and then Harry muttered, "Jesus," and I knew our friendship was over that morning.

When I heard he died later, in the war, I felt bad for him. I missed him, too. We had done our time together, and that's a bond that remains even after death.

I wonder if he ever got over the sight that had greeted him when he stepped out of the ordinary world of red light night and into that motel room of me tied up and a dead woman on the floor.

But now, he's in the Dark Game.

SUDDENLY, LIKE AN OVERNIGHT CELEBRITY, I BECAME revered among the Enemy in our camp.

No longer made to sleep in the hole, I had a straw mattress beneath me, and I ate regular food with some of the lower officers.

More of my own countrymen arrived at the camp. I observed them as they trooped in, proud and wounded. Some of them spat at the ground as they marched by me.

THE CAMP SPREAD ACROSS A FLAT WETLAND AREA
with long planks laid across muddy ground, rising to low
hills where most of the buildings sat, and behind which on a
kind of plateau, dotted with the holding wells for prisoners.

The commander's headquarters sat at the highest point
of one of the hills, and I got to calling it Mount Olympus.
The pits and holes where the Americans were kept, I called
Tartarus.

I taught Hoax about the various levels of Hell, and he
and I cooked up a scheme to begin a new set of torments
for my countrymen.

WE WOULD TAKE *DANTE'S INFERNO*, WHICH WAS EASY
enough to find even with the supposed anti-European
sentiment of the Enemy and from it create elaborate Rings
of Hell for the prisoners.

Next, I talked about the cannibal torture. I suggested a
whole new way to do this.

Why even use the Axeman? For despite his pleasure in
the art of cutting flesh and bone from a live victim,
wouldn't there be a more effective Host of such theatrics?

Why not *me*, their countryman?

What would be more horrifying than a well-fed
compatriot slicing off the lips of his fellow American in
front of the remnants of a once-proud platoon?

A USO show from Hell, I called it. We'll make it a

grand show, a hot ticket in the hot jungle. A feast for the eyes and ears. We'd entertain Hoax's soldiers, as well as mesmerize my American friends.

It took Hoax several days to see this as the grandiose and intriguing idea that it might be.

But then he smiled and nodded. "Yes, my friend Gordon, this might be quite a wonderful and acceptable entertainment."

The USO Show from Hell would begin.

WE'D HAVE BEAUTIFUL GIRLS DANCING FOR THE BOYS.

Then, we'd have the main event. I'd do a comedy routine, I told Hoax.

I'd strip them of their dignity. I'd cut off bits and pieces of the happiest, sweetest guy they knew, the youngest of their friends, the ones they thought of as mascots and baby brothers.

Right before their eyes.

"They'll tell you what you want to know," I said. "They'll divulge their mother and father's addresses if you want, once we do this."

Hoax, not suspicious in the least, was thrilled.

Yet, he still didn't completely trust me, for he felt the Axeman should be there to do the slicing.

I wasn't to be handed knives or razors. I was still a prisoner, albeit a *Friend of Our Country*, as they proclaimed loudly, nightly, into the pits and holes of Tartarus, making sure that every single captured American soldier knew my name and where I'd been born and what I'd done for my newly adopted fatherland.

Once everything was set, the prisoners began building the stadium.

I OVERSAW ITS CONSTRUCTION, AND THEY WORKED tirelessly and swiftly, for I told them that it was a monument to their Dead.

That it was their Memorial and that they must take pride in it.

I spent some nights with them, talking of how we were going to be well-treated by our captors, and that they must trust me, despite appearances.

They didn't trust me at all, I could tell, but they had the resignation of those who wait for freedom to come from outside their sphere. The helicopter raids from the sky, perhaps, they hoped. The end of the war itself was not too much to wish for in their current state.

They had lost all will to escape. They were broken, yet capable men.

They did as I told them to do.

I also spent nights with them, playing the Dark Game.

I needed their minds. I need to bring them into a state of calm and of service.

I needed for them to hear only *my* voice among all the voices of their prison.

The bleachers went up, the theater backdrop created.

WITHIN TWO WEEKS, IT WAS, BY THE STANDARDS OF the jungle, a beautiful imitation of an amphitheater, and could seat forty or fifty men.

The night of what I called *The Most Magnificent Show in the Universe*, finally arrived.

A banner announcing this, painted from human blood, hung from the wall.

THE CELEBRITIES OF OUR DAMNATION WERE THERE: the Commander, with his long face and inscrutable gaze; my friend Hoax, a chubby, round-faced fellow who whispered in the Commander's ear, no doubt about the show to come; the Enemy soldiers, dressed as if for an evening at the theater.

No doubt the women with some of them were not wives, but girlfriends who lived in the nearby Enemy Town, just beyond our Doom City.

The girls had fine red or blue dresses on, as if they would go to a celebration after the show. The men were dressed in full military garb. Cocktails were served, a rarity at this outpost, but the liquor had been distilled from a local flower, and left behind a scent in the air like jasmine.

The atmosphere fairly crackled with the electric moment to come.

I felt as if we were going to stage a great Broadway show. Or a spectacular Fourth of July fireworks demonstration.

It would be, I was certain, the inauguration of some

wonderful event that might be remembered and talked about for years to come.

Was I nervous? Of course. How could I pull off such a scheme? What if I were found out?

What if somehing went wrong?

If one thing had gone wrong, one tiny thing, all of it would fall like dominoes and it would make stepping on a mine seem like a walk in the park.

THE USUAL EXCITEMENT OF OPENING NIGHT SPREAD, even among my countrymen. They were brought in, roped at the hands, shackled at the legs, shuffling to their seats, although I kept a contingent backstage, those American actors in the drama to unfold.

Footlights consisted of small fatty candles laid in a semi-circle around the stage floor.

The backdrop, an enormous canvas that had once been an officer's tent covering but was now painted with scenes of the Enemy's Great Leader, stepping on all symbols of the USA. There was a ragged Statue of Liberty crumbling, there Uncle Sam, blinded and toothless his top hat a wreck, and there along the edges was our president being corn-holed by one of our great generals.

Just seeing the backdrop made the Enemy guard cheer and raise their glasses.

What they didn't know, of course, was that I had made sure that a quite a bit of the opium water that I had grown to know well was stirred into their drinks.

I led them in their national anthem. They stood and

sang bravely and happily, they drank – all, including the girls – I could tell from their expressions that they had begun to go into a blurred state – the strong alcohol and the poppy milk made themselves known.

As the crowd quieted, and the lights came up, I announced from my perch at the edge of the stage:

"We are gathered here for a momentous occasion! This is the inauguration of a great moment of historical significance!

"We are all the proud and the brave who have learned so much from our new masters, our friends and who wish to teach us the error of our ways and the true path of life! Here, on this very stage, you will see the wonders of transformation!

"You will see the magic of the ancients! The famous tricks of the fakirs of India! The secrets of the alchemists of old Europe! The mystical wonders of the sorcerers of ancient Mesopotamia!"

I spouted all the bullshit I could, and Hoax stood up and translated every word for the Enemy. They laughed, and brawled while some of my countrymen portrayed the President and our military leaders. They tripped, simulating intercourse with each other, acting like buffoons and idiots, all at my command.

The laughter from the stadium was enormous, even from Americans, whom I had brought into a state of the Dark Game just for this evening.

Hoax probably laughed the hardest, and once, when I glanced up at him, I saw the Enemy Commander slap him on the shoulder and whisper some approval in his ear that made Hoax beam.

The dancing girls came out next – they writhed and gyrated for the men. I had given them unhealthy doses of the local drink, and they began touching each other and taking off their clothes until they were nearly naked. This got the Enemy to cheer further, and the girls threw garments up to them.

My own countrymen sat quietly, as I had commanded for them to do in the Dark Game.

I could see that their eyes were glazed over, and they awaited my word.

Finally, to the delight of all, I announced the evening's entertainments.

"Tonight, good gentlemen and ladies, for your pleasure, the Axeman and I will carve up several Americans before your eyes. They will devour one another, as that is the way of our kind, and you will see how corrupt in our very beings we truly are. But first, I ask for volunteers from among you. For I want you to participate greatly tonight. Do I have any takers?"

The Enemy ranks roared approval, and many leapt from their seats to volunteer. But I wanted a special man to come forward. I wanted an important man.

"Commander!" I called out.

"Yes!" cried my countrymen, "Commander!"

Hoax laughed, clapping his hands, turning to his leader.

"Commander!" he said.

∾

THE COMMANDER SHOOK HIS HEAD VIOLENTLY,

laughing the entire time.

While he resisted coming forward, I brought the few remaining men from my own company out on the stage. They were further along in the Dark Game than the other prisoners.

Each was blindfolded, and they held each other's hands. I had spent four nights with the three of them to make sure that their minds were switched into another realm, so that my voice and my mind was their only guide.

"Commander!" I cried out again, and even the Axeman, coming up beside me, raised his glinting blade as it caught the last of the sunlight and called the Commander by full name.

FINALLY, GOADED, BLURRED FROM DRINK, THE Commander came down from the bleachers.

I raised a hand and called out a word of cheer, and all the Americans began clapping for him, and soon the guards clapped as well, whistling, as their beloved leader stepped up on stage.

"We have a magic show tonight!" I shouted to the noisy audience. "But we must have silence, now! Absolute silence!"

Within a minute or two, those in the bleachers quieted.

I glanced up at Hoax who smiled and nodded as if watching his prize protégé.

I THOUGHT OF MY FRIEND HARRY, BLOWN TO BITS BY a landmine. I thought of little Davy, tortured in front of me, tormented until his last breath left him.

I crouched down at the edge of the stage and blew out more than half the candles.

The sun had begun its descent and a gradually-creeping darkness seeped in like a dreadful mist.

Only six or so candles remained flickering, providing scant illumination to our stage. It was an effect I'd worked on – the backdrop now seemed ominous and evil – the Commander's face on the backdrop seemed to have gone in shades into a diseased, corrupt form rather than the healthy look that backdrop had when sunlight was upon it.

The crowd quieted even further, although I heard murmurs among the Enemy that set my teeth on edge.

They had begun to feel uneasy.

THE COMMANDER STEPPED UP NEXT TO ME, PATTING me on the shoulder.

He announced to the crowd that I was a shining example of the realignment procedure that had been developed in the Great City.

I told the Axeman that it was time to begin the carving of the Americans.

He brought the blade up to the ear of one of my boys.

I stopped him, and announced, "Why an ear? Can you make a good purse from it, ladies?"

A tittering came from the women in the bleachers as if

this were the cutest of jokes.

"I think not! Why not flay him alive? Right now? But even better, see how his friends," I pointed to the other two men, "don't know what's to come? Their ears are stuffed with wax. Their eyes are covered! Why not have them skin their friend for the delight of the Commander?"

Cheers went up, as I had expected.

In the dark, of course, it was the Americans who began the cheer, but in a stadium, cheers and claps become contagious. People want to be enthused about a show, and so the Enemy began crying out for more.

Then, when they quieted, I asked the Axeman for his blade.

Now, this was the point when my nerves nearly destroyed what I was about to do.

What if?

I felt sweat break out along my back. If he didn't pass me that weapon, none of this would work. If the drinks and the crowd didn't work on him, if he suspected anything…

The Axeman gave me a strange look, but his commander, the Supreme Leader of the camp, nodded to him, and shouted in their language.

The pressure of an audience watching did exactly what I wanted it to do – the Commander was caught up in the magic of the theatrical moment. He wanted the show to go on as planned.

Reluctantly, the Axeman passed me the blade.

It was heavy and its edge, sharp.

"You will now see," I announced, "one of the Corrupt Americans be skinned before you, and before your Commander, by his own compatriots!"

The audience went silent as I passed the blade to one of my blindfolded men.

Quickly, however, I took it back, and whispered to the three men whose ears were not, in fact, blocked, "Now. To your left."

I turned with the blade, and stabbed the Axeman in the groin, and then cut my way up into his belly and sternum –

As the audience began to gasp –

The three men, blindfolded, grabbed the Commander and tore at him as if they were wild dogs.

In their heads, they were wolves, in fact, and they believed that they were tearing at a stag in the hunt.

The commander screeched, but the men were strong, and in the darkness of the stadium, the Enemy rose, panicking, but it was too late.

They had drunk the opium and liquor, and my countrymen had already risen up with gnashing teeth and a strength that they had never known they'd had in their bodies.

I wanted to see Hoax one last time, to see the look on his face when he knew that this had not gone his way. That he had misplaced any trust he had in me.

But I couldn't find his face in the confusion.

I heard what sounded like wolves tearing at bleating sheep in the dark.

THE BEAUTY OF THE ESCAPE OF MY MEN — MEN FROM various platoons who now thought of me as their hero — was that none could remember the show at all.

By dawn, not all the prisoners had survived. Many had died in the fight.

But those who lived, blood on their faces and blotching their clothes, awoke without memory of the past year.

They didn't know the atrocity committed against them, neither did they know of their own savagery, which had killed the Enemy in the camp.

By dawn, I commanded the men, still under the influence of the Dark Game, to set fire to the last of Hell.

MEMORY:

I was sixteen, and my father lay dying in his bed.

My mother, who had to take up work now, needed me home to help nurse him while he was in pain.

I sat each day with him, and one morning, when I brought his breakfast, which he barely touched, he told me, "You're an evil son-of-a-bitch, Gordie. You show the world how good you are, but I know who you are on the inside. I've seen it since you were a baby. You have the Devil in you, and you spend your time hiding it."

I sat with him, patiently, nodding so that I might not appear to be the bad child.

Then, when he was through talking about my evil and how I was going to Hell, I offered him a glass of water.

He drank it, greedily, and passed the glass back to me.

"I still love you, dad," I said.

"I know you do," he said.

In the afternoon, he died, peacefully, in his sleep.

I missed him terribly.

His lifeless body, in that bed, made me remember the day he had me shoot my dog and had taught me about how sometimes, Death could be a friend.

THERE.

I've told you it all.

I've told you about the war, and the young woman, and my father.

My youth, pulled from the drawer, so you can look at it and judge me.

I should be tied up.

Bound.

Whipped.

It is the only way for me to go out of this body, the freedom of my mind to wander.

It intensifies the Dark Game for me.

I don't want to remember anymore.

I want to close the drawer now.

I want to lock up the past.

I give to you, my wife, Mia, the key.

READ THE NIGHTMARE CHRONICLES

O nce you've enter these nightmares, there's no way out...

Meet Oliver, whose dead wife waits for him down a dark alley.

Or Jane Boone, traveling to a distant country to meet a brutal killer – or is he a god?

Or Nix, an inmate using the geometry of night itself to escape...and more in this multi-award-winning collection stories.

FROM *THE NIGHTMARE CHRONICLES*

...We were subletting the place on Thirty-Third Street, just down from Lexington Avenue—it was not terribly far from my job across from Madison Square Garden, where I was an ink-stained drudge by day before transforming into a novelist by night.

Jenny was getting day work on the soap operas; nothing much, just the walk-on nurses and cocktail waitresses that populate daytime television, never with more than a word or two to say, so it was a long way to her Screen Actors Guild card.

But she made just enough to cover the rent, and I made just enough to cover everything else, plus the feeble beginnings of a savings account that we affectionately named *The Son'll Come Out Tomorrow,* because at about the time we opened the account, Jenny discovered that she was pregnant.

This worried the heck out of me, not for the usual reasons, such as the mounting bills, and the thought that I might not be able to pursue writing fulltime, at least not in this life, but because of a habit Jenny had of sleeping with other men.

It will be hard to understand this, and I don't completely get it myself, but I loved Jenny in a way that I didn't think possible.

It wasn't her beauty, although she certainly had that, but it was the fact that in her company I always felt safe and comfortable. I did not want to ever be with another woman as long as I lived; I suppose a good therapist would go on and on about my self-image and self-esteem and self-whatever, but I've got to tell you, it was simply that I loved her and that I wanted her to be happy.

I didn't worry if I was inadequate or unsatisfying as a lover, and she never spoke openly about it with me. I was just aware she'd had a few indiscretions early in our marriage, and I assumed that she would gradually, over the years, calm down in that respect. I felt lucky to have Jenny's company when I did, and when I didn't, I did not feel deprived. I suppose that until you have loved someone in that way it is impossible to understand that point of view.

So I wondered about the paternity of our child, and this kept me up several nights to the point that I would slip out of bed quietly (for Jenny often had to be up and out the door by five a.m.), and go for long walks down Third Avenue, or down a side street to Second, sometimes until the first light came up over the city.

During one of these jaunts, in late January, I noticed a curious sort of building—it was on a block of Kip's Bay that began in an alley, and was enclosed on all sides by buildings. Yet there were apartments, and a street name (*Pallan Row*, the sign said), and two small restaurants, the kind with only eight or nine tables, one of them a Szechwan place, the other nondescript in its Americanized menu; also, a flower stand, boarded up, and what looked like a bit of a warehouse. The place carried an added layer of humidity, as if it had more of the swamp to it than the city.

I am not normally a wanderer of alleys, but I could not help myself—I had lived in this neighborhood about a year and a half, and in that time had felt I knew every block within about a mile and a half radius. But it was as if I had just found the most wonderful gift in the world, a hidden grotto, a place in New York City that was as yet undiscovered except by, perhaps, the oldest residents. I looked in the windows of the warehouse but could see nothing through the filthy windows.

All day at work, I asked friends who lived in the general vicinity if they knew about Pallan Row, but only one said that she did. "It used to be where the sweatshops were—highly illegal, too, because when I was a kid, they used to raid them all the time—it was more than bad working conditions, it was white slavery and heroin, all those things. But then," she added, "so much of this city has a history like that. On the outside, carriage rides and Broadway shows, but underneath, kind of slimy."

On Saturday, I convinced Jenny to take a walk with me, but for some reason I couldn't find the Row; we went to lunch. Afterward, I remembered where I'd led us astray, and we ended up going to have tea at the Chinese restaurant. The menu was ordinary, and the decorations vintage and tacky.

"Amazing," Jenny said, "look, honey, the ceiling," and I glanced up and beheld one of those lovely old tin ceilings with the chocolate candy designs.

The waitress, who was an older Asian woman, noticed us and came over with some almond cookies.

"We're usually empty on weekends," she said. She glanced up at the tin ceiling, having noticed Jenny's interest. "Nice, huh? This was part of a speakeasy in the twenties—the cafe next door, too. They say a mobster ran numbers out of the back room. Before that, it was just an icehouse. My husband began renting it in 1954."

"That long ago?" Jenny said, taking a bite from a cookie. "It seems like most restaurants come and go around here."

"Depends on the rent." The woman nodded, still looking at the ceiling. "The owner hasn't raised it a penny in all those years."

She glanced at me, then at Jenny. "You're going to have a baby, aren't you?"

Jenny grinned. "How'd you guess?"

The woman said, "I can see it in your face. You'll have a boy, I bet."

After she left the table, we finished the tea, and just sat for a while. The owner's wife occasionally peeped through the round window of the kitchen door, and we smiled at her but shook our heads to indicate that we weren't in need of service.

"When the baby comes," she said, "Mom said she'd loan us money to get a larger place."

"Ah, family loans," I warned her.

"I know, but we won't have to pay her back for a few years. Can you believe it? Me, a mother?"

"And me, a father?" I leaned over and pressed my hand against her stomach. "I wonder what he's thinking?"

"Or *she*. Probably, 'Get me the hell out of here right now!' is what it's thinking."

"Babies aren't 'its.'"

"Well, right now it is. It has a will of its own. It probably looks like a little developing tadpole. Something like its father." She gave my hand a squeeze. I kissed her. When I drew my face back from hers, she had tears in her eyes.

"What's the matter?"

"Oh," she wiped at her eyes with her napkin, "I'm going to change."

"Into what?"

"No, you know what I mean. I've been living too recklessly."

"Oh," I said, and felt a little chill. "That's all in the past. I love you like crazy, Jen."

"I know. I am so lucky," she said. "Our baby's lucky to have two screw-ups like us for parents."

Now, it could be that I'm just recalling that we said these words because I want her memory to be sweeter for me than perhaps reality will allow. But we walked back up Second Avenue that Saturday feeling stronger as a couple; and I knew the baby was mine, I just knew it, regardless of the chances against it.

We caught a movie, went home and made love, sat up and watched *Saturday Night Live*. Sunday we took the train out to her mother's in Stamford, and then as the week was just getting under way, I walked through the doorway of our small sublet to find blood on the faux Oriental rug…

Available in print & ebook.

ABOUT THE AUTHOR

Douglas Clegg is the *New York Times* bestselling and award-winning author of *Neverland*, *The Priest of Blood*, *Afterlife*, and *The Hour Before Dark*, among many other novels, novellas and stories. His first collection, *The Nightmare Chronicles*, won both the Bram Stoker Award and the International Horror Guild Award. His work has been published by Simon & Schuster, Penguin/Berkley, Signet, Dorchester, Bantam Dell Doubleday, Cemetery Dance Publications, Subterranean Press, Alkemara Press and others.

A pioneer in the ebook world, his novel *Naomi* made international news when it was launched as the world's first ebook serial in early 1999 and was called "the first major work of fiction to originate in cyberspace" by *Publisher's Weekly*, covered in *Time* magazine, *Business Week*, *Business 2.0*, *BBC Radio*, *NPR*, *USA Today* and more. His book *Purity* was the first to be published via mobile phone in the U.S. in early 2001.

He is married, and lives and writes along the coast of New England.

Find the Author Online:
www.DouglasClegg.com

facebook.com/DouglasClegg

twitter.com/DouglasClegg

bookbub.com/authors/douglas-clegg

Printed in Great Britain
by Amazon